'NAM

*a novel of self-discovery
in a time of chaos*

by
William J. Millman

SB

Sunset Beach Press

SB

Sunset Beach Press

Manufactured in the United States of America

Cover photos: James Dung - Nat'l Archives; Colourbox - JuNiArt

ISBN: 978-0-9857918-9-6

TO ALL MEN AND WOMEN,
EVERYWHERE, WHO FIGHT FOR
FREEDOM AND JUSTICE

If you only experienced warfare through history books, you might think that wars are just a series of bloody, frightful battles contested by young men and women sent to strange lands by old men and women, to kill or be killed. But the lives of soldiers in wartime are more than just bullets and bombs; the vast majority of time is spent preparing... and waiting. And as Tom Petty so eloquently put it, 'Waiting is the hardest part.'

PROLOGUE

Kontum Province, Vietnam

The nights are the worst.

Lying here stretched out in a shallow foxhole, you feel like you're half-buried already. The ground's too hard to get any sleep, and even if you could the sounds of the surrounding jungle are so loud you couldn't hear the VC if they drove up in a deuce and a half. Insects chirping, animals screaming, the occasional breeze rustling the leaves up high – it's like goddamn Times Square out here.

There are days in Vietnam like days in other places. But with all that happens here on most days, it's difficult for me to remember that. You'd think I'd be used to it by now. Used to the lack of sleep, all the night sounds, the fear. But somehow you never really get used to it. At least I haven't. It gets better, no denying that. When I see newbies straight off the boat, crapping in their pants every time a mortar shell explodes nearby or a Long-Range Reconnaissance Patrol calls in a Victor Charlie sighting within 100 clics, I realize how far I've come. All of us, really. From a shell of a unit, reconstituted with over 90 per cent new blood, we've become pretty damn good. I'd trust just about every man in the company with my life. Hell, I do, most every day.

But 'used to it'? Nah. I can sleep nearly anywhere I drop, but almost never for more than 2 hours at a time. I don't have the shakes yet, but I still feel the creepy-crawlies in my gut every time I know we're going out on an operation. Not without reason, either. I've seen a First Sergeant who survived the Chinks in Korea come out here and step on a punji stick his first time out. Or a medic splinting a broken arm catch shrapnel from an incoming mortar round. Or just about anyone get bitten by the wrong damn mosquito and wind up in a field hospital shivering like it's twenty below.

Just last month I saw a grunt running through the elephant grass holding his guts in with one hand while firing his M-16 with the other. A while before that I saw the remains of a unit that had called in air support and got napalmed right along with the black pajama'd bastards they'd engaged: nothing more than charcoal briquettes left. Couldn't even tell some of them had been human.

I've seen too much. We all have. Most of us were kids when we got here. Not anymore.

Worst of all, I volunteered for all this.

What does that say about me?

CHAPTER 1

The sun shone brightly over West Point, the June sky a cloudless electric blue reflecting the overwhelming optimism of the 1968 graduating class.

They were good, they knew it, and after all the pomp and circumstance was over they were going out to kick some Viet Cong ass.

As the firstie seniors in their dress uniforms formed-up outside the gates to Michie Stadium at 0830, there was an audible buzz of excitement. Four years of hard work, unwavering discipline and endless hours on the marching field were about to pay off. Of course most of the class had been sworn-in as second lieutenants the day before, so the graduation ceremony was largely symbolic. Largely, but not entirely. Technically speaking, the school still held absolute control over their every move until the ceremony was over. That very morning a rumor had swept through the ranks that one of their own had been threatened with expulsion just the night before.

But what had the cadets really pumped-up was the idea of seeing family, friends, and most importantly *girl*friends after what had been months of enforced celibacy.

"So, how'd it all work out? Darla coming for the big show?" Mason Landry asked his closest friend and freshman year roommate, Josh Daniels, as he craned his neck to try to identify the civilian guests entering the west side of the stadium. Landry was a big guy: 6' 5", broad shouldered, with the dark eyes and square jaw of the Baton Rouge Landrys. He'd played tight end on the football team until a torn ACL his junior year put an end to "all that foolishness," as his father had so succinctly put it.

Josh smiled, his alert blue eyes hidden behind reflective shades, his sun-bleached chestnut hair cut Army-short. He wasn't a small man by any means, but compared to Landry he felt like one of the Munchkins.

"She'd better be," he said with just the right swagger for a newly-minted officer. "I basically told my old man either she comes along or you don't."

Landry smiled. He knew full well that Josh was BS-ing him. Mark Daniels was a U.S. Congressman, a retired full bird colonel, and one tough SOB. No one *told* the congressman what to do, probably not even the President, who he supposedly knew on a first name basis. The senior Daniels had been at both Inchon and Chosin Reservoir, receiving two Purple Hearts and a Silver Star for his two-tour service. Landry only asked because the congressman had made it very clear on multiple occasions that he thought of Darla as a 'distraction'. But he let his friend's bold words stand. *'No reason to bring him down on this beautiful summer day.'*

The order was given to form up, and in moments the amorphous blob of milling cadets crystalized into perfectly ordered ranks, ready to march into the stadium. Josh kept eyes-forward as the cadets came out through a short tunnel onto the brilliant green turf of the football field, but let his vision dart to the thousands of cheering spectators dotting the lower reaches of the bleachers surrounding the riser and rows of temporary seating. He felt a swell of pride as the Army anthem blared from the loudspeakers, then listened intently as General Harold K. Johnson gave the formal address.

He'd dreamed of this day; he'd known it was his destiny to attend the Academy from the time he'd been a little boy. The biggest day of the year in his father's household was the day Army met Navy in the yearly football classic. His father always invited the same four old war buddies over to watch his oversized Motorola color TV, and his Mom prepared chicken wings, brownies and popcorn to "keep the troops provisioned" during the three hour gridiron battle. His father and his friends would swig Budweiser beers from the bottle, yell at the TV screen whenever the game threatened to deviate from their desired script, and slap hands maniacally whenever the cadets scored.

But what he remembered best, and most fondly, were the rambling conversations that took place after the game was over, the food eaten, the TV set turned off. It was then that the old war stories popped up in one long, intoxicated, guffaw-filled bull session. His mother tried to usher him out of the room before the five old friends lapsed into the 'rough' language she so disliked, but he always found a way to sneak back in and make himself invisible while The War came alive through their tall tales. They laughed, they shouted, they covered their heads and dove into sofa cushions that stood-in for foxholes, and – sooner or later – one or more of them would cry. All except his Dad. The Colonel never cried.

It was unsettling for Josh, to see those older men with tears in their eyes, sometimes blubbering incomprehensibly. But it was also magical. What was so powerful about war that even twenty years later it could make grown men cry? It was probably then, during one of those post-game debriefs, that he'd decided he would go to the Academy. Not that it really mattered what he decided. The Colonel had probably decided on the day he was born that he would go to West Point. Maybe even before.

As Josh got older the Army-Navy booze-a-thons moved from their house to each of the buddies' on a rotating schedule, until finally, a couple of years before the Colonel ran for Congress, he stopped going entirely. Josh still wondered if his father had known that far in advance that he was going to run for office, and that booze-fueled bull sessions might not look good on his political résumé. The Colonel had been well-known for his planning and tactical acumen. So maybe he had known. Whatever the case, he'd won the seat in suburban Dallas, and had kept winning ever since.

Josh told himself he was scanning the crowd to catch Darla's eye, but he knew it was his father he was looking for. As much as he tried to live his life outside the gravitational pull of his bigger-than-life father, he knew deep-down that he still orbited the 'old man' with all the independence of Sputnik. Josh shook his head and let out a deep breath. How the hell could he ever stand on his own two feet when everything he did was always compared to the Colonel?

"See her?" Landry asked when he noticed his friend's line of sight.

It took a moment for Josh to realize who he was talking about. "Nah, too many people. But she's up there – I can feel it."

When all the chatter onstage was finally over, when everybody had been thanked and the entire stadium had fallen silent to honor the graduates of the Academy who'd died in combat during the preceding twelve months, it was time to say goodbye. Josh knew that some small, sick part of him would miss that place, but not for long.

"Class dismissed!" the order exploded from the loudspeakers, and like a flock of park pigeons flushed from their cozy perches, nearly 1000 white hats flew into the vivid blue sky.

Josh turned to Landry with hand extended.

"We did it, Lan."

Landry took one glance at the offered hand and with a cat-ate-the-canary grin grabbed his friend in a massive bear hug, lifting him off the ground.

"Sure did!" he yelled so loud that Josh flinched. "Bastards don't control our lives no more!"

For a few minutes Josh wandered among his classmates, giving and receiving congratulations. He felt elated, almost drunk with satisfaction. The grass seemed greener, the sky bluer, the air sweeter than he'd remembered them moments earlier. So it was somewhat disorienting when he felt a tap on his shoulder and found himself face-to-face with an underclassman he didn't recognize.

"Commandant sends his regards," the cadet began as soon as Josh turned, "and wants you to know that Congressman Daniels and family will be joining him in his office effective immediately. Your presence is *requested*."

Josh tried to keep the scowl off his face. Son of a bitch! Even on his graduation day the Colonel had managed to upstage him. Well, there wasn't much he could so about it. He knew full well that the *request* was in fact an order. Besides, he assumed that Darla would be there. H*oped* was probably more accurate.

"Hey bro, come on over to the civvie section and say hi to my family," Landry interrupted, oblivious to the little drama that was transpiring right in front of him. Josh saw the messenger's eyebrows arch up in ill-disguised surprise. He hesitated.

"Yeh, sure, I'd like that," he decided after a quick cost-reward analysis. "One second." He turned back to the cadet. "Please tell the Commandant that I'll be there in just a short while."

"You sure you wanna do that?" the cadet asked, both his expression and tone suggesting he did not agree.

"I'm sure. Thanks for bringing the message."

With that he slapped Landry on the shoulder. "So, let's go commiserate with the poor folks who've put up with your crap for all these years."

The big man laughed heartily and led Josh in the direction of the visitors' stands. The cadet messenger watched them go with a sad shake of his head.

Josh had met Landry's parents a few times during the four years they'd spent at the Academy. They were pretty much what he'd expected from knowing their son: simple, kind, friendly folk from rural Louisiana. His father was big like Landry, but all the muscle from his youth had gone to fat and he carried a few six-packs in a sizeable paunch right up front. His mother was somewhat of a surprise. Shorter than Josh had first expected, she was also prettier and quite a bit younger than his father. Luckily, Landry's little sister took after their mother. She was a heartbreaker for sure.

They chatted about a whole lot of nothing for several minutes, mainly sharing what Landry had told each about the other. Josh tried to focus on what they were saying, but he couldn't help hearing the tick-tick-tick of his inner clock as he envisioned the Commandant and the Colonel making small talk to kill the time until his arrival. When Mr. Landry snapped a couple of photos of the two freshly-minted lieutenants, and various combinations of family members, Josh had to try his hardest to come up with a smile that didn't look like an impatient grimace. As soon as he felt he'd shown sufficient deference and good will toward the Landrys, he excused himself to go see his own folks.

"I'm sure they're around here someplace," he dissembled.

"Maybe we can all get together later this afternoon," Landry's Dad suggested with a warm open smile that made Josh feel somehow dishonest when he answered, "Yeh, maybe so. I'll see if they have anything planned."

"His Dad's a congressman," Landry said as if the title explained everything. Apparently it did.

"We know, son," his mother said sweetly. "But if he and his wife have a moment we'd love to say hello. We've heard so much about them." She addressed the last directly to Josh.

If anything, her words made him feel even worse. His father *always* seemed to have something planned.

"In any case, it's been great seeing you again," he said, anxious to bring things to a close. He reached out for one last handshake. "You've got a great kid here, Mr. & Mrs. Landry," he said. "He's been a good friend, and I'm sure he'll be a great officer."

Landry looked at him with a hangdog smile that almost brought tears to his eyes. It was the smile from Landry's mother that made his day, however. Josh nodded and turned on his heels, the day suddenly bright once more.

*****

"Well, well, well, Second Lieutenant Daniels," the Commandant intoned as Josh made his entrance to the large, imposing office of the Academy's top administrative official. "Come on in."

Josh took in the tableau with a glance: the Colonel and his mother seated on a black leather sofa with the general positioned directly across from them in a simple visitor's chair; his younger brother, Kyle, seated to the general's right, and Darla – looking every bit as beautiful as he remembered – perched elegantly to his left. An empty chair sat at the far end of the heavy low coffee table that separated his parents from the others. The Commandant motioned him to that seat with a welcoming smile that Josh had rarely seen during his four years at the school.

The Colonel, on the other hand, showed the pressed lips and narrowed eyes that Second Lieutenant Daniels was all too familiar with. He was pissed.

"Sorry it took me so long to get up here," Josh began, hoping that a sacrificial mea culpa might defuse the situation. "Landry's family wanted some photographs."

"I'm sure they were very happy to spend some time with you," his Mom said. Josh noticed her hand slip ever-so-gently onto the Colonel's, tapping it lightly.

"We were just saying how most of your class will likely spend some time in 'Nam," the Commandant said to fill the sudden silence. "Of course, not all," he added with a bit more emphasis. He noticed the Commandant glance at his father with a look that seemed to suggest a subtext he didn't quite grasp.

He bent down and pecked Darla on the cheek, receiving a wink and a broad smile for his effort. The warm glow of the moment was extinguished in a heartbeat.

"What about you, Lieutenant? What duty station and school have you selected?" the Commandant continued as Josh positioned himself in his seat.

"I don't believe that he's finalized those decisions just yet," his father stated in a tone that was clearly meant to be more statement than hypothesis.

Josh hesitated. Part of him knew it would be wiser to go with the flow, let his father win the point. He knew he was already in hot water. No need to make it worse. And yet...

"Actually, like all of us Infantry types I put in for Ranger School at Ft. Benning," he announced. "With the idea of an onward assignment in Southeast Asia."

'Southeast Asia' was the Army's way of saying Vietnam without actually saying so. It was clear from the slight widening of his father's eyes that he understood the implication all too well. His mother, as was so often the case, missed the point entirely.

"Oh? Did you have a country in mind?" she asked without any hint of irony. It was as if he were booking a graduation trip to the islands and she wondered if he'd be staying at the Hilton or the Radisson.

"He means Vietnam," his father said with an edge to his voice. "Exactly when did you make this decision?"

"Not long ago," Josh lied. In fact, he'd decided on Ranger training way back at the beginning of his third year. The decision on 'Nam had been more recent.

"A chip off the old block," the Commandant said with a smile, hoping to defuse the tension between father and son.

The Colonel stared at Josh for several seconds. Seemed a lot longer to the younger Daniels.

"When's the drop-dead date for assignments?" the Colonel asked, his gaze only belatedly turning to the Commandant.

"Well, I believe that some modification could be made right up until the boys report to their duty station…" It was clear he was kowtowing to the congressman.

"May 1 was the last day for submitting our requests," Josh said.

"We'll talk it over," the congressman said, directing his words to the Commandant. His tone brooked no disagreement. "Get back to you."

"Of course, of course, Congressman," the Commandant agreed. He didn't look the least perturbed by the prospect of the Colonel's blatant interference with the assignment process. In fact, he looked absolutely thrilled that he could *serve*.

Josh wanted to barf. Was there nowhere that his father couldn't intervene? He'd thought that maybe the Army was big and tough enough to stand up to the Old Man, but now he saw that even the top-dogs were as susceptible to his threats and manipulations as everyone else.

He kept tight-lipped for the remainder of their audience with the Commandant, responding in concise phrases and nods whenever something came his way. As usual, the Colonel carried the burden of the conversation, weaving his stories and opinions with just enough affected interest in the general to make him feel like an active participant instead of a puppet on a string – which is what he was. By the time the Colonel announced that he and his family "unfortunately" had to attend to other business, Josh was more than ready to go just about anywhere to end the tedium of the mock exchange. Ready, despite knowing full well he'd be the focal point for a blast of his father's well-known displeasure as soon as they got out of sight of the Commandant.

After handshakes all around (and one last salute from Josh for his former commanding officer), the family filed out of Washington Hall in relative silence. Josh felt that his mother and brother knew full well what was coming, while Darla must have sensed the tension in the air. She slipped her hand into his without a word and walked beside him as if to announce she was willing to share whatever grief the Colonel wanted to dish out. Josh loved her for that.

It didn't take long. Almost before the door to the building had swung shut, the Colonel sidled up to Josh on the side opposite Darla and said in a quiet but unquestionably pissed voice, "What the hell do you think you're doing?"

Josh was tempted to play dumb, to feign ignorance of the offense for which he was about to be so thoroughly reamed. But he thought better of it. Darla's gentle squeeze of the hand helped him face the music.

"You know I've always wanted to be a Ranger," he said without any hint of emotion. "Like you." He added the last hoping that it might mitigate the Colonel's anger. It didn't.

"Don't give me that… crap!" the elder Daniels spat, struggling to stop himself from lapsing into the Army language with which he was so intimately associated. "It isn't a game they're playing over there in Viet-nam," he continued, pronouncing Vietnam with the accentuated second syllable made popular by his old buddy, LBJ.

"I've spent my whole life getting to a position where I could help you avoid that garbage, and I'll be damned if I'm going to let you throw it all away on some flea-brained idea of chivalry, or bravery, or whatever the hell is going on in that head of yours!"

"Mark Daniels!" his mother reprimanded her husband. "There are women present!"

The Colonel glanced at Darla with ill-concealed irritation but took a deep breath and stepped-down a notch.

"My apologies, but I find it very difficult to stand by and watch as my oldest son throws his life away."

Josh couldn't help himself. Sometimes he thought he carried the Daniels' gene for self-righteousness. Or was it self-destruction? "Throw my life away?! I can't believe I'm hearing this from you! Who was it that said, 'There is no more satisfying career than that of a U.S. Army officer.' I seem to remember it was you, just four years ago at my JROTC Change of Command ceremony!"

Josh dropped Darla's hand and turned to face his father. His cheeks burned red with indignation, and maybe just a little disappointment at the Colonel's admission.

For a long breath-held moment father and son stared at each other, anger simmering just beneath the surface. Then the Colonel blinked and turned aside. "You're not old enough to understand. You don't have any idea of what you're letting yourself in for."

Josh struggled to control his anger. "I guess I'll just have to grow up and learn," he said, his voice modulated to demonstrate resolve, not defiance.

"He's not a little boy anymore, Mark," his mother said.

"You're not *defending* his crazy ideas, are you?"

The look on his mother's face made Josh blink away the pain. "No," she answered, "but we can't just tell him what to do anymore. He's a young man now." She looked past her husband with a tenuous, satisfied smile.

"I just hope you're not doing this to make me proud, or some such crap," the Colonel added.

"I'm not doing this for you at all," Josh said. "I'm doing it for me."

"Can't we talk about this later?" Kyle spoke up from behind them all. Josh had almost forgotten he was there.

The Colonel glanced back with a look primed to kill, but he held his temper in check. "You can be sure of that," he said. He stomped off without another word, a few steps ahead of the others.

Mother and son exchanged a surreptitious glance, Josh grabbed Darla's hand, and they all hurried to follow.

CHAPTER 2

Josh felt both exhausted and exhilarated. It was finally all out in the open: Ranger training, Vietnam – all of it.

"A penny for your thoughts," Darla said as she ran her hand along the short stubble at the back of his neck. They sat in Josh's green '67 Cougar with floor shifter, tilt steering wheel and black vinyl top, looking out over the Hudson River in the distance.

He realized he'd been staring into space and turned to meet her questioning look. "Sorry. I guess I drifted off for a second."

"What were you thinking about – your Dad?" It was as if she had ESP or something. She seemed to know what he was thinking before he ever said a word.

"Yeh. I'm just glad it's all over."

"Telling him about Vietnam?"

"I knew he wouldn't take it well. He has other plans for me."

"Don't all our parents?" She smiled and kissed his earlobe.

"Not like the Colonel. He's used to command. You give an order, someone obeys. It's just that simple."

"It's been a long time since he was in the Army. He can't possibly believe that people will still react that way."

"Maybe not people, but me, oh yeh…" He tried not to sound put-upon but couldn't really pull it off.

"Poor baby," she teased, tickling his neck with her finger. "Anything I can do to make you feel better about your big, mean Daddy?"

He smiled. "I need to be consoled."

"You mean, like this?" She kissed his neck and tickled inside his ear with her tongue.

"Something like that," he said. He took her in his arms and kissed her with all the passion he felt for her and all the anger he felt for his father. It was a strange mix, but it did the trick.

*****

The stars had come out and a sliver of moon shone down on the Hudson Valley. Even with all the windows cranked down the inside of the Cougar had steamed-up like a sauna.

"It's just one year, right?" Darla asked, breaking the spell of the moment.

"What's one year?" Josh asked, even though he was pretty sure he knew what she was asking about.

"A tour in Vietnam. It's just one year – right?" There was a catch to her voice, a bit of emotion that caught him by surprise.

"Yeh. It'll go by fast."

"Not fast enough."

He looked down at her face, just inches from his own, and smiled. "Don't you think you should wait for me to leave before you start missing me?"

Her smile was more a pout. "I don't want to start missing you."

His smile disappeared. "I know. It's hard. But this is what I signed-up for. I'm a second lieutenant in the United States Army now."

She traced his eyebrow with a finger. "And a darned cute one too."

"I'll write. Call when I can, although from what I've heard that might not be too often."

She was quiet for a while. "You won't forget me over there, will you?" she asked.

He pulled her even closer. "Now how could I do that?" He glanced at his left hand as it cradled her wavy brown hair. His brand new graduation ring shone even in the faint moonlight.

"Here. I want you to have this," he said, shifting his weight so he could pull off the ring and hold it up for her to see.

Her eyes opened wide and her mouth dropped in shock. "Oh Josh!" she cried out before grabbing the ring and slipping it on the fourth finger of her left hand. It was much too large but she balanced it carefully as she held it up to take a closer look. "It's beautiful!"

"Not as beautiful as my girl," he said, and before he knew it they were kissing and she was unbuttoning his shirt…

CHAPTER 3

The days between graduation and the beginning of Ranger school passed in a rush of activity. True to his word, the Colonel had not let up on his campaign to dissuade Josh from attending Ranger school, or from seeking assignment in Vietnam. But the unrelenting pressure only hardened Josh's resolve. He was going, and no one was going to stop him.

He and Landry worked out together during the time leading up to their departure, trying to get in the kind of shape that would allow them to meet the demands of the course – and the steaming hot temperatures in Georgia – without puking their guts out. Josh had half-expected his friend to back out once it became clear that the Ranger training was going to be one helluva tough time, but had to admit he was damn happy he hadn't. It would be good to have a friendly face down there at Benning.

The G2 on the course was that they needed to know every detail of the operations order and needed to be ready for more hikes and less sleep than they'd probably ever experienced in their young lives.

"You think we're ready?" Landry had asked not long before they were scheduled to ship out.

"Nobody's ever ready for Ranger training," Josh said. "But we're less unready than most of the bozos they'll get down there."

"Hoo-ah," Landry replied.

As the days before their departure dwindled to a scant few, Josh's mother became less and less talkative as she padded about the house helping her son get ready to leave. It hurt Josh to see her shut down like that, but there was really nothing for him to do short of request another assignment, and he wasn't going to do that. His father, on the other hand, reacted in the exact opposite way. He became more and more vocal, as if his son's decision to go to Vietnam were a personal affront. Josh tried his best to avoid the old man. Kyle seemed unsure of how to react. At times he sounded excited, perhaps even a little jealous that his big brother was about to head off to war. At others, he retreated into himself, becoming as quiet as his Mom.

Darla was the only one to keep up a reasonably good front, though Josh could sense how much her supportive attitude was costing her. She looked tired all the time, her cheeks pale, her eyes dark and puffy; every once in a while he'd catch her staring off into space, seemingly a million miles away. As soon as she realized he was looking, the smile jumped back into position and she tried her best to act as if his assignment were just another life event, not all that different from moving to a new dorm room or finding a summer job.

Truth be told, all the tip-toeing around his family was beginning to wear on Josh. He spent more and more time with Landry and some old high school buddies, and less and less at home. He had to force himself to keep his composure even around Darla, not so much because he didn't want to be with her but because he knew full well he was the cause of her poorly-hidden anxiety. While everyone around him seemed to dread his upcoming departure date, he found himself looking forward to it with increasing eagerness.

'Just get me out of here,' he mused. *'Once I'm over there they'll realize I made the right decision.'*

*****

Finally the day arrived. Josh had planned to take a bus from Dallas to Ft. Benning like most everyone else in the course, but his father had other plans.

"They're gonna run your ass ragged once you get there," he announced a few days before his son's departure, using language that only revealed itself when his mother – and the voters – weren't around. "May as well save some of your strength for the Rangers." He handed him a plane ticket.

Josh realized that his father thought he was doing him a big favor. But he had committed to traveling with Landry, and he wasn't about to back out just because his father had the money to send him by plane.

"Dad, thanks. I appreciate it. But…"

"But?" the Colonel interrupted, a look of impatience matching his tone.

"But Landry and I are traveling together, and…"

His father reached into his pocket and pulled out a second ticket. "I'm not really the SOB you think I am," he said with what might have been a hint of a smile. "If there's one thing I appreciate, it's a good friend, and it's clear Landry fits the bill."

Josh was struck dumb. His father hadn't done anything so unexpected in recent memory. To be honest, it was more than a little confusing.

"Thanks… Dad," was all he could eventually manage to squeeze out of numb lips.

"Well don't go getting all teary-eyed," the Colonel said, his usual gruff intonation returning. "I just want to be sure you and Landry represent this family and all of Texas with the kind of effort that does us proud. And getting there with an ounce of energy left in the tank is a good way to start."

"Don't worry on that count. Landry and I are ready." Josh tried not to sound cocky, but only half-succeeded.

This time the smile was more obvious. "We'll see. A lot of good boys have gone to Benning thinking the same thing. Not all of them have left covered in glory."

"I don't know about glory, but we'll hold our own."

His father nodded thoughtfully. "I think you will. Both of you."

It was probably the nicest thing the Colonel had ever said to him, at least since he'd gone to the Academy. His father didn't often share his feelings, other than displeasure, of course. That was one emotion he took no pains to hide. But praise? And concerning Ranger training? Josh felt an unmistakable glow as he shook his father's offered hand.

So on this auspicious day they had gathered at the Dallas airport, not the Greyhound terminal. Landry was coming with his own family, but up till that moment Josh hadn't seen any sign of them. The Colonel was pacing, as usual, glancing at his watch as if the gesture would speed the Landrys' arrival. His mother was sitting off by herself, her face a blank mask of acceptance. She'd been married to the Colonel long enough to know how a good military wife – or mother – handled such departures. Stoically. Kyle was babbling something to him about how cool the whole Ranger experience would be, but he was only half-listening. Darla hadn't taken her eyes off him since they'd all gotten in the car that morning, as if she were trying to memorize every minute feature of his face. He glanced down at her and saw his Academy ring hanging from a gold chain around her neck. It made him smile.

"Hey Josh!" a familiar voice called out from down the hallway.

Everyone turned to see Landry striding determinedly in their direction, a huge duffle bag slung over his shoulder, his family scurrying along in his wake carrying various smaller bags, purses, cameras, etc. It looked to Josh like one of those photos of a family arriving at Ellis Island.

"Hey man, all ready for the big trip?" He sounded pumped.

"As ready as I'll ever be, I guess," Josh answered, moderating his enthusiasm to show Darla, and his Mom, that he'd miss them. Although, to be honest, he was pretty pumped too.

The Colonel jumped into action almost immediately, shaking Mr. Landry's hand, then Mason's, and nodding to Mrs. Landry with a reassuring confidence.

"Let's get you boys all checked in," he said, indicating the nearby airline counter. "Don't want you to miss your flight."

"Hell, Mason's so excited he could probably fly there without the plane," Mr. Landry said with a smile.

Mason grimaced good-naturedly. "We'd save a few bucks," he said.

"Probably end up in Colorado instead of Georgia if Mason were flying," Landry's younger brother said, and everyone laughed. The brother received a sharp punch to the shoulder for his attempt at humor.

Check-in went smoothly, with the attractive young woman behind the ticket counter showing special consideration for the two young officers dressed in their Army greens. In fact, she showed a bit too much consideration for Darla's taste. She went over to Josh at the counter and snuggled up close to his side as soon as the blonde airline employee started making too much small talk for her liking.

"Looks like Darla's seeing a bit of green," Mrs. Landry whispered to Josh's Mom.

"She's just anxious that they'll be gone for all these months," Mrs. Daniels replied with a sigh that suggested she understood her anxiety all too well.

Finally, with the boarding passes issued and the bags checked, Josh and Mason said their goodbyes to their siblings, tried to calm teary-eyed Moms, and shook hands with their Dads one last time.

"Make us all proud," the Colonel said as he crushed Josh's hand in his own. "And keep your head down."

"Stay safe, honey," his wife added with one last hug.

Then Josh turned to Darla, who stood a short distance away from the others.

"Guess this is it," he said, holding her by her shoulders. She was doing a good job of keeping her emotions in check, but he could see red rimming her eyes.

"You take good care of yourself, you hear?" she said, her voice thick with emotion.

"Don't worry, I'll be back in no time." He wasn't sure he believed his words himself, but he needed her to believe.

He leaned down and kissed her gently on the lips. "I'll miss you, babe," he whispered.

"I'll miss you too," she answered, tears beginning to pool in the corners of her eyes. He gave her one more big hug, and then pulled away. It was time to go.

He and Landry gave a last wave to the assembled well-wishers, and then turned toward the waiting plane.

"You be sure to write!" his Mom called out.

"You too, Mason!" Landry's Mom chimed-in.

"Wow, you'd think we were going to 'Nam, instead of Benning," Landry said.

"Yeh," was all Josh could spit out, his thoughts stuck on an ancient Chinese saying: *The longest journey begins with a single step.*

He put one foot in front of the other and boarded the flight.

CHAPTER 4

Columbus Airport was small, but fairly new and located a hair over ten miles from Ft. Benning. What struck Josh – and struck him hard – was the heat. He had survived his share of Texas summers, so it wasn't as if he'd never worked up a sweat just by walking fifty feet to a parked car. But this Georgia heat was something else. As soon as he stepped out of the plane and started down the rolling stairway, perspiration began to drip down the back of his neck as he wiped beads of sweat from his forehead.

"Feels like a steam room," Landry said from a step behind.

"With the thermostat set on high."

By the time they'd collected their gear and reported to a sergeant with a 'RANGERS' sign in his hands who led them to the drab green school bus that would take them the twelve miles to Benning, their uniforms were ringing wet. First thing Josh noticed, after the heat, was how little regard the sergeant seemed to have for his newly-minted officers. Sergeant Jackson was a solid six foot two of attitude. A black man from New Jersey, Jackson took one look at Josh and the eleven other Ranger School candidates who got off planes from all over the South, and shook his head with evident disdain.

"You boys look like you was ridden hard and put away wet," he announced to no one in particular.

"Sir," one of the other candidates, a tall, square-jawed kid from Mississippi said.

"I ain't no officer," Jackson answered.

"But *we* are," the Mississippi kid said with no hesitation. He stared at the sergeant as if daring him to contradict his words.

"I suppose that be true. But to me you're nuthin' but new meat."

"Sir," the kid repeated.

Jackson looked as if he might spit, but instead cracked a tiny sarcastic smile.

"Siiir," he drawled, stretching the word to the breaking point. "Now do you think all you shiny new officers can get your asses up on this bus so we can get you back to Benning?"

The kid, who had maintained a stony expression throughout the give-and-take, smiled and reached out his hand.

"Edwin Rand," he said. "Lieutenant Edwin Rand."

Jackson looked at the offered hand for a moment as if it were some kind of rotten fish, but finally grabbed ahold and gave it one slow pump. "Sergeant Jackson. I be your den mother for the next few days."

"Good to know we're in good hands," Rand said.

"We'll see what you be sayin' in a week or two," the sergeant answered without a hint of humor. Then he turned to the rest of the incoming candidates. "Come on, all you newbies, get yo' officer butts up on my bus and we'll get you off to Ranger school. There be some folk there want to make yo' acquaintance." He chuckled to himself. "*'Make yo' acquaintance'*. That a good one."

Landry snuck a surprised glance over at Josh. "If the sergeants are this hard-ass, what do you think the officers are like?" he whispered.

"Don't think about it," Josh said, but even as he did he couldn't help thinking about the Colonel.

The ride to Ft. Benning was hot, bumpy and loud. The would-be Rangers were quiet enough as an air of reflective anticipation settled over most of the young men, but the bus's transmission teamed with the driver's blaring radio to generate a wall of sound that would have made Phil Spectre proud. Josh stared out the window at the green vegetation and red soil that sped past in a blur, dotted here and there with tumbledown one-room shacks, small general stores with more booze than food on the shelves, gas stations surrounded by the rusting hulks of smashed cars and shiny new pick-ups, and the occasional Depression-era red brick elementary school. Landry kept up a monologue that suggested he was more than a little nervous. If anyone had pressed him hard enough, Josh would've had to admit he felt a few butterflies as well.

All the nervousness didn't come close to preparing them for the actual arrival at Benning. Oh, the first few minutes were okay, although the way their instructors barked at them made them wonder why they'd bothered to graduate from West Point. It was a lot like being a plebe back at the Academy. From the first moment the rickety old bus ground to a stop in front of their barracks, someone was screaming at them every minute of the day – and night. They barely had time to drop off their gear before the circus began. First up was the fitness evaluation. Push-ups, sit-ups, chin-ups, running with 60-pounds of gear, swimming in your uniform – and never enough food or sleep. And then there was the marching! Sweat pouring off your body during the day, eyes on the verge of closing at night, mile after mile up and down rugged hills. Despite all the prep he and Landry had put in during the weeks leading up to the course, Josh had never been more tired. And hungry. He'd put himself on a limited calorie intake diet for weeks before the course, but it hadn't come close to matching the tiny amounts of chow the school provided.

One of the worst moments in those first few days was when they had to climb up to a tiny platform perched high above the rugged hills, shimmy across a narrow bridge and then jump on a zipline to slide pell-mell down the other side. Of all the physical demands of those first days, that was the one that got Josh in the guts. He'd never had trouble flying, and he didn't remember any problems with heights, but the narrow crossing followed by the zipline got his adrenaline pumping so powerfully that for a moment he thought he might be sick.

'*Screw these guys,*' he thought as he struggled to keep the meager contents of his stomach in place. '*I'm gonna finish this course if it kills me.*'

There were times he thought it might. From Benning they marched up into the mountains. Only a little over half the guys who'd started still remained. Funny thing was, nobody talked about the wash-outs. It was an unspoken taboo: talk about the guys that crashed and burned, and you'd be next. Some of the West Pointers complained that the Ranger instructors were harder on them than the ordinary stiffs, but neither Josh nor Landry could tell the difference between their constant harassment and anyone else's. Josh was better prepared for the heights at that stage, but preparing to repel down a steep cliff face carrying almost half his body weight still made his knees weak. Or was it the lack of sleep? Landry seemed unfazed. The silly grin he kept plastered on his face started to annoy Josh, until he reminded himself that his buddy wasn't trying to show him or the others up, it was just his way. The constant drilling on tactics and strategy came as a welcomed relief from the sheer pain of the physical side, and besides, Josh was good at it. Damn good.

Two weeks in the mountains felt a lot like two months in hell, albeit an often wet, freezing cold hell, but nobody clamored for the next phase: the swamp. By the end of the mountain course they'd all heard stories about what awaited them in the Everglades: snakes, lizards and gators, all wrapped up in a sweltering hot swamp with more insects than any of them had ever seen – or felt. Less than forty per cent of the original class took the flight to Elgin Air Force base in northwestern Florida. By the time they'd hiked through waist-deep water a dozen times and led patrols through terrain that even the local Indians wouldn't set foot in, the remaining soldiers were stronger, tougher and a helluva lot smarter than when they started. A final field exercise put everything they'd learned to real world use. As Josh put it in a letter back home, 'The Academy made us book smart; Ranger school made us war smart.' Or at least that's what they hoped.

Graduation Day brought the real world to Elgin. Josh's mother cried when she first saw him in his loose-fitting uniform.

"You're so thin!" she moaned, tears sliding down her cheeks.

"Lost 22 pounds," Josh said with more than a hint of pride.

"I lost 26!" Landry chimed in from a few feet away where his parents were getting their first look at the soon-to-be Ranger.

"That's only because you had more to lose," Josh grumbled.

Despite all the hubbub with families and girlfriends milling about and chatting and taking photos with their loved ones, the Colonel didn't say much to his son but seemed to have gotten over his disappointment at his choice of school. The only remaining question was whether he'd get used to a SE Asia deployment. As usual, the senior Daniels spent most of his time chatting with the big brass, who gravitated to the visiting congressman like moths to a flame.

When it came time for the class to receive their Ranger tabs, the Battalion Commander called "Congressman Mark Daniels" to come up and do the honors. The Colonel looked pleased with himself as he answered the call, but even Josh had to admit that his smile was noticeably wider as he pinned the patch on his son's shoulder. The black and gold tab weighed heavily on Josh, both because of all the effort that went into earning it and because of all the responsibility it symbolized. Yet it was a weight he accepted gladly. He'd always been a leader; even among his fellow Ranger candidates he had been recognized as one of the best of the best, and whether the Army recognized it with early promotions or not, he would be a leader wherever he served.

The Daniels and the Landrys went out to dinner together that night. Mason was as jovial and relaxed as ever, but everyone from his parents to Darla noticed that Josh seemed a bit withdrawn, a little less freewheeling with his jabs and replies.

"I'm just tired," he replied when his mother asked. But later that night, when he and Darla were finally alone, he opened up about what he was feeling.

"They say Ranger training is the closest thing to warfare you can experience without getting shot at," he said as he sat sipping a beer in her room long after the rest of the family had gone to bed. "But a few of the NCOs I talked to who've actually been over there said Benning is a walk in the park compared to 'Nam. It's not like I don't think I can take the heat, or the lack of sleep, or even the gooks shooting at us. But I don't know how I'll react when one of my men gets shot, or killed. I mean, what if something happens to Landry?"

"Don't talk like that!" Darla chastised, her tone a mix of indignation and sympathy. "You'll jinx him."

"Maybe I already have," he said, his voice soft, reflective. "I mean, do you think he would've signed up for 'Nam if I hadn't led the way? I'm not sure. He didn't say a word about Ranger training until I brought it up. And now 'Nam." He sipped his beer. "I don't know if I could look his parents in the eye if something happened to him."

Darla rubbed his shoulders and sighed. "Landry is a full-grown man, Josh. A Second-Lieutenant in the United States Army. You're not responsible for him, any more than he's responsible for you."

"That's easy to say. But it's not how I feel."

Darla nuzzled his ear. "I know. That's one reason I love you. And why you're gonna make one heck of an officer."

He turned to her and smiled. "I bet you say that to all the guys."

"Just the ones whose ring I'm wearing." She tugged on the gold chain that held his class ring and pulled it out from under her sweater. She held it up to the light to inspect it one more time.

"Is it wrong to be jealous of a ring?" he drawled, stifling a yawn. He rubbed the spot between her breasts where the ring usually sat.

"If you play your cards right, you might get to spend some time down there."

"If we're going to do any playing, it better be soon. I'm fading."

"Oh no you don't!" she said with mock horror. "I expect to see you at attention and saluting, soldier."

"Yes sir!" Josh said, re-energized. It was quite a while longer before he slipped silently back to his own room and fell into a deep, dreamless sleep.

CHAPTER 5

The Oakland Army Terminal wasn't much to look at, certainly not when compared to the Golden Gate Bridge only a few miles away. The infrastructure at the base looked every bit its 40 plus years. The Army was good at throwing paint on anything that looked too worn, but replacing stateside buildings and runways didn't align well with the current needs of the Pentagon. With over half a million U.S. military personnel stationed in Vietnam, and many more in support roles in various countries surrounding the small Southeast Asian country, the focus was on men and materiel overseas, not at home. Of course, it didn't really matter to the majority of men and women heading in that direction. Most of them were too nervous to pay much attention to the Terminal's condition. Some were too excited.

Josh was a bit of both. He and Landry had flown out to Oakland the day before, a three hour jaunt from Dallas. It had been a difficult departure from Texas, more so for the families of the two young officers than the men themselves. Josh knew that the Colonel had given orders to his wife to keep the "waterworks" under control, and for the most part she had succeeded. He could still see the strain around her eyes when she'd given him a final hug and kiss, but the tears stayed hidden. Until, that is, Darla began to sob as Josh and Landry moved past the gate to board the flight to California. Then the damn broke and both Moms – Landry's as well – started to wipe at their eyes and blow their noses surreptitiously. Josh was taken aback when he took one last glance at the family before stepping onboard the 707 and saw his father hugging his mom, apparently trying to console her.

'Next thing you know, he'll be letting his hair grow,' the younger Daniels said to himself with a smile, but deep inside he was happy to receive confirmation that the Colonel's heart did more than just pump blood.

The flight was uneventful, putting them at the Oakland Terminal pretty much on-time. In-processing was relatively quick, especially considering the hundreds of other young soldiers on their way to Vietnam. The only discordant note was a disturbance that could be heard off in the distance. When Josh asked an older NCO who was working the processing what was going on, he sneered, "Protesters. We get 'em nearly every day."

"Damn hippies," Landry chimed in. "We fight so that assholes like them can protest."

Josh nodded. "Screw 'em."

It was nighttime before they boarded the chartered DC-8 that was going to take them to war. For Josh the entire experience was more than a little surreal: the plane was a regular commercial jet, even down to the stewardesses, but row after row of seats were filled with nothing but soldiers. The talk was light, from time to time boastful, but much more reflective than in the processing center a few hours earlier. Guys who'd never seen each other before shared stories of their families, their high school or college exploits, and most often, how their number had come up in the lottery and they'd learned they'd be drafted. It seemed to Josh like half of all the soldiers on his plane were draftees. They were young, most even younger than he. But most of them weren't all that enthusiastic about the War, or President Johnson. Many of them had high hopes that if Nixon were elected he'd end the War within a year of two.

For his part, Josh wondered how he'd be able to lead men who didn't want to be in Vietnam. It would be hard enough to order young guys to do something that could leave them dead or wounded. What would it be like with guys who thought the whole War was "just a joke, a stupid, fucked-up joke," as one of them had complained.

The idea of going into battle was intimidating enough without having to worry about some headcase fragging his platoon leader. Which in this case might be Josh. Or Landry. Josh tried to imagine what it would be like have to explain to Mrs Landry that her son had been killed by some American kid just a few younger than he was, and not a North Vietnamese regular. The thought left him feeling more than a little numb. He snuck a glance over at his friend as he read a Time magazine. For the first time it really struck him that Landry, or Josh himself, might not come back home from the War.

He shook his head and let out a deep breath. *'Won't do me any good to get into that mindset,'* he thought. Instead he cracked open a book that a friend had recommended: *One Flew Over the Cuckoo's Nest* by some hippy guy named Kesey. He kept the cover tilted down low so no one walking past his aisle could read the title. He didn't know what reaction he'd get if someone caught him reading it, but he didn't want to chance making any enemies that early in his tour.

Every few hours the stewardesses would ramble down the aisle pushing a cart loaded with chow or sodas. A few soldiers always tried to joke with them and shoot the breeze, but the relative rarity of such attempts underscored the thoughtful rumination of most of the passengers. Eating and drinking helped pass the time, but nothing could make the 22 hours in the air pass quickly enough. From California they flew to Hawaii, Wake Island and Okinawa, before they finally closed in on their final destination: Bien Hoa Air Base, Vietnam.

"We are sixty miles off the coast of Vietnam and about to make our final descent into Bien Hoa," the pilot's voice came over the intercom. "Check to make sure your seatbelts are securely fastened – due to security requirements, this may be a steeper approach than you are used to." For the first time since they'd taken to the air, a buzz of energy surged through the ranks.

"Steeper approach?" Landry said, looking to Josh for guidance. "What's that all about?"

Before Josh could answer, an older NCO with a Vietnam Service medal prominently displayed on his uniform turned around from the row ahead of them. "It means the gooks have supposedly scored more Grail shoulder-fired anti-aircraft missiles and we're going in with a non-existent glide path to give them less time to blow us out of the air."

He said it matter-of-factly, but Josh thought he heard a hint of taunt in his voice. 'See if the new kids got any balls,' or something like that.

"I'm good with that," Landry said.

"Me too. The steeper the better," Josh agreed.

"Well drop your cocks and grab your socks, because this might get hairy," the NCO added as he turned back to his own seat.

Hearing the old vet put it so bluntly inspired both Josh and Landry to pull their seat belts an inch or two tighter, until they could barely breathe. The lights in the cabin dimmed; the sudden quiet was eerie. Moments later the pitch of the engines rose untold octaves. The nose of the DC-8 dipped at a forty-five degree angle and a few of the men groaned loudly.

"Just like a roller coaster," Landry whispered, but his knuckles showed bright white where he held the arms of his seat in a death grip.

Down below them, in the early morning light the turquoise waters of the Pacific bumped headfirst into the stunning green vegetation surrounding the urban sprawl of Saigon. Sprawl that was coming up to meet them very, very quickly.

"Hope we don't have to pay extra for this ride," Landry said through clenched teeth.

"I just hope the pilot has done this before," a young draftee sitting next to them answered in a weak voice.

Suddenly the nose of the plane pulled up violently and they felt as well as heard the tires slam into the landing strip. The plane bounced once and then settled down onto the asphalt, the thrust reversers screaming as the pilot slammed on the brakes. A smattering of applause broke out throughout the cabin.

"Welcome to Bien Hoa Air Base," the pilot's voice announced over the intercom. "Please remain seated until we come to a complete stop."

The vast majority of first-timers stared out the tiny plane windows at the bizarre panorama that swept past as the plane taxied to the terminal. Even in the early hours of daylight most of the GIs who worked on the tarmac – pushing, pulling, loading, and unloading an incredible assortment of pallets, crates, boxes and God-knows-what from point A to point B – were shirtless and sweating profusely. The first impression that struck Josh was of an ant hill swarming with activity. Make that a fire ant hill.

"Jesus H. Christmas," Landry said with a whistle. "We ain't in Dallas anymore."

From near silence the buzz of conversation grew exponentially as first impressions swirled about the plane. A rolling stairway came up alongside as several drab green buses with something resembling chicken wire welded over the windows pulled up and idled. An officer with close-cropped black hair greying at the temples hopped out of a Jeep and started up the stairs, followed closely by an enlisted man carrying a clipboard. Dim morning light streamed into the plane as the front hatch swung open. A stewardess passed the intercom mike to the officer, who stood in the aisle to address all the new arrivals.

"What's this action?" Landry asked. Josh was wondering the same thing.

"Listen up!" he said with a voice accustomed to command. "I am Major Norman Eastly, Exec Officer here at the base, and on behalf of Colonel Slade, our Commanding Officer, I want to welcome you to Vietnam. I know you're tired, but before we do anything else we're going to get you processed-in. Corporal Heddlemeyer here will explain the procedure. Follow his directions to the T and this will be a painless process. Then, and only then, we'll get you to your barracks for some rack time. Corporal?"

Heddlemeyer read a laundry list of directions that Josh barely followed. He wondered how many of the other men would absorb it all. Glancing out the window he saw a half-dozen EMs pile off one of the buses and station themselves between the stairs and the buses, each carrying a cardboard sign with large writing on it. *'Should've known they'd make it idiot-proof,'* he thought. Somehow that made him feel better about the entire experience.

As the men filed out of the plane, row by row, Major Eastly stood by the cockpit door and nodded to each man as he went past. When Josh approached, he could see the major glance down at his name tag and then up at his face with a look of pleased recognition.

"Daniels, how was the flight?" he asked.

Josh blinked. "Uh, not bad, sir, not bad."

"Good, glad to hear it. Colonel Slade asked me to grab you before you got caught up in the processing and take you over to his office. That ok with you?"

Josh got the distinct feeling that the last was pure pro-forma. It wasn't a request. "Yeh, sure… Is there a problem?"

Eastly smiled. "No, no, nothing of the sort. The colonel just wanted to welcome you himself."

Josh saw a PFC glance over at him with a questioning look as he stepped past to exit the plane. It wasn't until that moment that he realized Landry was waiting at the top of the stairs, clogging the egress for all behind him.

"Problem?" he asked loud enough for the major to hear.

"Friend of yours?" the major asked Josh.

"We went to West Point together."

"Good. It's good to have a buddy here. But tell him you'll catch up to him."

For about an instant Josh considered asking if Landry could come along too, but the look on Eastly's face quickly dissuaded him. Josh did as he was told. Landry climbed downstairs and went toward the appropriate bus with a nod of his head.

With new arrivals still deplaning, the major turned the meet-and-greet over to Corporal Heddlemeyer and led the way down to a waiting Jeep. Josh followed compliantly, wondering what had sparked the high-level reception. He had an idea, and it didn't make him happy.

Even after Texas and Georgia, Vietnam was unbelievably hot and humid. His uniform started to show large damp spots under his armpits before he got halfway down the steps. *'This is really something else,'* he thought as he glanced at the activity all around him. *'Oh yeh, definitely something else.'*

The major tried some small talk as the Jeep bounced its way across the tarmac, but Josh was in no mood for a chat. He answered every question politely, but offered nothing with which to extend the conversation. After a few tries Eastly gave up, and they drove the last few minutes in silence. When they pulled up in front of a large, two-story white office building topped by orange tiles, the major wasted no time hopping out of the Jeep and leading the way inside. "Admin," he announced. "Commander's office is on the second floor."

Josh followed Eastly up the steep interior stairs to a small outer office where a thin, wiry corporal manned the reception desk.

"Second Lieutenant Daniels to see the colonel," Eastly told the corporal.

"I'll let him know right away, sir."

The corporal picked up a black phone and pushed the intercom button. "Major Eastly is here with Lieutenant Daniels, sir," he said. His head bobbed as he listened to the reply on the other end. As soon as he hung up he turned to the major. "You can go in now, sir."

As he walked past the reception desk, Josh reached out his hand to the corporal. "Josh Daniels," he said. His father had always told him that the keys to any organization were held by the receptionist, and he wanted this soldier to see him as a person, not just another junior officer.

"John Walker," the corporal answered after a moment's surprised pause.

As Josh looked up, he saw what might have been an annoyed glare from Eastly, but chose to ignore it and followed the major into the Commander's office.

It was immediately clear that Colonel Slade liked weapons, all kinds of weapons. Pistols, rifles, even grenades and knives were displayed all around the sizeable room. Most of them looked like VC or NVA. Slade's desk was massive, a huge chunk of dark brown wood that must have been locally made, Josh thought. The colonel was glancing at some paperwork on his desk, and kept his eyes glued to the documents just long enough so that the major and Josh had to wait a moment before he acknowledged them.

"Lieutenant Daniels," he finally said, standing with hand extended. "What do you think of our little corner of the world?"

Josh shook the older man's hand and was impressed by the strength of his grip. Reminded him of the other Colonel back in

Dallas. With that in mind, he was extremely circumspect in his response.

"Seems like you've got one heck'uv'an operation going here, Colonel. Very impressive."

Josh saw the smallest glimmer of satisfaction in the colonel's eyes. "In both number of flights and total tonnage we've got the busiest airport in this part of Asia," he said proudly. "Have a seat, have a seat." He gestured to one of two black leather chairs stationed in front of the desk. "You want to sit-in, Chet?" he asked Eastly.

The Major hesitated a second as if he were considering the invitation, but apparently thought better of it. "Thanks, sir, but I'm up to my shorthairs in paper," he excused himself. "I'm sure I'll have other chances to talk to the lieutenant."

"Well, thanks for bringing him over. And Chet, would you ask Corporal Walker if he'd bring us some coffee?" He turned to Josh. "Coffee work for you, Lieutenant?"

"Thank you, sir. Help me keep my eyes open."

"Feeling the trip, are you? I remember the first time I flew over here. I slept for about 12 hours straight once I got to my bed. Felt like I was walking on sponge cake." He smiled, seemingly proud of his analogy. Josh heard rather than saw Eastly open the door behind them.

"Major Eastly," he called over his shoulder. "Thanks. Appreciate it."

"No problem," the major said with a nod. "Just don't get used to it."

He and the colonel exchanged a knowing smile.

"So, you're a West Pointer, eh?" the colonel started right in before the door even shut. "Top ten per cent, is that right?"

"Yes sir."

"I graduated in '44. Thought I'd be going to the Pacific, but by the time they got me all trained up and processed-in, the War was over. Did two tours in Korea, though."

"My father fought in Korea," Josh offered. He figured he might as well bring up the elephant in the room before the colonel did. "Colonel Mark Daniels? 4th Battalion, 17th Infantry Regiment?"

Slade nodded. "Never met him, but I have been made aware that he's now a Congressman from Texas. You must be very proud."

"I am," Josh answered, waiting for the other shoe to fall. He didn't have to wait long.

"Of course, the Congressional liaison office at DOD informed us that the Congressman's son would be joining us here. I suppose you were aware?"

"Actually, no. But I'm not surprised."

"To be honest with you, neither am I. We haven't had all that many politicians' kids come through – oh, a few joined the National Guard, sure, but not so many Infantry officers request this posting, and fewer still Rangers. I gotta tell you, you're something of a rarity around here."

"Is that a good thing, or a bad thing?" Josh asked, remembering the hazing he'd received at the Academy when he'd first arrived and the upperclassman learned of his father's position.

"Probably a little of both. But I've instructed your Company Commander, Captain Reed, to keep an eye out for any *unusual* treatment – good or bad. I don't know if it's possible, but I'd like your tour to be as normal as any other soldier's. If you can call anything here normal."

"Thank you. That's all I could ask."

"If you run into any trouble, you tell Reed – okay?" When Josh started to object, the colonel talked right over him. "I know, I know, you don't want to snitch on anyone. But listen, Lieutenant, it's hard enough trying to win this war without all the black on white, young on old, rich on poor crap that goes around. Oh, we know it's here. But if we can do anything to keep it to a minimum, that's what we're going to do. Understood?"

Josh wanted to explain why he didn't want to be put in a situation where the big brass looked to be covering his butt, but at the same time he couldn't very well deny the Commander's logic. "Yes sir, I understand. If anything happens to jeopardize our unit's field capability, I'll talk to Capt. Reed."

A small smile appeared on the colonel's face. "You're starting to make me think this politician stuff might be genetic. You danced all around that commitment."

"Look, Colonel, I don't think it'll be an issue. And if it is I'll try to take care of it. But if it gets too bad for me to handle, I'll talk to Reed. Really."

"Good. They said you were a solid officer. Maybe they were right this time."

"I'll do my best, Colonel."

"I'm sure you will, Lieutenant."

The base Commander didn't have much else to say, but when Corporal Walker brought the coffee he needed to fill some time. After a few minute's pro forma gab he dismissed Josh to finish-up his in-processing.

When Josh left the colonel's office he found a sergeant waiting for him in the reception area.

"Lieutenant Daniels? Master Sergeant Fisher. I've been assigned to get you over to in-processing and show you the ropes."

"They afraid I'll get lost?" Josh asked with his best effort at a disarming smile.

Fisher snickered. "You wouldn't be the first, sir. This place is like a maze inside a maze inside a…" he hesitated, trying to think of an appropriate choice.

"A labyrinth?" Josh suggested.

"Yeh, right, a labyrinth. That's just about right. You know, there's a story about Daze-eyed Joe..." he began, ignoring Walker's rolled eyes. "They say he deplaned here from a non-stop out of California in '65 and he's still wandering around trying to find his unit. Folks only see him late at night."

"After they've finished-off a pint of whiskey and a few beers," the corporal chimed in.

Sergeant Fisher shrugged and raised his hands in mock surrender. "Maybe. But the point of the story is true enough – this place is a… labyrinth." He raised his eyebrows, self-impressed.

"Well then I appreciate your expertise, Sergeant. Shall we get to it?"

"No time like the present, sir."

With the sun barely rising above the buildings that surrounded the airstrip, the heat reflecting off the tarmac was already nearly unbearable. Sgt. Fisher noticed Josh wiping beads of sweat off his forehead.

"Hot enough for you? You'll get used to it. Kind of," he said. "Just make sure you stay hydrated. You don't drink enough out there," he continued, indicating an indefinite space outside the perimeter of the air base, "and you'll find yourself passing out. Not a good thing when you've got a few thousand VC trying to blow your head off." He smiled.

"Don't sugar-coat it for me," Josh said.

"Hate to lose a new West Pointer in the first few days. Too much paperwork." Josh smiled.

The sergeant filled him in on the basics of life in Vietnam as they walked; he seemed to know his way around. "How long you been here?" Josh asked during a lull in the orientation.

"Nam? Sixteen months. This is my second tour. Couldn't get enough the first time."

"How come?"

"Why'd I re-up? I don't know. Kind of missed the guys I guess. And the States seemed too damn boring."

"And having people shooting at you doesn't put you off?"

The sergeant shrugged. "You get used to it. Kind of. Depends on the people around you. I guess I've been lucky. I've had good people all through both tours. Where are they putting you?"

"First Air Cav, Company E," the lieutenant said proudly.

"You're a Ranger?"

"Trained as one, anyway."

"Hmmm. Would'a thought a Congressman's kid would've taken a nice desk job back in the Pentagon."

"Can't type worth a damn."

Fisher smiled.

"You may wish you did after a few months out in the rice paddies."

"We'll see."

Moments later they arrived at the white stucco building that housed the in-processing facilities. Long lines of new arrivals faced portable tables manned by unsmiling soldiers.

"Reminds me of the first day of gym in high school," Josh said.

"Something like that."

Much to his chagrin, Fisher led Josh to the front of the C-D line. He tried to ignore the icy stares coming from the soldiers who'd been waiting their turn.

"Hey, what is this shit? Get in line," one of the less patient newbies called out.

"Shut your face or I'll have you running so many laps you'll think you're on a merry-go-round," the sergeant yelled back. The young private glared but didn't say another word.

"Name, rank and serial number," a corporal behind the desk droned.

"Daniels, Joshua A, Second Lieutenant, 4217714," Josh barked without hesitation.

The enlisted man rifled through a shoebox bull of folders and pulled out Josh's.

"Daniels, you've been assigned to the First Infantry, 16th Division," the corporal read from one of the many pieces of paper in the folder.

Josh reacted before he could stop himself. "What? I was supposed to go to First Air Cav, Company E."

The corporal didn't even look up. "Take it up with your CO," he said, pushing a sheaf of papers in his direction. "Sign everywhere there's a red X."

"But…"

The corporal held up his hand. "Nothing I can do. Sorry. At least you've got a good unit with the Big Red 1. You could've landed with one of the MACV units babysitting the ARVN."

He only knew the Military Assistance Advisory Command by reputation. What he'd heard hadn't made him want to volunteer. Rumor had it that the South Vietnamese had unusual ideas of how and when to engage the enemy, and some of those ideas could get people killed. Still…

"Sign the papers, Lieutenant. We've got a lot of soldiers to process this morning."

Josh took a deep breath and did as he was told.

"Good. The sergeant here will get you organized. That right, Sergeant?"

Fisher looked down at the corporal as if he were inspecting a dirty latrine. "Come on, Lieutenant," he said to Josh, "let's get out of here."

Josh kept his mouth shut until they'd left the building. But then he couldn't hold it in any longer.

"First Infantry?" he said aloud to Fisher. "They don't even *have* a Ranger unit. Do they?"

Fisher shrugged. "We got Rangers scattered all over the place. Might be just a typical snafu, or maybe they changed their minds. Like the corporal said, take it up with your CO if it bothers you. Just remember, there are over a half-million soldiers in this stinking little country right now, and you're just one of them. Congressman Daddy or not."

Josh almost lashed out at the NCO, but caught himself. "If I were using my father's influence I wouldn't even be here," he said levelly.

Fisher looked at him and nodded. "Suppose that's true enough. But whether that makes you a friggin' hero or an idiot, I'm not sure."

'Neither am I,' Josh thought. *'Neither am I.'*

*****

By the time he'd checked out his weapon and a rucksack full of other equipment, the sun was already low in the sky. Not that it felt the least bit cooler, but at least the shadows were longer. Fisher had pushed him through the system about as quickly as humanly possible, and it had still taken four hours. He pitied the poor guys still standing in lines sweating their asses off.

Sgt. Fisher guided him once more through the maelstrom of activity to the temporary officers' quarters where he'd bunk until the powers-that-be decided to ship him out to his unit.

"Could be tomorrow. Could be next week," Fisher said. "Depends on what they're doing and how bad they need bodies."

Josh picked-up on the cynicism, but by that time he was so tired and drained that his head was spinning and he barely understood the words.

"Whatever," was all he could mouth.

By the time Fisher made sure he was situated and had a bunk, it was all Josh could do to stay upright. After thanking the sergeant and listening to his final words of advice ("Keep your head down, your rifle clean, and don't die until someone kills you,") Second Lieutenant Joshua Daniels barely pulled off his sweat-drenched uniform before collapsing onto the narrow cot.

'Wow, I'm in friggin' Vietnam,' was the last thought that skipped across his vanishing consciousness before sleep overtook him. *'Friggin' Vietnam.'*

*****

When he awoke the next morning, his eyes nearly glued together by the fine red dust that seemed to coat everything in sight, it took him a few seconds to orient himself. The tin-roofed barracks was already hotter than Dallas in mid-July and his mouth felt like it had been sandpapered. He was just re-establishing a tenuous reality when a voice piped up, seemingly out of nowhere:

"So you're Daniels?"

Josh craned his neck to see where the sound originated. His eyes came to rest on a skinny young guy with a long, narrow nose and short red hair that stood straight on end, about his age, sitting on the cot next to his. He sported a big green and red tattoo on one forearm. At that angle, Josh couldn't read it.

"Yeh, I'm Daniels. Josh. You?"

"Wentworth. Mark. You just come in last night?"

"Yeh. Flew in from Oakland. You?" He sat up to see Wentworth without working up a crick in his neck.

"Got here two days ago. Seems like they've screwed up my assignment. So I have to wait until they figure it out." He tilted his head. "Got a cigarette?"

"Sorry, don't smoke. Want a piece of gum?"

Wentworth shook his head with a look of disgust.

For a long moment the hooch was silent. "They screwed up my papers too," Josh finally volunteered.

"From what I hear, they screw up just about everything. You ROTC?" he asked, nodding at the lieutenant's bars on the uniform slung over the bed post.

"West Point," Josh answered. When he saw Wentworth's eyes open wide, he regretted mentioning it.

"I went the Rot-see route," Wentworth explained. "Ohio State. Played cornerback."

Josh was impressed. "I played a bit at Army. Not that it's quite like playing for the Buckeyes."

Mark waved one hand lazily. "Football's football. The guys just get a little bigger and faster the higher you go."

Turned out he'd enrolled in ROTC as an insurance policy against a low lottery number in the draft, and he'd hit the jackpot. "I pulled #22," he explained, "so I'd've been over here one way or the other. Figured I might as well go as an officer."

Josh tried not to make any first impressions, but after all the rah-rah of the Academy, Wentworth's story seemed less than inspiring. Not that he held any negative feelings for draftees; he knew a lot of people thought the War was a mistake. Some folks thought any war was a mistake. But he thought officers should have greater motivation. How could they lead men, especially guys who didn't want to be there, if they were only half-committed themselves?

He was pondering how to respond when a knock on the hooch door saved him from saying something he'd probably regret.

"Come in!" he called out.

The door swung open and a familiar smiling face strode in looking like he owned the place.

"Daniels! They got you over here too?" Landry asked as he slapped a high five and surveyed the spare furnishings of the temporary housing.

"For the time being. They're sending me to First Infantry." He tried not to sound disappointed or petulant, but only half-succeeded.

"They screwed you over too?" the big Texan asked, his tone more excited than outraged. "I thought I was the only one."

"No shit. Where're you going?"

"Big Red One," he said with what might have passed for a hint of pride.

"Damn, and I thought I'd finally gotten rid of your sorry ass," Josh said with a big smile.

"Can't get rid of me that easy."

"Or me, it looks like." Wentworth had been watching the scene without expression until that point.

"How do you mean?"

"Another 'volunteer' for Big Red," he said, pointing to himself.

"You're kidding?!" Josh said. "What did they do, lose all their officers in one week?"

"Probably replacing all the KIAs from the Tet Offensive."

Landry glanced over at the skinny redhead. "Who's your friend?" he asked Daniels.

Josh glanced back over his shoulder. "Wentworth, this big old cowboy is Mason Landry, a friend of mine from back at West Point. Landry – Mark Wentworth."

The two men nodded at each other and Wentworth mumbled hello.

"Looks like we might be seeing a lot of each other," Landry said.

"Hard to say. First Infantry is huge. Depends on the Battalion."

"I'm assigned to the first of the second," Josh offered.

"No shit!" Landry came back. "Me too."

"Well, as of now they've got me in the 16th. So we may or may not see so much of each other."

'Wouldn't break my heart,' Josh thought acidly. Wentworth might turn out to be a good officer, but first impressions die hard.

"That's if they even send us there," Landry offered. "Probably change our assignments three more times before we ever get out to the field."

"Speaking of getting out," Josh interrupted, "have you seen any of the Base yet?"

"Just what we saw coming in yesterday. By the time I got done with all my paperwork all I wanted to do was crash."

"Want to take a look?"

"Sure thing," Landry said.

"You, Wentworth?" Josh asked after a moment's hesitation.

"Seen it. Not much out there except a ton of sweating GIs and more materiel than you've ever seen in your life."

"That might be interesting. Let's go take a look." He got up off the cot and headed to the door.

"See you on the rebound," Landry said to Wentworth, who shrugged as if he couldn't care less.

No sooner did the hooch door close behind them, than Landry started-in on his friend.

"What's with that guy?"

"I don't know. Has a stick up his butt from having to do ROTC to avoid getting drafted. Not a happy camper."

"Then can't say I'm sorry he's not coming with us to the 2nd."

"That makes two of us. We'll have enough problems without a whiner."

The two young soldiers walked all around the huge air base, sticking to the shade as much as possible to keep from melting into the tarmac. Their second impressions were pretty much the same as their first: a big, wild, sweat-drenched nuthouse, with no one inside the gates overly concerned with security.

"I guess the VC would be kind'a nuts to try to attack this place," Landry said as they surveyed one of the main gates, complete with towering white concrete columns more befitting the entrance to a concert hall than an air base, with concertina wire topping the whitewashed walls.

"They already did," Josh said matter-of-factly.

"What?!"

"Last January. Dropped 150 mortar and artillery rounds on the base and tried to overrun it down by runway 27."

"You're shittin' me."

"Read about it before we left Texas. If it wasn't for our helicopter gunships it could've been a real cluster flick."

"Are those guys nuts!? Did they really think they could take this base?"

Josh looked at his friend with a slow shake of his head. "You're kidding me, right? The VC think they're gonna take the whole *country*, man. This is just one stop on the way to downtown Saigon."

Landry didn't say anything for a long while. Josh let him cogitate, enjoying the quiet time to check out their surroundings.

"We've really got our tit in a ringer, ain't we?" he finally said after they'd made their way most of the way back to their hooches.

"It's a mess, that's for damn sure."

Both men continued on in thoughtful silence. It was one thing to study the history and tactics of the War at the Academy, and even at Benning, another to see, and feel, and smell the reality: a heady mixture of piss and sweat and disinfectant wafted on the humid breeze. But they were young, and they believed.

And they were thirsty.

"Buy you a beer," Josh offered when they noticed an officers' club looming in the distance.

"You've got yourself a deal."

The club was nothing to write home about, just a big room with concrete floor and tin roof. But it was dark, Credence Clearwater was playing on a jukebox, the air-conditioning worked, and the beer was cheap. Josh and Landry were sitting at the bar, sipping a cool one while they tried to imagine what tomorrow would bring, when out of nowhere Sgt. Fisher suddenly appeared.

"Lieutenant Daniels?" he said, standing just behind Josh's bar stool.

"Sergeant! Did you take a wrong turn?"

Fisher smiled. More a sneer. "Wouldn't be caught dead in a half-ass O Club unless I'd been sent here to haul your ass back to processing. Seems they want you out with your unit. Now."

Landry looked stunned. "What about me?" he said to no one in particular.

"Your name Daniels?" the Sgt asked.

"No. Landry. But I've been assigned to the same unit."

"Well, Landry, I'd say get your ass back there too, and maybe we can save the government the cost of shipping the two of you out there on separate copters."

"That's *Lieutenant* Landry, Sergeant," Josh said with just enough attitude that Fisher paused for a second, wondering if he'd overstepped his bounds. But then Josh laughed and slapped the sergeant on the shoulder. "We'll give you a pass, this time," he said as he threw down a few dollars to cover the beers and pushed off his stool, "but don't make it a habit."

When the three of them got back to Processing they learned that the Big Red One had been in fierce fighting upcountry and that the division commanding general's copter had been shot down, killing the general and all his closest aides.

"Wentworth wasn't far off the mark when he said they needed us," Josh said softly to Landry when he heard the terrible news. "They're short officers."

As if to give credence to that opinion, two NCOs hustled them back to their hooches to collect their equipment and rendezvous at a copter pad for the short trip north of Saigon to someplace called DiAn, which was where the First's in-processing unit was located. They expected the usual 'hurry up and wait' they'd already grown accustomed to in the Army, but to their surprise the copter crew was already in place an waiting for them when they arrived at the pad.

As the small Hughes Loach copter lifted off, Josh could see the sprawling air base unfold beneath them. In minutes they were clear of the city sprawl and flying at a surprisingly high altitude ("prefer not to get my bird shot up by some bored VC," the pilot explained), as the deep greens of the vegetation below swept past in a blur of rice paddies, fields and jungle. Josh looked over at Landry, who stared out the front bubble of the copter as if it were a ride at an amusement park. Reality was, it didn't seem all that real to him, either. Just a few days earlier they'd all been drinking beers, and bs'ing, and hanging out in Dallas. And now this. Josh kept thinking of that line from *Wizard of Oz*...

Suddenly the copter banked abruptly and the engine began to scream as they struggled to gain altitude.

"What's going on?!" he shrieked, barely loud enough to hear himself over the engine and the rotors slashing the air above them.

"We're taking fire from the ground," the pilot said almost calmly, but with just enough adrenaline edging his voice to alert Josh to the seriousness of the situation.

Josh looked out the side window at the lush greenery below. How was it possible that people he'd never even seen before were trying to kill him from a half-mile away? The surreality – or was it absurdity? – of it all hit home hard. They were trying to kill him, and soon, he'd be trying to kill them. Weird.

In less than a minute the copter stopped its crazy gyrations and levelled off to resume their journey. The entire trip only took ten minutes or so, and then they found themselves plummeting to earth like a meteorite from outer space until the copter pulled up with a roar just a hundred feet or so from the ground. Slowly, softly, almost gently, they floated down to the LZ.

"Hope y'all enjoyed the flight," the co-pilot said light-heartedly as the engine whine died down and the rotating shadows above slowed to a halt.

"Quite a ride!" Landry shouted a bit too loudly.

"Yeh, thanks for the lift," Josh added as he threw off his seatbelt.

"You boys take care of yourselves," the pilot said. "I'm sure we'll see you around."

The in-processing unit was just a bunch of smaller tents surrounding one large one, all surrounded by red dirt, tall grass, and jungle. The smell of latrines, helicopter exhaust and his own sweat made Josh nauseous at first, but as he moved further away from the copter his stomach settled. A smiling major with a black scarf tied around his neck came out of the large central tent and greeted the two new arrivals.

"Lieutenants Daniels and Landry, is that right?" he asked, extending his hand as he asked.

"Yes sir!" both men answered, coming to attention and snapping off a sharp salute before shaking his hand. The major's smile widened.

"Appreciate the salute, gentlemen," he said, "but out here we're a little more... relaxed with all that stuff. Or at least I am. It might be best if you salute your CO, but for the next couple of hours treat this place like your home away from home. I'm Major Thompson, the XO of the First. Come on, let's get you started."

Josh glanced around as they made their way to the main processing tent. It was certainly a good deal less hectic outside Saigon, that much was immediately obvious.

"Isn't it warm for a scarf?" Landry asked as they passed several of the smaller tents, the blazing sun already baking the red earth beneath their feet into a slab of fired clay. Josh shot him an *'are you kidding me?'* look that Landry ignored.

Thompson chuckled. "Good thing you asked me that here," he began, "'cause some of the guys in the field might get a little… prickly if you brought it up there."

"How's that?"

"The scarf is the symbol of this unit. I take it you two didn't read-up about our history before coming out here."

"Didn't know we were coming until yesterday," Josh explained.

"Not a lot of time for reading," Landry added.

"Ah, got waylaid from another unit? Where did you think you were headed?"

"First Cav – Ranger company."

"Ah, Rangers, eh? Good! We can use some new blood with Ranger training. We're a little short just now."

"We heard. Sorry about the general and his people."

Thompson shrugged and nodded sadly. "And that's just the latest. We had some real tough sledding during Tet. Kicked the bastards' butts pretty good, though." The pride in his words and face made Josh feel a little better about the changed assignment. At least some of the people in the Division showed spirit.

After completing additional paperwork, Josh and Landry were sitting around shooting the bull with a few of the admin guys when the tent flap opened and in strode a tall, muscular, tough-looking captain. They all jumped to their feet and saluted. The captain snapped off a quick acknowledgement.

"You Daniels and Landry?" he asked.

"Yes sir. I'm Daniels – this is Landry."

"I'm Captain Ellison. Jeff. I'm the CO in Bravo Company." They shook hands.

"Is that where we've been assigned?" Landry asked.

"We just learned we were coming to the First yesterday," Josh quickly explained before the captain started to think they were idiots.

"Major Thompson told me. Rangers, huh? Well, I can't tell you that you'll get all the thrills and chills that those boys over in E Company get, but I can tell you that if we get even half of what got thrown at us during Tet, you won't be bored. Not hardly."

Josh looked at the wrinkles around the Captain's eyes and the weathered creases of his skin. It took him a moment to realize that Ellison was only a year or two older than he was.

"No picnic, huh?"

"Anything but. Don't let anybody kid you," he said, looking around casually to check if anyone was listening to their conversation. "The VC might be small, and they might wear black pajamas and recycled tire treads on their feet, but they're tough little mothers. You get a handful of them dug into their tunnels and you'd better be ready for a fight to get them out."

Josh could imagine. No, actually he couldn't. For the moment, he wouldn't even try.

"You boys ready to head out and meet your platoons?"

What could they say? "Yes, sir."

This time there was no helicopter to fly them to the encampment. They piled into the back of a deuce and a half truck with seven new enlisted men and piles of food and equipment. The captain rode up front. The truck looked like something out of Alice In Wonderland, heavily sandbagged all around.

"Expecting a flood?" Landry asked, indicating the leaking brown bags.

"Mines," a PFC answered. "Blow you all to hell if you're not careful."

"Great," the tall Cajun mumbled as the truck lurched its way through the countryside.

The trip out to the unit's base camp near an abandoned rubber plantation was only about ten miles as the crow flies, but it took over an hour to get there. The dirt roads were rutted and rock-strewn; the truck never got above 20 mph. The soldiers in the back with Josh and Landry carried on an easy dialogue as the truck passed through flooded rice paddies and dense green jungle. It was hard to believe that the VC might be hiding anywhere along the route, waiting to ambush them. But they knew it was true.

After first introductions, the grunts kept pretty much to themselves unless Josh or Landry asked them a question. Then they answered briefly and to the point. Josh didn't know if such interaction was the norm for those guys, but it felt strange. He figured they'd loosen up once they got to know them.

When they arrived at division base, it was like something out of a novel: the grunts had cut out a huge swath of jungle and a small tent city had sprung up in its place. A line of bare-chested young men were hard at work with machetes chopping away at the dense underbrush even as they pulled up in the truck. Smoke rose from smoldering fires all along the brush line.

"All right! Fresh meat!" one of the machete-wielding privates yelled out. Cat calls and whistles followed.

"Shut your yaps and keep clearing the brush!" a sergeant overseeing the work responded. The soldiers did as they were told.

Josh stood in the back of the truck for a moment, using the elevated platform to see what was going on around him.

"Impressed?" Captain Ellison asked from down below him.

"Yeh, actually. How long have you been here?"

"Three weeks."

"You've done a lot."

"Have to. We've had a few VC patrols probe the edges of the camp, so the CO ordered it moved out another 100 yards. Should get there in a day or two."

Josh looked at a broad green expanse where several helicopters loaded and unloaded supplies. Around the edge of the LZ he saw a sea of tents and make-shift huts.

"What you're looking at are artillery, medical, engineers, admin, and division headquarters," Ellison explained. "The infantry battalions are over there," he continued, waving his arm in a broad arc at the nearby tent city.

"How many men?" Landry asked.

"I don't know. We're supposed to be at 5000, but I'd guess we're more like 3500 or 4000. Hasn't been a good month."

First stop was headquarters. The new CO, Major General Irwin, greeted them personally.

"Glad to have you here with us," he said as soon as an aide showed them into his small, bare office. "We need officers with your training."

"Glad to be here," Josh said.

They exchanged a few moments of small-talk before the general got down to business. "Now look, Daniels, I don't believe in beating around the bush, so let's get something straight, right here and now. I know your father's a Congressman – we've had the 6th Psyops guys all over us since they decided to send you out here. They want to show the American people – and everyone else I guess – that this war's not just being fought by poor high school dropouts. They want everyone to know that congressmen's kids are fighting here as well. Only problem is, most of them aren't. So that means they want to do stories about you. Take pictures. The whole works. You okay with that?"

"Do I have a choice?" Josh asked, smiling to let the general know he wasn't complaining.

"Not really. We'll try to keep them out of your way, but their orders come from back in Washington. Which means we all have to salute. If it gets too intrusive, you let me know. Got it?"

"Yes, sir. Thank you, sir."

"And Daniels..."

"Yes, sir?"

"Don't go getting yourself killed. It wouldn't look good in the press." This time it was the general's turn to smile.

"I'll do my best, sir."

And just like that, their audience with the CO was over. Landry had only said about two words, but it was clear he wasn't expected to talk. Just listen.

As they left headquarters, Josh tried to keep his expression reaction-free. He'd known that his family ties would come into play, but even he was surprised how much and how quickly. *'Not much I can do about it,'* he thought as they led him to his tent. *'Just try to follow the general's orders.'*

Stay alive. Always Rule #1.

CHAPTER 6

Sept 28, 1968

We made our first foray out into the jungle yesterday.

Preparation began before dawn; the CO tabbed me to lead a recon patrol out beyond the barbed wire. Our Intel people picked up on rumors that suggest the VC might be moving people in our direction. For what? Nobody seems to know. But the Old Man (Irwin) wants to keep the perimeter clear, so out we went.

The men were quiet in the dim light of early morning, some smoking, some checking their gear. It's been a while since I lugged a pack and so much ammo, since Benning, actually, and I'd forgotten what a bear it is to drag it on patrol. It weighs a ton; with all the heat and humidity I started sweating before I took two steps. I wasn't alone in that, but the men were used to it and I didn't hear any bitching at all. In fact, I've got to say, they're a good group. I've got 33 men at this point. The old-timers tell me the number has varied from 28 to the mid-50s, but this is the most they've had since Tet.

I briefed the men on our mission, turned the organization of the platoon over to my Top, Sergeant Hernandez, and we set off. (I'm not sure why they gave me Hernandez instead of one of the lower-ranked sergeants; maybe they're baby-sitting me because of Dad. Wish they'd just let me be.) At first we swept back and forth through the thick underbrush beyond the perimeter, our point guys chopping their way through a green wall of vegetation. The breeze doesn't penetrate the dense plant life, and the air is so thick it almost feels like you're breathing water. There is always animal and insect noise coming from all around, and when there isn't, when it gets deathly quiet for even a few seconds, the old-timers throw off their safeties and start looking around like the Devil himself was on our tail. I've got to say it felt more than a little claustrophobic, with leaves and stems and roots all around you, and who knows what hidden behind them. But as the day went on I got used to it a little and it didn't bother me all that much. Most of the time, anyway. At one point I brushed against some big leafy plant and the next thing I knew my neck was burning! Turns out they've got ants over here kind of like the fire ants back home. Sting like hell! Our medic put a lotion on the bites and the pain went down considerably, but I can still feel them now, a day later.

When we were pretty sure no enemy forces had penetrated the immediate surrounding jungle, we headed up-country a short ways. There's an old trail that supposedly leads west to the Cambodian border. The VC have been using it since the time of the French. To get there, we had to pass through a rice paddy. No fun. You walk on the built-up earth dikes of packed mud that separate one flooded area from another, but sooner or later you've got to walk through the paddies themselves and then you find your boots sinking into a foot or two of stinking, slimy mud that slows everyone down and makes the simple act of walking a real chore. Worse yet, a young private from Iowa, Jeffries I think is his name, stepped on one of those damn sharpened punji sticks the VC place just under the water. The steel shank to his boot protected the bottom of his foot, but the stick stuck through the leather at his ankle and laid him up good. Had to call in a chopper to medevac him out.

Then, when we got to the end of the flooded fields and were taking five, I turn around and see the men peeling off their boots and socks and rolling up pant legs and shirt sleeves. When I realized what they were up to I did the same, and sure as heck I found a couple of big dark brown leeches sucking away on my legs. Used a lit cigarette to burn them off, but just knowing they were there gave me the heebie-jeebies.

We found the trail, and the Top showed me a few abandoned tunnels nearby that the VC had used in the past to store materiel and hide from the French (and us?) They looked long-abandoned, but I can understand how it'd be damn hard to get them out of there once they were inside. Hernandez says the tunnels can go on a half-mile or more!

We bivouacked right there within shouting distance of the trail, but kept squads out patrolling 24/7. At first the noise in the jungle kept me awake: insect chirps, animal calls, loud screams of who knows what. But I was so damn tired from carrying my gear and hiking through all that growth and mud, I finally conked out.

The trip back to base camp was uneventful. Just long, hot and wet. So we all survived our first patrol — except for Jeffries. Went to visit him at the field infirmary and he's doing okay. No sign of infection.

I think we did okay. I think **I** *did okay.*

CHAPTER 7

The days and weeks passed in a blur of recon patrols and grunt work. Their CO kept the men chopping brush around the perimeter until they had it pushed back over 100 meters. A couple of times Josh took a walk out there to check on how his guys were doing, just a casual visit with some idle chit-chat, a question or two about their progress, a comment on the music blaring from portable radios (usually Hendrix, or Credence Clearwater, or one of the black groups.) Nothing too heavy. But once, about two weeks after he'd arrived, he thought he caught a whiff of marijuana. He wasn't sure – he'd never smoked the stuff himself – but he was pretty sure. He was about to read them the riot act, remind them how they were putting not only themselves but all their buddies at risk, when he remembered something the Colonel had told him back in Texas: "especially when you first get out there, don't do anything drastic unless it's a real emergency. Talk to your NCOs; see if it's worth the effort." So he did.

Sergeant Hernandez listened to him with a slow nod of his head.

"So – what do you think?" Josh asked when he'd finished recounting the facts.

Hernandez threw his hands up in a show of consternation. "Probably was, pot. A lot of them smoke that shit. Usually, unless we catch them using it when they're on patrol, we let it slide."

"Let it slide?" His Academy sense of outrage at any abuse of the rules and regs bubbled to the surface. He tried not to show it. "You think that's wise? What if there's a surprise attack? Do we really want a bunch of spaced-out potheads shooting live ammo at who knows what?"

Hernandez smiled. "What would you like better: them shooting at 'who knows what' or at you?"

Josh was taken aback. *'Shooting at me? What the…'* "Are you telling me that our own men would take a shot at an officer for reporting their drug use?"

"Or a grenade." The sergeant said it without blinking. "It happens, you know. Not often, but every now and then we get an officer back in a body bag and no one knows how he died. A mystery. We figure it's fraggin', but can't prove it."

"We can't let fear of a few potheads keep us from enforcing the regs," Josh said, sounding prissy even to his own ears.

Hernandez held his hands open wide, a silent plea. "Look, you're new. Give 'em a few months to get to know you. And you to know them. I'll make sure none of them gets loaded outside the wire. After a while, if you still think it's worth taking on, you can bring one of them up on charges. Maybe an article 32 investigation, which leaves you with a lot of leeway. Put the fear of God into them. But now… Maybe not such a good idea."

He looked at Josh with the kind of questioning expectation that a parent might use for a good but unthinking teenager. For an instant Josh felt like putting Hernandez in his place, asking him who the hell he thought he was, but he knew deep-down that the sergeant was only trying to help.

"Yeh, okay," he agreed. "But if I catch anyone with those sleepy eyes and a shit-eating grin outside the Green Line, it'll be his ass."

"That's cool… sir," Hernandez said with a smile.

Josh smiled back, in spite of himself. "This is one screwed up place, eh Sergeant?"

"And they say you West Pointers are a little slow." His smile widened.

"They say wrong."

"Might be. Just might be."

*****

The plan was simple: reconnoiter trails the VC were known to have used to move men and supplies into the Saigon area, probe for tunnels, and head home. Problem was, even the simplest plans rarely worked as they were drawn-up. This one certainly did not.

Josh led his patrol as they swept the jungle northwest of the capital. He sent one team ahead to scout, another two on the wings to provide protection. The day was hot and humid, like every day, but a brief shower in the early morning had wet them down just enough to make everything heavy as hell; the jungle camos chafed, the boots squeaked, and the mood was generally pretty shitty. They had already been at it for nearly five hours when one of their point team came upon a tunnel system that wasn't marked on any of the maps.

"Looks abandoned," Sergeant Hernandez said when he and Josh took their first look. "Probably hasn't been used for a few months at least."

Josh scanned their surroundings and got down on his hands and knees to peer into the tunnel opening at his feet: no signs of recent activity on the trail leading to the tunnel, no scrapes or trash to suggest anyone had been inside the tunnel for quite a while, no reason to think it remained active.

Still...

"Sarge, let's get someone in there to take a look-see."

Hernandez didn't look thrilled, but he called for their team tunnel rat, a PFC whose family had worked in the Kentucky coal mines for generations. He no more feared going into the tunnels than taking a walk on the streets of Saigon. Probably less.

"Elliot, probably nothing to it, but we need to be sure. Go scout it out – make sure no one's down there."

Private Elliot actually looked pleased to get a chance to go underground. He slipped out of his pack, stripped off his leaden shirt, and slithered on his belly into the narrow confines of the tunnel. Josh told the others to take five, except for a handful of men who patrolled the perimeter.

For ten minutes or so the platoon relaxed in place, smoking, snacking, just taking a load off. But then, seconds before Josh was going to tell Hernandez to get Elliot back there so they could resume their sweep, the tell-tale sound of muffled gunfire drifted up out of the tunnel opening.

"Did you hear that?" Hernandez shouted.

Josh held up his hand. All conversation stopped dead. Moments later, more gunfire.

"Get someone down there – now! And send a squad out that way," Josh continued, pointing in the direction the gunfire seemed to come from. "See if they can find another entrance."

Men scattered in organized chaos as more shots rang out. Josh grabbed his radio operator and called in the contact. He was told to stay put; they'd send out helos to try to spot any enemy sneaking out of the tunnel via other exits.

For several long minutes the patrol waited. The sudden silence of the jungle was even more nerve-racking than the shooting. At least they had some idea of where Charlie was located when they were shooting. Quiet could mean a lot of things, most of them bad.

Finally, the whirring of helicopters approached. Josh ordered Hernandez to toss a smoke grenade to mark their location. The copters were no more than a clic away when a thundering explosion sent a shudder through the ground where they stood.

"What the hell was that?!" one of the men said aloud, the same thought every man in the unit was thinking.

Just as Josh turned his head, smoke begin to billow from the tunnel entrance. In the near distance, from the direction he'd sent the relief squad, the staccato report of gunfire rang out.

"Sergeant, defensive positions! Set a perimeter!" he ordered, unsure exactly what was happening.

Hernandez barked orders to his squad leaders; they led their men out into the jungle to find cover. In minutes they were ready to face whatever was out there. Overhead a deafening wave of sound washed over their position as three gunships closed on the smoke.

The radio crackled to life. "Got eyes on your position," one pilot announced. "What's your situation?"

"Unknown!" Josh yelled over the rotor wash. "Possible contact with Victor Charlie about two hundred meters to our west. Over!"

"Roger that. We'll go take a look."

The Cobra gunships separated and swung to the west, their bristling armaments silhouetted against the blue afternoon sky. Moments later the jungle exploded in a symphony of miniguns and 40mm explosive rounds.

"Wouldn't want to be those poor bastards," Hernandez said to Josh as they watched black smoke begin to rise above the treetops.

"Enemy engaged," came a matter-of-fact report over the radiophone.

For a minute or two the jungle became a madhouse of explosions and roaring engines, the pitch and volume of the sounds constantly shifting with the attack vectors of the helos. And then, once again the jungle fell silent except for the sounds of the circling copters. Columns of black smoke soared into the sky.

Despite the quiet Josh kept his men on alert, waiting for an update from the Cobras. "Caught a handful of tunnel rats coming out of their hole," the pilot finally radioed. "They are no longer a threat."

"Roger that, Cobra leader. Can you guys hang around for a couple of minutes? We may have casualties."

"Let me see what command says." A few seconds later he returned with permission for one helicopter to stay behind while the other two returned to base.

"Let's get some people in the tunnels," Josh told Hernandez as soon the news reached him.

"Captain, the smoke's still pretty thick in there. Maybe another five minutes until it clears out a bit?"

Josh was anxious to pull any survivors out and get them medical attention, but he understood his sergeant's reluctance.

"Okay, five minutes. Then send them in from this entrance and the one those VC came up out of."

As it turned out, it wouldn't have made any difference if it were five minutes or five hours. There were no survivors.

"Got a crater ten feet across in there," the corporal who'd entered the tunnel from their end explained. "Probably an ammo cache." His report was echoed by the GI who entered from the other end. Josh nodded silently.

As soon as all the members of his unit had regrouped, he sent the Cobra back with their thanks and called the men together for a moment of silence for Elliot. Several of the men wanted to say something, a eulogy of sorts, but there was no time – they had a mission to finish. It was a solemn, emotional platoon that continued on into the lengthening shadows of late afternoon.

If anything the air seemed hotter, the brush thicker as they pushed further along the VC trail that had led them there. Even the sounds of the jungle seemed subdued, as if the myriad creatures sensed the sadness so many of the men felt. The shadows grew longer and longer as they pushed deeper into the heavy undergrowth. Josh was just about to call another break, to give his tired and demoralized men a breather, when two scouts came rushing back to where he stood.

"A village, Captain, just over a clic to our east!" one of the men reported.

"Might be where those VC were holed up," the other man suggested.

A mumbling from a handful of grunts standing nearby alerted Josh to the platoon's state of mind. "Let's not jump to conclusions," he said, attempting to calm the situation. "They might not have even known they were in the area."

"All the gooks look out for each other," a private muttered.

"They knew," another added.

"We don't know that," Josh continued, ignoring their comments. "For now, it's standard operating procedure – initial sweep, stand-off guard, all the while winning hearts and minds. Understood?"

Unintelligible muttering. Josh was having none of it. "I said, is that understood?!"

"Yes sir," several of the men answered half-heartedly.

Josh decided right then and there that he needed to keep a tight rein on the platoon. He'd heard too many stories about pissed-off GIs taking their frustrations out on whatever locals they stumbled upon.

"Sergeant!" he summoned Hernandez. He motioned him off to one side away from the mass of men. "Take five or six of your best people and check out the huts. And get your squad leaders together and have them calm their men – I don't like the feel right now."

"The men are angry, Captain. It's understandable."

"Understandable but not acceptable. We're here to make friends, and that's what we're going to do." The words rang false even to Josh, but he had his orders.

"Understood, sir."

Hernandez passed the word. The mumbling that broke out as the men divided into squads worried Josh, but he trusted the NCOs to tamp down any bad blood. He gave the order to 'take five' and had just broken out his canteen when a shot rang out in the direction of the village. Heads turned and shoulders stiffened. Moments later a private came running back to where they rested.

"We're taking fire!" he yelled out.

"I only heard one shot," Josh began, but no sooner did the words leave his lips than a torrent of automatic weapons fire exploded in the distance.

"Take me there – now!" he ordered the private. "Sergeant, you're in charge!" he directed one of the squad leaders as he hurried along a dirt path that disappeared into the lush greenery.

Josh slipped the safety on his M-16 off and braced for a firefight. But when the village came into sight a minute or two later, the cacophony of explosions suddenly stopped. He signaled the private to get down and the two of them moved stealthily to the perimeter of the small circle of ten or twelve huts. What he saw made Josh's stomach crawl.

Two huts at the far side of the circle were fully ablaze, smoke pouring from the straw thatch. Perhaps two dozen people, mainly women, children and the elderly, sat or knelt on the red dirt in the center of the circle. Five grunts covered them with their weapons. Josh took it all in in an instant.

"What the hell is going on?!" he asked Hernandez, who was interrogating a village elder with the help of a corporal who spoke some Vietnamese.

"A sniper took a shot at us," the sergeant explained. "The guys responded."

"Responded?! They took out half the goddamn village!" The village elder stared at him with stark fear in his eyes. Or was it hatred? "Is there anyone in those huts?"

"We didn't get that far."

Josh shook his head. "What's the old man say? Anything worth a crap?"

"He says they don't know anything about any VC in the area. He says they don't help them." The sergeant did not sound convinced.

"You think he's lying?"

Hernandez shrugged. "Could be. Hard to tell."

"Keep at him." He wanted to send some men to check the two burning huts, but the flames were leaping twenty feet into the air. The heat from fifty feet away was overpowering.

About an hour later Hernandez finished his interrogation of the village elder. He didn't get anything more out of him. The two huts lay in ruins, still smoldering. A third adjacent hut lost one wall and part of its roof.

Josh was meeting with his squad leaders to try to come up with some way to mollify the stunned villagers, when a heart-rending scream suddenly cut through the whimpering and tears of the locals.

An elderly woman who stood by one of the burned huts dropped to her knees, her hands thrown high above her head in despair. "What the hell is that?!" he called out to the nearest GI.

An interpreter hurried over to the spot. "Her daughter and grandkids were inside!" the interpreter yelled back.

"Christ!" Josh muttered under his breath. He left the squad leaders and walked over to the hut. There, in the midst of charred wood and scorched palm fronds he could just make out three black mounds curled up against each other, one larger, two small. Part of one skull shone off-white in the black ashes. He felt short of breath, his guts churning.

He turned to the interpreter, nodding toward the sobbing older woman. "Tell her we're very sorry." Then he faced Hernandez. "And get her back to the others. Then get some men to dig a grave – make that three graves. Anything in the other huts?"

"Not that you can see from out here."

"Have someone go through the ashes. And do it respectfully!"

Josh turned and walked away, struggling to keep his composure. He bit down hard on his lower lip to regain self-control. Bit hard enough to draw blood. What the hell was going on? He'd seen dead bodies before – lots of them. So why were his guts trying to leap out his throat and his eyes stinging as if they'd dusted the place with CS?

*****

Later that afternoon, after they'd buried the woman and her two kids, Josh talked to the villagers, all together in one group. He apologized, his voice fluttering despite his best efforts. He tried to explain that it was the fault of the person who shot at his troops, but it was clear they didn't believe him. He only half-believed it himself. Two middle-aged women, relatives of the dead, screamed something at him, tears streaming down their faces. He stood there and took it, unblinking. He didn't even ask the interpreter to tell him what they said. He knew.

He had his platoon stack their MREs in a pile and offered them to the villagers as compensation. Not a single local stepped forward to accept the plastic-wrapped meals. When one small child tried to investigate, his mother yanked him back by the arm.

The GIs finally pulled out of the village just before sunset. As they marched back into the jungle, the Buddhist chants of the friends and families of the dead echoed in the village behind them.

Josh knew even then that those chants would stay with him for a long time. Maybe forever.

CHAPTER 8

Time passed in fits and starts, racing ahead in a haze of patrols and firefights, then slowing to a crawl. It was proving troublesome for Josh to shake the daze that enveloped him after 'the village incident', especially the nightmares. His Top Sergeant finally had had enough.

"Get your ass out of these quarters! Your attitude is affecting the men."

Josh knew he was right, but it was difficult to forget. No matter where he went, the images of those burned bodies never left him. The investigation said it wasn't his fault, but he'd been in command. They were *his* men.

*****

Even though their two platoons were housed within a few hundred yards of each other, Josh hadn't spoken to Landry for over a week when the two bumped into each other at the Officer's Club – a dark little hangout where the officers could drop most of their command persona and just be themselves for a short while. Since Josh didn't drink all that much, and he'd been a virtual recluse, he hadn't made it over to the Club for weeks; Landry was more or less a regular.

"Jesus H. Christmas, if it isn't Second Lieutenant Daniels," Landry called out when he saw Josh enter the Club. "I was beginning to think you'd gone back home."

"Good to see you too," Josh said, putting out his hand to shake his friend's. But Landry tried to grasp his hand in a fancy new grip that some of the black enlisted men used, and for a moment the two hands fluttered and fretted like confused birds. Finally, they aligned and met in a warm greeting.

"What's with the shake?" Josh asked, nonplussed.

"Brother Landry gettin' some soul," a young black lieutenant joked from the table where Landry was sitting.

"When in Rome…" Landry said.

"… Do like in Detroit," the young black man quipped, and Landry almost bust a gut laughing. Josh managed a small smile.

"I see you started without me," he said when the laughter subsided, nodding at the empty beer bottles that dotted the small bar table.

"Unless you've changed your ways, the party always starts without you," Landry said, glancing down at the lieutenant. "He almost never drinks."

"Wow, that's sad. I hope you're not smoking any of that shit that's going around. I hear it can really lay you up."

"Marijuana?" Josh said, surprise tinged with irritation. "I don't smoke it, no."

Landry put his arm around Josh's shoulder. "His idea of a party is two Dr. Peppers and a bag of chips, but he's a good man, no matter what they say. Daniels, this is Lieutenant Charles White from Oklahoma. White, Josh here is from the great state of Texas."

"I might've heard of it," White said, and reaching out with a broad smile of exceptionally white teeth he grabbed Josh's hand in the same odd grip and shook it furiously.

"Charles is celebrating."

"It's Hump Day!" he said. "Six months left and I'm outta this dump."

"No kidding. Congratulations."

"Thank you, thank you. Now if I can only keep them damn VC from blowin' my head off for another 182 days, all will be right with the world."

Josh sat with Landry and White, and for an hour or more they swapped tales of their first days in 'Nam. Charles talked about one kid who got so scared on his first patrol he dropped a load in his pants. "Said it was worms, but we said it was Cong," White laughed. "Told him to watch out he didn't get court martialed for using chemical weapons." Landry matched leech scars with Josh, and wondered aloud how much brush cutting and latrine cleaning would be necessary to win the War; both agreed that life in 'Nam wasn't quite what they'd imagined. That touched off a long bitch session about everything from the heat and humidity to the rations. The list of complaints was so long, Josh started to feel embarrassed thinking what the Colonel would say if he could hear their grumbling.

"All considered, it's not so bad," he said by way of a semi-apology after the session had run its course.

"What *are* you smokin'?" White asked. "If this ain't bad, remind me not to visit Texas."

All three men laughed, and for a short while they could almost forget that they were not in a bar somewhere in Austin, or Oklahoma City.

Almost.

*****

Time was a strange commodity in 'Nam. Each day crawled along like a loaded truck in the heavy Vietnamese mud. Sometimes, in a battle, each minute seemed to last an hour. But then, sometimes a month slid by with scarcely a second thought. That's how it was for Josh.

It was exactly five months into his tour, five months to the day since he'd taken over command of his patrol. They got briefed-up on a major operation that'd have them air assault into the lowlands bordering Highway 13, an important supply route they'd nicknamed Thunder Road, in a multi-divisional operation called Atlas Wedge.

They formed-up at the LZ by company. Bravo – Josh's crew – would head out first and seal off the northern end of the Highway so that nothing could come down on them from that direction. Alpha would follow and establish a secure LZ. Charlie would take key bridges, leaving Delta – and the Battalion HQ – to come along last once the LZ was secured.

It was 0500 hours when line after line of Huey copters came roaring in to take them to their positions. These were slick troop carriers with no seats, just a bare studded floor and two M-60 machine guns for defense. They packed as many soldiers into each copter as weight and space allowed, and then roared off in a swirl of exhaust fumes and blade whoosh. The men were quiet, both anxious and tired. Josh was sure he wasn't the only one who hadn't slept well the night before. They hadn't been out on a big mission like this one since he'd arrived. For the old-timers, it was the first multi-company action since Tet.

They flew low through the silver-gray darkness of pre-dawn, the tops of palm trees skimming the copter's skids. About a third of his platoon was aboard his copter, including Sgt Hernandez – not surprising. He went just about everywhere Josh went. Some of the men had started calling him The Baby Sitter, though not to his face. Josh had mixed feelings: he didn't want to look like he needed a sitter, but he liked Hernandez and appreciated his savvy.

As they approached their LZ, the pilot informed Josh that the 1st Cav was going to run a few copters across the site to strafe with ARAs. "We think it's cold," he explained, "but no use in taking chances."

In the distance Josh saw the bright burst of explosions as the rockets peppered the LZ. He motioned to Hernandez, who gave him a thumbs-up. He didn't feel the same optimism as the sergeant, but he didn't have much time to ponder his feelings. In just moments the sound of the copter motor changed and the nose pitched abruptly downwards. They were going in.

"Get ready to move as soon as we touch down!" Hernandez yelled to the entire platoon over the roar of the engine. "Safeties off!"

Josh checked his M-16 and watched out of the corner of his eyes as the rest of the men in the unit did the same. Before he could even brace himself, the copter bumped down hard in the tall grass and he and Hernandez jumped out to lead the men away from the whirling blades. All around him he could see other copters disgorging their soldiers, a crazy Chinese fire drill of men and machines that did not seem real.

By the time the last of the Hueys had disappeared into the blinding red glare of the rising sun, the LZ was secure. No incoming. No sightings. In fact, it was eerily quiet. But not for long.

"Let's form-up and move out!" Josh yelled, and almost before he could finish his order Hernandez was herding the men into formation for the move to a position above and to the east of the Highway. Platoon leaders all across the LZ repeated the same order, and like some kind of reverse cell division the disparate units all flowed together into one large creature with thousands of legs crashing through the chest-high grass and verdant green undergrowth.

"Piece a' cake," Hernandez said as he moved past Josh, his helmet tilted jauntily to one side as if they were headed out on a nature hike. Jeff cringed and then berated himself for giving in to superstition. He caught a glimpse of Landry off to their left, pushing his platoon on a parallel course. The presence of his old friend made him feel a little more secure, but not enough to stop worrying about Hernandez' premature boast.

It took them about twenty minutes to settle into the coordinates they'd been assigned.

"Dig in!" Hernandez ordered before Josh could even suggest it. "You too, Lieutenant," he added under his breath as he did the same.

The earth was damn hard up on that shelf, fifty feet above the thin line of pot-holed asphalt they'd been sent to guard. He chopped at the rocky ground with his collapsible shovel until his hands cramped, just managing to gouge out enough of a trench to lie down in when his point man, Corporal Hilford, came running back to him, eyes wide.

"We've got movement back up the hill," he whispered, breathing hard. "Looks like VC."

"How many?"

"Don't know. We only saw two, but that doesn't mean much." The VC were like rats, Josh thought. Even if you only see one, there's probably a dozen more hiding in the jungle or in holes beneath it.

Josh motioned to Hernandez who was listening from his half-dug foxhole a few feet away. "Send a recon squad out there and get my RTO over here now! We've got to let the other platoons know we're not alone."

The sergeant organized the recon unit in seconds and PFC Ellis appeared from nowhere with the bulky radiotelephone and its antennas looking like a huge insect sitting squarely on his back. Josh called in the sighting to Captain Ellison, who was coordinating the company's activities from a base on the other side of the Highway. In moments Ellison had alerted all three platoons; half the men were diverted from digging their foxholes to guarding their individual perimeters. As soon as the first group finished excavating, they switched-off with their buddies.

A half-hour passed since the first sighting, with no follow-up.

"Maybe they were seeing things," Hernandez offered when he saw Josh pacing.

"Maybe. But if I were the VC I wouldn't want us sitting here choking off any traffic north or south."

"I suppose. But..." Hernandez didn't finish his words. From out in the direction the recon squad had gone, the tell-tale sound of gunfire echoed through the dense greenery. One particularly loud rapid-fire sequence stopped Josh in his tracks.

"DK?" he asked Hernandez.

"Sounds like it."

Josh thought it through for just a second. "Get everyone down in their holes until we can find out what's going on. Tell them stay ready but stay alert – we've got a squad out there that I don't want getting shot by our own guys. Got it?"

"On it," the sergeant said as he took off to tell the platoon to hunker down, even though he knew most if not all of them had hit the ground with the first burst of fire.

"Crap Shoot, Crap Shoot, this is Bravo 1," he called out over the radio. "Automatic heavy weapons fire a few hundred yards to our north. Sounds like a DK. Trying to evaluate the situation. Over."

"Bravo 1, Roger that. I'll try to get ahold of air support, just in case. Keep me informed. Over."

"Roger, wilco. Bravo 1 out."

Hernandez came running back toward Josh. From the look on his face, Josh knew it was bad.

"We've got VC all over the place out there! Our squad is cut off. Not sure how many, but there's crap-load of 'em."

"How's our perimeter?"

"We're dug-in pretty good, linked up with Charlie Platoon, with the two M-60s angled for a decent kill zone. But if they've got DKs, you can bet they're at strength – company at least."

Josh nodded. He felt his heart thundering in his chest, but he concentrated on slowing his breathing. "I'm going to call in air support," he finally said.

"We've got men out there…" Hernandez began.

"I know that!" Josh said, more harshly than he'd intended. "But we've got a bunch more right here that are going to be in deep shit if there's a company of VC out there headed our way."

"We don't know if it's a company."

"Do you want me to wait until we're sure?" He stared at the sergeant.

"Damn it. I'll tell our guys to keep their heads down." He took off running.

Josh got Ellison on the radio. "Best guess is we've got a company out there," he said as calmly as he could muster. "We're gonna need some air support right quick or we're gonna be in deep doo-doo." He gave the coordinates.

"Did you get your squad back yet?" the company commander asked. His tone was neutral – no sense of blame or incrimination.

The question inspired him. "We're working on it. I'm gonna lead a squad to try to break them free, but we'll need the support in any case."

"That's a negative, Bravo 1," the captain answered. "No rescue missions. Sit tight until air support arrives."

Josh heard the reports of intense gunfire not 300 yards away. He wasn't going to let those men die so close to the main unit. "You're breaking up," he said into the radio, covering part of the mike to deaden his voice. "Repeat last!"

"I said, SIT TIGHT!" Ellison answered, but Josh had already flipped the volume off and covered the mike with his hand. "Radio seems to be malfunctioning," he told PFC Ellis. He ripped the wire to the battery off its connection. "You're coming with me. Let's see if you can get this working in, say, ten minutes?"

Ellis nodded with a smile. "You got it."

Josh patted him on the shoulder and took off running for Hernadez' last known position. He found him rallying the men, shouting orders and encouragement.

"Sergeant. I need five men to come with me, now!" he ordered. The sergeant looked at him from the corner of his eye.

"Assignment?"

"We're gonna go give our squad some support," he said. "That okay with you?"

Hernandez smiled. "I'm with you all the way, Lieutenant." He jumped up and cleared his M-16. Josh realized he intended to go with him.

"I need an experienced man back here," Josh began, but Hernandez cut him off.

"Corporal Russell's been out here for the better part of two tours, right Russell?"

The corporal gave him a thumbs-up. "He can take care of these boys nearly as well as I can."

Josh hesitated, just a moment. "Fine, Okay. No time now for an argument. Get me four more men and let's move!"

Josh half-expected Hernandez to insist that he take the point, but the sergeant seemed to understand that his platoon leader was determined to do it himself, and so settled-in just off his shoulder, his eyes on a pivot searching the greenery in every direction. Josh set a fast pace, but not so fast as to be reckless. As they halved the distance between them and the trapped squad, he sent two men off to scout ahead. In minutes they were back, looking none too happy.

"VC, lots of 'em, not 200 yards to our north!" a grizzled sergeant reported.

"Any sign of our squad?"

"Couldn't get close enough, but there's a shitload of firing so I'd guess they're still holding the fort."

"You have a plan?" Hernandez asked.

"Not really," Josh admitted. "Just... maybe create enough of a diversion to make them think the cavalry has come to the rescue, and then drop some air support on their heads."

"That's a plan," the sergeant said with an appraising nod. "I'll take Sgt. Koons here and one other man out to our left. We'll cut loose with everything we've got and start yelling and screaming like banshees. You take the others off to the right and do the same. Okay?"

"Yeh, yeh that sounds good. But give me a couple of minutes once you're in place. As soon as I can get a fix on our squad's coordinates, I'm going to call in the air support. Tell your guys to keep their heads down."

"You got it – sir." Hernandez smiled.

"Good luck, Sergeant."

Hernandez gave a thumbs-up and tapped his two other men before heading off into the brush. Josh called his RTO and a corporal who'd been in-country for over a year to him and explained the situation. Then they set off.

The dense green foliage created a living screen separating them from the mayhem they could hear just a short distance away. They were picking their way through the jungle as fast as they were able, hoping that Hernandez wouldn't get to his firing point too soon, when out of the corner of his eye Josh saw a flash of black. He barely had time to turn his weapon in the direction of the movement when he saw the barrel of a rifle come up, pointing directly at him. Without a moment's hesitation he let loose with a burst from his M-16. He saw the VC soldier jerk backwards and disappear into the greenery.

"There's more!" he heard the corporal yell, and shots rang out.

For what seemed like an eternity they fired into the brush at anything that moved, or might have moved. He heard bullets whistle past his head and slam into the thin trunks of palms. But then, as quickly as it had begun, it stopped. The corporal raised his weapon as if to fire, but Josh placed his hand on top of the rifle stock and pushed it down. "Wait a second!" he whispered, none too sure of his full voice. For several seconds they squatted there in the bush, sweat pouring down their bodies, hearts thundering. The sounds of a vicious engagement up ahead continued unabated. But there, and in the jungle surrounding them, it was still.

"Let's move – slow, and eyes open!" he ordered. Maybe they'd gotten all the enemy. Maybe the main body of VC hadn't heard their short firefight over the sounds of their own battle. Maybe…

They found three bodies sprawled on the ground, eyes glassy or closed, faces contorted in fear and pain. Josh motioned for his men to move on. They pushed through the ferns and bushes and trees until they were just 100 yards from where their squad still held-on against overwhelming odds. Josh saw that his men had chosen their defensive position well – *'They must've seen Charlie first. Lucky.'* If you could call it luck.

They were backed up against a rocky hillside, with the enemy holding positions all around them. He motioned for Private Ellis, who handed him the radio handset.

"Crap Shoot, Crap Shoot, this is Bravo 1, over!"

"Bravo 1, this is Crap Shoot – where the hell are you?!" Ellison sounded either pissed or worried or both.

"Crap Shoot, we need air support NOW!" he whispered hoarsely into the radio. He gave the coordinates.

He was afraid the captain would debate the issue, or counter his request. He didn't. "I'll call it in. Won't be long - they've been waiting on you. Keep your heads down."

As soon as he handed the handset back to Ellis, he turned to his two man squad. "Spread out and yell and scream while you hit 'em with everything you've got. Understood?!"

Not unlike his counterparts at the Battle of Fredericksburg a hundred years earlier, he began to yell at the top of his lungs as he opened fire. As soon as he did, he heard Hernandez and his two men, their voices barely audible over the firing, launch their diversionary attack from off to the left. Suddenly a wave of fire swept in their direction, with screaming bullets ripping leaves and bark from plants all around them. The three men hit the deck, then bounced up and fired again before being driven back down. It quickly became clear to Josh that their attack would not end well unless the air support he'd requested appeared soon. Very soon.

The undergrowth was shredding all around them as if a giant tornado had settled in their midst. He no longer bounced up to shoot, but just raised his M-16 from where he lay on his back and fired randomly in the direction of the VC.

"They're flanking us!" the corporal yelled, pointing to a snaking line of black pajamas barely visible moving through the jungle about twenty yards to their right.

"Come on, Captain. Get that support here now!" Josh whispered through clenched teeth. He didn't want to die like that, not there, not then. With bullets screaming all around him, Josh held up his rifle and fired in the direction of the flanking VC. In an instant all hell broke loose as the world turned into an angry bees' nest, the air coming alive with enemy fire. He fell back to the ground and hugged the cool moist earth, as an insistent clock ticked off the seconds in his head, the seconds until his position would be overrun and he would die. He chanced another burst of blind fire and heard a grunt in the near distance as if his shots had found a mark. But the firing didn't let up.

Now as he fired short bursts, he prayed. Prayed that the air support was on its way; prayed that Hernandez could hold them off their left flank for just a few seconds more...

A burst of light flashed in front of his eyes at the same time a red-hot poker jabbed him in the side and a sucker punch took him in the side of his helmet, driving his head back into the soft earth. For just an instant he tried to focus his eyes as the roar of battle slowly faded...to black.

CHAPTER 9

When Josh opened his eyes, at first he thought he'd gone blind, or died. He saw nothing, heard nothing.

Then he tried to sit up. Pain crashed through the top of his head and his left side; he fell back with a groan.

"He's conscious," a familiar voice called out, seemingly from very far away.

So he wasn't dead. He reached up and touched a gauze bandage wrapped around the entire top of his head, effectively walling him off from the outside world.

"Daniels, Daniels can you hear me?" the same voice repeated from much closer.

"I... I..." he tried to speak, but his mouth was so dry the words stuck in his throat.

"Here, just take a sip." The lip of a canteen pressed against his lips. He tried to draw-in a mouthful, but the cool metal jerked away immediately. "Just a sip!" the voice scolded.

"Wha... where...?" He couldn't seem to formulate his words.

A hand patted his shoulder. Another voice: "Take it easy, Daniels. We think you caught some shrapnel to the head and a clean shot through your left abdomen. You've lost a lot of blood." He thought it was Captain Ellison speaking, but Ellison was over on the other side of the road...

"The squad?" he croaked.

A hesitation. "Three dead. Two wounded."

"Hilford?"

"You just rest, Lieutenant. We've got a dustoff on the way to get you and the others out of here. It won't be long now."

Josh lifted his head. "Hernandez?"

A hand gently pushed him back down. "Rest."

A needle pricked the inside of his forearm. And then he slept.

*****

The starched hospital sheets seemed like artifacts from another place. Another time. He tried to shake the cobwebs from his head, but the same stabbing pain reminded him why he shouldn't do that. He labored to push himself up to a sitting position, leaning back against a pillow.

"Hey, is anybody out there?" he croaked. Through the muffling of his bandages he heard footsteps approaching rapidly.

"Lieutenant Daniels," a woman's voice responded with more irritation than concern, "you lie back down this very minute!" He detected a slight southern accent. Texan?

"Where... am I?" he asked, ignoring her direction.

"You're at the division field hospital," she answered, a bit softer, a bit more sympathetic. "You've been injured in a firefight. Now let's skooch you down some." Small but strong hands grabbed his shoulders and slid him down onto the mattress. She fluffed his pillow. "There. Now you just rest a bit until we can get one of the doctors to come take a look at you."

"Thirsty."

"I'm afraid we can't give you too much to drink until the anesthesia's worn off, but I think we can manage a sip of water. Hang on a second."

As if he were going anywhere. In seconds she was back. She lifted his head by the back of his neck and put a plastic cup to his lips. He sipped slowly.

"That's enough," the nurse said after just a few tablespoons, pulling the cup away and laying him gently back on his pillow. "Now you get some rest."

"What… what's your name?"

There was a long pause. "Whittaker, First Lieutenant Angela Whittaker," the nurse answered. "And that's the first and last question I'm answering until you've had some sleep. Agreed?"

"Yeh, okay." He was too weak to argue.

"Good. I'll check back on you in a little while."

As her footsteps padded away, he tried to remember the specifics of the firefight. It was all a little jumbled, but he remembered a big explosion close by… In minutes he was asleep.

When he next awoke, it was from a firm hand shaking his shoulder. This time it didn't feel like Lt Whittaker, or any nurse for that matter. At least not a female nurse.

"Lieutenant, hate to interrupt your sack-time, but we've got to check your temp and blood pressure," a male voice announced. Even as he spoke, another person – Whittaker? – stuck a thermometer in his mouth and started to wrap a blood pressure cuff around his left arm. "How're you feeling?"

Josh took a moment to run a quick inventory. "Not too bad. My side aches a bit."

"Not surprising. But you got lucky there. Bullet passed right through your love handle. No major damage. How's the head?"

"Ok, unless I move."

A barked laugh. "You know the answer to that one: don't move."

"Are you a doctor?" Josh asked. He didn't mean to sound doubtful, but as soon as he said it he realized it might be interpreted that way.

"Captain Fortunato. Jeremy Fortunato. And before you ask, yes I was a doctor before joining the Army. At Johns Hopkins."

Josh bit his tongue. Was it a coincidence he'd been assigned to an experienced doctor from an elite hospital, or had his family name preceded him? Whatever, no need to bite the hand that would get him better.

"Good hospital," he mumbled.

"We think so. Now, I'm going to take off some of this gauze, but I'd like you to keep your eyes closed until I tell you to open them. Understood?"

"Uh huh."

The doctor began to unwrap the bandage. It came free easily at first, but then grabbed as if glued to his skin. Fortunato swore under his breath, dampened the gauze and without hesitation pulled it loose from the scabbing, apologizing when it restarted the blood flow. Finally the last length of gauze pulled free; as Fortunato lifted two cotton swabs from his eyes, he detected a dim halo of light through his lids.

"I'm just going to swab your eyes, get the gunk off them," the captain said softly, beginning even as he spoke. Seconds later the cleaning was done. "All right, now you can open them – slowly."

The first thing Jeff saw was a blurry tableau of two faces staring down at him. He lifted his hand to rub his eyes, but was intercepted by Lt. Whittaker.

"Uh-uh, just a second. Let me wipe those fingers before you go touching your eyes." As soon as she finished he massaged his eyes until they regained focus.

"How's the vision?" the doctor asked. "Any halos or other distortion?"

Josh glanced around, for the moment thrilled to see at all.

"Pretty good," he answered. "Still a little blurry."

"That's to be expected. We put drops in your eyes and it'll take a little while for them to clear out. But other than that?"

Josh looked over at his nurse. She was young, probably even younger than he, with short brown hair and piercing green eyes. Cute. "It's good," he said, flashing Whittaker a smile. "Really good."

"He seems to be recovering nicely," Fortunato said blandly.

"I can see that," the lieutenant agreed.

"Okay then, I'll leave him in your capable hands." He turned to Jeff. "You listen to the lieutenant, Daniels. Even if you start to feel better, I don't want to hear you've been trying to get out of bed. Not for another day or two. Got it?"

"Yeh. Okay."

"Okay, sir!" the captain prodded with a smile, patting him on the shoulder. "Don't worry about it. You can catch up with the formalities when you're up and about. I'll come back to pay you a visit in a few hours."

"Thanks – sir."

"Mental faculties are improving. Better watch yourself," the doctor told Whittaker with a wink.

"I'll keep my sidearm cocked," she joked. He chuckled as he turned and walked away.

As soon as Fortunato had left, the nurse went back to taking his blood pressure.

"Didn't you just do that?"

"It was a little high. I want to see how it is when no one's prodding and pushing you."

"Does that include you?" he asked, and got a thermometer stuffed back in his mouth for his efforts.

"Good. 123 over 94," she said, pulling off the stethoscope. "You're coming around nicely. But as the captain said, you stay here in bed until he says otherwise. Head wounds aren't always predictable. Don't want to have to scrape you up off the floor if you pass out."

"I'm not going anywhere for a while. At least not 'til my head stops throbbing."

"Glad to hear it. I'll be back in an hour. Give a yell if you need anything."

Josh watched her walk away, her swaying rear quarter providing the most entertainment he'd had in weeks. One thing led to another, and his thoughts turned to Darla; he wondered what she was doing just then. He began to daydream about the good times they'd spent back home in Texas, and the next thing he knew, he was asleep.

*****

"Hey, Sleepin' Beauty, wake up. You gonna' lay there all day?"

Josh opened his eyes to see Landry, Hernandez and Corporal Walker all standing over his hospital bed like a scene from Wizard of Oz.

"What happened – they take a time-out from the War?" he asked, struggling to sit up without reviving the headache.

"Uh oh, he sounds like he's getting better fast," Landry said, turning to Sgt Hernandez. "Too fast for you."

"Oh, I don't think we'd mind getting him back in the platoon," the sergeant drawled. "We're not so overstaffed that we couldn't use one more soldier, even if it's an officer."

Josh smiled. "Did you just come down here to pick on a poor bed-ridden second lieutenant?" He had to admit – to himself, not them – that he was happy to see them. At least Landry and Hernandez. What the heck was Walker doing there?

He didn't have to wait long to find out. "General Irwin and Colonel Slade send their best wishes," the corporal volunteered during a lull in the conversation. "They'll try to stop by when they get some time."

"Stop by?" Landry said out loud what everyone in the room was thinking.

"Congressman Daniels has been notified," Walker continued, as if to answer Landry. "I imagine either the general or Colonel Slade will bring you a message from your family."

"I... I appreciate their concern," Josh said, trying to choose his words carefully, fighting the light-headedness that rushed back whenever he moved too quickly, "but I'm sure they have more important things to do than visit a second lieutenant who's already feeling a lot better."

"Not my call," Walker said.

"No, don't imagine it is. Well, thank them for me, would you?"

"No problem. How're you feeling? Really."

He sighed. "I'm okay. Side hurts a little, and if I move my head too fast I get one hell of a headache and my vision blurs a little, but much better than two days ago. It was two days, right?"

"Yes, sir." Hernandez answered.

"How're the men?" Josh asked, his platoon leader brain taking over.

"Better than they have any right to be," the sergeant answered, sounding more like the senior NCO that he was.

"You're being a bit tough on 'em, aren't you?" Landry asked. "They did fight off a company-size ambush and kick some Charlie butt."

"But they almost got themselves – and me – killed. Next time someone orders an advance after air support, they'd better get *their* butts moving or I'll be kicking some!"

"How many did we lose?" Josh asked quietly.

Hernandez' anger drained visibly. "Lost three from the recon squad, two others wounded, and three KIA and seven wounded in the main body."

"Could've been a lot worse," Landry chimed in. "Your air support blasted the hell out of everything in the vicinity. Of course, I wish they'd kept their fire concentrated a bit further east – I thought for a while there they were going to take us out as well."

"How many VC?"

Hernandez shrugged. "Like usual, they dragged off most of their dead and wounded, but we counted twenty-two confirmed, and from the tracks our guys estimate another few dozen."

"Sounds like they got the worst of it."

"You should'a seen 'em when the bombs and rockets started fallin'," Landry said with a proud grin, "they got outta' there like a hound smellin' a skunk. A smart hound, anyway."

"I'm glad," Josh said, his mind only partly on his friend's words. "Sergeant, would you get me the names of the fallen so I can draft letters for the captain to sign?"

"That's being taken care of," Corporal Walker interrupted.

"You sure?"

"SOP."

Of course. With so many soldiers dying, they would have to have a standard procedure. As sick as that sounded.

"Okay gentlemen, that's enough for today," Nurse Whittaker announced as she strolled up to his bedside with a handful of pills and the blood pressure cuff on a small tray. "Lieutenant Daniels needs rest, not a rehashing of the firefight."

All three men eyed the lieutenant with appraising glances. She ignored them completely.

"I think I feel a case of Uncle Ho's Revenge coming on," Hernandez joked. "I think I'll need to spend some time in here."

"All you'll get is a shot in the butt and an IV in the arm overnight," Whittaker said. "To each their own."

Everyone else laughed; Hernandez sighed with a resigned shrug.

"Guess we'll see you when we see you," Landry said, grasping Josh's hand. He turned to the nurse. "You take care of him, hear? He might not look like much, but he's a good guy." He winked at Josh and then led the others out of the ward.

"Those are your friends? I'd hate to see your enemies," Whittaker griped when the threesome was barely out of earshot.

Josh smiled. "Sometimes it's a little hard to tell one from the other." *'But you **can** tell,'* he said to himself, *'you **can** tell.'*

She shrugged half-heartedly and went about her business. When she was done poking, prodding and testing him, she left Josh to get some rest. But rest didn't come easy. He couldn't help but relive the attack again in his mind, wondering if he could've done anything differently to save lives. He wondered if he'd ever get used to it: sending men into battle, knowing some of them weren't coming back. It had seemed so easy back at the Academy. Not so easy anymore

CHAPTER 10

Weeks of bandage changes, bedpans and IVs were followed by extended rehabilitation back in Saigon. As happy as Josh was to get out of that hospital bed, he couldn't help but wonder why they'd sent him to rehab when he hadn't been wounded in an arm or leg. It made no sense, but he figured the doctors knew best and went along as cooperatively as possible. As one week became two and wandered into three and then four, he began to get itchy to get back to his men. Finally, he confronted Capt. Fortunato one afternoon when he'd stopped by to watch Josh go through his therapy.

"Captain, I'm feeling good as new. How about you release me back to my platoon?"

Fortunato looked at him and nodded, his lips pressed tightly together as if were debating how much he could share. "Not my call," he finally said. "You need to talk to your Division people."

"Division? Since when do they make medical decisions?" He tried to sound casual, but his mind was whirring.

"They don't," the captain admitted. "It's not a medical decision. Not anymore. Don't quote me, but from my point of view you could've gone back last week." To his patient's confused look, he added: "we've had word to extend your rehab – indefinitely. I guess they were just wondering how long you'd put up with it."

"Who do I need to talk to?"

"I really don't know. How about your XO? He's the one we get our orders from."

"Major Thompson."

"The one and only. Good luck." He didn't say it with much conviction, but at least he patted him on the shoulder before he walked away.

Josh toyed with the idea of *requisitioning* a Jeep to make his way out to the First's base camp north of the city. But he realized that the MPs might not take kindly to him borrowing a US military vehicle, and if he was right about what was going on he could be pretty sure no one would take him there. That left... Corporal Walker.

"Corporal, Lieutenant Daniels. How're you doing?"

"Daniels," the startled voice came over the hospital payphone, "what a surprise. I guess we owe you an apology – the colonel's been very busy these last couple of weeks..."

"No, no. I'm not calling to complain. Actually, I need some information."

"What kind of information?" Walker's voice became much more officious.

"How do I get ahold of Major Thompson from BR1?"

"How do you mean, 'get ahold'?"

"I need to talk to him, but I'm still under medical orders and can't go running around trying to find him. I guess what I want to know is if you can find out for me when he's going to be down here in Saigon."

A long pause. "Yeh, I suppose I can check with some people I know up there. Can I ask why -- you need to talk to him, I mean?"

"Let's just say he has something I need. That good enough?"

"Sounds like it'll have to be. How do I get back to you?"

"I'll call you. Tomorrow okay?"

"Yeh. If I can find out anything, I should know by then."

The next day Josh took pains to ensure he was alone and unwatched before making his way to the payphone to call Walker. Turned out Thompson was in Saigon that very afternoon to meet with his Bien Hoa counterpart, Major Eastly, at 1400 hours.

"I just may crash that meeting," Josh explained. "You know where it'll be?"

"Lieutenant, I'm not sure that's a good idea…" Walker began, but Josh cut him off.

"Corporal, this is something I've got to do – understand? Where will they be?"

Another pause. "I assume in Major Eastly's office, but I didn't tell you – any of this."

"Understood. And thanks."

At 1300 Josh announced he was going out for a jog around the base, loud enough so that anyone who might be listening could hear. He did just that for a half hour or so, covering enough ground so that if anyone were following him, they'd be tired, at least. Then he ducked into a series of alleyways to be sure, arriving at Major Eastly's office a few minutes after 1400 hours. He was sweaty, winded, and ticked-off.

When he walked into the major's reception area a young woman NCO greeted him with usual Army camaraderie.

"You have an appointment?"

"Just tell the major that Lieutenant Daniels is here to see him and Major Thompson."

The assistant started to object, but Josh held his hand up. "They're expecting me, believe me. Just tell them." She stared at him as if trying to decide whether Josh were some kind of nutcase. "Please?" he added with a winning smile. She frowned, but gave in. She picked up the phone and dialed the intercom.

He wasn't lying, exactly. He was sure that Thompson, at least, would be expecting some kind of confrontation when Josh realized what they were up to. Maybe not today…

"They'll see you," the assistant said, her eyes narrowed as if to add, *'but if it were up to me, you'd be out the door in two seconds flat.'* Luckily, it wasn't up to her.

When he walked into Eastly's office, the two officers were already standing, looking his way.

"Why Lieutenant Daniels, what a pleasant surprise," Eastly said, walking over to shake his hand. "I'm glad to see you up and around again."

Thompson sidled up as well. "Lieutenant – looking good."

"Sorry to interrupt your meeting."

Eastly mumbled some nonsense about it not being an imposition, but the way the two of them just stood there, waiting, it was clear they were eager to get back to their discussions.

"May I speak?" Josh asked, reverting to protocol when all else failed.

"Didn't think you came here just to stare at us," Eastly said good-naturedly. "What's up?"

"Well, as you can see, I'm back on my feet again, feeling good, and ready to get back to my platoon. But I understand there's some administrative snafu that's keeping me in therapy. So I thought I'd come talk to the two XO gurus in my chain of command to see if there's some way to expedite matters." He tried to sound nonchalant and looked from one to the other to make clear each understood he was included in his request for help.

"Mark, I think you might want to address this one," Eastly said to Thompson.

Josh saw Thompson's eyebrow arch and his head tilt ever so slightly to one side.

"I'm sure the doctors are just being extra cautious…" he began, but Josh was in no mood.

"Sorry to interrupt, sir, but I've talked to my doctors. They said word has come down from your office."

Thompson glanced at his counterpart, who'd sat behind his desk. Eastly shrugged.

"Lieutenant, I guess you'd say what we have here is a situation," Thompson began. "Just like you, we follow orders, and our orders are that you should stay in therapy for another couple of weeks."

"But why?" Josh asked. "I'm fine."

"Look, Daniels, you're something of a hero around here. And a congressman's son."

Josh sighed and shook his head in despair.

"I know, I know. But as a recovering hero, you're an asset to the Public Affairs people here and back at DOD. A good human interest story, I think they'd call it."

"I'm an infantry officer," Josh insisted.

"Of course you are. But we all have to do what's best for the war effort, and the powers-that-be have decided that what you can do is stay here, for now, and get completely healthy."

"For how long?"

The major vacillated. "I don't know. A couple of weeks, maybe more."

"So now I'm just a REMF, is that it?"

Eastly interrupted. "You were wounded leading an assault that turned back a VC company," he said as if explaining to a 10-year-old. "That's newsworthy."

"And I'm a congressman's son," Josh added, petulance leaking into his voice.

"We all have our cross to bear."

"Is it him, my father, who's behind all this?"

Thompson raised his hands as if to ward off the question. "I don't know. Really. By the time the word gets down to us, we have no idea where it originated."

"Damn it!"

"Look, Josh, I understand you want to get back out there, but I'm afraid it's not going to happen. At least not for a while. Why don't you take advantage of your stay here in Saigon and relax a little? Get some down time? I'm sure your doctors could be persuaded to let you wander off base every now and then."

"Our company is short of officers." He knew it wouldn't make any difference to the two XOs, but he had to say it.

"We know. But like Andy said, we all have to play our part."

Josh wanted to say more, to argue, to cajole, anything to get him back out in the field where he belonged. But it was useless. The two XOs were majors, but that wasn't near enough rank to override Washington's *interest*. He took a deep breath.

"This sucks," he muttered, barely audible.

Thompson shrugged. "Our is not to reason why..."

"Apparently I can't even do that," Josh snapped. "Thanks for the explanation. I think I know who I have to talk to."

He saluted and pivoted sharply. The two majors exchanged a glance as the office door shut behind him.

"Is this going to be a problem?" Eastly asked.

"We shall see."

*****

"I know you had something to do with all this!" Josh said to his father, his voice barely under control.

"You know no such thing," the colonel said calmly. "I inquired about you, as any father would, but I never told them to pull you off the front lines. Although I can't say I'm disappointed they did."

"If you didn't, who did?" He knew he was being unreasonable, but he didn't care. He was pissed.

"I have no idea. Why don't you ask General Abrams, or maybe Secretary Clifford? They might know."

"Right. As if they'd talk to me." A thought came to him. "But they might talk to you. Will you call Clifford?"

"Josh, this isn't like grade school where a parent calls the principal. They give the orders, and you follow them. Surely they taught you that at West Point." The Colonel had always made it clear that he didn't think Pointers were the be-all and end-all of the military.

Josh wasn't going to surrender that easily.

"Will…you…call…them?"

The Colonel exhaled in exasperation. "I'll try. But like I said, I don't necessarily think it's a bad idea to let you recover a while longer."

"The doctors say I'm fully recovered. This isn't a medical decision."

"Fine. I'll call."

"Thank you."

As much as he was tempted to hang-up at that point, before his father could find a reason to back out of his promise, Josh continued a somewhat civilized conversation, mostly about the rest of the family and Darla. His mother came on the line at one point, but she could only talk for a few minutes "because the roast is about to come out of the oven."

He smiled. He could almost smell the roast, surrounded by potatoes… It made him homesick, for an instant. By the time he finally replaced the receiver, he felt better. Not good, but better.

That night, he decided to heed the majors' advice and get out of the hospital compound for a while. He cleared it with Capt. Fortunato, who seemed to think it was the very thing to keep him on the fast-track to full recovery and secured a pass for him. Only trouble was, he had no idea where to go. He hadn't been to a single bar in the city, and he didn't feel like stopping by the base Officers' Club and having to explain twenty times why he was still on medical leave if he was healthy enough to go out. Then he thought of Walker.

The corporal seemed thrilled that Josh would deign to go out to a club with an NCO.

"Nine o'clock?" Walker suggested.

"Kind of late to get started, isn't it?"

The corporal laughed. "Late? Most of the action doesn't start until close to midnight. Before nine I'm not even sure the bartenders will be working."

Josh was in no mood to argue, so he agreed to meet Walker at the base gates at 2100 hours.

By the time Josh showered, dressed and made his way to the main base gate, he was debating whether it was really such a good idea to go out partying. After all, he'd only just recovered from his wounds, and his conscience kept nibbling at the back of his head: *'My guys are still out there. Am I becoming a real REMF?'* Standing there in civvies only exaggerated his guilt.

But before he could change his mind, he found himself at the gate with a very enthusiastic Corporal Walker. In fact, the corporal was so jazzed that Josh could barely recognize him as the sedate soldier he'd seen a few hours earlier. The wild shirt and bell-bottom jeans didn't help any.

"Looking good, Lieutenant!" Walker called out before Josh could even get close enough to express his misgivings. "Let's go get us some Tiger beer!"

Josh smiled and shook his head. *'What the heck...'*

Walker chatted non-stop as he led the way out into the rabbits' warren that was the street scene surrounding the base. Vendors tried to sell them everything from green oranges to VC black pajamas. Small children begged for change, while slightly older girls – and boys – offered themselves for only a few Dong more. Smoke from open fires swirled in the darkness as motorbikes sputtered up and down the main drags carrying anything from single riders to entire families. After having spent a month in the hospital, the whirl of activity made Josh's head spin. The noise, the smells, the chaos: it was almost overwhelming. Thoughts of reneging bubbled-up in his over-stimulated brain, but even as he was considering turning back to the base Walker pulled him by the arm into a dark cave of a club with strobes flashing, American rock music blaring, and young, attractive, barely-dressed women dancing on raised platforms.

"What do you think!?" Walker had to yell to be heard. "Pretty cool, huh?"

That wasn't Josh's first reaction. "It's not Dallas, that's for sure."

Walker took that for agreement, and so continued on inside until he'd managed to find them two sets at a tiny bar table with an unobstructed view of the dancers. *Proud Mary'* blared over massive loudspeakers.

They hadn't been seated for more than a minute or two when a waitress, wearing the shortest mini-dress Josh had ever seen, stopped by to take their order.

"Tiger beer?!" Walker yelled to his tablemate.

Josh shrugged. He'd never had Vietnamese beer, and in fact had only sampled good ol' American brew a few times back in the States. He didn't really like the taste all that much, and Tiger's reputation wasn't too good, with an aftertaste that reminded most of formaldehyde. But he didn't want to rain on Walker's parade. Besides, he liked to make up his own mind.

The beer came quickly, though after one sip Josh wasn't sure that was a good thing. As advertised, the beer had a nasty chemical taste that might well have been formaldehyde.

"Not bad, huh?" Walker shouted after downing half a glass in one swallow.

"Different," Josh answered diplomatically.

After an hour or so of shouted small-talk and another two drinks (Josh switched to seltzer water, which was marginally more potable), both men had grown sufficiently tired of having to yell to make themselves heard to just kick-back and watch the bizarre show that went on all around them. Aside from the dancing, which evolved from lackadaisical, almost bored going-through-the-motions to seductive, raunchy bump-and-grind as the night wore on, there was the 'side trade' that kept the clientele churning. A small army of (for the most part) attractive young women plopped themselves down at random tables to ask "Can girl get beer here?" in heavily-accented English. The answer was almost always "Sure!' and after a beer or two (probably well-watered and massively overpriced), the girl leaned over and whispered in a GI's ear. If the answer to her question was 'yes', the two would disappear for a short while; if 'no', the girl turned to one of the other soldiers at the table without missing a beat. Josh never heard what the girls said, since the girl who landed at their table apparently made a tactical decision that Walker seemed a more likely target for her advances and so the young corporal received all her ministrations. Finally, after extended public foreplay, the girl dragged an unprotesting Walker off to God knew where for God (and everyone else in the place) knew what.

"I'll be back soon!" he yelled.

"I may not be here!" Josh answered, but Walker responded with a smile and wave that suggested he either didn't hear or didn't care.

Josh waited a while, probably only about fifteen minutes though it seemed much longer, before he decided to call it a night. He was tired, the blare of the music was becoming tiresome, his eyes were burning from all the cigarette smoke, and there was no saying how long Walker might want to hang around. He left a substantial tip (by Vietnamese standards) and headed off into the Saigon night.

The city was relatively quiet, at least as quiet as that part of the urban maze ever got. There were few people on the street, probably because it was too early for the late partiers and too late for the early birds. It felt good to escape from the onslaught of sight and sound and smells, although it wasn't noticeably cooler outside. He felt his shirt begin to stick to his skin before he'd walked half a block. Every few feet another somewhat attractive young woman, all of them wearing too few clothes and too much makeup, tried to lure him into one of the dingy clubs that lined both sides of the block. After a short while the constant harassment began to feel depressing, so Josh turned and walked a couple of blocks off the main drag.

Immediately the flashing neon and blaring music faded, replaced by an older, dingier Saigon, the city as it must have existed before the Americans, perhaps even before the French arrived. Older, grimmer faces peered out from doorways, some hidden beneath the ubiquitous wide straw hats worn by nearly every rural Vietnamese he'd seen. The smells changed from beer and cigarette smoke to fish and open sewers. He was beginning to wonder if perhaps he should've stayed on the streets more traveled when he heard, rather than saw, a small dispute just ahead of him.

A woman said something in the loud, high-pitched whine that seemed to be the preferred delivery of most Viet women, followed by a gruff response by a man, apparently American.

"Listen, bitch, I will pay! Do you understand, I gottem' money!"

Back came the woman, even more upset. "No go with you! You go!" she began before switching to a stream of invective in her native tongue.

Josh was debating whether to get involved when he saw a hand lash out and heard skin strike skin – hard. The woman cried out, and Josh found himself running in their direction.

"Hey, what's going on there?!" he yelled out, hoping to fluster the attacker into taking off without a confrontation. No such luck.

An angry black face turned to him. He saw sergeant's stripes on the sleeve. "Mind your own business, white boy!" the soldier yelled back, but Josh was having none of it.

"Stand down, soldier!" he ordered, using his best command voice. It wasn't good enough.

"I said, mind your own business!" the soldier repeated, turning to him with hands balled into fists.

"I wouldn't do that, Sergeant," Josh said, modulating his voice. "Striking an officer is a court martial offense." He saw some doubt creep into the sergeant's eyes.

"This ain't none of your business, white bread, officer or not."

"I'm *making* it my business, soldier, and unless you want to spend the rest of your time here in-country in the brig, I suggest you move along. Am I making myself clear?!"

He could see the man weighing his options; he could almost hear the wheels turning. Josh didn't exhale until he saw the NCO's fists slowly unclench.

"All you chink bitches the same," he muttered to the attractive Vietnamese woman standing defiantly in the shadows behind him. With a last smoldering look at Josh the sergeant walked off down the narrow street, mumbling to himself as he wove his way drunkenly into the warm, humid night.

When it was clear he wasn't coming back, Josh turned to the woman. She may have been scared, but you sure couldn't tell it from the look she gave him.

"Are you okay?" he asked, a large red mark on the side of her face suggesting otherwise.

She looked him straight in the eyes with a stare that might have been fear but might just as well have been defiance, then turned and hurried into the dilapidated building behind her without a word.

"Guess you are," Josh said to himself as he watched her disappear up a rickety set of stairs. "Nice meeting you."

As the adrenaline slowly faded from his system, Josh made his way back to the base hospital. Whether it was the beer, the after-effects of his wounds, or his encounter with the NCO, Josh could barely strip off his clothing before falling into bed. The last think he saw in his mind's eye was the face of that Vietnamese woman, shaken but unbowed.

*****

The next morning Nurse Whittaker had to shake Josh awake to get ready for his daily rehab session.

"You look like crap," she said as she watched him struggle to shake off the cobwebs from the night before.

"Did some local sightseeing last night," he managed between yawns.

"Did Captain Fortunato know about your *sightseeing?*"

"He did… more or less. Maybe not the specifics, but he's the one who signed my pass."

Whittaker busied herself straightening up his side table. "We're not going to have to get you penicillin shots, are we?" She seemed only half-joking.

"Nah, nothing like that. Had a beer. Watched some dancers. That was it."

"You do remember that you were wounded just a few weeks ago, don't you?"

"You know as well as I do that I'm 99 per cent back to normal. They're just keeping me here for… I don't really know what."

"Maybe they know more about medicine than you do?"

"It's not about medicine."

"And you know this how, exactly?"

He didn't want to rat out Dr. Fortunato, so he evaded. "I just know."

"So what, you want them to send you back out to the field? Half the guys in here would give their big toe to be in your shoes."

He smiled at the phrasing. "I'm not most guys. I want to get back to my men."

She looked at him sideways. "You're not going for a psych discharge, are you?"

"I just want to get back out to my platoon. That's all. I don't see why everyone around here seems to think that's so crazy. Isn't that why we're all here, to win this war?"

The lieutenant looked at him appraisingly. "That's what they say. But it's not what I hear from a lot of the guys who pass through here. And I mean a lot. They think the War is a big screw-up and the draft is proof that the American people don't support it."

Josh winced. He'd heard the same from some of his men, though not to his face. A lot of them had been backing Nixon in the recent election, hoping he'd change LBJ's policies. But Whittaker had never shown him anything but impartial professionalism.

"We're soldiers. We get paid to do what we're ordered," he explained. "Once respect for the chain of command breaks down, the entire system fails." He sounded moralizing even to himself. Whittaker didn't challenge him, however.

"I guess it's good we've got some soldiers here like you," she said, "or this place would be even crazier than it is now. But try to let your body heal. You're no good to anyone if you don't get healthy."

"Yes, ma'am!" he said with a mock salute.

"You Academy grads," she said as she walked away, "you all think you're Superman."

"Batman!" he yelled after her.

She flashed a broad smile over her shoulder.

*****

Orderlies distributed the mail every Monday, Wednesday and Friday, bringing it to each patient's bed. Josh waited expectantly for his. It was so boring lying there in bed that even a letter from his little brother provided much-needed distraction. In his most recent missive he told of his high school routine, his inept basketball team. His mother talked about the family, and added "Dad says hi." Nothing from Darla.

*****

Rehab was a real bitch that morning, or maybe it just seemed that way because he had a throbbing headache and felt half asleep. Every stretch, every exercise was an effort. But he kept at it, shamed by his own words to follow the doctors' orders. He didn't necessarily like it, but he did as he was told, for a while anyway.

He was deep in thought, midway through a set of dumbbell curls, when a disturbance at the entrance to the large open therapy room snapped him out of his reverie. A group of officers filed in, accompanied by more hangers-on than seemed customary. When Josh took a second look, he saw stars shining on one of the officer's shoulders. Another few feet closer and he realized it was his CO, Major General Irwin.

'*What the...?*' he thought as the entourage headed in his direction. It stopped directly in front of him.

"Captain Daniels," the general announced, tipping his head in Josh's direction.

"It's lieutenant, Sir," Josh said before he could censor himself. "Lieutenant Daniels."

"Not anymore," Irwin said. He motioned to an aide standing beside him, who passed the senior officer a small box. He opened it and took out a gold medal attached to a red, white and blue ribbon.

"Daniels, it is my honor, representing the President and the Secretary of Defense, to present to you the Silver Star for conspicuous gallantry during combat on the 16th of January, 1969. Congratulations." He handed the medal to Josh, shook his hand, and turned to allow a photographer to snap a flash photo of the presentation. Before the dots in front of Josh's eyes had even cleared, the general turned back to his aide. "And in recognition of your bravery and leadership," he continued, accepting two small double silver bars from the aide, "you are hereby promoted to the rank of captain. Congratulations." He handed the captain's insignia to Josh and posed for another photograph.

"Sorry this is a bit... unorthodox, *Captain*," the general explained as soon as the photo was finished, "but the Deputy CO of MACV has had an unexpected opening on his staff, and you've been named to the position. Major Thompson will fill you in. I'm sure you will be a credit to the Academy, the Army and your family. Now, I'm afraid I have another meeting to attend, but I'm sure we will have other opportunities to talk. Captain." Josh snapped off a salute as the general pivoted and headed back out the way he'd come in, trailed by the herd of hangers-on like a mother goose with her goslings. Josh stared down at the Silver Star and the captain's bars.

"Things move fast around here, sometimes," Major Thompson said as he moved to Josh's side.

"This is crazy," Josh mumbled.

"Crazy or not, General Rattling will be expecting you tomorrow morning, 0800 sharp, at his office. That's in the main MACV building, if you didn't know."

"Is all this because of my father?"

Thompson shrugged. "Above my pay grade. Ask the general. He might know."

"I just may do that."

"Up to you. But I might wait at least ten minutes before pissing the old man off."

Josh smiled despite himself. "I might be able to wait ten minutes."

"Good. Then that's settled. Congratulations, Captain." He shook Josh's hand. "Try to make the Big Red One look good over there with the big brass."

"I'll do my best."

"That's all we can ask. Chin up: this may not be your ideal assignment, but it's not Khe Sanh either. Show 'em what you can do, and you might get another chance in the field – if you still want it by then."

"Thanks, Major. You're right – it's not my ideal assignment. But I'm a soldier and I follow orders. I'll do the best I can, you can count on it."

Thompson patted him on the shoulder. "Go get 'em, tiger."

As soon as the major left, most of the other rehabbing soldiers and medical staff came over to offer their congratulations and see the Silver Star. Josh was as gracious as he could be given the fact that he was furious at his father and feeling more than a little guilty, but the back-slapping dragged on interminably. When the last well-wishers finally went back to their exercises, Josh picked out Captain Fortunato across the room and made straight for him.

"Did you know about this?" he asked the captain, his anger bubbling over.

"Don't blame me," Fortunato said. "I just found out this morning. We were kept in the dark just like you."

"I suppose I'm medically fit to take the job?"

"No one asked us, but yes, you are."

"This sucks."

The doctor nodded in sympathy. "Sorry about that."

Josh took a moment to gather his thoughts. "Yeh, well thanks for all your help these past few weeks. You and your staff have been great."

"We do what we can. Now take care of yourself, Captain. I've heard the jungle over at MACV is almost as dangerous as the one outside the gates."

Josh forced a grin. "I'll keep my eyes open."

The two men shook hands and Josh left the center to return to the hospital to start packing. Lieutenant Whittaker and a couple of the other nurses were waiting for him there, as was a chocolate doughnut topped by a single candle.

"We hear our star patient is leaving us," Whittaker said when Josh came through the ward doors.

"Looks that way."

"We all wanted to wish you the best of luck." She leaned over and kissed him on the cheek. "Take care of yourself."

Josh blushed. "I will. And thanks, to all of you." The other nurses followed the lieutenant's lead and gave him a little hug and kiss on the cheek.

At their urging he blew out the candle as they sang, 'For He's A Jolly Good Fellow.'

"Afraid we've got to go take care of some *really* sick people," Whittaker said even as the smoke from the candle still drifted lazily toward the distant tin roof. "This war doesn't wait for anyone."

"Maybe see you around."

"You never know." Her smile and the glint in her eye made Josh blush again.

What's going on?' he wondered. It was a question that needed more answers than he could give.

CHAPTER 11

I see Darla – she's sitting in the passenger seat of a yellow Corvette; she has the window rolled down. She's waving at me and smiling, but she doesn't call out to me and the car doesn't stop. I try to see who is driving, but I can't make it out. Something tells me it's a man.

"Darla, wait!" I cry out, but the car rolls slowly on, and her window rolls slowly up.

"It's me, Josh!"

The car slowly disappears, as if dissolving, and I find that I'm standing in front of our childhood house in Dallas. "Mom, Dad, I'm home!" I yell, and I run toward the front door. But when I throw it open there's no one inside. So I run upstairs, calling out, "Mom, Dad, Kyle!" but no one answers. I look from room to room, but the house is empty. Until I look in my own room.

There I see myself, looking into a mirror. But where I should be reflected, there is nothing. Just the empty room behind me.

I feel panicky, but at that moment I suddenly know who I can talk to: Landry! I find myself outside, running down the sidewalk toward his house even though I know he doesn't live in Texas. I feel cool air rushing past my face as I arrive at the Landrys' front door. I don't knock, or ring the bell, but just turn the knob and step into the house. Right there, in the living room, I see a casket covered by an American flag. No one is there. It is eerie, but I have to know. I walk up to the casket, roll back the flag, and pry open one corner of the wooden box. It's heavy, but I struggle to lift it. Inside, all is dark. Black actually, as if I'm staring into a hole. And as I look, suddenly Landry's face, all pale and lifeless, pops up out of the darkness. I step back but trip over some piece of furniture and fall, fall, fall…

I awaken, my face covered in sweat. It takes me several moments to orient myself, to realize it was all just a dream. Then I sit up, and my mind begins to whirl: why didn't Darla stop for me? Why was our house empty? And why did I see Landry dead in a coffin? I'm not much for psychology, but I can't help but wonder.

CHAPTER 12

Josh was up before 0600 and on his way to the MACV headquarters building by 0730. He toted a green canvas duffle stuffed with the few belongings that had caught up to him at the hospital. The rest were out at Division Headquarters. He'd have to get someone to take him out there as soon as he knew which way was up at his new assignment.

He caught the drab green shuttle bus with wire-reinforced windows that took him from the hospital complex to Tan Son Nhut. Across the street stood a block-long white two-story stucco building that looked more than a little like an oversized chicken coop: Military Assistance Command, Vietnam, as the sign on the top of the building proclaimed.

'Great. Just like home,' he thought as he crossed the busy boulevard, dodging the constant stream of pedicabs, taxis, Jeeps, trucks, bikes, and even the occasional buffalo cart that called the streets of Saigon home.

He made it to the other side with effort, sweating both from the heat and humidity and the struggle to avoid being run down. The guards at the front entrance were efficient if not overly friendly, but it was the air-conditioning inside the building that made his day.

"Lieutenant Daniels, reporting for duty with the Deputy Commander's office," he announced to the receptionist. The middle-aged woman looked down at a visitors' list and then up at his shoulders.

"Would that be *Captain* Joshua Daniels?" she asked.

Josh followed her gaze to the double silver bars. "Oh, right. Sorry, I was just promoted," he stammered.

"Well congratulations," the woman said with little enthusiasm. "Second floor, turn left."

He nodded his thanks and headed straight for the large staircase that led upstairs. As he moved through the entranceway he glanced left and right to get a feel for the place: scores of soldiers, and not a few sailors, moved helter-skelter through the narrow corridors. He was a little surprised to see how many were officers.

Upstairs he found more of the same, though perhaps the movement through the corridors was somewhat less hectic. As he'd been directed, he turned down the left hallway and soon found himself at the Office of Deputy Commander, MACV. As he stepped through the door an attractive young woman looked up and smiled.

"Captain Daniels?"

This time he didn't hesitate. "Reporting for duty."

The young woman saluted and then held out her hand. "Corporal Nancy Wilding," she introduced.

"A pleasure."

The corporal stared at him with such obvious interest he began to wonder if something were amiss.

"What, did I miss a spot shaving?" he finally asked.

"Oh, no, sorry," she explained. "It's just, well, we'd all been wondering who all the rush-rush fuss was over, and it turns out it was you."

'Rush-rush fuss?' "I'm afraid I don't understand. What fuss?" Josh asked.

"Well, I mean, we only got word…"

Just then the back left door that led off the reception area opened and a tall, thin major stepped out and turned toward them.

"Captain Daniels?" he called out. "Welcome to MACV."

He came over and shook Josh's hand, even as Corporal Wilding ducked her head and feigned filing work.

"Max Winshotz," the major introduced himself. "Glad to see you. We can use someone with your background."

Josh wondered what background he was referring to, but held his tongue. "Pleasure to be here, sir."

"I realize you're probably a bit disoriented, what with the quick change of orders and all…"

"A bit," Josh admitted.

"I'm sure General Edwards will be able to clear things up. Let's go introduce you."

Without waiting for a reply, the major pivoted and walked briskly back to the door he'd come through. When Josh caught up to him, he found himself standing at the doorway to the MACV Commander's private office.

"I thought I was supposed to see General Rattling," he whispered to the major.

"Change of plans," Winshotz whispered back.

"Come in, come in!" Major General Edwards welcomed him as soon as he saw the newly-minted captain peer through the doorway. "Any trouble finding us?"

"No sir. This is probably the best-known building in Saigon." He snapped to attention in front of the general's desk and saluted. "Captain Josh Daniels, reporting for duty, sir."

The general smiled as he returned the salute with a relaxed wave of his hand. "Look, Daniels, we'll be seeing a lot of each other over the next few months. If you salute me every time we see each other, we'll both waste a lot of valuable time. So let's just say once in the morning and that's that here in the office. Sound ok?"

"Yes sir."

"Good. Have a seat. Max, do you think you can give us a couple of minutes?"

The major nodded. "You got it, sir. Buzz Corporal Wilding when you want me."

"Thank you."

As soon as Winshotz closed the door behind him, General Edwards sat heavily in his large high-backed leather desk chair.

"Can I get you anything: Coffee? Water?"

"No sir, I'm fine, thank you."

Edwards looked down at his desk as if ordering his thoughts. When he looked up, his gray eyes were sharp and focused. "Daniels, I know this assignment was unexpected."

"Completely," Josh interrupted.

Edwards nodded. "And if the grapevine is accurate, you would have preferred to have gone back out to your platoon. Is that right?"

Josh debated denying it, but decided to let the chips fall where they may. "I'm an infantry officer, General. I trained as a Ranger. I think I can make a difference out there."

"I'm sure you could, son, I'm sure you could. But I think you can make a bigger difference right here. You were top ten at the Academy, right?"

"Yes sir."

"And the way you handled yourself out in the field had already brought you to the attention of your superior officers even before that firefight out by Thunder Road."

Josh couldn't help the quizzical expression that twisted his face. *'It had? Is he BS-ing me?'*

The general leaned forward. "Captain, we've got a lot of good soldiers out there. Men, and women, who can follow orders and are brave and responsible out in the field. What we don't have are enough people who see the big picture. Who can see two steps ahead. You've had top-notch strategic training and have shown an innate tactical ability in the field. People like you need to be here, helping us plan this war. I'd never say you were wasted out there in the field, but it isn't the *best* use of your abilities."

Josh fidgeted. "Permission to speak?"

"Of course." Edwards leaned back into his chair.

"I'm sure you know that my father is a congressman from Texas."

"I do."

"He and I... disagreed about my tour here."

"Understandable."

Josh tried to weigh his next words, but he couldn't find another way to say it. "Is this his doing? I mean, did he pull strings back in Washington to get me placed here with you?" As he spoke his ears began to burn.

Edwards shot forward, his eyes burning. When the general's eyes narrowed, Josh felt like sliding down into his chair and hiding.

"Look, Captain. Josh. As I'm sure you're aware, the U.S. role in this little pissing match is coming to an end. We're winding down, turning the fighting over to the South Vietnamese, no matter what the consequences. That's not for us to decide. It's for people, like your father, back in DC. But as long as we have American soldiers and civilians on the ground here, I'm going to do my damnedest to make sure they are protected. And I don't give a rat's ass if a congressman, or a senator, or even the President tells me to put someone on my staff, I'm only going to do it if I'm pretty damn sure they can do the job. That they can help keep our people safe. Am I clear on that?"

Josh eyed the man closely. What he saw made him nod his head.

"Yes sir, perfectly clear."

"You're here to help us get every last American out of this hellhole, alive and well if possible."

"I'll do my best, sir."

Edwards relaxed. "Good. That's all we can ask. And for your information, I have not heard a word from your father. Though I imagine he'd be proud of you."

"Thank you, sir. I hope so."

"I'm sure of it." He rifled through some papers. "So now that we're done with that, how about we discuss this damn war." He pulled out a folder marked TOP SECRET and plopped it down on the desk.

"Sir?"

"I've decided you're too valuable to stick over there in General Rattling's office, pushing paper. I want you close by where we can pick your brain. That sound okay with you?"

"Absolutely, sir."

"Good." He picked up his phone. "Corporal, would you tell Major Winshotz he can come back now? And tell him to bring the rest of the people."

Ten officers, most of them colonels and above, filed into an adjoining room chatting with the easy back-and-forth that suggested this was a regular, perhaps daily event. They went straight to a long meeting table without even a cursory salute to the CO. Apparently General Edwards was as good as his word as far as the trappings of rank in meetings he chaired.

But when the general finally got up from his seat and made his way over to the table – the last one, save Josh, to do so – all the others stood at their places.

"Sit, sit," Edwards directed with an impatient wave of his hand. "As most, if not all of you already know, we have a new member of our little planning group with us today: Captain Joshua Daniels, taking Jerry's place. I'm sure you will all do your best to get him up to speed and make him feel welcome." It was an order, not a suggestion. "Now let's get down to business." Josh scanned the officers lining the table and received a small nod of recognition from several.

It all seemed so surreal. A month ago he was a platoon leader out in the elephant grass. Now, there he sat, surrounded by the core group planning military strategy for the entire war. He thought of the ancient Chinese saying: Beware of interesting times. He wondered just how interesting things would get.

*****

When the planning meeting broke up some two hours later, Josh's head was swimming with people, places, jargon and acronyms.

"Hold on just a second," General Edwards said when he stood to leave. The general finished some last business and sent the final member of his group out to begin implementation of their decisions.

"So, what did you think?" he asked Josh when the office door closed.

"Very impressive. A little confusing."

Edwards nodded. "You'll catch on. Won't take long. After a while all the units and commanders and the ARVN and even the NVA – they all become like part of your family."

"It's a lot to take on."

"Is that why you didn't offer any recommendations or opinions?"

Josh wasn't sure whether the general was angry or just inquiring.

"I don't like to talk until I know what I'm talking about."

"That's a good policy. But you should know that I expect all my group members to contribute – after they know what they're talking about."

"I'm not the shy type," Josh said, "not once I get my feet under me."

"Good. Then I expect to start hearing from you in say… three days?"

"I… Yes, sir. Three days it will be."

"Go talk to some of the other members of the group – Colonel Henry would be a good first choice. Pick his brain. Then be back here at 1400 hours. I'll set up a briefing by some of the guys in the group to catch you up ASAP."

Josh knew enough about the chain of command to realize that a private briefing for a captain by high-ranking staff officers was almost unheard of.

"Fourteen hundred hours. Yes, sir." Josh answered at once. He saluted and turned to leave.

"And Captain," General Edwards added before he could take a step toward the door, "what I said about not caring if the President told me he wanted someone on my staff – scratch that. I might have been a little overzealous on that one."

Josh looked back and smiled. "Yes sir."

*****

The first few days at MACV flew by in a blur of new responsibilities, new people, new quarters – new everything. His reception had been, for the most part, quite friendly and convivial. A couple of the senior officers on the planning staff were hard-asses, but Colonel Henry more than made up for them. He'd taken Josh under his wing and introduced him to the entire MACV operation.

In fact, the only fly in the ointment was the only other junior officer on the team: Captain Alfred Harris, a nasty, conniving, insecure little man from some farm town in Arkansas. It seemed he'd taken an instant dislike to Josh. His attitude seemed to be that all Academy grads were idiots, and he didn't hesitate to make his opinion clear – in private of course. In front of senior officers he was all sweetness and puke, a real Bravo Foxtrot kind of guy.

But Harris was just an irritant. Josh had too much to do, too much to learn, to be rattled by one puissant little ROTC graduate. When Day 4 of his new assignment brought him once again to the planning meeting in General Edward's office, he was fully prepared to show his stuff. He'd crammed for hours the night before on one particular operation – a continuation of the same Thunder Road mission that had landed him in the hospital, and indirectly in his current assignment.

"All right, now let's take a look at Toan Thang 3," the DCO announced, and as soon as he did, Josh spoke up.

"Actually, I have some personal knowledge of the terrain where Atlas Wedge will take place," he said, purposely downplaying his experience. He could see Harris grimace and roll his eyes.

"You do, don't you, Captain," Edwards jumped in. "What're your thoughts?"

Josh had already run his thinking past Colonel Henry and had fine-tuned it with the colonel's input. So when he laid it out to the group, stressing the political implications of Vietnamization, he was reasonably certain that no one could do much more than pick at the periphery of his words. To his great satisfaction, it was Harris who tried to find fault.

"This is a war, Daniels, and we're soldiers," the Arkansas native intoned, staring at Josh with a look of assured superiority. "Political considerations are the politicians' responsibility."

General Edwards looked like he was going to reply, but Josh didn't wait.

"Vietnamization is the end game to this war, Captain, whether you like it or not. And Atlas Wedge is the leading edge of that policy. The only way the Vietnamese are going to support the ARVN and their political bosses is if they get some sense that their lives will be better under their rule than under the NVA. The only way *that* is going to work is if we have enough time to help them establish some semblance of order here in the South. And the only way we're going to get the time and resources to do that is if the *politicians* back in Washington think that our strategy will both get us out of here as soon as possible and at the same time have a reasonable chance of keeping the Communists out of power – at least for a while. *Politicians*," he stressed the word as if it described some foul creature, "don't want to have to tell their constituents they lost a war. And that, Captain, is why the political considerations are just as important, if not more important, than military strategy."

Josh stared at Harris, daring him to contradict him. Harris stared back, but didn't say a word. Out of the corner of his eye Josh saw several other members of the group look to each other with unspoken acknowledgment of the acuity of Josh's presentation. But only one man's opinion really mattered, and for a few heartbeats General Edwards was silent. Josh's pulse began to race. Had he gone too far?

"No other objections?" Edwards finally asked. He looked around the table and got nothing but shakes of the head. "Good, because the captain's analysis is spot-on. We've got to make sure that our tanks, and mechanized artillery, and gunships target only our NVA and VC friends – NOT the locals. If we have to keep our kill zones tighter than we'd like, then that's what we're going to do – understood?"

Mumbled "yes, sir" and nods greeted his question. The general looked to Harris.

"Understood, Captain?"

Harris looked like he'd just swallowed nuoc mam, the noxious sauce that the Vietnamese poured over almost everything they ate even though it tasted like rotten fish.

"Understood, sir," he managed to squeeze out through clenched teeth. The look he shot at Josh was pure venom. He'd taken his best shot and lost.

"Good. Then let's see how we're going to accomplish that," Edwards continued as if nothing had occurred.

*****

"Good presentation," Colonel Henry congratulated Josh when the meeting concluded. "The Old Man seems to like you."

"He wanted me to talk…"

"Oh, I think he's going to want that more than ever, now. Unless I'm mistaken one of the reasons he roped you into this meeting is because you've been exposed to the political theater back in Washington."

"That's my father's thing," Josh said. "Not mine."

"Maybe not, but you seem to have a better feel for it than most of the rest of us, so I wouldn't go belittling your insight, or your contacts, for that matter."

"My father and I don't talk much."

"You should. If for no other reason than to get a sense of what the politicos back there are thinking. The general and the CO are fighting two wars – here with the NVA, and with the politicians in DC. We've got to help them win both."

Josh sighed. This was going to be harder than he'd thought.

*****

At the next meeting of the strategic planning group, Captain Harris's seat was occupied by a freshly-minted captain about Josh's age. Colonel Henry leaned over and whispered in Josh's ear.

"The Old Man doesn't like sniping," he said. "Rumor has it Harris is on his way to a fire base up north somewhere." The colonel smiled.

Josh had mixed feelings. He wasn't sorry that Harris was gone by any means, but at the same time he almost wished it was him headed for the fire base instead of Harris. He'd come to Vietnam to fight, damn it, not sit in meetings! Yet, if he was honest with himself, he had to admit that the responsibilities of the planning meeting were more satisfying than he had expected. Not quite the adrenaline rush of a platoon leader, but something different, something important.

As the days dissolved into weeks, Josh found his voice in the meeting and a place at the table. Not only General Edwards, but most if not all his fellow officers treated him as an equal. On some subjects, like politics, they considered him the group guru, rightfully or not. On others, he held his own. Almost without a second thought, Josh acclimated, both inside the meeting and out.

At first he was assigned to temporary quarters, but after Harris's unexpected departure he got his own room – not a perk he'd thought much about, but a welcome one nonetheless. At first he'd felt guilty about the private digs, not even bothering to put up a single photo or personal possession to brand it as his own. But a photo of his family opened the floodgates, and by the middle of 1969 the room looked like home.

It was in that room, with framed photos of Darla, the family, his grandparents, and his Academy graduating class, plus posters of Willy Nelson and Charlie Daniels, that Josh was relaxing one afternoon sipping a beer and listening to music, when a loud knock on his door brought him face to face with an old friend: Landry.

"Well, well, well, look what the cat dragged in," Josh said as he grabbed his fellow Texan by the shoulders and gave him a big hug. As he stepped back, he saw that his buddy looked a good deal the worse for wear. His sunken eyes were outlined with dark circles, and he'd lost a good fifteen pounds. As he stepped through the door, Josh saw his eyes quickly scan the room.

"Life is good," he said softly. Josh couldn't tell if it was merely an observation or whether a hint of sarcasm tinged his words.

"Can't complain. Come in, come in – have a seat!"

The tall, lanky Texan did as he was directed, but his slow gait and tentative attitude worried his old friend.

"Can I get you a beer?"

"Yeh, sure, thanks," Landry said as he flopped down on a brightly upholstered easy chair.

"Bud okay?"

"Yeh, sure, anything." Even his words were slow, without the animation and enthusiasm Josh remembered so fondly.

"So, what brings you to the big city?"

Josh's attempt at small-talk fell flat even to his own ears.

"Just a three day pass. Our unit had some trouble. I guess they thought I needed a break."

Josh waited for his friend to elaborate, but he didn't.

"Trouble?" he coaxed. "What happened?"

Landry took a long swig of beer and then stared at nothing in particular for several long seconds. Josh was just about to repeat his question when Landry began to talk, slowly, softly.

"We were running a recon patrol just north of here, near an old rubber plantation." Josh nodded; he knew the place. He'd seen it marked on maps and had heard it discussed in the planning meeting. "Nothing special, just part of a bigger operation to start turning things over to the Vietnamese. I usually would have sent my Top with the squad, but he was down with worms and so I decided to go with them. It'd been quiet for a long time, and I guess I was getting antsy." As he talked, Landry continued to stare off into space, but his words picked up tempo and volume.

"For the first few clics everything was good – the men were relaxed, rested. My pointman was solid, experienced. Second tour. But we still stepped in it, big-time. We walked right into a VC ambush. They had us pinned down for hours – couldn't break out, couldn't go back, and my RTO took a bullet that passed right through the equipment in the first few minutes of the fight. Saved his life, but we couldn't even call in support. I don't know how many of them there were, at least a couple of dozen, maybe more. They just kept hammering at us with small arms fire, a heavy machinegun, and then mortars. Were chewing us up pretty bad; we took a lot of casualties. So when darkness fell I decided to try again to get a squad out to go back for help. Asked for volunteers and got four. We laid down heavy cover fire, and for a while I thought maybe they'd gotten through."

He stopped, his head low, his lower lip quivering. Josh wanted to say something to console him, but no words came.

"It was maybe a half-hour later we started hearing the screams. I knew it was Williamson the second I heard it. Terrible sound." His eyes darted back and forth as if he was reliving the moment. "Lasted for almost an hour. Some of the men wanted to go after him, ride to the rescue, you know?" He looked up with a pained grimace. "But I told them no. Couldn't risk any more men. We'd fired off more than a dozen signal flares – I kept hoping someone was looking. But no one came." He shook his head and sighed.

"Wasn't until hours later, around 2200, that gunships came in and lit the place up. A short while later a platoon of Rangers dropped in and mopped up the VC stragglers. Most of 'em had taken off once the barrage started. They found 13 KIA. Who knows how many wounded they dragged off."

"And you?" Josh didn't want to ask, but he had to.

"Eighteen dead. Sixteen wounded bad enough to medevac out." He bit his lips and his voice lowered to barely more than a whisper. "Worse thing was when they found Williamson. They'd cut off his ears, slit open his gut and pulled his intestines out. Then they just left him there to die. But he was still alive…" Josh saw tears well-up in his friend's eyes.

"It's this war, Mason. There's not much we can do about it."

"I sent him back there!"

Josh spoke softly. "He volunteered, Mason. He was a good soldier, just like all the others. The VC killed him – not you."

Silent sobs shook Landry's shoulders.

*****

The two men talked for hours, draining beer after beer in the process. Josh hadn't downed that much alcohol since high school, but he thought it might help his friend open up as he tried to convince him that the ambush wasn't his fault. Only problem was, he wasn't sure it wasn't. Josh knew that scouting reports had mentioned major movements of VC in the area; he'd heard of them all the way back at MACV. Surely Landry had been warned. Should he have assigned more advance scouts to warn them of an ambush? Who could say? Josh knew he didn't have the intel to decide one way or the other, but he was confident some review board somewhere would investigate. Maybe even a full court martial. It all depended on what his men said back at their base camp.

The one thing that worried him was Landry's description of his men "looking at me with dead eyes. They blamed me; I could feel it."

If that was true, his buddy might be in big trouble. But for that moment, in those quarters, Josh was determined to give his friend peace of mind, or at least help soothe the pain. Between his words and the beers, he thought he'd done some good. When Landry finally dozed-off in the easy chair, Josh draped his legs over the end of a coffee table and covered him with a blanket before turning off the lights. In the darkness of the tiny room Josh listened to Landry's heavy breathing as he struggled to sleep himself.

It would be a long night.

*****

When the alarm startled him back to consciousness at 0630, Landry had left. All the beer cans had been neatly stashed in the trash and the general mess had been straightened.

'Damn, why didn't you hang around a little longer,' Josh mused as he dragged his pounding head out of bed and stumbled to the shower. He was worried about his friend. Landry rarely let anything get him down. But he was down now. Real down.

He thought about using his position to get word to Landry's CO, but thought better of it. Even with the best intentions, a word from Headquarters that a platoon leader was showing signs of emotional problems would likely get him pulled from the field and a notation placed in his file: *headcase.* That wouldn't help anyone. So he decided to find a reason for going up to the 1st Division HQ and paying his buddy a visit. The only question was, when? *'Soon',* he promised himself. *'Real soon.'*

By the time he reached MACV, his head was almost screwed on right and he felt halfway human. Corporal Wilding brought him right back to reality, greeting him with her usual respectful welcome.

"You look like crap," she said, shaking her head. "Too much fun last night?"

"I wish. A buddy stopped by – he was having a bad time."

"And you played shrink?"

"Friend," he said. Wilding didn't follow-up.

The day dragged by as his thoughts constantly wandered to Landry. Once General Edwards called him on it, in a nice enough way; the others around the table noticed his lack of focus as well.

"Hangovers are frowned upon," Colonel Henry told him at a break. "The general doesn't drink."

"I don't drink all that much either," Josh responded. When the colonel looked at him with obvious skepticism, he went on to explain about Landry's visit. Henry listened thoughtfully. He was Josh's go-to guy in the meeting; he was the one person who seemed to give a damn.

"So now I'm in a quandary – do I just ignore his situation, or do I try to do something to help him?"

"Sounds to me like you've already decided."

"I just don't want to cause him any trouble. He's a good officer. His platoon needs him."

"And he's your friend."

"Yeh, that too."

Henry agreed that a personal visit up to the Big Red One's field HQ was "the tactic most likely to bring positive results." When Josh asked him how he could get up there without raising unwanted questions, the colonel told him he'd take care of it. "We've got to take care of our own," he said, patting Josh on the shoulder. "No one else will."

The conversation left Josh with mixed feelings: he was pleased that Henry had promised to help, but he'd never heard him sound so… cynical. Were things really getting that bad?

As if that weren't enough, Josh's day went from bad to worse as the general called him into his office at the conclusion of the planning meeting. He braced for a dressing-down, but the CO surprised him.

"Looks like you're a little under the weather," he commented as soon as Josh sat down. Josh knew he owed the general an explanation, but debated how to respond; after some hemming and hawing, he explained, briefly, what had happened the night before. He didn't mention Landry by name, and only gave the vaguest of descriptions.

"Well, then I guess we have to give you a pass for today. What you need is something to lift your spirits a little. Tonight the Ambassador is having a reception for some local businessmen. He's asked us to come up with a half-dozen officers to pad-out the guest list. Feel up to it?"

In fact, Josh didn't. He wanted to tell the general that receptions weren't his thing, and today of all days wasn't the time. But the Old Man looked at him with such expectation he couldn't say no. Besides, he wasn't really given the option.

"Captain, this isn't an invitation, it's an order," Edwards finally said after waiting long seconds for Josh to respond. "You need a change of pace, and I need some presentable officers to fill out the invitation list. Understood?"

"Yes sir. I'll be there."

"Good. And Captain, try to smile every now and then. We don't want the civilians to think we're all a bunch of moody nut cases."

Josh smiled. "I'll see what I can do."

"I'll expect a full report tomorrow."

Josh saluted, just to tweak the Old Man. He smiled and nodded his dismissal.

That night, Josh showered and changed into his dress uniform at 0630, all the while mumbling to himself about his bad luck. When he finished and looked at himself in the mirror, he saw a scrawny, hung-over soldier who looked about 5 years older than his dog tags indicated. The uniform hung loosely on his diminished frame; even after all the time that had passed since he'd been released from the hospital, the effects of his four months in the field still showed.

'*Nice, real nice,*' he continued his internal dialogue. '*They'll think I was a POW or something.*'

There wasn't much he could do about it – too late for a tailor – so he sucked it up, tucked his cap under his arm, and headed off to the Embassy. The night was warm, as always, but relatively quiet. The corner of Thong Nhut and Mac Dinh Chi Streets was in the high-rent section of Saigon, not far from the French Embassy and the Presidential Palace. As Josh got out of the Jeep he and two other officers had corralled to take them to the reception, he looked for the spot in the wall surrounding the compound where Viet Cong sappers had blown a hole just over a year earlier and invaded the Embassy grounds, killing several defenders before dying themselves. It seemed surreal that the VC could penetrate all the way to the heart of Saigon with so many US and South Vietnamese military running around. But they had.

Inside, Embassy staffers were still scurrying to finalize preparations for the big to-do. They'd arranged fresh flowers in crystal vases all around the large reception area, and stationed glittering silver food heaters on a long banquet table in an adjacent room. A full colonel from MACV was the senior military officer, and his entire briefing to the other officers present was, "don't eat too much and only talk when spoken to." Not exactly motivational.

At 1920 hours the first of the invited guests began to arrive. Josh learned from one of the junior Foreign Service Officers at the Embassy that the reception was being held for the Saigon business community, and one glance at the first arrivals convinced him that business was good in Saigon, despite the War. Several gentlemen wore tuxedos, while all the women present – a small minority – sported gowns and jewelry that would've made Paris jealous. As the long line of invitees passed through a security checkpoint the room gradually filled up, until by 2000 hours the place was jammed. A jazz trio played old American standards from Count Basie and the like, while blank-faced South Vietnamese waiters circulated through the multitude with finger food and drinks.

At 2020 the Ambassador gave a short welcome speech, something about the need to maintain strong economic ties and a healthy business community so that the South could recover quickly after the War was over. Josh thought the man sounded overly optimistic, but he knew it's what politicians did. An Ambassador was the closest thing to a full-fledged politico that diplomatic life produced, especially a political appointee, as all recent SV ambassadors had been. Everyone, including Josh, applauded politely when the Ambassador finished, but the speeches weren't over.

A short, graying Vietnamese gentleman wearing a very expensive tuxedo stepped to the mike, apparently to speak for the local business community. A consecutive interpreter moved to the microphone next to him, an attractive young Vietnamese woman, probably in her mid-20's, wearing a form-fitting black cocktail dress and tall high-fashion heels. As she repeated the man's speech in both English and French, Josh got the feeling he'd seen her before. He edged a little closer to where she stood to get a better look. Although she was dressed much more elegantly than when he'd seen her last, and her makeup was now impeccable, he was pretty certain it was the very same person he'd 'saved' from harassment in the dark alley just weeks earlier. But instead of the pidgin' English she'd used to harangue the sergeant who'd tried to coerce her, this woman was speaking both English and French with an ease and skill that could only come from considerable repetition. What was going on?

He waited until the businessman finished his talk and then slid inconspicuously over to where the interpreter was stuffing her copies of the speech into an expensive-looking black leather briefcase. Before he could say a word, she glanced up at him with an expression that neither invited nor denied communication.

"I thought that was you," she said as she snapped the briefcase shut.

"I wasn't sure if it was you," he admitted. "You look... different."

She smiled, though whether it was from humor or self-satisfaction, he wasn't sure.

"As do you. Although I would consider finding another tailor." She eyed the loose-fitting uniform from top to bottom.

Josh shrugged. "I lost some weight." He held out his hand. "Captain Josh Daniels," he announced, "U.S. Army."

The woman stared at his offered hand for a moment before taking it loosely in her own. "Kim-Ly Tran," she said. "Interpreter." As opposed to most Vietnamese women he'd met, Kim looked him straight in the eyes. And what eyes they were: a deep, bottomless green.

"You were very good. Translating. A little more... refined than last time we met."

This time the smile was genuine. "Interpretation, not translation," she corrected. "And 'different strokes for different folks' – isn't that how you say it? I have found that soldiers, of any army, respond better to simple words delivered forcefully."

"I guess it works. Can I buy you a drink?" He didn't know why he asked her, the words just seemed to pop out. Not that it mattered.

"I believe the beverages are free, are they not? In any case, I must be going. My work is done."

"Do you have to leave?" Even to his ears the question seemed impertinent, though he justified it by reminding himself how boring the reception had been until that moment.

She eyed him closely. "I was not invited."

"Please, stay. As my guest."

"Thank you, but I don't think so. I must get home."

"Ah, okay then. Husband waiting for you?" *What am I doing?'* he asked himself.

She paused as if debating whether to answer. "No, no husband. But my father will worry."

"You're a good daughter."

She smiled. "It was pleasant talking to you again, Captain…"

"Daniels."

"Yes, Daniels. Enjoy the reception." She bowed her head ever so slightly and left before he could continue. Josh stood there, looking after her as she made her way gracefully through the packed room. Just as she got to the door leading out of the Embassy, she glanced back over her shoulder, directly at Josh.

He could have sworn she smiled.

*****

A few well-placed questions led Josh to the Embassy Public Affairs Officer responsible for arranging the sound system and interpretation for the reception. He was talking with two local invitees when Josh sidled up to him and waited for a lag in the conversation.

"Good party," Josh said as soon as he could politely interrupt. "I'm Captain Josh Daniels." They shook hands. "Are you the guy who set all this up?"

The PAO seemed embarrassed. "Not really. The residence staff did most of the work. I just arranged for the music and the PA system."

"And the interpreter?"

"Kim-Ly? She was excellent, wasn't she?"

"She was. Excellent. I was thinking that we might use her the next time we needed interpretation over at MACV, but she snuck out of here before I could get her contact info. You don't happen to have it, do you?"

"Not on me, but I'm sure we have it back at the office."

"Do you have a card?" The PAO dug one out from his jacket pocket. "Thanks. Mind if I give you a call tomorrow? To get the interpreter's contact info."

"No problem. Glad to help."

Josh continued chatting for a few more minutes, until the PAO's contacts demanded his attention. Josh excused himself and made his way out into the humid Saigon night.

Without even knowing it, he was whistling.

CHAPTER 13

Josh found it difficult to concentrate in the morning meeting. His thoughts kept returning to the reception and the attractive young interpreter who had barely given him the time of day. He tried to distract himself with the details of the latest operations, but he found himself staring at his watch, impatient for a break. Finally, at 1030, they were allowed to take five. Fifteen, actually.

Josh headed straight for his office phone. He pulled out the PAO's card and dialed his Embassy extension.

"Hi, it's Captain Josh Daniels, from last night?" he said, trying his best to sound calm and relaxed.

"Oh, sure, Josh. How're you doing?"

"I'm fine, thanks. You?" He hated the phone niceties that turned every call into an exchange of pabulum, but he understood the necessity.

"Good, good. How can I help you?"

Josh felt irritated that the FSO didn't remember why he was calling. How could he forget?

"You said you could get me the contact info for that interpreter last night?"

"Oh, right, right! Hang on a second."

Josh tapped his toe anxiously and tried to slow his racing heart. *'This is really weird,'* he thought as he waited. *'What am I doing?'* For perhaps an instant he thought about Darla, but he dismissed any feelings of guilt out of hand. *'Haven't had a letter from her in months. And Mom doesn't even mention her. I know something's going on there.'* Justification? At that precise moment, he didn't care.

Just then, the PAO came back on the line. "Okay, here it is." He gave him her address and phone number.

He thanked the FSO, engaged him in the least possible small talk necessary to satisfy telephone etiquette, and hung up. In seconds, his palms damp with sweat, he was dialing her number.

"Chao?" It was an older man's voice. Probably her father.

"Hello! May I speak with Kim-Ly please?"

The man said a string of unintelligible Vietnamese words. Then, "wait."

He heard footsteps moving away from the phone. He waited. "Bonjour," Kim-Ly finally answered.

"Miss Tran?"

"Yes, this is Miss Tran. To whom am I speaking?"

"This is Captain Josh Daniels. We met at the Embassy function last…"

"Ah yes, Captain Daniels," she cut him off. "This is a surprise." Something in the way she said it told Josh it wasn't all that much of a surprise.

"A pleasant one I hope." He waited for her response and panicked when nothing was forthcoming. "I, ah, I thought it was quite a coincidence that we saw each other again last night." It sounded lame, but it was the best he could do given the circumstances.

"Do you believe in coincidences?"

He mentally flipped a coin. "Of course. Don't you?"

She laughed, a warm, light-hearted sound that slid his heart down from his throat to its proper place in his chest. "Of course. But some people would say that all events in life are preordained, that what seems like a coincidence is in fact fate."

"Is that what you think?" He stepped lightly, trying not to scare her off before she could get to know him better.

"If all things are preordained, then where is the adventure in life? And what is life without adventure, don't you agree?"

He felt his head swimming. *'All I wanted was to ask you to go out with me,'* he thought anxiously. *'Not discuss world philosophies.'* "Sure," he said, "adventure is the spice of life."

"I thought that was *variety*," she said, and laughed again. The sound of it left him short of breath.

"You're probably right. My English needs some work." Her laughter reverberated in his ears. He decided to cut to the quick. "Hey, I don't want to seem too..."

"Pushy?"

"Yeh, pushy. But I was wondering..."

"My schedule is very full just now," she interrupted. "But I might be able to fit you in."

"I don't really have a job for you right away," he quickly answered. He didn't want to lead her on with the possibility of interpreting work.

"I wasn't talking about work, *Captain*."

He blinked as if whacked between the eyes. This woman was proving to be anything but predictable. "How about a cup of coffee?"

"May I drink tea?"

"You may. You may even add sugar, if you want." He smiled, the back-and-forth reminding him that a world still existed outside the War. What he wanted to know was how a young woman living right in the middle of Saigon could escape its grasp.

"How could a woman say no to such a tempting offer. When?"

They agreed to meet at a small French café mid-way between the MACV headquarters and her apartment. Noon, the next day.

"I am already looking forward to it," Kim-Ly said when they'd finalized the location.

"So am I," he said. When he hung up he was already picturing it in his thoughts.

*****

When Josh arrived at the café, she wasn't there.

Josh's heart skipped a beat, until he glanced at his watch and realized that he'd arrived ten minutes early. He told the impatient server he was waiting for "a friend" and resisted the urge to order until she got there. As he waited, he glanced around at his fellow customers: mainly young professional types, all Vietnamese. He was the only 'round eyes' in the place. He caught a couple of wondering glances but ignored them, acting as if he belonged there. Try as he might, he felt like a fish out of water – an American Army officer, in uniform, sitting in a small café surrounded by young, affluent South Vietnamese. He hoped that no superior officers or MPs happened by – he didn't want to have to listen to a lecture on security considerations.

He was just starting to get fidgety as the minute hand clicked past the '2' on the expensive Omega watch his parents had given him as a graduation gift, when a familiar face appeared at the entrance.

"I'm *so* sorry," Kim-Ly said as she hurried to the table where he was sitting. "I had a last minute phone call I had to take."

"Nothing to be sorry for," Josh said as he pulled out her chair for her. "I only just got here myself a few minutes ago."

"Oh? Then good. A happy coincidence."

"If you believe in coincidences." He didn't hide his smile.

"I forget," she played along, "do we or don't we – believe in coincidences?"

"Free will is alive and well at this table."

"I'm glad. I'd hate to think this was all preordained."

"If that were the case, your tea would already be here, wouldn't it?"

She laughed, and he felt the sound reverberate in his chest. "I hope we won't be debating philosophy all afternoon."

"Not on my account. What *would* you like to talk about?"

She shrugged. "How about you? Tell me about yourself, your family."

Josh felt the urge to compress his life into a few pithy phrases, but her expectant look and unwavering attention convinced him to be more forthcoming. He talked about growing up a military brat, moving from base to base, never staying in one house, or one school, for more than a couple of years at a time.

"Was that hard?" she asked, her eyes wide at the very idea.

"Sometimes. I mean, I liked going to new places, and meeting new people, but it was hard leaving friends behind."

"Such a life would be almost unthinkable here in Vietnam," she suggested with a pained expression. "I lived in the same house, the same village, until my father moved us here when I was in high school. If it hadn't been for that, I might still be there today."

"Did you ever want to visit other places?"

"Every now and then I will see an advertisement, or someone will talk of a trip they've taken, and I'll wonder what it must be like to travel to other lands, experience other cultures."

"But?"

"But... I haven't seen all of Vietnam yet, and I meet new people all the time. Like last night, for instance. And here I am, talking to an American Army captain. Is that so different from traveling?"

He nodded. Until he'd come to Vietnam, he'd rarely experienced a situation where he'd thought of himself as an 'outsider'. Even surrounded by northerners at the Academy, he didn't feel particularly out of place. And yet there he was, the 'different thing' as they used to call it in the old children's magazines. It was easy to forget that his new experiences were also new to all the people around him.

"Somehow I don't think that new people or places would be much of a problem for you."

She smiled. "Is that a compliment? You Americans are very penurious with compliments. Unlike the French. A Frenchman will tell you that you have eyes like emeralds, hair like silk and a smile that rivals the sun, just upon a casual meeting on a bus." The smile she beamed at him warmed him like the sun.

"I like your finger nails," he said, only partly in jest.

"Oh ho! My father has warned me against smooth-talking foreigners like you!"

"Your father is obviously a wise man."

"There's more to you than meets the eye, Captain Daniels," she said mischievously. All thoughts of a witty retort disappeared into her hypnotizing green eyes.

The next two hours passed in non-stop laughter and small talk; all too soon the lengthening shadows on the street outside the café signaled an end to their visit.

"I'm afraid I have to go," he said with a hurt puppy dog look that was not in the least contrived.

"As do I. But I enjoyed our little tête-à-tête. We should do it again sometime."

Her reply knocked him back a step. Wasn't *he* the one who was supposed to say that?

"I'd like that," he managed to squeeze out. "When?"

She laughed. "You Americans. Always in a hurry."

"There are some things worth hurrying for," Josh said, surprising himself with, what for him, was flowery repartee.

"A poet? Mon dieu, what have I gotten myself into?" she teased. "How about Saturday night?"

"I'll have to check to be sure I can get a pass," he began, but she waved off his explanation.

"Call me. You have the number." She pushed back her chair and stood. "I hope you can come. It's my birthday." She smiled broadly.

"Are you kidding me? Is it really?"

"Really and truly. My family will have a small party for me. You'd be most welcome."

A party? With uncleared South Vietnamese? Josh didn't know if the MPs would even allow him to attend. But he knew he was going to find out.

"Thank you. I'll let you know as soon as I'm sure one way or the other."

She nodded to him, and with one short step leaned in and up to kiss him on the cheek. "A la prochaine," she said. With a flip of her head and one last glance, she was out the door.

He wasn't sure what she'd said, but he knew a sergeant from Vermont who spoke some French...

*****

Josh went straight from lunch to MACV headquarters, and Major Winshotz' office.

"Captain Daniels!" the major called out when his admin assistant announced the new arrival. "To what do I owe this unexpected visit?"

Josh saluted. "Major. I've got an admin question. Or maybe it's a security question."

"Okay. If I have the answer. What's up?"

As Josh explained the invitation from Kim-Ly, he watched closely for any reaction from Winshotz.

"How well do you know this woman?" was all he asked.

"Not well. But Public Affairs over at the Embassy hires her all the time."

Winshotz raised an eyebrow. "Oh? That's a plus. They must have run her through a security check, so that hurdle might be eliminated. Do you know who else will be there?"

"She just said a few family members."

"No names, addresses?"

"She invited me to a birthday party, Major. I didn't do a background investigation." As soon as he spoke, he regretted it. It wasn't the major's fault.

Luckily, Winshotz laughed. "Seems you really want to go to this party, Captain. I take it the young lady is attractive?"

Josh's ears burned. "Very. And funny, and smart..."

Winshotz held his hands up to defend against any further description. "Okay, all right! I get the picture. Let me give the Provo a call and we'll see what we can come up with. That okay with you?"

"Thank you, sir. Appreciate it." He turned to leave.

"Just one thing."

Josh stopped, his smile fading. "Sir?"

"Try to pay a little more attention to the War in our planning meetings, and a little less to the young lady. Think you can handle that?"

The smile returned. "Sorry sir. Won't happen again."

"I doubt that, but at least now I'll know what's got you staring into space. Dismissed."

Josh saluted and pivoted to the door, his hopes alive.

He had barely cleared the reception desk in the outer office when he was intercepted by a loud shout. "Captain Daniels!" Col.

Henry called out from halfway down the opposite corridor. "Got a minute?"

Josh knew the question was rhetorical; he wanted to talk, now.

"Everything all right?" the colonel asked when he'd closed the distance between them. He nodded in the direction of the offices behind him. He must've seen him coming out of the CO's office suite and figured there'd been a problem.

"I'm fine, sir. Yourself?"

"I'm doing well, thank you. Hey, do you still want to go up to the First's field camp?"

Josh's thoughts had been so far from the field it took him half a second to remember why it was he wanted to travel to the big camp north of the city: Landry.

"Yeh, sure! You've got a lift for me?"

"Better than that – I've got an assignment. Real work."

"Great. What would that be?" He wanted to sound enthusiastic, but he had questions.

"General Edwards has decided that he wants an on-site evaluation of Atlas Wedge. He wants someone to talk to both the CO and his staff and some of the platoon leaders, to get both the big picture and the grunt-eye view. Think you can handle it?"

This *was* real work. Big-time. He was a little surprised that they'd assign a captain to such an important job.

"Would I be accompanying a senior officer?" he asked to clarify his position in the pecking order.

Henry laughed. "You think we want you to carry some senior's bags? Actually, we think you're the perfect choice. You've got the heft of the MACV planning group behind you, and yet as a captain and recent platoon leader you should be able to get the real low-down on how things are going on the ground. So, interested?"

"Yes, sir!" This time the enthusiasm was genuine. "Is there a timeframe?"

"I've got you scheduled to fly out with a resupply copter tomorrow at 0800. You'll have Sergeant Whitten and Corporal Anderson with you, for support. Work for you?"

Josh barely knew the two NCOs, but he was still about to agree when he remembered his weekend 'date' with Kim-Ly. "Uh, how long do you think this should take, sir?"

Henry looked at him with narrowed eyes. "Why – you have a hot date on the weekend?"

Josh's face burned, even though he knew Henry was joking. But the blush did not escape the colonel's eye.

"My God, you do?" He shook his head with a disbelieving smirk. "Look, you should be able to wrap things up in 3 or 4 days if you push them. Does *that* work for you?"

"Yes, sir – works just fine. And thank you, sir."

"Just don't short-change us on the evaluation. This Vietnamization is the big thing in Washington these days. Don't want to disappoint them."

"Our evaluation will be thorough and accurate, sir. I guarantee it."

Henry patted him on the shoulder. "I'm sure it will be, Daniels, or we wouldn't be sending you up there in the first place. Now why don't you go talk with Whitten and Anderson to start roughing out your strategy. I've got them standing-by downstairs in 203."

"You were pretty sure I'd go, then?"

"This is the Army, Captain. I knew you'd go. I just wanted to see how enthusiastic you'd be."

"Right," Josh answered, slightly flustered. "I understand, and I can assure you, I'm *very* enthusiastic, sir."

"Glad to hear it. Now take this," he added, handing Josh a thick manila folder, "and go, talk to your team."

Josh saluted and headed downstairs. Behind him, Colonel Henry shook his head in amusement.

Although Josh had seen Sgt. Whitten and Corporal Anderson a number of times at MACV, it had always been in passing as either they, or he, were running somewhere else. So when he stepped into room 203 they all recognized each other but no one knew what to expect. Both NCOs jumped up and saluted. Josh was pleasantly surprised; saluting wasn't high on General Edwards' agenda and his relaxed attitude had filtered down to many of the other soldiers in the building. Apparently it hadn't reached those two, or perhaps they were just covering their backsides until they got to know him better.

"Sergeant, Corporal, looks like we're headed north tomorrow morning."

"Yes, sir, that's what we've been told," Whitten answered. "But truth is, they didn't tell us much more than that. Said you'd fill us in." Anderson nodded – it was clear he deferred to the more senior man.

"Sit, sit," Josh directed as he did the same. "What do you know about Atlas Wedge?"

Whitten spoke without prompting. "Just that it's part of turning the War over to the Vietnamese."

"The *South* Vietnamese," Anderson corrected. Whitten shot him an exasperated glance.

"Well, that's about it in a nutshell, actually. But there are a lot of moving pieces up there. A lot that has to happen if the ARVN are going to take over operational control of the War anytime soon. We're going to go see how all that's going."

"Will any... more... *senior* officers be joining us?" Anderson asked hesitantly. Whitten shot another glance but didn't say a word.

Josh chuckled. "What's the problem, gentlemen: think a captain is too... lowly to take on a big assignment like this one?"

"Oh no, no sir!" Whitten jumped in with both feet. "I'm sure Anderson just wanted to be sure we were aware of all the participants in this visit. Isn't that right, Anderson?"

Anderson's wide-eyed expression said it all. "Yeh, that's right, Sarge. Absolutely. Just wanted to be aware."

Josh let them stew for a second. "Well I'm afraid it's just the three of us on this run. Sink or swim. Think you can handle that?"

"Yes, sir!" the two men answered in synch.

"Good. Because I don't have any intention of sinking," Josh continued, dropping his voice and staring at the two men with his most intimidating glare. "Do I make myself clear?"

"We'll be swimming, sir, I can assure you of that!" the sergeant said.

"Good. Then let's take a look at what we should expect to find up there and how we'll go about it."

Josh opened the thick file that Col. Henry had given him and spread the papers across the desk.

*****

The sun had dropped behind the jagged green mountains to the west when Josh finished briefing his two-man team and made his way to an office telephone. He had to find the number; the phone rang three times before a familiar voice answered.

"Kim-Ly!" he said with more enthusiasm than he'd meant to show.

"Captain Daniels," she answered, her voice welcoming but utterly controlled. "What a pleasant surprise."

"I was just calling to let you know that there might be a problem with this weekend."

She paused. "A problem?"

"I have to go out of town for a short while. I hope to be back in time, but… there's a chance I might not be able to."

Another pause. "I understand. That would be most unfortunate, but I'm sure it can't be helped."

He thought he heard a note of blame, or was it just disappointment, in her words.

"There's still a pretty good chance I can make it."

"I will save you a piece of birthday cake." Noncommittal. Angry?

"I didn't know the Vietnamese ate birthday cake. I thought that was a western tradition."

She laughed lightly. "We Vietnamese don't celebrate western-style birthdays at all. Just at Tet. I'm afraid I've infected my family with my French and American influences."

"I'm guessing they'll forgive you."

"We shall see. They have overlooked my *idiosyncrasies* for a number of years now, but this may be the year they change their minds."

'Because of me?' he thought. "I guess I'll just have to get back here to defend you."

"Hmm. An American soldier defending the honor of a South Vietnamese family. I can almost hear the discussion in the neighborhood now."

"Should I come in disguise?" He grimaced. He'd be coming in his uniform, like it or not.

"You shouldn't confuse them. Come as you wish."

"Well, as I said, I'll do my best to get back. I'd really like to be there."

"I'm sure my father would be *honored*."

He could almost see her smirking through the phone.

"I'm sure. But not half as much as I would."

"Let us see what you say when you get here."

'What did she mean by that?' "Yeh, well, hope to see you Saturday night."

"Until Saturday, then. And Captain," she continued after a brief pause, "take care of yourself."

"Always."

When he hung up he caught sight of his reflection in an office window. He was smiling.

CHAPTER 14

Josh climbed aboard the waiting copter, followed closely by Whitten and Anderson. They'd met at the Golf Course LZ at 0745 sharp, and after some last-minute fiddling with cockpit electronics ("always inspires confidence," Anderson whispered) they'd gone airborne at 0833. The flight plan was slightly reconfigured from his first trip up to the First's camp. VC infiltration had been detected to the north and west, so they flew out to the east, skirting the blue-green waters of the Gulf before cutting back-in to their destination a few clics north of Saigon.

Before the dust and debris from the rotor wash had even settled, Major Thompson appeared from the tent-city just a short distance away.

"Major!" Josh addressed as he snapped off a salute, his two NCOs following suit a step or two behind him.

"Well, well, well, if the bad penny hasn't returned," he smiled as he shook all three men's hands. "How're you doing, Captain? Hey, I'm sorry we didn't get down there to the hospital while you were recouping…"

"No sweat. From what I hear you've kept busy."

"And that's what you're up here to check-on, is that right?"

"Yes, sir. General Edwards just wants to be sure that our ARVN brothers will be fully prepared to begin assuming more of the fighting load in the near future."

"The *very* near future, if what we hear from Washington is any indication."

"There does seem to be some urgency," he smiled.

"As LBJ knows all too well. Come on, come on. The old man is waiting to talk to you."

The major led them back into the maze of tents and temporary shelters to the CO's digs. Major General Irwin was, indeed, aware of their arrival.

"Captain Daniels! Good to see you again. Welcome home," he said reaching out his hand.

"Sir." Josh answered with a crisp salute. "Glad to be here."

"And your two aides?" He looked at Whitten and Anderson, who seemed dazed to be in the presence of a major general.

Josh introduced the two, and the general nodded in their direction before turning his attention back to Josh.

"So, General Edwards wants to be sure we're turning this whole ball of wax over to the Vietnamese on schedule?"

"Something like that, sir. I believe MACV is getting a good deal of... interest from Washington."

"I'm sure they are. Well, I'm confident they'll be happy when they get your report. The ARVN are doing a good job moving into our positions in this sector, and I think I can say with confidence that the turnover should proceed as scheduled. Isn't that right, Major?"

Major Thompson nodded energetically. "Yes sir! Right on schedule."

Josh restrained a grin at the general's little dog and pony show. He had no reason to doubt the success of the mission, but to think that the major would say anything to disagree with Irwin right there in his office was more than a stretch.

The general sat them all around a small table covered with maps and had an aide bring in coffee and sodas. He gave a short history of Atlas Wedge, placing it in the larger picture of pacification and Vietnamization. "We've got a number of people out in this area right now," he indicated, pointing to a map coordinate less than four clics from where they stood, "going hut to hut winning hearts and changing minds." He said the last without even a hint of sarcasm, but Josh knew that the long-running slogan had begun to fray badly in light of recent incidents.

"Any chance Bravo Company is working out that way?" Josh asked.

"Those were your guys, weren't they?" Irwin asked. The CO's grasp of his command impressed Josh.

"Yes sir. Thought we might stop by and say hi if we get a chance."

"I don't see any problem with that. Mark," he said turning to Major Thompson, "see what we can do about getting them out there. Tomorrow ok, Captain?"

"That would be fine, sir." Josh went on to request several other inspection and interview visits all along the Atlas Wedge front. "Yes, good," the general agreed. "Make sure he gets whatever access he needs, Major."

And just like that, they were on their way to temporary quarters – officers' for Josh, enlisted men's for his two NCOs. Josh had prepped Anderson and Whitten to move about the base camp to talk with like-graded soldiers, with the idea that corporals would be more likely to talk with other corporals, and sergeants with sergeants. That left Josh to interview the officers. With carte blanche from the CO, he had access to pretty much whoever was in camp at the time.

It was an eerie feeling for Josh, being back in the field, even if it was a semi-permanent encampment. As he walked through the narrow pathways between tents and tin-roofed huts, he couldn't help but experience a flood of memories as familiar sights, sounds and smells assaulted his senses: the heavy earthen scent of the campsite, the heady mix of disinfectant and body wastes that floated out from the latrines, the indelible odor and rumbling roar of diesel engines, the glistening bodies and stench of sweat out on the periphery where the men worked on shoring up defenses. It seemed almost like a dream as he floated amidst shades of a former life.

But the shades came alive when he sat down to interview them.

"Goddamn gooks don't have their hearts in it!" one fellow captain explained when Josh pinned him down in the Officers' Club after the officer had had a few beers. "We take a sector, hand it over, and two weeks later we're back taking it again! They're afraid of the VC, let alone the NVA. Hell, I'd much rather fight with the Koreans than these shifty bastards."

When he noticed some of his fellow officers staring at him with wide eyes, he refused to back off.

"What?! You want me to BS the dude just because the Big Brass want everything to be hunky-dory with our *allies*! Bullshit!"

With that a gruff-looking major appeared at their table and hustled the captain to his feet.

"Come on, Captain. I think you've had one or two too many," the major said as he pulled the officer by his arm.

The captain was having none of it. "What!? Can't tell the truth, even to our own guys? People are getting killed out there, Major, you know it! All because our *allies* don't have the stomach for it!"

"That'll be enough, Captain!" the major ordered, his voice clearly indicating that he was no longer asking. The drunken officer eyed him warily for a few seconds, before spitting on the Club floor.

"Yeh, maybe it is."

"Sorry, Captain," the major apologized to Josh, "he's had a little too much."

"No problem," Josh said, but as the major tried to hustle his drunken colleague from the OC, he couldn't help but wonder whether the captain's tirade was more than just the beer talking.

Josh tried to strike up conversations with several other officers after the altercation, but whether they weren't interested in talking or they'd gotten the message from the major's intervention to keep away from him, he got nothing more.

On his way back to his quarters he stopped by the enlisted men's barracks to leave a message for his two NCOs. Turned out they were already back at their bunks.

"That was fast," he said when he stepped into the long dormitory-style tent. He waved the two men off when they jumped up to salute. "Not much happening out there?"

Whitten scanned the lines of bunks to be sure they were alone. There were a couple of other men horsing around at the opposite end of the barracks, but they were far enough away to be out of earshot.

"Nothing anyone would talk to *us* about," he said pointedly. "I don't know if everything is hunky-dory or if they simply don't want to show their dirty laundry to outsiders."

"Everyone was perfectly friendly and all," Anderson added, "but the second we talked about Atlas Wedge, or Vietnamization, they turned off."

"I got one officer talking, a captain in Charlie," Josh said, "but the second he started bitching about problems with the ARVN, a major showed up and towed him away."

"Kind of makes you think there may be problems, don't it?" Whitten said.

"We may have to make these interviews a little more formal than we planned."

Anderson's eyebrows arched. "Maybe a lot more formal."

After they finalized their plans to interview soldiers from his old Charlie Company the following morning, Josh set off to talk to General Irwin – or so he thought. When he got to the CO's hut, his aide had other ideas.

"Josh!" Lieutenant Edward Hastings said when the corporal in the reception area announced him over the intercom. "I'd heard you were back here." The two men shook hands. "So, what can we do for you?"

"Well, I'm sure you know why I'm out here…"

"You mean it's not just to say hi to your old buds?"

"Not entirely," Josh said, his smile meant to be disarming. "We're taking a look at Atlas Wedge, and Vietnamization in general."

"So I've heard. How's it going?" There was something about the lieutenant's chipper attitude that didn't jibe.

"As a matter of fact, that's what I was hoping to talk to General Irwin about."

"Maybe I can help." It was increasingly obvious that Hastings had been sent out to run interference. Josh decided to see how far he'd go to insulate his boss.

"I don't think so. I think the CO's the only one who'll be able to help me on this one."

"Well, you know, Josh, the general is very busy just now, what with Atlas and all…"

Josh had had enough. "It won't take but a couple of minutes. And Ed, tell the general I was assured of his cooperation by General Edwards. I can have *him* call the CO, if that's what's necessary."

Hastings' eyes narrowed. His smile was gone.

"Let me see if the Old Man has a minute or two. I'll be right back."

Out of the corner of his eye Josh saw the corporal manning the reception desk purse his lips in surprise. Captains rarely called a general's bluff.

A couple of minutes later the lieutenant was back. "The general will see you now," he announced, his tone noticeably cooler. He held the door for Josh, but closed it behind him without following him into the CO's office.

General Irwin sat behind his desk, stacks of paper piled high on all sides. Josh couldn't help but note that he looked a heck of a lot busier than he had just 24 hours earlier.

"So, Daniels, I hope this is important," Irwin began as soon as the door closed. "As you can see, I'm swamped."

"My apologies, sir, but I felt I needed to bring something to your attention."

At that the general's eyes widened a hair. "Oh? What is that?"

"General, my directions from General Edwards were to interview a broad cross-section of your men, from privates all the way up the line, to get a broad sense of how Atlas Wedge is proceeding."

Irwin nodded his head impatiently. "Yes, I am aware of that. Go ahead."

"Well, sir, my men and I are getting the feeling that some of your people are being... less than forthcoming in their responses to us."

Irwin's eyes narrowed. "In what way?"

"Well, sir, every time we raise the subject, we run into a brick wall. People suddenly have no opinions, aren't willing to talk."

"Oh, I'm sure you're exaggerating, aren't you Captain? You've been here less than a day – how many of our people could you have talked to?"

"Enough that it's pretty obvious that they aren't being fully cooperative. I was hoping you might pass the word that we're not the enemy."

For an instant the general stared at him, his look unreadable, but then a smile crept across his lips and he sat back in his chair.

"Of course not, of course not. I'll get the word out that you're to have the full cooperation of all our people. Will that take care of the problem?"

"Thank you, sir, I'm sure it will. But, off the record, I feel I have to ask why your men would be reluctant to discuss the operation with us." He knew he was pushing his mandate, but he had a job to do.

It was immediately obvious that Irwin was not used to being questioned by subordinates. "Look, *Captain*, I realize that General Edwards has given you a big assignment here, and I understand very well how important this is – not only to Saigon but to Washington. But, to quote a visitor from down South, *we're* not the enemy here. I reject your implication that there's some kind of… conspiracy here to keep any information from your little investigation. We are proud of what we're accomplishing up here, and I will not have *anyone* casting aspersions on my people."

The general kept his voice level, but hard as steel. Josh had lived his entire life listening to just that sort of response from the Colonel, however, and he barely blinked an eye.

"No one is casting aspersions, General," he said, trying to sound as conciliatory as possible. "And I'm sure that General Edwards will be very pleased to hear of your successes."

The general eyed him coolly. "I'm pleased to hear that, Captain. Now, is there anything else I can help you with? If not, I have to get back to work."

It was clear that the conversation was over, but also clear to Josh that he'd touched a nerve. This was no time to probe further, however. "No sir. And thank you, sir." He saluted, receiving a limp wave in return, and pivoted from the room.

He found Lieutenant Hastings waiting for him in the outer office.

"Did you find out what you needed to know?" he asked before Josh could even make it to the reception desk.

"I think so," Josh said, knowing full well everything he said would be transmitted directly to Irwin.

"If there's anything I can do to help with your interviews…" Hastings began.

Josh waved him off. "I don't think so, Lieutenant, but thanks for the offer. If anything comes up, I'll let you know."

"Yeh, you do that."

As Josh left the office he could feel two sets of eyes watching him go.

CHAPTER 15

He was back leading his platoon, moving them through elephant grass that towered high over their heads. It seemed almost as if they were swimming through dense green water, the grass closing up behind them as if they'd never passed through. The sounds of birds and insects filled the sky above.

"Captain, there's an ambush up ahead," a voice suddenly announced, and when he turned it was Corporal Hilford, the point man from his old platoon.

Josh knew he needed to lead the men on a different path, to flank the ambushers. But somehow he didn't know how.

"What should we do?" he asked Hilford. The corporal looked at him quizzically.

"Why are you asking me? Aren't you the captain?"

But when he looked down at his uniform, he was only a lieutenant.

"No, I'm not!" he said.

The corporal nodded. "I see. Then follow me."

Before Josh could answer, Hilford took off into the elephant grass, his rifle held chest-high. Josh hurried after him.

"Where are we going?" he whispered.

"To find the answer."

"What answer?"

"You'll see."

The going was slow as the grass gave way grudgingly, but when Josh looked behind him there was no one there. He was about to call out when suddenly he realized that the rest of the platoon hadn't followed them. The two of them were alone.

He turned back to tell Hilford, but the corporal was gone too. For a heartbeat he almost panicked, but just that quickly he decided to push onward through the green river of vegetation. Step after step the grass gave way in front and closed up behind him. The air was hot, moist, nearly suffocating. And then he heard rather than felt his foot land in water, just a small puddle at first, but with each step the ground softened until his boots sunk up to his ankles, and then his shins. He could barely pull them free from the stinking, sucking goo when he suddenly stepped out into a broad opening, the grass ending like an oriental screen.

"Where've you been?" Landry asked.

Josh looked up and there was his old friend, looking like crap, sitting on a tree stump a few yards ahead.

"I was lost."

"You're never lost," Landry said.

He wanted to argue, but felt his boots sliding deeper into the muck.

"Can you give me a hand?" Josh asked, reaching up for Landry's help.

"Me, help you?" He tried – unsuccessfully – to smile. Not a happy look. He reached out his hand, but their fingertips barely touched. Josh tried to move closer, but his boots were locked in the mud.

"Come closer," he said.

"I can't," Landry said. "You'll have to do it."

"Go ahead, Josh, you can do it!" cried a woman's voice, and when he looked to his left he saw Darla, parked in the same yellow Corvette.

"I can't!" he called back to her.

"Too bad," she said, and with a sad wave the Corvette drove slowly away, disappearing into the elephant grass.

He reached out toward the disappearing car, as if to hold it there even a moment longer, but suddenly he was sinking — faster! He turned back to grab Landry's hand, but there was no one there! He felt the mud pulling him down, down, the stinking goo so close now that he could barely breathe, barely suck air into his aching lungs. He was sinking too fast, too fast! He couldn't get out, couldn't get OUT!

CHAPTER 16

Josh awoke drenched in sweat, his mouth pasted shut, his legs flailing at the bed sheets. It took him several seconds to get his bearings and realize where he was.

'That was strange,' he thought as he made his way to the john, *'very strange.'*

He met his two NCOs for breakfast, Josh breaking protocol by 'slumming' at the enlisted men's mess. He didn't share details of his dream with them, but did explain that he was "going to be dragging today. Didn't get near enough sleep."

They seemed sympathetic, but were more interested in hearing a play-by-play of his meeting with the CO.

"Doesn't sound like he's all that supportive of our assignment," Anderson said when Josh had finished.

"Really? Jesus, Anderson, sometimes you can make the obvious sound like rocket science," Whitten jabbed.

"I'm afraid you're right, Corporal," Josh interrupted, ignoring the sergeant's cut. "Looks like we're on our own with this one. But that only means we've got to dig a little deeper and push a little harder."

"With Irwin on our ass?" Whitten asked with eyes open wide in disbelief.

"*General* Irwin is a soldier, and he'll follow his orders. Maybe just to the letter, but he'll follow them. It's his subordinates who may think they're doing him a favor by stonewalling us. But, we'll just have to convince them otherwise. Ready, gentlemen?"

When the three men arrived at the designated assembly point near the XO's hutch, they found a Jeep waiting for them driven by a Corporal Eddings.

"Out to Bravo's MOA, Captain?" Eddings asked immediately after saluting.

"Looks that way, Corporal. Is it a long haul?"

"Fifteen, maybe twenty clics. Take us an hour or so – provided we don't run into any surprises."

"We don't like surprises," Whitten said. "Feel free to keep it completely cool."

"Cool it is," the corporal agreed, and as soon as they'd thrown their gear in the back the four men set off.

The ride through the countryside at that hour of the morning was a welcomed change of pace for Josh. The contrast of the brilliant blue sky and the shocking green of the jungle, the living symphony of a thousand different creatures starting their day, and draped over it all the constant hum of the Jeep's engine and transmission turned the morning into a welcome escape from the smoke and dust and grating roar of the average day in 'Nam. Josh scanned the greenery on all sides for unwelcome 'surprises', but his mind turned back to the dream of the night before. It only struck him then that he'd pictured Darla very infrequently in his recent dreams, or in his waking thoughts, for that matter. Somewhere deep in his gut he accepted the realization that their relationship had cooled considerably during the six months since he'd left home. Whether it was his fault or hers, or both, he felt a slight flutter in the stomach when he admitted to himself that he was no longer the same person who'd kissed her goodbye in what seemed now like another universe, and neither was she.

Josh was so lost in his thoughts that he started when heavy machine gun fire and what might have been mortars sounded in the distance directly ahead of them.

"Bravo?" he asked the corporal.

"Could be. That's about where we had them camped last night."

Josh ordered his men to ready their weapons.

"We going up there?" Eddings asked dubiously.

"Damn right we're going up there. Those are my men, or were, and I want to know what's going on with them."

Josh saw Eddings look to Whitten and Anderson with a questioning glare in the rearview mirror, but there were no more complaints to be heard. He knew his actions were endangering the other three men, but there was no way he was going to turn tail and run, at least not until he'd reconnoitered the area. Eddings took a deep breath and punched the gas.

The Jeep rattled and bucked its way along the unpaved roadway, the undergrowth so thick it slapped at the sides of the vehicle as it plowed forward. The shooting grew louder with each passing minute.

"How close?" Eddings asked when the explosions were only a few hundred meters ahead.

"Until someone takes a shot at us, or we see them first," Josh said. This time the corporal shook his head but held his tongue.

Within minutes the battle seemed to have engulfed them, as multiple bursts of weapon fire shook the jungle all around them.

"This close enough?!" Eddings yelled to be heard over the gunfire.

"Everyone out!" Josh ordered, signaling Whitten and Anderson to move to their left. "Let loose with everything you've got as soon as you can see where the enemy's located," he added. "Let's make 'em think the 7th Cavalry has come to the rescue!"

"You're with me," he informed Eddings, who grabbed his M-16 with something approaching disdain.

Josh picked his way through leafy ferns and thick, stunted palms that completely hid the battle that roared on no more than 100 meters ahead. A bullet whizzed through the greenery inches from their heads, sending both him and Eddings diving to the ground.

"I don't think it was meant for us!" Josh yelled inches from the corporal's ear when no other enemy fire came their way. "I don't think they know we're here!"

"Neither does Bravo," Eddings suggested. "We're gonna have *two* armies firing at us!"

The point had crossed Josh's mind. But there was nothing he could do about it. They were going to do what they could to help Bravo, no matter what.

Finally, just as it seemed they couldn't possibly approach any closer without stumbling into the midst of all the shooting, Josh stepped past a huge elephant fern to find himself facing the back of a VC firing line! Three black-pajamaed fighters, their conical straw hats tilted every which way, fired on Bravo Company with such complete concentration that they didn't even recognize the danger they were in. For the briefest of instants Josh hesitated, some childish sense of chivalry questioning the morality of shooting the VC in the back. But before he could give it a second thought, Eddings opened up on automatic, jarring Josh into action. In seconds the three were down, and Josh heard himself screaming at the top of his lungs like the Confederates at Gettysburg. Eddings looked at him as if he were crazy, but then joined in with his own insane shouts. From off to their left, a hail of gunfire and what sounded like a grenade. Then more yelling.

Suddenly all hell broke loose as bullets began cutting through the leaves and branches all around them. Pieces of bark and chunks of leaves fluttered to the ground, some of them hit a second time before they could reach the soft jungle soil. Josh threw Eddings to the ground and fell down next to him as the jungle virtually exploded.

And then, as quickly as it had begun, it stopped. A few spurts of automatic weapons fire in the distance, probably M-16, and then a shouted order: "Hold your fire!"

The quiet was eerie.

"What now?" Eddings whispered after a few seconds.

"Stay put."

Josh crawled on his stomach to a point where he could see the three dead VC clearly, and in the distance a hint of movement through the trees. He froze, trying to make out whether it was their people or the VC, but the brush was too dense. He couldn't quite see...

"I should've known it was you," a familiar voice said softly from a few feet behind him.

Josh turned quickly to find himself staring at Landry, his face blackened, a knife dripping blood in one hand, a hacked ear in the other. His stare was wide-eyed, yet frighteningly calm.

"Landry? What the hell...?"

A smile, so detached that it sent shudders down Josh's spine, was his only answer.

"Are you... hurt?" he asked, unable to form any other words.

"I knew you couldn't stay away. Here." He handed the severed ear to his friend.

"I... think we'd better leave that here," Josh said, his voice as level as he could manage. Eddings looked over at him with undisguised horror in his eyes. "Can you take me to your CO?"

Landry's smile broadened. "CO's dead."

Josh nodded toward the battlefield ahead of them. "What happened up there?"

Landry turned mechanically. "We chewed 'em up. They thought they could ambush us, but they were wrong."

Josh tried to grasp the situation, but his mind kept coming back to the trophy ear. "Let's go see your men," he finally said, taking Landry by the elbow and directing him up the path. His friend acquiesced without a sound.

"Go find Anderson and Whitten," he told Corporal Eddings, who seemed more than eager to be somewhere else.

When they reached the perimeter of Bravo's lines, it became immediately obvious that the VC weren't the only ones chewed up. Bloodied and bandaged GIs dotted the jungle floor, with three medics running between them in a frantic race against the clock. Josh scanned the men, looking for an officer, any officer. Finally he identified a First Lieutenant who seemed to be in charge.

"Lieutenant, what's your status here?" he asked the officer as soon as they'd approached close enough to catch his attention.

The lieutenant seemed genuinely surprised to see Daniels, and Josh realized he'd never met the man. *'Must have arrived since I left.'*

"Sir," the lieutenant said, snapping a weary salute, "eleven dead, 19 wounded. No report yet on enemy casualties."

"Are you in command?"

"Captain Ellison was CO, sir, but he's been wounded. I believe you are now." He glanced at Josh's captain's bars as if to justify his evaluation.

"Yeh, I guess I am," Josh said, his head spinning until his instincts kicked in. "Let's get some copters in here for a Dustoff, and we need to check the perimeter to make sure our sentries are alert so Charlie can't sneak back for a second strike. Can you do that, Lieutenant?"

The officer looked relieved. "Yes sir. Get right on it."

The lieutenant spoke to an E-5, who grabbed two men and ran off into the jungle. Then he lassoed an RTO and started to call-in the medevac.

"What should *I* do?" Landry suddenly asked from just off Josh's left shoulder. His voice was dead, lifeless.

Josh thought about leaving his buddy with a medic, but he knew that a Section 8 would be a possibility if they saw him in his present condition. "Let's go check on your platoon," he said. "They'll be wondering what happened to you."

By asking among the men, they soon found their way to Landry's unit. The Top had rounded them all up and was busy giving out tasks when Josh and Landry appeared.

"Captain Daniels, what the hell...?" the sergeant began, until he saw Landry half-hidden behind Josh. "Lieutenant! Are you. . okay?"

Josh leaned in close to the sergeant's ear. "Can you get him to some place out of the way for a while?"

The sergeant looked from Josh, to Landry, and then back to Josh again. "He needs a medic to take a look at him," he said softly.

"The medics are a little busy right now," Josh said impatiently. "Let's let him unwind awhile, and then we'll go from there."

The sergeant shrugged. "If you say so, Captain. But this has been coming on for some time now. I don't think a *rest* is going to do it."

"Maybe not, but it's the best I can come up with right now. Understood?"

The sergeant nodded. "Yes sir."

Josh turned to his friend. "Go with your Top," he said to Landry. "He knows what comes next."

Landry didn't argue, but followed Josh's direction without a word. As Daniels watched his friend walk away, he felt a lump ball-up in his throat.

"Looks like somebody forgot to tell the VC about this Vietnamization thing," a familiar voice said from just behind him. Josh turned to see Sgt. Whitten looking after Landry, with Corporals Eddings and Anderson a few steps behind him.

"A real cluster flick, huh?"

"What's our next move?"

Josh thought for a second, glancing around at the mayhem that surrounded them. "First, let's make sure these guys get air-lifted out of here and that Bravo sends some reinforcements. Then, we do what we came here for. Sergeant, you three split up and do a quick tour of the battlefield. Make sure no wounded or KIA are left behind and that the rest of the unit has their defensive positions in good shape. Meet back here at… 1200 hours?"

"Yes sir. We'll get right on it."

Whitten saluted and herded Anderson and Eddings back toward the heart of the ambush. Josh watched as they stepped over body parts and abandoned weapons to slowly make their way back to the front line of the battle. He shook his head. *'If this is the best we can do, we've got trouble,'* he thought grimly. There was no way they'd be able to turn the war over to the ARVN if they couldn't hold a position just a few clics north of Saigon. So what were the alternatives: stay and watch the States fall apart over a continued War, or pull out and watch the North walk all over our allies? Not much of a choice.

Josh spent the next two hours overseeing the medevac and re-positioning the remaining Bravo troops. He called back to base camp and got a promise that they'd send some backup to hold the fort, but it wasn't at all clear when the new men would arrive. The remainder of Bravo would just have to do their best, and everyone would have to hope Charlie didn't return for another visit.

He was feeling pretty good about the situation by the time a half-dozen Huey Slicks roared into the makeshift LZ, discharging 70 fresh troops and a small mountain of munitions. He was relieved by a grizzled captain, whose look of irritated displeasure did not bode well for the exhausted and drained Bravo troopers.

"Charlie chewed on 'em pretty bad," Josh explained to the new officer, trying to steer him in the right direction without getting his back up. "They could use a breather."

The new arrival looked at Josh with ill-disguised contempt. "This is the Army, Captain, not Sunday school. If they can't pull their weight, maybe they shouldn't be here."

Josh barely stopped himself from tearing into the pompous ass standing in front of him. He knew it wasn't his place to lecture an experienced officer, yet still...

Soon after the new CO finally left to review his troops, Josh was interviewing a Second Lieutenant about Atlas Wedge when Sergeant Whitten and the two corporals returned. He told them to grab some chow and begin debriefing the troops.

It was after 1300 by the time Josh finished up with the lieutenant and made his way to a quiet tree stump where he could eat his C-rations in peace. Something the lieutenant had said echoed uncomfortably in his head: "The ARVN aren't bad soldiers," he'd explained, "it's just that they don't seem to have the stomach for prolonged action or ongoing campaigns. They like to fight hard for a while and then take a break, like it's some soccer game or something."

'Soccer game?' He'd seen more dead and wounded soldiers of every stripe than he'd care to remember, and they thought of it as a 'soccer game'? He tried to keep his motivation unshaken, to ignore the words and actions of a few dumb ARVN. But deep in his heart, he couldn't shake the sense that they were fighting the wrong war, in the wrong place, at the wrong time, with the wrong partners. What the hell does it say when the people you're fighting to protect care less about the outcome than you do?

As soon as he finished his rations he set out to interview another handful of officers, hoping against hope that they'd have a different spin on the War than those who'd come before. Somehow he couldn't quite make himself believe it.

*****

It was mid-afternoon before Josh had talked to enough soldiers to have a pretty good idea of what was right, and what was wrong, about Atlas Wedge and the whole process of Vietnamization. The general consensus was pretty much the same across all ranks, age groups, race and religion: it wasn't working, at least not as well as Washington had hoped. Josh wondered how the powers-that-be would take the news, or if they'd even receive it in an intelligible package.

Josh cut his three NCOs free to do as they wished for the hour or so he figured he'd need to chase down Landry and try to figure out what was going on with his old friend. As he made his way toward the area where Landry's platoon was said to be watching the perimeter, he couldn't help but note the change that had come over the battlefield in just a few hours: the bodies were gone, the abandoned weapons and gear had all been neatly stacked, and for all intents and purposes the site had reverted back to its natural state. Well, almost. The broken tree limbs and bullet-scarred trunks were tell-tale signs of what had transpired, but unless someone was paying close attention they'd probably walk right through the place and not even suspect the utter carnage that had ravaged the jungle earlier that morning.

Walking through the thick foliage, Josh's pulse began to race and a tingle crept up the back of his neck. It had been a while since he'd been out in the boonies by himself with VC in the area, and he felt the lack of exposure acutely.

'Getting' soft,' he admitted as he scanned every fern and palm for black pajamaed Charlie. By the time he got to Landry's platoon, he remembered full-well the kinds of experiences that had pushed his friend to the dark place he now seemed to inhabit.

He saw the Top before he saw Landry.

"How's he doing?" he asked the sergeant.

"Better. Still not good, but better." The sergeant was stony-faced.

"Can he stay in the field, or do I need to find a reason to get him back to Saigon for some R&R?" Normally he wouldn't ask an NCO such a question, but the Top had fought in Korea as well as a previous tour in 'Nam, and Josh knew that he was probably a better judge of combat readiness than anyone else he was likely to run into out there.

The Top stared off into the indefinite distance. "I think he'll make it," he finally said, softly but with certainty. "I'll keep an eye on him. If it gets any worse, I'll send word."

Josh nodded. "Thanks."

"You've known him a long time?"

"We were in the Academy together."

The sergeant lingered, as if he had something on his mind. "He's seen some bad shit out here," he said after a long silence.

"We all have." The images of some of the horrors he'd witnessed flashed through his memory, triggering a wave of unease that swept across his stomach. "You take care."

"You too, Captain." The Top saluted quickly and turned to leave. He'd only taken two steps when he stopped and turned back. "See if you can make those people back in Washington understand that this isn't just some political chess game. People are dying out here. And worse."

Josh wanted to reassure the man, tell him that the politicians understood what was going on. But he couldn't. From the few conversations he'd dared have with his father, he knew full well that elected officials had a different outlook on the War. Domino Theory. Cold War. And a lot of equally irrelevant nonsense. To be honest, *he* hadn't really understood what was going on until he'd been out in the field. Until he'd seen men dying for a cause the locals barely understood and certainly didn't appreciate. Democracy. Freedom. They may as well have been discussing nuclear physics. It wasn't that the Vietnamese people wouldn't appreciate a western style government if someone handed it to them. It's that they had no point of reference with which to evaluate the prospect. The majority of the people he'd seen just wanted to be left alone.

Josh debated whether to go see Landry again, but the shadows were rapidly growing longer and he knew the pilots wanted to get back to base before sundown.

'Not *much I can do anyway,*' he thought, but even as the idea crossed his mind he wondered if he was being realistic or just giving himself a good excuse for leaving the heavy lifting to the Top.

The trip back to Saigon was a quiet, solemn affair, with Josh struggling to make sense of his responsibility to Landry while pondering how he would present the team's findings to the General. He wouldn't be pleased, that much Josh knew for a certainty. The only question was whether he'd accept their conclusions or just write them off as so much unwanted noise. Even though Josh had spent literally hundreds of hours with the man, he didn't really know him at all. One thing Josh had learned at MACV – point of view oftentimes derived from your position in the chain of command. Every soldier thought he – or she – knew best what their unit, or even the whole army should be doing in 'Nam. But each of them only saw their own little corner of the world, while Commanders like General Edwards or General Abrams saw the big picture from a hundred different angles.

He hoped they hadn't forgotten the little picture as well.

*****

When the helicopter landed back at base, Josh dismissed his three NCOs with thanks, and then made his way back to his quarters. He was pleasantly surprised to find that one of the guys had delivered his mail, a small pile of envelopes resting in the middle of his neatly-made bed. His interest was piqued when he saw Darla's familiar handwriting on one of the letters.

'It's been a while,' he groused as he flopped down on the cot and tore open the envelope. He knew he couldn't complain *too* much since he hadn't exactly been the best correspondent either. In fact, he pretty much only sent letters in response to those he received. Of course, he had his reasons. The folks back Stateside couldn't really grasp what was happening there on the ground. And Josh couldn't bring himself to share all the nasty goings-on. What was he supposed to write: *'Things here are much the same as always. Killed a half dozen gooks and saw my buddy get his head blown off.'* No, that wouldn't be well-received.

As he pulled out the letter a small object wrapped in tissue paper fell from the envelope. He picked it up and tore off the paper. It was his Academy ring. He took a deep breath and turned back to the letter.

Dear Josh:

In the year since you've been gone, so much has changed. I know I have, and I'm sure you have as well. We aren't the same people as when you left.

When I finally sat down to write I thought of a million ways of saying this, but finally decided to just say it: I've fallen in love with someone. No one you know. I only met him a few months ago. I wasn't looking for anyone; just the opposite. But, things happen. His name's Dirk, and I met him through my church. But you probably don't want to know all that.

I just wanted to tell you that I'm sorry. I feel guilty that I couldn't wait for you, but I can't change the way I feel. You're a great guy and I'm sure you'll find someone else as soon as you get home.

Stay safe. I'll pray for you.

Darla

Josh let out the breath he didn't realize he was holding. He went back to the top of the letter and scanned the meager lines once more. He waited for their impact to hit him – a flutter in his stomach, lump in the throat – something. But there was nothing. He felt… nothing. Oh, perhaps a vague sadness, but compared to all he'd seen and experienced, this was just a blip on the radar screen.

He had to admit he wasn't surprised. After the first few months he'd been in-country, there had been fewer and fewer letters. Part of it was his fault. He knew that. But now? Now it didn't really matter whose fault it was. Funny thing was, now that he thought about it, he felt a little relieved. She was right: he had changed. More than she could imagine. How could he ever explain to someone who hadn't been there?

He crumpled the letter and tossed it into the trashcan next to his desk. His ring lay next to him on the taut beige blanket. He picked it up and inspected it, for what he didn't really know, and then slipped it onto his finger. The heavy weight felt good, a reminder of his four years at West Point. A reminder of his bond to all his fellow grads, all his brothers in arms.

His stomach growled, reminding him how long it had been since he'd eaten. A glance at the mirror on the wall revealed a familiar face, more tired and worn than when he'd first arrived in 'Nam, but not so bad. He smiled and watched himself as if he were watching a television show. With a shake of his head, he flipped the light switch on the wall and headed off to mess.

*****

That night, for the first time in quite a while, Josh went into the city. He secured a pass ("What's the big occasion, Daniels? You celebrating something?" his CO had asked), and made his way through the narrow darkened streets to a place he'd heard some of the men talking about: the Kangaroo Club. They said it was the kind of place you could have a drink, listen to the music and forget who and where you were. Sounded good.

But when he was about halfway to the club, he suddenly changed his mind. Out of the blue he started thinking about Kim-Ly. He was only a few blocks from her apartment, so he didn't have enough time to back out before he found himself standing at the front door to her building. He hesitated a moment before pushing the button on the intercom. Nothing. He waited a while and pushed again, longer this time.

He was just about to leave, his determination wavering, when a familiar voice emerged from the battered speaker.

"Là có những người?" she asked. Josh's Vietnamese was shaky at best, but he thought she was asking who was ringing her bell.

"Kim-Ly? It's me, Josh Daniels." Even as he said it, he realized how unexpected his visit might seem.

The long pause that followed unnerved him. He was about to apologize, when she finally answered. "I thought our date was for tomorrow night."

He smiled. "It is. I was just walking in the area and... thought I'd stop by. If this is a bad time..."

"No, no it's not a bad time." Her answer came faster, and it sounded sincere. "Come up. 3b." The door buzzed and he pushed it open with a soft nudge.

The stairway was a mess: peeling paint, cigarette butts scattered everywhere, the faint smell of urine on the first landing. He was surprised. Kim-Ly seemed like the kind of person to live in a nicer place. But maybe that was just Vietnam.

When he got to the third floor she was standing in the half-open doorway.

"This is an unexpected pleasure," she said with a welcoming smile.

"Is it?" He meant 'a pleasure'. "I hope I'm not intruding…"

"No, no. Come in. Please." She stepped back and opened the door more fully to allow him to pass. He looked down at her and smiled as he stepped into a room that couldn't have been any more different than the stairway he'd just left. Floor-to-ceiling bookcases covered two walls in a large, open room with two big windows that looked out to the wide boulevard on the other side of the building. Expensive-looking artwork dotted the walls. The furniture was sparse – a black leather sofa and matching easy chair – but it fit the apartment perfectly.

"Nice place," he said. A warm floral scent drifted on the fan-churned breeze.

"It's my father's," she explained, shutting and locking the door.

Josh nodded toward the books. "He likes to read, I take it."

"He's a journalist. Writing is in his blood." She motioned to the sofa. "Please. Sit."

He did as directed. "May I get you something?" she asked.

"No, thank you. Unless you're having something?" He tried not to sound too eager.

"I was thinking of having a cup of tea. Would you be interested?"

"Yes, please."

She nodded and left the living room by a doorway to the left. "So," she called back as he heard the sounds of tea being prepared, "you were just in the neighborhood?"

When she said it, it sounded so… phony.

"Yes, yes I was." He thought about making up some convoluted story that would paint him in the best possible light, but decided against it. The truth. Better to stick to the truth. "Actually, I was headed to the Kangaroo Club – ever hear of it?"

"Of course! Half the American soldiers in Saigon spend time there, or so I've been told. I'm sure the women are very... attractive." The last caught him by surprise.

"I wouldn't know. I've never actually been there. I don't go out much." Defensive. He sounded defensive.

"So what brought you out tonight? A special event?"

"No, not really," he said. Too much truth might not be healthy so soon. "I just needed to get out of my quarters."

"Everything okay?" she asked, appearing with a small tray on which sat a large plate of banana cake and candied fruit.

"Yeh, yeh, it's all... okay."

She noticed his hesitation but chose to ignore it. "I hope you have, what is it called, sweet teeth?"

He chuckled. "A sweet tooth. Yeh, I've got one, all right."

"Good. Begin. I'll go get the tea."

He watched her leave, her skirt swaying gracefully as she returned to the kitchen.

"Where's your Dad?" he asked.

"He is visiting friends," Kim-Ly answered, moments before reappearing with a delicate ceramic teapot and two small cups. "They play Tiến lên a couple of nights a week." To his crinkled brow she replied, "It's a card game. Very popular in Vietnam."

"Ah, like poker night in the States."

"Do you play?" She poured them each a cup of tea and handed one to Josh.

"Occasionally. I'm not too good. Don't have the patience."

"Oh? I would've thought you were a very patient man." She looked into his eyes and smiled.

"Sometimes, if it's something important enough to me." He watched her closely to see her reaction, which, quite unexpectedly, seemed inordinately important to him just then. She showed nothing.

"That's the only time a person should be patient," she said. "Patience with the unimportant leads only to unease."

"What's that, something from Buddha?" He felt foolish as soon as the words escaped his lips.

"From someone even more inscrutable – my father," she said with the same light laugh that had intoxicated him at their last meeting.

"I bet you'd be a good poker player."

"Oh? Why is that?" Her wide-eyed stare could have been innocence, or was she mocking him?

"You have what they call a good poker face."

"And what does that mean?" Her mock indignation made him smile.

"It means you only show what you want to show. You're hard to read."

"A woman must be 'hard to read'. Otherwise she is susceptible."

"To what?"

She crossed her legs and leaned back into the chair. "To life, Captain Daniels. I've never traveled to your country, but here in mine a woman's path is difficult, even dangerous. You men think the earth revolves around you. We women are just moons in your orbit."

Josh shook his head. "Wow. You sound like you don't like men very much."

She smiled, her straight white teeth gleaming in the dim evening light. "I didn't say that. Just that a woman needs to be careful."

He suddenly knew what a ball of yarn must feel like as it's batted around by a cat. He was out of his depth.

"I think *I'd* better be careful. I'm told Vietnamese women are very… persuasive."

She laughed. "Who told you that? One of your friends from the Kangaroo Club?" She said the last with such scorn he jumped to respond.

"I've never even been there!"

The tiniest of smiles painted her lips and shone in her eyes. She was enjoying herself, making him squirm!

"Then where do you go, when you're not fighting this War? You must have a favorite place."

He shrugged. "Not really. I don't have all that much free time, and I don't enjoy bars, for the most part."

"Then why were you going to the Kangaroo Club?"

She was *very* persistent.

"It's a long story." His emotions must have made their way to his face, since she reacted immediately.

"You are in a hurry?"

He took a deep breath. At first he thought to dance around the breakup with Darla, so instead he recounted his encounter with Landry and the firefight they'd all just survived. She listened attentively, reacting with a soothing sympathy that eased his anxiety and gradually broke down the barriers he'd intended to keep strong. Before he knew it, he was telling about the letter he'd received and the end of his relationship with the girl back home.

"You must be very sad," she said when he finally stopped.

He was about to respond with an appropriate cliché, but something made him reconsider. "Not really," he heard himself say. "I guess I knew it was over a long time before I got that letter. I just didn't want to admit it."

He glanced up at Kin-Ly to judge the impact of his admission, just in time to catch a tiny smile flicker across her face. Or was he imagining it? When he looked again, it was gone, her features a mask of pained concern.

"Still, it must be painful for you. I am sorry, but I'm glad you felt comfortable enough with our... friendship to come here and share your thoughts with me."

Her words brought a flutter to his chest. He hadn't thought it through, coming there; it was as if his feet had just carried him to her. He looked into her eyes and knew the truth of what she'd said.

"There's no one else I could talk to," he admitted, to himself as much as her. "Sad as that might seem."

Her lips twisted into an angry frown. "It is not sad at all!" she snapped with such vehemence that he leaned back in surprise. "You honor me with your confidence. I am happy that you came."

He felt a weight lift from his chest. "I am too," he whispered, "I am too."

Kim-Ly gently stroked his clenched hands. He stared into her green eyes, his pulse racing.

"Would you like some more tea?" she asked.

*****

Hours later, by chance more than design, Josh glanced at his watch and realized he only had twenty minutes before he was due back on base. Kim-Ly noticed the look.

"You must go?"

He turned up his hands in surrender. "I'm afraid so. I..."

Just then a key turned in the front door and an older man, a face he recognized from several photos he'd seen on the bookcases, took two steps and froze in place. His stare focused directly on Josh.

The old man said nothing for a heartbeat, then spit out something in Vietnamese that sounded anything but welcoming. Kim-Ly responded in kind.

"I, I was just leaving," Josh said as he jumped to his feet. He was keenly aware of the uniform he was wearing.

"You do not have to go," she said defiantly, staring at her father.

"Actually, I do. Like I said, I've got to get back."

Kim-Ly looked to him, and then to her father. She pointed to Josh and spoke in Vietnamese. The old man's face did not soften. He stared at the young captain with what might have been interpreted as anger.

"Captain Daniels, this is my father, Su'u Bao Tran," Kim-Ly introduced.

The old man stood his ground, leaving Josh hanging in no-man's land, so he took a step forward and put out his hand. The old man was having no part of it. He dipped his head minutely in recognition and then stomped out of the room with just a burning glance at his daughter.

"I'm sorry," Kim-Ly said as an interior door shut loudly, "he's… often angry these days."

"Hey, I understand. If I did anything…"

"It isn't your fault," she interrupted. "It's just this War."

"Well, I'm sorry if I upset him. Please apologize for me."

She sighed deeply. "I doubt it will matter to him. You see, his older half-brother, Phan Khắc Sửu, was Chief of State here for a short time – until a coup overthrew him. He died a few years later. My father blames the U.S. for supporting the military dictatorship that took control of our country."

"Wow. I can see why he wouldn't be happy finding an American soldier in his living room."

Kim-Ly smiled. "I'm not sure he would be happy finding *any* man alone with me in his living room. He's very conservative in his beliefs."

"Great, so I upset him twice before I even opened my mouth."

"He'll get over it. Despite appearances, he *is* a rational person."

"Except where you are concerned."

She shrugged. "I am his only daughter. My mother is dead. He tries to be both mother and father to me."

"Sounds like a good man."

"A very good man. But an angry man. Don't worry, I will explain. He will understand."

"You sound pretty sure of yourself."

"Vietnamese women are very... persuasive, or haven't you heard?" Her smile was reassuring.

"I remember hearing that somewhere. But I'm afraid I really do have to go. They'll string me up if I get back to base late."

Her smile faded to a pouty frown. "I'm starting to dislike the U.S. Army as well."

"Don't do that!" he teased. "At least not all the Army."

The smile was back. "I'll see what I can do. Perhaps I can grant a pardon to selected individuals."

"Good decision. So – are we still 'on' for tomorrow night?"

"Of course! Unless you are afraid of my father..."

"I'll leave him to you. 7:30?"

"Perfect. I will see you then."

For an awkward moment Josh was caught between wanting to lean down and kiss her good night and his unease that her father was just a few feet away and might reappear at any moment. He'd done enough damage without even trying; he didn't need to double down.

Kim-Ly settled the debate when she stretched up on tip-toes and kissed him on the cheek.

"Be careful," she said softly.

"Always."

As the door closed behind him, Josh jogged down the derelict stairs, his head spinning. What a crazy world!

For the first time in ages he felt a bounce in his step. Maybe Vietnam wasn't such a bad place after all.

CHAPTER 17

When Josh got back to his quarters he found a note from General Edwards taped to the door. He'd been called to a special meeting of the planning group at 0830 at MACV. What was going on? No such meeting was on the weekly schedule. They almost never met on Saturdays. The thought crossed his mind that someone had already snitched on their visit to Bravo Company. But why then meet with the entire group?

The next morning he was up early and at MACV headquarters by 0815. Although he didn't think he had anything to worry about from the Bravo interviews, he'd been in the military long enough to know that everything depended on the CO – how he'd slept the night before, whether his guts were working properly, even whether his wife had been on his back for some real or imagined transgression. He could only hope that the general was having a good day.

When he arrived at the conference room there were already five members present. Thankfully, one of them was Col. Henry.

"So, how'd the trip up north go?" he asked before Josh could even get seated.

"Other than a major firefight with multiple KIAs on both sides, and a general consensus that Vietnamization isn't happening, not bad."

The colonel's face twisted into a pained expression. "Whoa. Not what the Old Man was hoping to hear, I bet."

"I haven't told him yet."

"Ah. Something to look forward to."

"Into every day a little crap must fall."

The two men chatted while the rest of the standing group filtered in, until General Edwards made his entrance a few minutes later.

"Gentlemen, we've got a problem," he began, and Josh immediately assumed that he'd gotten word from up north. But the real reason was even more worrisome.

"It looks like Charlie has been moving right back in behind our Wedge pacification operations. We've got air intel and eyes-on IDs. We're going to have to go back to a number of the villages and teach our good friends a lesson."

He went on to describe a new operation, Atlas Power, that would put a good-sized armor force under Big Red One and send B-52s out to hammer the entire area where the VC had re-infiltrated. Then the First would go out in force to sweep the area clean once and – hopefully – for all.

There wasn't much debate. Once the general had fleshed-out an operation to the extent that he'd already called-in support from other units, the only real discussion concerned the details. Josh thought of Landry and his platoon, wondering whether he was doing either any favors by hiding his friend's problem. He'd decided to reach out to Landry's Top to get his input when the general interrupted his reverie.

"Daniels, when we're done here I want to hear about your trip north – I understand it got a little hairy."

"A little bit, sir."

"Anyone else have anything to bring up to the entire group?" No one moved a muscle. "All right then, group dismissed. Daniels, in my office."

"Good luck. Keep your left up and your head down," Henry whispered as he walked past.

Josh made a necessary stop in the head before making his way to Edward's office.

"He's waiting for you inside," his assistant informed him before he could ask.

"Daniels! So, tell me all about it," the general greeted him as he entered his office and saluted. "I just read the morning take – how bad was it?"

Josh tried to keep his report short and to the point. He'd already learned that Edwards liked to hear every detail of good news but just a brief description of anything that had gone wrong.

The general listened intently, his face showing no sign of emotion. He asked several spot-on questions and digested Josh's answers.

"And the interviews? What's the general take?" he asked when he'd heard enough about the ambush.

"Well…" Josh hesitated, fumbling for a way to deliver the bad news. The look on Edward's face told him the CO understood the implications.

"Damn it!" he shouted, pounding his fist on the big wooden desk. "All I've been getting has been good news: the ARVN are pulling their weight, the countryside is coming under control, the North Vietnamese are pulling back. So tell me, what's the real story?"

He stared at Josh as if daring him to contradict his field commanders' reports. But Josh had no alternative; he decided to keep it short and to the point.

"The South Vietnamese are inconsistent fighters at best, utterly disinterested at worst. The rural communities have a very primitive understanding of the conflict and more than anything just want to be left alone. And, if the ambush yesterday is any indication, the PAVN or VC or whoever they are can still operate with impunity right under our noses. In a nutshell, that's what we learned." He felt a trickle of sweat drip down his back. It suddenly seemed way too warm in the office.

The general stared blankly for several seconds before easing into his high-backed chair with a deep sigh.

"These observations were widespread?"

"Just about everyone, sir. After some initial bashfulness, we didn't even have to push them. They were more than ready to trash our allies, the operation, the entire strategy of the War."

Edwards nodded. "How bad's morale? Can we still depend on our own units to hold the line?"

Josh didn't hesitate. "I think so, yes. But the grunts made it clear that they're not fighting for their commanders, or even for the people back home – they're fighting for each other. Particularly the draftees, but enlisted men as well. They've had enough, and just want to go home."

General Edwards steepled his fingers and stared at them as if trying to find elusive answers.

"I guess I can't say I'm surprised," he finally said, his voice low and pained. "Fraggings are up, Section 8s have skyrocketed, we can't even process all the Article 32s. No matter how many battles we win, it always seems like those bastards come back at us with just a little bit more. If it's frustrating to me, I can imagine what it must be like for the men in the field."

"They're good men, sir."

"I know they're good men!" Edwards barked. "But those SOBs back in Washington don't seem to give a damn about them." Josh saw his CO catch himself and start back-peddling. "Not all of them, of course, but... This conversation is off-the-record, Captain, understood?"

"Understood, sir. And for the record, I think most politicians are SOBs too. But not all." He didn't clarify in which group he placed his father.

The general's shoulders relaxed as he opened a drawer and pulled out a box of cigars. "Cuban," he said, offering them to Josh. Josh wasn't much of a cigar-smoker, but it seemed like a good time to take up the habit. They lit up and the conversation drifted to specific units, strategies grand and small, and then to families, and how the War had impacted military life for all concerned. It was growing dark outside by the time the general called it quits and dismissed Josh.

The young captain hurried back to his quarters to shower and change. It was getting late by the time he made his way off base and into the crowded streets and narrow alleyways of Saigon. Even with the sun long-set, the lights and sounds of the city made it seem like daytime. At least on the larger streets. Once Josh turned onto the alley that led to Kim-Ly's apartment, however, darkness engulfed him. Maybe it was all that had happened recently, maybe just that he was paying more attention. But the closeness of the buildings created a sense of claustrophobia that hurried his step and increased his wariness. Even if the VC weren't an immediate threat, more than a dozen soldiers had been mugged in recent months, their glittering gold chains and expensive watches easy targets for the thieves of the city.

It was with a sense of relief that he arrived unscathed at the apartment door. This time the buzzer was answered almost at once. By the time he climbed the stairs to her floor, Kim-Ly stood in the doorway, leaning languidly against the doorframe. She wore a long black silk gown, embroidered with spectacular red and green dragons.

"So my father did not scare you away," she said with a sly smile.

"Wow. If I knew you cleaned-up like this, wild horses couldn't keep me away," Josh said, pausing to take in the whole scene at the top of the stairs.

Her smile widened just a hint. "I thought it was Vietnamese women who were known for their persuasiveness. It seems as though American GIs have some talent in that direction."

Now it was Josh's turn to smile. "Just telling it like it is."

"Come in, come in."

Josh half-expected Kim-Ly's father to be waiting for him in the living room, a shotgun cradled in his arms. But the room was just as he'd left it the previous night – no sign of the gracious Mr. Tran.

Kim-Ly watched him scan the room, a twinkle in her eyes. "He's not home," she explained. "He decided that he'd prefer to play cards once again."

"He'd probably prefer to pluck chickens than talk to me."

"My father does not pluck chickens," she said, "even if it means confronting the round-eye invader."

"I'm glad to hear I rank above chicken plucking at least."

"He is a good man," she said, more seriously now. "But it may take time for him to accept a stranger in our midst."

"Especially a round-eyes."

"Yes, especially."

Kim-Ly and Josh sat and sipped snake wine while they chatted about her day and how Josh found the Vietnamese and their capital city. Both of them studiously avoided any mention of the War. Of course, after a few sips of the potent wine the War seemed very far away indeed. They laughed and traded snippets of their younger lives, before Kim-Ly decided that they'd had enough wine. "Time to go dancing," she said.

Josh couldn't imagine how anyone could even walk in the form-fitting gown Kim-Ly had chosen to wear, let alone dance, but he was more than willing to watch her try. So they locked up the apartment and made their way down to the maze of streets below. Kim-Ly took his hand and led him through a half-dozen interconnected alleys, to all appearances unfazed by the stares of dozens of Vietnamese who passed by or watched them from their stoops. She flagged down a rickshaw ("a cyclo" she corrected him), and gave the driver an address.

"Where are we going?" Josh asked, his question perfunctory. He was so enchanted by the beautiful woman at his side and the intoxicating blend of sights and sounds – and smells – that she could've taken him anywhere. He didn't really care.

"Oh, you will see," she said easily.

The ride was only about 15 minutes, with a maximum speed of no more than 5 mph in the packed streets of the downtown city. Josh wasn't sure how to position himself in the tiny seat, but eventually eased his arm up and around Kim-Ly's shoulders. She didn't object, so it stayed in place the rest of the trip.

When the cyclo finally pulled to a stop, Josh helped her out of the cramped vehicle and reached into his pocket to pay the driver. Kim-Ly stopped him.

"He will charge you double. Perhaps triple," she said. Then, turning to the driver, she carried on a heated discussion that lasted until the exasperated man surrendered to her unyielding logic. She told Josh a ridiculously low amount, which he quickly paid – slipping an extra bill into the payment to assuage his guilt.

Only then did he look up and see the glowing red neon sign: Kangaroo Club.

"You're kidding!" he shouted above the incessant cacophony of the street.

"You said you had never been here. Now you have!"

As he started to object, she took his hand and led him up the steps into the darkened club. Loud rock music assaulted them as they stepped through the door. In the day-glow gloom they could barely make out a circular bar with two young women – in various stages of undress – pole dancing in front of a few dozen raucous GIs, and a similar number of young women who were working that night. Heads turned.

"Lively," Kim-Ly shouted into his ear.

"Probably a little early for this joint," he yelled back, his cheeks burning. "Why don't we try someplace a bit more..."

"Civilized?"

"Exactly."

This time he took her hand and tugged her toward the exit. He exhaled deeply as the door shut behind them and the blare of the music was drowned out by the blare of the motorbikes, horns and trucks in the street.

"That's really not my scene," he apologized as soon as they reached the crowded sidewalk.

"No? Perhaps, then, I might suggest a different club?"

"Absolutely!"

Her teeth glowed in the neon lights of the club. "Follow me."

Kim-Ly led the way through the press of bodies that always seemed to congregate in that district of the city, everything from street peddlers and hustlers to druggies and MPs. Even with such a variety of bystanders, Kim-Ly stood out from the crowd. Josh felt both pleased and nervous as he trailed close behind her. She drew attention from nearly everyone they passed, more often than not eliciting a glance up at him with a scowl or questioning gaze. He'd heard of ugly scenes in which local men had taken exception to American GIs dating Vietnamese women, and he only hoped that they didn't bump into any drunks or angry young men with a score to settle.

Kim-Ly was oblivious. She moved through the crowds without hesitation, never making eye contact and yet showing no sign of anxiety or impatience. He followed closely in her wake, admiring her skill and marveling at her gracefulness in the face of such chaos. It was a full ten minutes before she came to a halt in front of an old French colonial building that had seen better days. The heavily sculpted façade was beginning to disintegrate, and the pale yellow paint that had once brought cheer to the neighborhood now peeled in long strips, revealing the dirt and grime that marked every building within view.

"What do you think?" she asked, looking up at the decaying building.

"It's… a classic," he said, trying to avoid insulting her if it should turn out the building was a personal favorite.

"It looks better inside. Come." She took him by the arm and led him up the worn marble stairs and through the carved oak front doors. He hoped he wouldn't be disappointed – for her sake. He wasn't. They found themselves in a huge high-ceilinged ballroom lit by a massive crystal chandelier; dozens of faux candles encircled a gleaming wooden dance floor. Circular tables covered by crisp white tablecloths dotted the edges of the room. Around 100 well-dressed men and women -- most all Vietnamese – listened or danced to a big-band orchestra.

"This is incredible!" Josh said in disbelief.

"It remains from the era when the French made Vietnam their home," Kim-Ly explained. "Though perhaps not as majestic as when they maintained the building."

"It's beautiful."

"I'm glad you like it. Though I apologize for my countrymen. Not many American soldiers come here."

It was only then that Josh noticed the many surprised and occasionally hostile stares.

"Are they afraid I'll bite?"

"Like most people, they are afraid of what they do not understand. But *I* am not afraid. Shall we dance?" She gazed up at him with the assured look he had come to expect from the stunning young interpreter.

"You got it."

He took her purse and his cap to a nearby table before leading her out to the dance floor. As the band played the old Benny Goodman standard, 'Taking a Chance on Love,' couples in their vicinity shied away nervously, leaving a broad no-man's land encircling the two.

"You dance well, for an American," Kim-Ly said as Josh tried not to crush her tiny feet beneath his spit-shined dress shoes.

"You know, I don't think they're looking at me at all," he replied, glancing around the room before his look settled back on her smiling face. "I think they can't take their eyes off the most beautiful woman in this entire room."

She dropped her gaze with a coquettish blush. "My father was right to warn me about you Americans."

"Wouldn't want to disagree with your Dad," he said just before taking her in his arms and swirling around the room with complete disregard for their fellow dancers, couples scurrying aside as if confronting a tornado. Josh had never moved that way in his life and was more than a little surprised how much he enjoyed it. That, and sticking it to the stiff-necked locals who still stared unabashedly.

By the time the music stopped both of them were panting from exertion.

"Perhaps we should take a short break?" she suggested.

"Why not? Give the rest of these folks a chance to use the dance floor."

"You are evil," she joked.

"Must be an American thing."

Josh led the way back toward their table, but before they'd gone halfway an older woman, her face a bizarre mask of pale powder and gaudy makeup, grabbed Kim-Ly by the arm and began a haughty lecture in Vietnamese. Kim-Ly was having none of it. She gave at least as good as she got, her voice rising an octave as she explained the facts of life in a rapid-fire burst of indignation. The shocked matron forced her nonplussed husband to leave at once, the woman casting furious looks at Kim-Ly the entire time.

"Looks like you made a new friend," Josh said, smiling broadly at the older woman as she and her husband stomped out of the club.

"Too many of their generation live in the past, afraid of any change. We must remind them that time does not stop and we must adapt."

They ordered drinks, a newfound habit that had crept-up on Josh – a bourbon for him that tasted more like the dregs of a homemade still, a martini for Kim-Ly – and joked about her confrontation with the older generation. Josh gave his perspective, assuring Kim-Ly that the same problem existed back in the States; he was thinking of his father, in particular. One thing led to another, and before they knew it several empty glasses dotted the tabletop.

"If we're going to do any dancing, we'd better get to it," Josh suggested, holding up his watch. "I've got to be back in an hour and a half."

She feigned a pout. "It isn't fair!"

"I don't think my CO gives a fig about fair, just about readiness. And a tired, hung-over soldier is usually not a ready soldier."

"Then we will dance!"

Josh could tell that Kim-Ly was feeling the effects of the drinks as she pulled him up out of his chair and onto the floor. Her eyes gleamed as she snuggled into his chest and held him tight while they moved to the rhythms of the music. He realized how much he'd missed such intimacy, and for the first time really relaxed and enjoyed himself. Perhaps because the two of them let themselves go, refused to be intimidated, the people around them gradually gave up their stares and treated them as just another young couple. For Josh, it was as if he'd been transported to another place.

He looked down at Kim-Ly's glowing face and felt at home for the first time since he'd arrived in Vietnam. He couldn't help but wonder if their relationship could survive the pressures of that time and place, but for the moment he was just grateful for whatever time they would spend together. His face must have shown his thoughtfulness, for Kim-Ly picked-up on it at once.

"Is there a problem?" she asked, her eyes showing worry.

"Nope. In fact, everything is *great*!" He swirled her around so forcefully that she let loose a small scream of excitement.

"Are you crazy?!" she asked through her laughter.

"Nope. Just Texan!"

They danced every one of the remaining dances in the 90 minutes Josh had available to him, everything from upbeat Latin-influenced jazz to an utterly traditional Vietnamese number that had Josh stumbling about like the oversized Westerner he was. But in place of the stern-faced disapproval they'd generated when they first arrived, their attempts to navigate the local dance brought good-natured laughter and even polite applause when Josh finally 'mastered' the steps.

Both of them were breathless and dripping wet when he finally hauled them off the floor.

"Afraid I have to call it a night," he said. "My chariot is about to turn into a pumpkin."

Kim-Ly looked at him with a mixture of confusion and regret.

"An old fairy tale," he explained. "It means my pass is only good until midnight."

"We will have to speak to your commanding officer about this!" she said with mock indignation. At least, he hoped it was mock.

By the time they made their way back to her apartment, it was already 23:40 hours and Josh was seriously running short of time. He asked Kim-Ly to tell the cyclo driver to wait while he walked her to the front door of her building.

"I had a wonderful time," he said, taking her hands in his.

"I did as well." Her voice was so low he could barely hear her over the rumble of street noise.

"So, do you think we can do it again sometime? Not necessarily dancing..."

"When?" she interrupted.

Josh was caught off-guard. "Well, how about next weekend? If I can get a pass."

"I will talk to your CO!" she said, and this time Josh was afraid she might actually do it.

"Let me take care of that," he soothed. "He's a pretty cool guy."

He was hoping she'd come back with some sort of reply while he tried to decide how to end the evening, but she just looked up at him with those dreamy green eyes and he was stuck. He realized full-well that Vietnamese society was considerably more conservative than what he was used to in Dallas, but Kim-Ly was very much her own person and he didn't want her to think he wasn't interested. He definitely *was*.

"I…" he began, but before he could get the words out she stretched up and kissed him lightly on the lips. He felt the thrill of her touch surge through his entire body.

"You are a good man, Josh Daniels. For a round-eyes."

With that she turned and ran up the apartment steps. She turned back as the door swung open and waved. The faint trace of a hummed melody was cut short when the door slammed shut.

Josh stood there in the busy street for several long moments staring after her. *'As one door closes, another opens,'* he thought, and whistling mindlessly he turned back to the cyclo for the short trip back to base.

CHAPTER 18

The following week dragged on endlessly for the young captain. He tried to call Kim-Ly the next night, but when her father answered he hung up immediately.

'This is ridiculous!' he thought as he stood there with the phone receiver in his hand. *'I'm acting like some lovesick teenager!'*

Of course he wasn't much older than a teenager, and there was no doubt he had feelings for the young interpreter, but love? He remembered all the lectures during training about how young men cut off from their own society and culture might be susceptible to the 'wiles' of foreign women. He was pretty certain that Kim-Ly's wiles were just what he needed.

His infatuation didn't escape the attention of those around him. His buddy Colonel Henry remarked more than once about his distraction during their planning meetings, and General Edwards made it clear through his exasperated glances that Josh was skating on thin ice. But perhaps because of the severity of the ambush up north he cut the captain a little slack. For the most part Josh was oblivious to his CO's displeasure, as Kim-Ly dominated every waking – and most sleeping – moments.

When Friday came around at last, Josh could think of little else. He stumbled around MACV with a moronic smile on his face, his other-worldness so obvious that officers he barely knew made jokes behind his back. And sometimes to his face.

"Hey Daniels, cat got your brain?" one major called out to him as he walked right past the entrance to their daily strategy meeting before realizing his mistake half-way down the corridor. Josh just waved to him happily, causing even more merriment among his fellow officers.

So it wasn't a complete surprise – from Josh's perspective – when General Edwards ordered him to stop by his office after the meeting.

"Oh, oh," one of the other participants said softly as soon as the Old Man left the room, "looks like Daniels got his tit in the wringer." If Josh had been even slightly more aware of his surroundings, he would've realized that more than a few of those officers took some satisfaction in seeing the young 'hotshot' get his comeuppance.

"It's about time," one commented as he watched Josh head off to Edwards' office. "The Old Man has been letting him get away with murder, just because his Dad is a congressman."

"And the fact that he's one of the best young field officers in the country," Col. Henry interjected, tired of hearing others grouse at Josh's success. He received an irritated glare for his efforts.

As Josh entered General Edward's office he was not particularly concerned about what had prompted the meeting. Despite appearances, he wasn't completely oblivious to how his recent demeanor had been received by his fellow officers. He *heard* their taunts, he just chose not to react to them. It wasn't worth the effort. But he was wrong about the general's concern.

"Captain, have a seat," he greeted Josh without even looking up from a sheaf of papers scattered across his desk.

For the first time in days, the dazed smile fell from Josh's face. He expected anger, perhaps even disappointment, but not the concern in the CO's voice.

"What happened, sir?"

Edwards finally raised his eyes. His lips were pulled thin with anxiety.

"Daniels, I have some bad news. Your buddy Landry, the platoon leader up with the First?" He stopped and Josh assumed the worst.

"Yes sir?"

"He's been reported AWOL. Left his platoon two days ago and hasn't been seen or heard from since."

Josh felt as if he'd been kicked in the stomach.

"Landry? No way!" he answered reflexively, but even as the words left his lips he knew in his heart that the Landry he'd last seen was not the man he'd gone to the Academy with.

"I'm sorry," Edwards continued. "I know you two were buddies. But I'm afraid there's no denying it. He's gone."

"Maybe he's been wounded, or the VC grabbed him," he flailed, trying to convince himself as well as Edwards.

The look on the general's face was sympathetic, but it was clear he was having none of it. "We've interviewed his entire platoon. Sent teams out to look for him. They haven't found a thing to indicate anything other than desertion."

The word sounded so hash in Josh's ears he winced.

"I still can't believe it."

The general nodded sympathetically. "I suppose I wouldn't either, if I were in your place. But we've got to proceed as if it's true."

"Meaning?" He knew he was dancing close to impudence, but he couldn't help himself. Just a flicker of annoyance flashed in Edwards' eyes.

"Meaning we're going to have to instigate an Article 32 investigation in absentia and follow it out to its conclusion."

"I volunteer to head-up that investigation," Josh said.

Edwards stared at him, his face the blank page that Josh had grown accustomed to seeing. "I'm not sure that would be a good idea."

"Please, sir. If the facts lead to a charge of desertion, I'll be the first to file them at the hearing – you've got my word. But I need to be there. I need to help find him."

The pain on his young captain's face touched the general. He took a deep breath. "It's against my better judgment, but okay, I'll talk to Major Winshotz about getting you named as officiating officer. But, Daniels…"

"Yes sir?"

"I don't want to hear about you or anyone else on your team risking their safety unnecessarily. Understood?"

"Understood, sir."

"Then go find him, Daniels."

Josh saluted and double-stepped out of the building.

*****

Josh spent all that day and most of the next developing a plan and lining up men to serve on his investigating team. He was able to spring Sergeant Whitten and Corporal Anderson from their day jobs, but getting General Irwin to release Corporal Eddings proved to be more of a problem. Josh didn't know if he'd already heard rumblings of their Vietnamization inquiry results, but whatever the reason he put up a fight.

"I need someone with knowledge of the area," he explained to Irwin over the radiotelephone. "Eddings fits the bill."

"So does just about every other member of the First encamped up here. Look, Captain, I know Landry is a friend, but everything I've heard makes me think he was losing it – had been for some time. I can't justify risking the lives of good men to look for a man who very probably took off and abandoned his command."

Josh waited a moment to compose himself. "I understand, General. But I know Landry better than anyone, and even if he was having problems, he's not the kind of person to abandon his men." He only hoped that was true.

The two men went back and forth for several minutes, the general showing more patience than Josh had feared. Finally Irwin had heard enough. "All right. You win. You've got Corporal Eddings – for 72 hours. But unless you can come up with intel that shows a situation different than the one I outlined, Eddings returns to this base at 72 plus one. Agreed?"

"Yes sir. Thank you sir."

"No need for thanks; just find him. And Daniels – good luck. I hope you're right."

When he hung up, Josh felt a rush of adrenaline. He would find Landry and bring him back. He didn't know how, but he would do it. Failure was not an option.

*****

Josh debated canceling his date with Kim-Ly that night, but decided he needed to see her, if only to explain what he was doing and why. And although he was reluctant to admit it, he knew full-well that her knowledge of the people and places north of the city was almost certainly better than his own. Perhaps she could at least point him in the right direction.

By the time he got to her apartment he was exhausted, more mentally than physically. He hadn't slept more than a few hours since he'd heard about Landry, and all his waking hours had been spent trying to understand what might have befallen his friend. Kim-Ly noticed as soon as he stepped in the door.

"You don't look good. Are you ill?" she said as soon as he appeared.

"I've had some bad news."

Her face dropped. "Come in, come in."

Josh hadn't been thinking about Kim-Ly's father, and so was taken aback when he found the older man seated in his living room, smoking a pipe and reading as if nothing unusual was taking place.

"We had a… discussion," she whispered to Josh.

He nodded and made his way directly to her father's chair.

"Sir, it's a pleasure to see you again," he said, this time keeping his hand to himself to avoid risking another snub.

Su'u looked up over his newspaper and nodded once. The captain waited several seconds for a follow-up, but the old man's eyes fell back to the newspaper without a word spoken.

"Yes… well, enjoy your paper," Josh muttered, at a loss where to go from there. Kim-Ly took his elbow and pulled him back toward the other side of the room. "Does he speak English?" Josh asked when he thought they were out of earshot.

"When he wants to," she whispered, tugging him down onto the sofa. "So, tell me, what has happened?"

Josh shook his head. "I think I mentioned my friend Landry, from West Point?"

"Yes, but just that he was having some problems."

"Yeh, well now he has big problems. He's disappeared from his unit and they want to charge him with desertion." Even saying it aloud made Josh's skin crawl.

"That is terrible! Why would they say such a thing?"

He shrugged. "They have no other explanation. So they chose the easy answer."

"And what is your answer?"

"I don't know," he had to admit. "But I know Landry wouldn't desert. I know it."

She considered his words. "What will happen now?"

"Now, I'm going to take a team and go look for him. We'll be leaving tomorrow."

He saw the reaction in her face. "You are going into the jungle? Where?"

He told her the rough coordinates.

"Isn't that where you said the Viet Cong ambushed a large group of your soldiers just the other day?"

He debated lying to her, but decided against it. "It is. That's where they last saw him."

Her eyes flew open. "That area is sympathetic to the North!" she said loud enough to draw an inquisitive peek from her father across the room. "You are crazy!"

"I've got to find him. He'd do the same for me if our roles were reversed."

"Do any of your men even speak Vietnamese?"

"I speak a little…"

"You speak Vietnamese like I speak German – badly. Without being able to speak to the villagers you will have almost no chance of finding him."

He knew she had a point, but he would find Landry, language or not.

"We'll just have to take our chances."

"Insanity! Doesn't the Army have language experts?"

"Not that they're willing to send with us. Like I said, they think he deserted."

She looked at him with thinly veiled anger. "An army that values its people so little is unlikely to win their loyalty. Even the Viet Cong make it a point to leave no soldier behind."

He wanted to argue with her, to make her understand. But he felt tired, spent, unwilling to ruin their night together. Besides, he wasn't at all sure he could win the argument.

"I don't disagree. But I've got enough on my plate right now – I can't take on the entire U.S. Army."

"No, of course not." She rested her hand on his arm. "I apologize. I was unfair to you."

He saw the concern in her look and felt a surge of emotion that he could barely hide.

"No, you're right to be angry. But sometimes we just have to play with the cards we're dealt."

"I know. And I am sure you will find him."

The two sat in silence for a short time, each lost in thought. "Can we change the subject?" Josh finally asked.

"Of course." She paused. "We could go out for dinner. Would you like that?"

Josh had just wolfed down some chow at the officers' mess a half-hour earlier, but he wasn't about to contradict her. "Sure!" he said. "You pick the place."

She laughed. "If you picked it we'd both likely wind up in the hospital."

The truce between them held throughout the evening. She took them to a tiny hole-in-the-wall café not far from her apartment that served the best noodle dishes Josh had ever tasted. After a glass of wine they talked, they laughed, they did their best to forget the War. It was exactly the kind of night Josh needed; the time passed much too quickly.

They didn't talk much as they walked hand in hand back to her place, the streets unnaturally quiet so early in the nighttime. Josh was happy just to share the moment with her. He didn't want to chance saying anything that might ruin it.

"I'm sorry for what I said earlier," Kim-Ly said as they stood at the top of the staircase to her apartment. "I was just... worried about you."

"I know," he said, stroking her long dark hair absently. "And I appreciate it. Really."

Her voice dropped to little more than a whisper. "I would be very… saddened if anything happened to you."

They kissed deeply, her thin arms holding him tight. For just that instant Josh thought of nothing but the two of them. It was as if the rest of the whole screwed-up world outside no longer existed. For an instant.

"I'll give you a call as soon as I get back to Saigon," he said, pulling loose from arms that seemed unwilling to let him leave. Then, kissing her on her eyelids, adding, "Good night."

Kim-Ly was still standing at the top of the stairs looking down at him as he left the building.

*****

The next morning Josh was up at 0600, rechecking his field pack and going over the map coordinates he hoped would lead them to Landry. His determination was as firm as ever, but deep in the back of his mind he felt a tiny stab of fear that the Landry he'd seen just after his unit had been ambushed was not the same person he'd known for so many years. What if he *had* deserted? He pushed the thought from his mind. He *would* find Landry, and he *would* get him the help he needed.

By the time he arrived at LZ Albany, all three of his NCO squad members were already in place. But from the very first, Josh knew something was up from the sly grin on Whitten's face.

"You didn't tell us we were going to have another team member," the sergeant said as soon as he'd saluted.

"What are you talking about?"

"The interpreter? She's waiting in the CO's office."

Josh stifled a string of expletives. "I'll be back." He heard his three NCOs exchange comments as he hurried off.

Before he even entered the hut, he saw Kim-Ly through the open front door. She was seated in front of the CO's desk, dressed from head to foot in black pajamas! General Irvin sat on the edge of his desk, hovering over her with a look of sheer enchantment.

'Oh, Christ!' he thought, seeing how well she had ingratiated herself in such a short time.

He was so fixated on Kim-Ly that he failed to notice Major Winshotz come up next to him.

"Where did you ever find her?" he asked, his voice pitched for Josh's ears only. "She's something else."

"She certainly is that," Josh answered distractedly, only realizing who he was speaking to after the fact. He snapped off a particularly aggressive salute to try to make amends.

"You know you really should've cleared it with me or the Old Man before recruiting her for your mission. I mean, it's fine and all, but Force Protection is having a bird that they don't have time for a background check. But the Embassy vouches for her, and I assume you know her well?" His eyes gleamed.

"Too well. And we'll see about the mission." He didn't wait for a reply, but left the XO standing open-mouthed and amused. Josh rapped on the open door and came to attention just inside the office.

"There you are," Irwin said with more good cheer than he'd shown in all the previous months Josh had known him. "I was just talking to your team interpreter. A real find, Captain." He glanced down at her with the look of a cat eying a canary. Kim-Ly smiled back, glancing out of the corner of her eye to see how Josh was taking her unexpected appearance.

"Yes, sir, that she is," he said, struggling to keep his face and voice free from reaction.

"Smart move, taking along a local who speaks the language and knows the area. Should greatly enhance the chances of success."

"I... certainly hope so, sir." He looked at Kim-Ly, who smiled nervously. "May I have a moment with my... interpreter?"

"Of course, of course! But I hope we'll see you again soon," the general turned his attention to Kim-Ly.

"I hope so as well, General. It has been a pleasure to talk with you."

Josh jerked his head ever so slightly, signaling her to cut the chatter and follow him outside. She took a deep breath and did as he asked.

Major Winshotz had to step back out of the way from his vantage point just outside the entrance to allow Josh and Kim-Ly to exit. Josh took her arm none to softly and half-dragged her out of earshot.

"What the hell do you think you're doing?!" he asked more gruffly than he'd intended. "Are you crazy?"

She kept her emotions under control. Not a twitch or even a blink.

"Not crazy. Vietnamese."

He suppressed a grin. Ballsy, he had to give her that.

"You don't really think we're going to take you out there with us?"

"As your general said, your chances of success will be much greater with my help."

"Kim-Ly," he said, more concerned than angry, "the VC are out there. Maybe even regulars. They're not going to give you a free pass just because you dress like one of them! Speaking of which, what in God's name is with this get-up?"

She looked down at the black pajamas. "If you mean these – I would prefer that the villagers don't shoot at us before we can ask them about your friend. Wearing these I will have a better chance of getting close enough to ask."

"Getting close enough! We can't guarantee your safety twenty-five feet beyond our barbwire, let alone out in the jungle. What happens if we get ambushed?"

"I am my father's daughter," she said matter-of-factly. "I learned to shoot at age 11. I killed my first wild boar at age 15. I can take care of myself."

He looked down at her in utter astonishment. "That's all well and good," he continued as soon as he regained his equilibrium, "but shooting a wild boar isn't the same as killing another person."

She stared deeply into his eyes. "If anyone tries to kill you, they will die." A chill raced down his spine. He believed her. Who *was* this woman who just the other night had moved around the dance floor so gracefully and now offered to kill to defend him? He was thrown completely off balance.

"Kim-Ly, I can't let you do this…"

She laid her hand gently on his arm. "Josh, I *must* do this. Not just for you – for *all* of you."

He wanted to argue more, to talk her out of it, to make her understand what she'd be risking. But one look at her steely determination and he knew he had no chance. And with the general's blessing, he didn't even have his chain of command to fall back on as an excuse.

He exhaled. "All right, okay. But you will do as I say or we'll send you packing. Understood?"

She kissed him gently on the cheek. "I understand. Thank you."

His mind whirling, Josh led her back to General Irwin's hut to give a quick readout of his plan.

"I hope you're right, Daniels," Irwin said when he'd listened to the proposal. "Landry was a good officer – I'd like to bring him back in one piece."

"We'll do our best."

"I'm sure you will. And Ms. Su'u – you take care of this soldier. We'd kind of like to see him back here in one piece as well."

Kim-Ly didn't smile. "We will come back. And we will find Lieutenant Landry if he is out there."

The general's smile faded. "Yes. I think you will. Good luck."

At Kim-Ly's request, Josh secured a 9mm pistol for her. She'd taken target practice on multiple occasions with a 9mm, she explained, and felt comfortable with it. He checked her out briefly to make sure she wasn't exaggerating, and came away convinced and impressed. He ran through his plan for searching the area surrounding the ambush site and answered several of her questions. She was sharp and seemed unafraid.

They met the other three members of their squad at the landing pad, where a Huey was already warming up to carry them north.

Josh introduced Kim-Ly to the others, who reacted with chivalry, surprise and ill-disguised lust.

What am I getting us into?' Josh thought as they climbed aboard the copter.

His trepidation increased when Kim-Ly grabbed ahold of his shirt sleeve as the Huey lifted off.

"I've never flown in a helicopter," she explained over the roar of the engine and the whirl of the blades.

"Don't sweat it!" he yelled back. "Everybody has a first time!"

He glanced surreptitiously at his three NCOs and saw only Corporal Eddings with a questioning look. The others had on their game face, totally into the mission. Josh relaxed a bit, turning his mind to the task at hand. In less than twenty minutes, they'd be on the ground.

*****

As the Huey flew off at treetop level, Josh moved his people off of the LZ and into an adjacent heavily forested area.

"All right," he began, opening his mission map to go over their approach one last time. "We will move out in this direction, toward this village about two clics out. Stay together and keep your eyes open. Sergeant, you take the point, followed by Eddings, then me and Kim-Ly, and Anderson, you bring up the rear. All clear?"

They all murmured their agreement. "Good. Let's go find Lieutenant Landry."

Despite no reports of VC sightings since the ambush, Josh felt ill-at-ease as they moved through the dense underbrush. Perhaps it was having Kim-Ly with them – although she moved through the jungle with more ease than he and his men could ever hope. Or perhaps it was his fear of what he might discover if and when they found Landry. Whatever the cause, he was uncharacteristically jumpy, his head swiveling from side to side with every animal cry, every unexpected gust of wind.

They made good time under the hot tropical sun, but his uniform was drenched within an hour. Anderson and Eddings looked even more wasted then he felt, while Whitten and Kim-Ly seemed to hardly notice the steamy heat at all. With sweat dripping down his back in rivulets, he called a break. The three NCOs split off a few yards to smoke and swap observations, leaving him and Kim-Ly to chat between themselves.

"How you doin'?" he asked, more to show he was interested than because he thought she was having any difficulties.

"I am fine," she said. Then, eyeing the dark green patches of sweat that dotted his uniform, added, "And you?"

He had to smile. "I'm okay. Sweating to death, but nothing unusual about that."

"You Americans dress too warmly."

"What would you have us do, wear pajamas like you?"

She didn't hesitate. "It would make more sense, yes. You lose too much water from your body. You will grow weak."

"I'll mention it to the general when we get back," he joked.

"Good. Maybe I will as well."

He twitched. As crazy as it seemed, he could almost see her doing it. "Uh, that might not be a good idea," he said. "Let me take care of it."

She shrugged and took a quick sip from the lightweight canteen she carried. "As you wish."

If anything, Josh was sweating even more heavily when they got started again after fifteen minutes. They moved along a well-worn path in silence, lost in thoughts as different as each of the five. With the noises of the jungle and their own rasping breaths as backdrop it was easy to fall into a casual routine, aware of their surroundings but one step removed from the reality of the War. So it came as more of a shock than it should've when Eddings sang-out in an energized whisper: "Captain! Movement in the bush!"

Josh pivoted and signaled for everyone to hit the deck.

"Down!" He turned to the corporal. "Where?"

Eddings pointed to an area to their left, a clump of palms and ferns that created a natural screen that could have hidden a platoon. Josh focused all his attention on the spot, but saw nothing. No movement. No Charlie. Nothing. After several long seconds, he motioned for Eddings and Anderson to move toward the trees from either side, while he signaled Whitten to stay put with Kim-Ly. He made his way at a quick crawl toward the dense greenery, half-expecting to hear gunfire at any moment. But none came.

By the time he reached the spot Eddings had indicated, both corporals were already in place, crouched down examining the soft ground beneath them.

"Footprints," Eddings said.

"Looks like sandals. Maybe VC," Anderson added.

Josh took a look at the well-defined markings. Sure enough, it was almost certainly a local, but whether friend or enemy it was impossible to tell.

"Someone surveilling us?" Anderson asked.

"Don't see what else they'd be doing out here," Josh said. "I think we'll take a short break and have one of you try to follow these tracks."

"Whitten's the tracker," Eddings said. "He's got eyes like a hawk."

Josh nearly barked at the corporal, but reconsidered. "Whitten!" he called out, motioning to the sergeant so he could make out their location through the foliage. "Come!"

Whitten had eyes on the tracks before Josh could explain what he needed.

"Recent. Someone's shadowing us," he explained. "He's wearing sandals. Maybe VC."

"No, not Viet Cong," Kim-Ly said. All eyes turned to her.

"How do you know?" Josh asked, modulating his voice to indict neither Kim-Ly nor Whitten.

She bent down and pointed to the tracks as she explained. "The bottom of the sandal does not have the design from the tires the Viet Cong use for their sandals. It is smooth. Most likely a villager."

Josh turned to Whitten. The sergeant nodded, surprise etched on his face. "She's right. I got ahead of myself. Charlie *does* use old tire treads for sandal soles most of the time. Could be a villager."

"From the depth of the tracks it is a male, perhaps 55 kilos," Kim-Ly continued. "Probably a teen age boy."

"Why do you say that?" Josh asked, trying to keep the amazement from his voice.

"See – here, here and here," she said, pointing to cracks and crevices in the soft earth. "The bottoms are worn, breaking in places. A younger son got them from his father or older brother."

Anderson whistled. "Looks like we got ourselves another tracker."

"She's got me beat," Sergeant Whitten admitted. "Where'd you learn to read signs like that?"

"My father is a hunter. He had no sons, so I often went with him."

"But why would a villager be out here shadowing us?" Josh asked. "I would think they'd want to keep as far away from us as possible."

"I don't know," Kim-Ly answered. "Maybe he watches for the Viet Cong. But perhaps we should follow him and ask."

"I think we're gonna have us one surprised kid," Whitten said with a smile.

Josh hesitated. He hadn't been convinced that bringing Kim-Ly on the mission was a good idea from the first, and now he was going to let her persuade them to head off on what might be a wild goose chase? They didn't have much time to find Landry. If she were wrong…

"Yeh, okay, let's do it," he finally agreed. "But let's pick up the pace a little."

He repositioned his team, putting Kim-Ly out front with himself virtually attached to her hip. She moved them through the thick undergrowth quickly, not once faltering or doubling back.

"The tracks are clear," she explained. "Whoever it is makes no effort to hide them."

Josh didn't know if that was a good thing or bad. There was always the very real chance that the kid – if it was a kid – was leading them into an ambush. It wouldn't be the first time. But the situation was strange enough that he had to check it out. For himself and his people as much as Landry.

They pushed through the jungle for over a half-hour, probably covering two to three clics – less as the crow flies. Josh was beginning to think they were spinning their wheels when Anderson called out from the rear: "Captain – smoke!"

Sure enough, off to their left Josh could just make out a thin gray stream of ash rising above the treetops. He called his team together. "Sergeant, you take Anderson and come at them from that direction," he directed Whitten. "Eddings, you and Kim-Ly come with me."

They picked their way through the dense foliage, keeping low and moving from one stand of protective trees and bush to another. It was only a matter of minutes before they saw the first thatched hut through a screen of leaves and branches. Despite telling himself that it was a different village and different situation, he couldn't help but flash back to an earlier time, a terrible time. A wave of nervousness swept through him. Or was it guilt?

He motioned for Kim-Ly and the corporal to follow his lead. In single file they circumnavigated their half of the village while Whitten and Anderson did the same on the opposite side. Nothing seemed out of place or unusual. Around twenty small thatched-roof huts dotted a clearing less than 100 meters across. Most of the villagers were probably out in the fields working, and the few that remained – mainly women with small children – were either in their huts or congregated in small knots, deep in conversation. But when he led the way out of the brush and stepped into the open space between huts, their reaction was anything but what he'd expected.

The women looked at him with no sense of panic or surprise, bowing respectfully in his direction.

"They knew we were coming," Kim-Ly said as she came up behind him. "The young man told them."

"It certainly seems like it," Josh answered. He remembered other villages and the screams and dread that had greeted his unit when they appeared. "Stay alert. We don't know if they're friendlies."

Josh motioned for Whitten and Anderson to stay on their side of the village. "Take a look inside the huts," he called over to them, "but no firing unless absolutely necessary." He didn't want a repeat of the mistakes of the past.

Meanwhile, Kim-Ly had moved toward the nearest small group of women: three of them, two with children.

"Kim-Ly!" Josh yelled after her. "Wait!" He hurried to her side, with a very nervous Eddings covering them as he scanned the surrounding jungle.

"Don't like this, Captain!" he called after Josh. "Something's not right."

"Hold your ground!" Josh ordered.

"I wanted to talk to them without all of you Americans standing around," Kim-Ly explained before Josh could say a word. "They're more likely to talk to me if I'm alone."

"They might. But don't go running off on your own again, okay? You're part of this team, and we don't want to lose you."

She smiled at his serious look and tone. "I am the last one likely to get lost. So, may I go speak with them?" She motioned toward the women, who eyed her and Josh warily but without open anxiety.

It was against his better judgment, but she had a point. "Yeh, go ahead. But keep your eyes open. This could be a trap."

Kim-Ly didn't wait for him to change his mind, but immediately approached the three local women with hands in plain sight. Josh kept one eye on her, the other on the surrounding jungle.

As soon as Kim-Ly got within hailing distance, she said something to the group that sparked a heated reply. Shouts back and forth spooked Josh and his four men, each of whom raised their weapon to an easier firing position. Kim-Ly wasn't deterred, however, and kept approaching the women, dropping her voice to a soft, persistent tone. Finally she was next to them, explaining with her hands as much as her words. The nervous initial reaction of the villagers gave way to grudging conversation. From a distance, Josh guessed Kim-Ly was explaining that they were looking for Landry and asking if they'd seen him. After a few minutes she nodded to the women and made her way back to where Josh was waiting.

"So? Do they know anything?" he asked before she could speak.

"I don't know. They say they haven't seen any American soldier, but they are nervous. I think they may be lying."

"I'd be nervous too, if a bunch of armed GIs wandered into my village and started nosing around," Eddings said.

Josh ignored him. "Why do you think they might be lying?"

"I am not sure. Something in the way they looked to each other for support before answering my questions. I just have a feeling."

"Oh great…" Eddings mumbled.

"Can it!" Josh snapped, receiving a nasty stare in return. He turned back to Kim-Ly. "Let's talk to some of the others. See what their story is."

Over the next hour Kim-Ly spoke with all the remaining villagers. Her opinion didn't change.

"They're hiding something. I know it."

"Another feeling?" Eddings jibed.

Josh glared at the corporal but didn't say a word. "What do you suggest?"

Kim-Ly hesitated. "I do not think they will tell the truth with the four of you standing watch. I think I should talk to them alone."

"Oh no you don't! We're not leaving you out here with who knows what."

Sergeant Whitten had been listening from just a few steps away and came over to touch Josh lightly on the sleeve.

"Can I talk to you a second, Captain?"

Josh looked confused, but agreed. "You stay right here," he ordered the remaining three members of the team. "I'll be right back."

Whitten led him just out of earshot. "Captain, the reason the woman is here with us is because she can talk to these people. Maybe you should let her do her job."

"Her *job*?!" Josh reacted so loudly that Kim-Ly and the two corporals turned toward them, alarmed. "She should never have been allowed to come with us at all," he whispered furiously. "She is not a GI!"

"General Irwin thought different."

"General Irwin doesn't give a shit about anything other than finding Landry before he can embarrass the Army!" Josh spit before he could stop himself. "Just like all the rest of the top brass."

Whitten stood silently.

"We want to find the lieutenant too," he finally said softly.

Josh felt the anger drain out of him. "Yeh, of course you do," he managed. "This damn war just has me all turned inside out."

"You're in good company."

Josh forced a smile. "That I am, Sergeant, that I am. So, I guess we let our interpreter go do her thing, huh?"

"Might help us accomplish our mission, sir."

"Yeh…" Josh went back to where Kim-Ly stood, watching them.

"So, you think you can get these people to talk to you?"

He saw the tension leave her eyes. "I think so. At least I can try."

"All right. We'll give it a try. The rest of us will be just over there a bit, out of sight but not out of shouting range. If anything goes wrong, if you feel anything strange, you shout out for us – okay?"

She smiled. "Yes sir!" She stretched up and kissed him on the cheek. "I'll be fine."

Josh saw the smirking reaction from his men but didn't give a damn. He just wanted Kim-Ly to be okay. There had to be someone not broken by this war.

"Come on – let's move out," he ordered his men. He led the way to the perimeter of the village and found a dense strand of elephant ferns to station the team behind. His heart began to pound as Kim-Ly walked back to the women. They talked for several seconds, until one of the villagers motioned to a nearby hut and the entire group disappeared inside.

"What the hell is going on?" Josh muttered to himself, just loud enough that Whitten overheard.

"They know we're out here," he said. "They may not show it, but they know. They probably just wanted to get out of our field of view."

"Maybe," Josh said, hoping the sergeant was right. "But I don't like it much."

From their vantage point the two corporals scanned the jungle surrounding them while Josh and Whitten continued to watch the hut. Several minutes later smoke began to drift through a hole in the thatched roof. No one went in, or out. Ten minutes went by. Then 20. Josh was getting twitchy when one of the women at last emerged from the hut carrying a large black metal container.

"Look alert!" Josh called out. "One of the locals is coming our way carrying a metal container."

"Explosive?" Eddings asked, pushing in closer to get a better view. All of them had heard of a recent incident in which a woman had approached a group of GIs and then pulled the pin on a grenade, killing 4 and injuring a half-dozen. It was fresh in all their minds.

"Not sure what it is, but she's carrying it gingerly. Let's let her get just close enough so we can identify what she's got. No shooting unless I say so – understood?"

Josh felt nerves jangling in the men, especially Eddings. He was a driver, mostly, not used to this kind of action. Josh didn't want anyone shot by mistake. As the woman came closer and closer, his own pulse quickened.

"Okay, that's close enough!" he called out to her when she'd come within 50 feet of their hiding place. He stepped out from behind the ferns and motioned with his hand. "Put it down, there!"

The woman looked baffled. Josh mimed holding a container and bent down to place the invisible item on the ground in front of him. The woman's eyes opened in understanding. She did as directed.

"Move back a little!" he called to her, motioning again with his hands. She stepped back a few feet.

Josh debated whether he should insist she move back further, but decided to risk it.

"Want me to go check it out, Captain?" Whitten asked.

"Nah. I'll do it." If it was a bomb, it was his responsibility.

Slowly, showing the woman his hands so she wouldn't be frightened, Josh approached the black metal container. His eyes jumped between the woman and her gift, either of which could put him in a body bag. It seemed to take an inordinately long time to cover those fifty feet, but finally he moved close enough so he could peer down inside the container. Before he could see anything, however, the smell hit him: the pungent, even rancid smell of duck blood soup. The woman was bringing them food!

He stepped closer to be sure nothing was concealed in the pot, stirring the contents with the long wooden spoon she'd left inside to be sure. A wave of nerves fluttered across his stomach.

"Thank you; cảm ơn bạn," he said, stretching his Vietnamese near the breaking point. The woman smiled, her rotten, blackened teeth aging her 15 years in 5 seconds.

Josh turned and walked back to his men.

"Duck blood soup!" he called out.

"Oh yum…" Eddings answered with little conviction.

"You *will* taste it," Josh said, confident the woman couldn't understand him. "All of you."

"And you?" Whitten asked with a small grin.

"*All* of us."

Although he was reasonably sure that the woman was a friendly, Josh split his team into two parts: he and Anderson did their duty first, eating as much of the soup as they could stomach, before Whitten and Eddings spelled them.

"Hey, this ain't so bad," the sergeant said, smiling and nodding to the watching villager.

"Glad I didn't grow up in your house," Eddings griped before forcing himself to swallow a spoonful of the potent mixture. He made no attempt to hide his less-than-enthusiastic reaction from the woman, who unexpectedly laughed hilariously.

"Looks like you made her day, Eddings," Whitten said.

"Glad to be of service."

Josh was about to thank the woman again and send her on her way, when Kim-Ly appeared from the hut. She motioned for him to come over. He tried to read her expression as he came toward her, but she was wearing her poker face.

"They've got him," she said when he was within speaking range.

"Who? Who's got him?"

"The villagers. They found him wandering in the jungle. They call him 'điên'."

"Meaning?"

"Crazy One."

Relief and distress flooded his gut. "So where is he?"

"They've got him hidden in a cave not too far from here. But they won't take us there unless you make them a promise."

Josh tried to hide his growing impatience. "Promise them what?"

"That you won't hurt him."

As she said it, the two village women emerged from the hut. The elder of the two said something to Kim-Ly.

"She asks if you enjoyed the soup." Kim-Ly smiled.

"Tell her it was... very tasty."

Kim-Ly relayed the comment, eliciting smiles and coos from both locals.

"So? Now that were all friends, will they take us to Landry?"

Kim-Ly interpreted his question. The smiles disappeared. The older woman responded, briefly.

"She wants to know if you will make the promise."

Josh resisted the urge to let loose on the two. "Yeh, yeh, I promise. He's my friend."

When Kim-Ly communicated his agreement the older woman nodded and then raised her hand above her head and yelled something in Vietnamese. Josh jerked around to look in the direction she was shouting. The other three team members brought their weapons to their shoulders and assumed firing positions.

The woman said something to Kim-Ly.

"She says you do not have to worry. She is calling to her son."

"I don't like it," Eddings said almost at once.

"What do we do here?" Whitten asked, scanning the jungle anxiously.

Josh forced his jaws to unclench. "Lower your weapons," he said softly, "but keep your fingers on the trigger."

"Captain..." Eddings began, but Josh cut him off.

"Lower your goddamn weapons!" he barked. Kim-Ly looked at him questioningly, but kept silent.

Moments later a teenage boy, perhaps 15 or so wearing ragged black pajamas, emerged from the jungle cautiously, his wide eyes darting to the weapons pointing in his direction.

"Tell him to put his hands where we can see them!" Josh ordered Kim-Ly. She relayed the message and the boy did as he was told.

The older woman protested indignantly, but Josh ignored her. "Tell him to come over here, slowly."

The boy approached to within 20 feet when Josh held up his hand to signal him to stop.

"Tell him I just want to check that he's not carrying a weapon," he told Kim-Ly. The kid nodded nervously.

"Captain, let me do that," Corporal Anderson volunteered.

"Hold your position," Josh said as he started across the short distance that separated them.

A strong sense of déjà vu struck him, as if he'd been there and done that before. He watched the teen's terrified eyes track his every move. *The kid's pissing in his pants, thinking I'm going to shoot him,'* he thought. *'And he's the reason we're here – to protect kids like him. Goddamn war.'*

The kid stood stiff as a board as Josh circled and flinched when he patted him down.

"Kid's clean," he called back to his men, who lowered their weapons.

The village woman said something to her son, who glanced over at Josh's team and answered her harshly. His reply was met by what Josh understood to be an order. The kid sullenly nodded, and ran off.

"Where's that little gook going?!" Eddings yelled, raising his rifle threateningly.

"He is going to tell the men watching Lieutenant Landry that we are coming – so they do not shoot us," Kim-Ly explained.

"That would be good," Whitten mumbled.

"So we're going to where he is?" Josh asked.

Kim-Ly nodded. "She will lead us there."

"We're gonna follow that gook into the jungle to God knows where, just because she says to?!" It was Eddings again.

Josh had had enough. "Look Corporal, if it bothers you to come with us, then you can stay here and stand guard over the village. Any of you others can do the same."

"I'm with you, Captain," the sergeant answered without hesitation.

"Me too," Anderson agreed.

Eddings looked like he might pout. "This stinks," he said, but he made no move to separate himself.

"Okay, if that's settled, let's go get our man," Josh said.

Kim-Ly talked to the village women, and the older woman handed her child over to her friend. "She says she is ready," Kim-Ly interpreted.

"You coming?" Josh asked Eddings.

"I ain't staying here," the corporal replied.

"All right, let's move out. But keep alert – we don't know what's out there."

Kim-Ly sidled up next to the village woman, who led the way into the jungle. Josh positioned his men just as he had previously, with the lone exception that Kim-Ly was now on point together with the village woman. He didn't much care for that, but he had no choice.

The sun was now straight up above the tops of the palm trees and the air surrounding them was a hot mist that brought out sweat from every part of the body. The village woman seemed to have a pretty good sense of where she was headed, picking out thin, nearly invisible trails without hesitating. Josh strained to hear the animal calls around them, hoping they'd give him notice if any non-friendlies crashed the party. He'd been anticipating a short hike, so after 10 minutes slogging through the thick foliage he was just getting antsy when the woman up front signaled them to stop.

"What's up?" he asked Kim-Ly. They'd stopped in a heavily overgrown area, no different than what they'd been seeing most of the way from the village.

Kim-Ly shrugged. Just then, the woman cut loose with a high-pitched screech that mimicked one of the jungle monkeys so perfectly that Josh wouldn't have known the difference if he hadn't seen her produce the sound. In seconds a similar cry responded from what seemed no more than a hundred meters from their position. The village woman turned and spoke to Kim-Ly.

"They are just ahead of us," the young interpreter informed Josh. "They will not shoot."

"Miracle of miracles," he heard Anderson mutter just behind him.

"Don't get lazy," Josh said. "They may be friendly, but we don't know that yet." He directed Whitten and Eddings to hang back as a rear guard while he and Kim-Ly and Eddings went to where Landry was supposedly being held. "If we're not back in 10 minutes, light 'em up."

Even though Josh had no reason to doubt the village woman, his stomach churned as they pushed the last few meters through the bush. Finally the woman led them to a small clearing: on the far side opposite to where they stood, the opening to a cave was barely visible as a thin slash in the side of an overgrown hillside. In front of the opening stood the teen from the village and a young man just a year or two older holding a rusty M2 carbine. They weren't smiling. Josh scanned the jungle on all sides.

"Is Landry in there?" he asked Kim-Ly, who passed his question to the village woman.

"He is, but he is ill," Kim-Ly passed the reply.

"Are we okay going in there?"

Kim-Ly asked, the woman shouted something to the kid with the gun, and he answered.

"He wants you to put your guns down right here. Then you can enter."

"No way, Captain," Eddings piped up, his voice a nervous squeak. "No way I'm giving up my gun."

Josh quickly evaluated the situation. The corporal had a point. "All right. You stay here. I'll go in," he said, laying his M16 on the ground and stripping off his pistol. "Keep your eyes open, but don't shoot anyone unless they shoot first! Understand?"

"I don't like this…"

"You don't have to like it," Josh spit under his breath, "just do it!"

Without waiting for an answer, he turned toward the cave.

"I'm going with you," Kim-Ly said. Before he could argue, she added, "If anything goes wrong, I may be able to talk us out of there."

It was too late to get finicky. "All right, but stay behind me. If anyone starts shooting, get the heck out of there."

Josh kept his eyes glued on the teen with the rifle as they approached the cave entrance. The boy returned the favor. When they were close enough for Josh to see the nervous sweat dripping down the kid's face, Kim-Ly spoke to him in a soft, soothing voice. He nodded in reply.

"We can go inside."

Josh nodded to the young guard and forced a thin smile. Nothing of the sort came back his way.

As they stepped from the shadowy sunlight into the near-blackness of the cave, it took Josh a few seconds for his eyes to adjust. The cave was bigger than it looked from the outside, stretching back from the entrance a good twenty feet. All the way in the back of the hollow he saw a body curled up on the dirt floor, a tattered blanket covering head and shoulders.

Josh hurried to his friend. "Landry?" he called out softly as he bent down to check, "it's me, Daniels."

The only reply was a soft groan. Josh reached out and gently touched the shoulder nearest him. Another groan.

"Is he injured?" Kim-Ly asked.

"Don't know. Only one way to find out." He rolled the body toward him, carefully guiding the limp extremities. Kim-Ly gasped.

It was Landry all right, but his face was drawn, nearly skeletal, and his blinking eyes stared unfocused. His lips moved silently, as if struggling to speak.

"It's gonna be okay, bro," Josh said soothingly. "It's gonna be okay. Just give me a second – I'll be right back." He jumped up and stalked across the cave toward the entrance. Kim-Ly darted after him.

"Josh, Josh! You must gain control of yourself!" He shook her hand from his arm and stepped out into the sunlight. The young guard started and raised his weapon when he saw the look on the American's face.

"Goddamn it! What have you done to him?!" Josh roared in the teen's face.

Kim-Ly interpreted, but it was the village woman who answered. "He does not eat," Kim-Ly told Josh. "They have tried, but he refuses."

Josh struggled with his emotions. The teenager looked ready to open fire. "Yeh, okay… all right," Daniels finally managed to say. "Eddings, we're going to need a stretcher!" he called out to the wide-eyed corporal. "See if you can cut us a couple of branches we can use for side poles."

The corporal seemed relieved to be able to leave the vicinity. Josh turned back to Kim-Ly. His temper was nearly back under control and he was already planning their next moves. "Tell them we appreciate what they've done for this soldier. We know they risked their lives helping him, and we won't forget that."

Kim-Ly passed his words and the woman smiled, nodding. The teen showed no reaction.

"Is it safe for us to take him back the way we came?"

The village woman answered Kim-Ly. "She says they have not seen any Viet Cong since the big battle several days ago. But that doesn't mean it is safe."

"Understood. Go keep an eye on Landry, please, and I'll go round-up Whitten and Anderson. I'll be right back."

She nodded her agreement and re-entered the cave. Josh looked after her. He was impressed how she kept her cool, never showing any fear or distress. But Asians were like that, he reminded himself, that's why they were such good gamblers.

He quickly backtracked to where his two men kept watch and together they headed back to the cave. The NCOs put together a makeshift stretcher in just a few minutes, while Josh and Kim-Ly worked with Landry, getting him propped up in a sitting position, cleaning his filthy face and trying to get him to drink some water. More dribbled down his chest than was swallowed, but it seemed a small victory when he downed a tiny gulp.

"He doesn't look too good," Eddings said from the cave entrance as he and Anderson brought the stretcher.

"Keep your opinions to yourself," Josh snapped. "Get that stretcher over here."

They loaded Landry much as they would a dead body, with just about as much assistance from the traumatized lieutenant. The village woman stood back at the other side of the cave, watching everything closely. As Whitten and Anderson hefted the stretcher, the woman said something to Kim-Ly.

"What now?" Josh asked.

"She says that now that she has seen you with your friend, she believes you will take good care of him."

"Yeh. A little late for that," Josh mumbled under his breath. "Come on. Let's move out."

The four male squad members took turns carrying the stretcher, with the two who were unencumbered scanning the jungle for any sign of ambush. With the village woman leading the way, they made good time and saw no sign of anyone – friend or foe. After having been surrounded by so many people for so long, it was strangely liberating for Josh to be with just the five other members of their little rescue mission in the middle of the jungle – six, if you counted Landry. He hadn't realized how penned-in he'd felt at the MACV headquarters, how much he missed being able to just hop in his car back home and head out for a drive.

"You are very quiet," Kim-Ly said after they'd passed through the village and left the women behind.

"Just thinking."

"About what?"

"I don't know, just how far Landry and I have come from back home."

"Your friend will recover, I feel it."

"I don't know…"

"Have hope," she said, taking his hand in hers. "Miracles happen every day."

He squeezed her hand. "I'd like to believe that."

By the time they got back to the First base camp, all four stretcher bearers were drenched with sweat and exhausted. Even Kim-Ly was unusually quiet. They brought Landry straight to the medics, who immediately transferred him to a hospital bed and set him up with an IV.

Josh dismissed Whitten and the two corporals, thanking them for their help.

"No soldier left behind," the big sergeant said. "Don't worry – I've seen grunts in worse shape bounce back. Landry will too."

Josh forced a smile and patted Whitten on his shoulder. It was soldiers like him that made it all worthwhile, or at least kept it from being a complete disaster.

Kim-Ly and Josh kept vigil for over an hour, waiting for a doctor to give them a status report. Finally, a tall, bone-thin major appeared from the medical tent.

"You Daniels?" he asked.

Josh nodded.

"Your Lieutenant Landry has severe dehydration, a few cuts and bruises – nothing too serious. However, he's suffering from a bad case of combat fatigue. He needs a long rest and counseling. I'd like to keep him here with us for at least a few days."

"Any reason why you can't?" Josh asked.

The doctor shrugged "We've already had some military police over here. They seem anxious to get their hands on him."

"For what?! Is it now a court martial offense to get shook up?"

Kim-Ly put a restraining hand on his arm.

"Yeh, sorry. I just get a little ticked off when I hear that MPs are trying to get their hands on a guy who's given so much for our country."

"No argument here. But we don't control the situation. We just do what we're told."

"Yeh, I know. I'm not blaming you. It's the damn system."

"We'll try to keep him here as long as we can, but we can't fight the big brass. Maybe we'll get lucky and they'll let him stay here for a while; sometimes we do. But it's usually a long, slow process. Best thing for him would be to ship out to the States and get some VA treatment there."

Josh tried not to show his frustration. He'd heard his father rail about the broken VA system for years and had very little faith in it himself. It wasn't something he'd bring up with the doctor responsible for treating his friend, however.

"Who makes that decision?" he asked instead.

The major hesitated. "Good question. The initial decision comes from the company Medical Officer, but if you're talking about appeals I'd guess it probably goes all the way up to the MACV Commander."

Josh saw a ray of hope. "Good to know. Thanks, Doc. Take good care of him, okay? We'll try to come visit as soon as we can."

"It helps, believe me. A familiar face, a friendly voice – all of it can help snap them out of it."

"Do they all recover?" Kim-Ly asked.

The major shifted his feet uneasily. "I wish I could say they do, but I'm afraid I can't. About 20 percent have severe lingering symptoms, and over 80 percent have some ongoing problems five years after treatment. We really don't understand the brain all that well. So we do the best we can."

Josh's heart fell. Landry would be one of the lucky ones. He'd see to it.

*****

Josh didn't talk much on the helo ride back to Saigon. Kim-Ly tried to make small talk at first, but the motor roar and rotor wash made it almost impossible. Besides, what was there to say?

When they landed at the air base Josh was more than a little surprised to see Major Winshotz waiting for them in a Jeep driven by a corporal.

"Daniels!" the major called out as soon as they'd made their way out from under the still-turning rotor blades.

"Major. What brings you out this way?" Josh asked.

"Thought you two might need a ride. Can I drop you somewhere?"

Josh knew that there was more to the visit than that, but he held his tongue. "Sure. Miss Tran here lives just off of Ham Nghi Blvd."

"I know. She told General Irwin before you went out looking for Lieutenant Landry. Hop in – we'll give you a lift."

Kim-Ly looked to Josh, who opened his hands in surrender. "Okay with me."

"Thank you. That would be very much appreciated," Kim-Ly said to Winshotz.

No sooner had they taken their seats in the open top green Jeep then the major turned and began to talk to Josh.

"So, I understand that Landry is pretty out of it. Is that about how you'd describe him?"

A twinge of unease twisted his guts. "He's... been better."

"Were you aware of any drug use – pot, LSD, anything like that?"

The twinge flared into a flame of anger. "What is this?! Landry has combat fatigue, like ten thousand other GIs."

"Okay, okay," Winshotz calmed, "take it easy. We're just trying to identify a possible defense for the lieutenant."

"Defense? Defense of what?"

Josh saw the major work to settle his expression. "He's going to be charged with desertion."

"What?! Driver, stop the Jeep!" Josh yelled at the corporal behind the wheel. The vehicle came to a head-jerking stop. "What the hell are you talking about?!" he yelled at the major. "Landry is ill – any fool can see that."

"He left his post without permission and did not return for an extended period of time. In fact, he showed no intention of returning."

"He's a fucking vegetable!" Josh cried out, his face a deep shade of red. "He had no intentions of doing *anything!*"

"He'll have a chance to defend himself," Winshotz said.

"He can't even swallow water! How the hell will he defend himself?"

"Calm down, Captain!" the major said, his tone more an order than a request. "Our doctors will fix him up."

"Oh sure they will. And after that they'll cure cancer."

Kim-Ly put hand on his knee. He glanced at her but turned immediately back to the major. "How can you people do this to him? He's been out there in the jungle more than any officer I know. He's been wounded twice – two Purple Hearts and a Bronze Star. And now you're going to court-martial him?"

"Soldiers cannot be allowed to leave their post without permission." The major seemed to be reciting the regulation. His heart wasn't in it.

"Ah, now I get it," Josh went on. "You're out here because General Irwin didn't have the guts to tell me himself. He sent you to deliver the message."

"Generals don't deliver messages to captains," Winshotz said calmly. "Majors do."

Josh stared at his superior officer for several long seconds. Then he grabbed Kim-Ly by the arm and pulled her out of the Jeep. "Come on – we're out of here."

"Captain…"

Kim-Ly turned to the major with an apologetic look, but Josh had no such inclination. "Tell Irwin that this was chickenshit, sending you to tell me about Landry," he shouted back over his shoulder as he half-dragged Kim-Ly in his wake. "And the charges are chickenshit too!"

Winshotz sat motionless for nearly a minute, watching Josh and Kim-Ly storm off into the crowded streets of Saigon. Not until they disappeared from view did he quietly order the corporal to return to MACV Headquarters.

*****

"If they think I'm just going to stand by while they screw with Landry, they've got another thing coming!" Josh raged as he paced back and forth in Kim-Ly's apartment. She'd never seen him so upset. "They're going to be sorry they ever pulled this crap."

"Will you contact your father?"

Her question stopped him in his tracks. His thoughts hadn't carried him that far.

"I don't know. Maybe."

"Why not? You said he is a big politician. Couldn't he help?"

Josh had to collect his thoughts. How could he explain?

"It's complicated. My father is… difficult."

"But if he can help?"

Josh closed his eyes for just a moment. The very thought of asking the Colonel to intercede made him ill. But it was for Landry…

"Yeh, all right, maybe I will. If it's absolutely necessary. But first I'm going to General Edwards. He knows everybody. He might be able to pull a few strings."

Kim-Ly put her arms around his waist and leaned her head on his chest.

CHAPTER 19

"He abandoned his post."

General Edwards' words were matter-of-fact, emotionless. To him it was purely a question of the regs. Josh stood at-ease in front of the MACV Commander's desk, his face drawn and eyes rimmed with red from lack of sleep.

"He's sick, General. Combat fatigue. The Docs can confirm it."

Edwards looked up at the young captain, his face revealing nothing. "Daniels, I've got a stack of Article 85 and 86s as high as this desk, and every one of them claims he's got combat fatigue. It's an epidemic, Captain, and we can't allow it to spread. We've received orders from Washington to prosecute every soldier absent without leave. Your buddy was AWOL, pure and simple."

"But…"

The general held up his hand. "I'm sorry, Daniels. Best thing you can do for him now is get him a good civilian lawyer."

"Over here?"

"There are a few, I'm told."

Josh bit his tongue. "Do you happen to know the name of any of those lawyers?"

"I don't. But Major Winshotz might. Give him a call."

"Yes sir. I'll do that. Thank you sir." Josh snapped to attention and saluted.

Edwards nodded. "We need to see this thing through, Josh. Some people may get hurt in the process."

"Yes sir."

"Go talk to Max. He'll set you on the right track if anyone can."

As Josh left the general's office he felt acid rise in the back of his throat.

*****

"So, have you cooled down since yesterday?" Major Winshotz asked as Josh entered his office.

"Yes sir. I apologize for that. I was upset."

"Yeh, I could see that. I'm sorry I had to deliver the message, Daniels, but we've got orders from Washington."

"General Edwards told me. He also said you might know some civvy lawyers who could help Landry's defense?"

"A few. But they charge."

"We'll find the money."

The major eyed him as though debating what to say next. "Captain, it's going to be a tough fight. I've already seen depositions from some men in his platoon saying he'd been bad-mouthing the War for months - criticizing everyone up to and including LBJ. And they saw him in the field, giving orders, as recently as the day before he left his post."

"He's sick! He didn't know what he was doing."

"He'll have the opportunity to convince the judges."

"Does it have to come to that? Can't he just get the treatment he needs?"

The major leaned back in his chair and crossed his arms. "Desertion is a serious charge, Captain. From what I understand he'll have to show the panel that he was unable to distinguish between right and wrong when he walked away from his platoon."

"He'll have to *prove* that?!" Josh felt the hairs on the back of his neck stand up.

"I'm afraid so. They've decided to make an example of him. Bad luck."

Josh felt the blood pound in his temples. *'Bad luck?!'* He wanted to scream, but Winshotz was a friend, or at least a sympathetic ear. "Yeh. So, can you give me that lawyer's name?"

When Josh left the XO's office five minutes later, he felt like a drowning man hanging on to a life preserver with one hand. It was not a pleasant sensation.

*****

By the time Josh arrived at Kim-Ly's apartment, he was exhausted. He'd spent the whole day chasing down the lawyer Winshotz had recommended, trying to contact his father to arrange a loan to pay the lawyer, and talking to a JAG captain who had experience in cases of desertion. One thing had become perfectly clear: Landry was in deep shit.

He'd called Kim-Ly in mid-afternoon to suggest they put off their date; he wasn't feeling much like socializing. But she insisted. Instead of going out, however, she had invited him to a home-cooked dinner at her place.

"You don't look so good," she greeted him at the door before giving him a quick kiss and hug. "Come, come."

"Been a rough day," he said, taking the glass of wine she offered and flopping down on the black leather sofa in the living room.

"So I understood from your call. How can the Army not understand Landry's situation? Can't they see he is sick?"

Josh shook his head sadly. "They don't care. They need a poster boy to put the fear of God into all the grunts who are having second thoughts about the War, and Landry pulled the short straw."

"Short straw?"

Josh smiled in spite of himself. Sometimes he almost forgot that English wasn't Kim-Ly's first language. "He got unlucky. His case came up just when they were looking for someone to make an example of."

"But it is obvious that he is ill."

"Yeh. Now. But they're going to claim he knew what he was doing when he walked away from his post. They'll say that any mental changes came *after* he'd deserted."

"Did you find that lawyer you were looking for?"

"Yeh, I found him. He wasn't overly optimistic. He basically said that the system is rigged – the Army has all the advantages."

"Will he work with Landry?"

"Oh sure – if we can get the money. Five grand, and that's just for starters." To her questioning look he explained, "Five thousand dollars up front. Possibly more if it goes to appeal."

"Does his family have that much money?"

"I don't know. Maybe not. But I haven't told his parents."

"Why not?! Certainly they would want to help their son."

Josh closed his eyes for just a moment. "Mason is their golden boy, their pride and joy. I can't be the one to give them the news."

"Wouldn't it be better than hearing it from the Army?"

Josh winced. She was right, of course. He'd been delaying, justifying, hoping to avoid the onerous task. But he owed them that much. "Yeh, you're right. I'll call when I get back to base."

The pain of the decision reflected in his eyes. Kim-Ly took the wine glass from his hand and stroked the side of his face. "You are a good man, Josh Daniels. Landry is fortunate to have you as his friend."

"I'm not so sure," Josh said in a whisper. "Would he even be here if it weren't for me? Would he even have stayed at the Academy?"

Instead of answering, Kim-Ly leaned in and kissed him deeply. He started to say something, but she held her finger to his lips.

"No. Don't talk, come." She took his hand and led him toward her bedroom.

"Your father…"

"Will be playing cards until late."

She closed the door behind them.

*****

By the time Josh returned to base, it was late – nearly midnight. It would be noon back in Texas. Since it was a Saturday, perhaps Landry's Dad would be home. He hoped so. He didn't think he could break the news to his mother.

The phone rang four times. Mr. Landry answered.

"Hello?" His voice seemed older than Josh remembered. Tired.

"Mr. Landry?"

"Yes…"

"Mr. Landry this is Josh Daniels – I'm calling from Saigon."

Silence. "Please don't tell me you have bad news." His voice was even slower, more tentative.

"Not that kind of bad news," Josh answered, aware of what he must be thinking.

"Then what kind?"

"Well, you see, Mason, well, he's got some legal problems. With the Army."

"Legal problems? What kind of legal problems?"

Josh clenched and unclenched his fist. "The Army may court-martial him."

More silence. In the background Landry's Mom asked her husband what was going on. "And what does that mean, exactly?" he asked Josh.

"Well, Landry was having some problems with his platoon here in Vietnam, and the Army thinks he left his post without permission." He couldn't bring himself to use the 'd' word.

"But, Mason's been a platoon leader for the better part of a year," Mr. Landry argued. "They even gave him a Purple Heart."

"Yes, that's right. But, you see, this War is a nasty piece of business, Mr. Landry. And every day you're here you see things, and sometimes have to do things, that are hard. Real hard. It seems like Landry had enough. Too much." As the words come out of his mouth, Josh couldn't help but wonder if they pertained as much to him as his friend.

"So, is it bad, this court-martial?"

Josh knew that Mr. Landry had never served in the military. He doubted he could possibly explain the details of the military justice system to his friend's father over the phone.

"It's pretty bad," he said instead. "We're trying to get him a good lawyer."

"But Mason wouldn't do anything bad," Mr. Landry said. "He's a good kid."

"He's a very good kid," Josh answered. "But the Army thinks he did something wrong."

Long, slow breaths at the other end of the line. A long pause. "What should we do?" he asked. He sounded determined. "How can we help?"

Josh had expected the question. "Call your congressman. Tell him your son is being court-martialed, and you want to be sure he gets a fair trial." There really wasn't too much else they could do. Except... "And send him a message – maybe a telegram. Tell him you believe in him and are behind him all the way."

"What about the lawyer? He doesn't have much money to pay a good lawyer."

"Don't worry about that right now. Some of his friends here are taking care of that." He didn't want them getting a second mortgage on their house, or anything else that would threaten their family. He would convince his father to help; he had to.

"Does he have a lot of friends?"

A lump swelled up in Josh's throat. "Yeh, sure thing Mr. Landry. Your boy's got lots of friends." Truth was, he wasn't sure. He always assumed Landry had a lot of friends, but he didn't really see him often enough to know for sure. Thing was, Josh didn't have that many friends himself, aside from Landry. Not too many at all.

By the time Mr. Landry hung up, the older man seemed slightly more settled. He understood the basic charges, knew that Josh was trying to get his son a lawyer, and had a game plan for his wife and himself. His voice was stronger; his attitude defiant.

"We'll show those military people that Mason didn't do anything wrong," he said just before disconnecting. "They'll see."

Josh just hoped he was right.

*****

Josh had planned to call his father as soon as he'd finished talking with Landry's dad, but he decided he needed a quick pick-me-up before he tackled the Colonel. He went over to the Officers' Club, expecting it to be somewhat subdued at that late hour. He was wrong. The place was jumping, with the jukebox blaring, a game of darts eliciting shouts more appropriate to a football game, and soldiers two deep at the bar.

He hoped to just slide in, get his drink and leave, but no sooner did he step inside than one of his fellow planning team members, another Captain just a year older than he, spotted him and yelled out a greeting: "Daniels! What are you doing up at this hour? Come on over! We need some new blood in this conversation."

Josh winced but knew he needed to make an appearance or risk alienating the obviously inebriated captain. He ordered a scotch on the rocks – a drink he'd just recently developed a taste for – and made his way over to the table where Captain Scott and three other officers engaged in a drunken debate.

"There you are! How they hangin' Daniels?"

"Couldn't sleep. Just stopped by for a drink," he said, keeping his tone subdued and noncommittal.

"Ah, needed a liquid sleeping pill, eh? I know that one! Guys, this is Captain Josh Daniels, probably the youngest captain in 'Nam and one of the sharpest tacks in the MACV planning meeting." He introduced Josh to a First Lieutenant, another captain and a major. Josh shook hands without enthusiasm. "Have a seat, have a seat," Scott insisted, pulling over a chair from a nearby table.

"I'm just here for a couple of minutes," he tried to explain, but Scott wasn't having any of it.

"So, this is what we're arguing about," he plowed ahead. "Ripley here thinks we shouldn't be tossing VC prisoners out of helicopters if they refuse to answer our questions. We say fuck'em, if they won't talk, they walk."

"Or fly," the major said with a drunken grin.

Everyone, except Ripley, laughed.

"What's your take, Daniels? You know what all those bastards back in Washington are thinking." He turned to the other officers at the table and put his hand up as though whispering a great secret. "His Dad's a congressman."

The other three looked to Josh as if he'd suddenly grown another head.

"You're shitting me," the lieutenant said. "What the hell are you doing here if you've got that kind of pull in DC?"

"Good for you!" the other captain said so loudly Josh wondered if he were just saying it for his benefit. "If we had more kids here who were sons of the bastards running this War, you can bet it'd be over before you could say 'body bag.'"

There was nothing Josh wanted to do less right then than join in on their drunken debate. But he'd sat down with them; he had to say something.

"I don't talk all that often with my Father," he found himself saying.

The men laughed. "No shit! What's the problem – different outlook on the War?"

"Yeh, you could say that."

His admission won him the admiration of the other four, who forgot about throwing prisoners out of helicopters and turned to what it was like being a congressman's son. After about five minutes of deflecting their questions, Josh had had enough.

"Speaking of my father, I need to give him a call," he announced in the middle of a discussion of why politicians' kids never seemed to get drafted.

"Got to give him the latest scoop, eh Daniels?" Ripley asked.

Josh went with the flow. "You might say that. Gotta make sure the politicians hear the real poop every now and then." Everyone agreed.

It took him a few more minutes to extricate himself from his new-found friends, but finally, after a round of back slapping and offers of another drink (that he firmly, and repeatedly turned down), he managed to push his way through the crowd and out into the early morning darkness.

The night air wasn't cool by any means, but compared to the sweatbox inside the bar, it was refreshing. At that point, it was exactly what he needed. The buzz from the alcohol had kicked in big-time, augmented by his exhaustion and the strain of Landry's predicament. He blinked to clear the blur from his vision and stumbled back to his quarters without encountering anyone who might recognize the normally staid and controlled officer.

He flipped on the lights and flopped down on his bed, silently cursing his idea to 'relax' by having a drink. He splashed cold water on his face and engaged in a couple of minutes of calisthenics to try to regain his knife's edge, but finally had to settle for a butter knife.

As the phone rang his stomach engaged in calisthenics of its own. It was his younger brother who answered.

"Josh! What's going on, man? When are they sending you home on vacation, or whatever they call it?"

Josh grit his teeth and forced himself to smile. "No vacation just yet, Kyle. Hey, is Dad home?"

"Yeh, he's here," the younger brother said with a distinct lack of enthusiasm that told Josh just how well things were going between those two.

"Can I talk to him?"

A pause. "You *want* to talk to him?"

"Yeh, sure. I've got something… important I need to discuss with him."

"You okay?"

Josh felt his brother's concern through 6000 miles of telephone lines.

"Yeh, I'm good. You?"

"Okay. Pretty sick of school, but who isn't, right?"

"Let me tell you, Kyle, it's a hell of a lot better than what's out here. Stay in school as long as you can." He wasn't sounding like the gung-ho Ranger he was supposed to be, but screw it. He was tired of being that person.

"What happened?" Even though Kyle was six years younger, the kid always could read Josh pretty accurately.

"Nothing. It's all okay. Just tell Dad I need to talk to him."

"Yeh, okay. Let me get him. And Josh? Take care."

"Will do. You too."

The phone rattled on the kitchen counter and then the voices of his parents came through in the distant background. A few seconds later the phone returned to life.

"Josh! Are you okay?" His father must've picked up on Kyle's unease.

"Yeh, yeh I'm fine Dad. But I need a favor."

"What's going on?"

Josh took a deep breath and focused on a photo of the whole family he kept on a side table. "Landry's in trouble."

Once he got that out, the rest poured out of him like a monsoon rain. The Colonel listened without another word, only interrupting for clarification. When Josh finished the whole sorry tale, he waited anxiously for his father's reply.

"So let me get this straight: Landry's probably going to be court-martialed, for desertion, and you want me to put up the money to hire him a lawyer. Is that about right?"

When his father explained it that way, he cringed. The Colonel was a politician. His life's blood was good press. Supporting a deserter, even at a distance, could cause him big problems with his conservative base. He shut his eyes tight.

"Yeh. That's about it."

"Jesus, Josh. You don't make it easy, do you?" Josh didn't know what to say, so he kept silent. He listened to his heart beat for what seemed like an hour. "I take it you don't think he's guilty?"

He exhaled. "Like I said, he's sick. I've seen guys with combat fatigue, and he's got it. Bad."

"Yeh. Alright. This is going to make a stink back here among some of my supporters, but like they say, if they can't take a joke…"

Josh wasn't sure he understood. "You mean…?"

"I mean I'll get you the five thousand for his lawyer. And if he needs more, we'll figure out a way. I always liked that kid."

"We'll pay you back, Dad. It might take a while…"

"We can talk about that once he's past these charges. For now, just tell me who to send the money to, at what address."

By the time he hung up the phone, Josh was stone-cold sober. He lay back on his bed, still buzzing from the adrenaline rush the call had generated. *His father had backed him, and in a situation that could turn nasty!*

It took a while, but he eventually fell asleep, his dreams a lighter shade of gray than in recent days.

CHAPTER 20

The next morning, after the daily planning meeting, Josh got permission to visit Landry at his medical holding facility. In essence, it was a prison hospital.

The building, tucked away in a corner of the Air Base, looked neither like a hospital nor a prison – more like a warehouse. The drab green exterior had few windows, and most of those were tiny slits high up on the concrete block walls. A chain link fence topped by concertina wire encircled the entire building, and an armed guard stood watch at the main entrance. It didn't look like a good place to be recuperating, Josh thought as he showed his ID to the guard at the entrance.

He had to present his ID a second time just inside the building at a reception desk manned by two young American women. An MP stood guard just behind them.

They directed him to 'the psych wing,' a long dimly-lit corridor of locked doors that reeked with a heady combination of urine, cleaning products and puke. He swallowed repeatedly to get past the first blast of stench, his stomach knotting and unknotting with each step. Carl, a big black dude wearing a blue medical uniform, accompanied him to Landry's room.

"You a friend?" the aide asked as he fumbled with a keychain trying to find the key to Landry's door.

"Went to West Point together."

"That guy went to West Point?" The way he said it made Josh's skin crawl.

"Yeh. Why?"

The aide shook his head. "No reason. It's just… when they get this way it's hard to remember they were ever different." He opened the door and stepped aside to let Josh enter. "I'll be right outside. Call out if you need help."

Josh thanked him and stepped into the darkened room with nerves jangling. He could see a body lying on a cot in the small cell-like room, but couldn't make out any features in the medicinal gloom.

"Hey, Landry, you awake? It's me, Daniels," he whispered. No reply. Josh walked to the side of the cot with such a strong sense of foreboding that perspiration began to bead up on his forehead.

"Hey man, how're they treating you?"

He looked down at his friend and his heart nearly stopped. Landry stared blankly into nothingness, spittle bubbling up at the corners of his mouth.

"Landry, Landry it's me!" he repeated, louder this time. He rested his hand on his friend's shoulder and shook him lightly. Landry didn't even blink.

"Hey, Carl, come in here!" he yelled to the aide out in the hallway.

"What?! What's going on?!" Carl answered anxiously as he rushed into the room.

"What the hell have they done to him?!" Josh asked, his voice nearly cracking. "He's a vegetable!"

"All right, all right, calm down," the aide soothed. "This is how it's done with guys like him. They keep them medicated for a while, until they can stabilize them a little."

"Stabilize?! They've turned him into a fucking zombie!"

"Yeh, well they'll gradually ease up on the medicine. He'll start coming out of it in a few days."

"A few days!? Fuck that! Who's in charge in this place?"

"Colonel Lesser is the CO," Carl said. "But good luck getting to him."

"We'll see about that. Come on, show me where his office is." Josh didn't wait for a response, but turned and stormed out of the room. The aide followed close behind, stopping only to re-lock Landry's door.

The colonel's office was hidden behind a hardline of wire reinforced glass and thick steel doors. An orderly even bigger than Carl stood guard.

"Something I can do for you, soldier?" the orderly called out as Daniels and the aide approached. It was clear from the look on the captain's face he was going to be trouble.

"I want to see the colonel!" Josh demanded before he even came to a stop. "Lesser – I want to talk to him!"

"The captain has some questions about Lieutenant Landry in D-417," Carl tried to mediate. The orderly wasn't having any of it.

"You have an appointment?" he asked.

"No I don't have a fucking appointment!" Josh exploded. "But I need to see Colonel Lesser!"

The expression on the orderly's face turned from professional disinterest to cold, hard dismissal. "No appointment, no chance," he said.

"Listen, asshole, my buddy is stuck in this prison for something that's not his fault and he's being drugged to keep him quiet!" Josh growled. "I'm not leaving without talking to the colonel!"

"Soldier, if you're not out of here in one minute I'll be calling the MPs and you can explain to them why you're causing a disturbance in this hospital," the orderly snapped.

"Go ahead – call 'em! I don't give a damn what you do, I'm going to talk to Lesser!"

Just then an electric lock buzzed and the solid metal door next to the reception desk swung open.

"It's *Colonel* Lesser, Captain," a wiry officer nearly as tall as Josh with close-cropped grey hair said as he stepped between Josh and the orderly. "And I suggest you lower your voice if you don't want to spend a day or two in the brig. We have some very sick people in here."

"Colonel, I'm sorry. It's just… they have my buddy drugged up and they're talking about bringing charges for desertion, and I know damn well he's not guilty…"

"Okay, okay, calm down Captain." He stared at Josh as if trying to see inside him. "You think you can control your temper long enough to talk about it?"

Josh took a deep breath. "Yes sir, I think I can."

"All right. Come on in, then." He turned to the orderly. "Atkins, if you hear any more screaming coming from my office, you call the MPs first and then come running. Got it?"

"My pleasure, Colonel." The orderly stared at Josh as if he wanted to tear his head off.

Josh ignored him, nodded to Carl – who looked like he might throw up, and followed the colonel back to his office. It was a small room, sparsely furnished with a beat-up old desk, a couch that had seen better days, and a couple of drab green filing cabinets.

"Have a seat, Captain." Josh did as he was directed while the colonel slid into the high-backed chair behind the desk. "What's your name?"

"Daniels, sir. Joshua A."

"Well Captain Daniels, that was one half-ass demonstration I witnessed out there in the corridor. I take it you have an explanation?"

"I'm sorry, sir. I... lost my temper."

"You lost your mind," the colonel said matter-of-factly as he eased back into the chair. "And you might've lost your freedom for a couple of days. This is a hospital, Captain, not the field."

"I understand, sir. And, like I said, I'm sorry for my outburst."

"Yes, well, let's hear what was so important you thought you could just bully your way in here."

Josh took a deep breath and started from the beginning. As he spoke he watched the colonel's face, hoping to find a clue to his thinking. Lesser nodded, raised his eyebrows, pursed his lips, but it was impossible to read the conclusions behind the expressions. When he came to the end of his story, Josh still didn't know if he'd made his point or not.

"And so Lieutenant Landry is sitting in D-417, drugged so heavily he can't do much more than drool, with a court-martial coming up in anything from a few weeks to a month," he closed. "He won't even know where he is, let alone be able to participate in his own defense."

He thought about asking the colonel directly for his help, but decided to let the officer come to his own conclusions.

He didn't have to wait long. "So, what do you want from me?" the hospital CO asked. "Obviously you have something in mind."

Josh fidgeted, gripping his armrest tightly. What he said next could determine not only Landry's future, but his own as well. There was no other way: he went for it. "Colonel, I have reason to believe that the powers-that-be intend to make an example out of Lieutenant Landry — to try to cut down on all the AWOLs and desertions they've been getting lately."

"And?"

"And I don't think they particularly give a damn whether Landry's guilty or not. I think they're out to make a point."

Lesser leaned forward in his seat. "That's a pretty serious charge, Captain. What, exactly, do you base it on?"

"Colonel, I work at MACV. I hear a lot of things, some of which are confidential."

"So you can't tell me where you got your info, just that it comes from people who should know – is that about right?"

Josh nodded. "Yeh, that's about it."

For several long seconds the colonel looked directly into Josh's eyes. What he was looking for, Josh could only guess.

"So, you want me to help get your buddy ready for the court-martial so he can testify to his... what? Innocence?"

"I want him to be able to tell them what happened. That's all. If he says he walked away from his post, so be it. But I know this guy, Colonel. I went to school with him. He isn't the kind of person to desert."

"This war changes people, Daniels. Sometimes changes them a lot."

"I know that, sir." He fought the urge to explain how much the War had changed *him*, but in the end kept silent. "But even if it's true, even if I don't know the man you've got all trussed up back there in his cell..."

"Room."

"Call it what you will, he deserves a chance. I owe him that. We all owe him that."

The colonel nodded minutely, and a charge of hope ran through Josh.

"Captain, despite its bars and locked doors, this is a hospital," Lesser began. "We try to make people healthy again – body *and* mind. I've read your friend's file. He's got problems. You know that. But we've had other soldiers in here with symptoms just as bad, maybe worse. Now I can't tell you we can cure your friend. I don't know yet if anything can do that. But I do know that we will try. I promise you that. And nobody, not from MACV or anywhere else, is going to tell us how to do our job." The colonel's face was red, his eyes narrowed. "If we have it in our power to make Lieutenant Landry whole again, we will do it."

Josh was struck dumb. He didn't have the words to express his feelings, so he jumped to his feet and snapped to attention. "Thank you, sir."

"You know, Daniels, that could be you, or me in that room," Lesser continued, his voice softer, more contemplative. "I know what I'd want, what I'd *expect* from the Army. And that's what Landry will get. Now get your ass out of my office and get to work helping that soldier defend himself."

Josh saluted and turned on his heel to leave. The last thing he saw before the door shut behind him was Colonel Lesser, staring thoughtfully out the small window behind his desk.

*****

The days passed in a mad rush, with Josh – helped by Kim-Ly and several GIs from Landry's platoon – struggling to collect information and testimony about Landry's unauthorized absence from post while still maintaining their normal duties and activities. A deposit of $5000 had arrived at the lawyer's bank as promised, and the lawyer, Tim Jacobs, was hard at work coordinating the defense strategy. He'd already taken sworn depositions from several grunts in Landry's platoon as well as from his company and division commanders. The one major detail still unaddressed was the lieutenant's mental state – both then and now. Jacobs had lined up psychiatric specialists in the Army and in the States who would testify that soldiers exposed to gruesome battlefield scenes were especially susceptible to combat fatigue: a generic term that amounted to a mental breakdown caused by war. The one troubling aspect of the expert testimony was that all the shrinks – private and military alike – agreed that the long-term impact of such a breakdown was unpredictable. Soldiers could bounce back in a matter of weeks, or they might never recover. There were stories of some WWII vets who still found it difficult to sleep at night and function in normal society – 30 years after their last combat experience!

True to his word, Colonel Lesser had ordered that Landry be weaned off of the painkillers and anti-depressants that had turned him into a drooling lump, and word from the hospital was that the young lieutenant was showing signs of recovering at least some of his previous acuity. Josh was chomping at the bit to visit his friend, but the medical staff was keeping him off-limits until they were confident he had stabilized and was headed in the right direction. Everything seemed to be coming together for the defense team, and so for Landry, until one afternoon some three weeks after he'd arrived at the hospital.

Josh was called into General Edwards' office right after the morning planning meeting. Josh didn't think anything of it, since he and the general frequently talked about strategic and political aspects of the War. So he was completely unprepared for the general's tack when Edwards brought up Landry's situation.

"So, Daniels, word has it you and your friends have put together a pretty good team to help defend your buddy, Landry."

Josh experienced a jolt of unease, but decided he was just being paranoid. "Yes, sir. His lawyer thinks he's got a good chance to beat the charges."

The general nodded. "You know, sometimes things like this are more... complicated than they appear. Sometimes what's good for the individual soldier isn't always good for the Army – or the country."

Josh couldn't keep the skepticism from his face. "How's that, General?"

"Well, sometimes what's good for one soldier isn't exactly what's good for us all. You can understand that, can't you son?"

"I'm not sure I can," Josh answered, sitting up more stiffly in his chair.

"Look, Daniels, you know we've got a big problem with soldiers going AWOL and, to a lesser degree, deserting. The media back in the States have gotten wind of the situation – there've been questions at Pentagon press briefings, and in personal interviews. And now the politicians are getting in on the act." He paused. "I don't mean to suggest that all politicians are out to make the Army look bad…"

"Don't worry, sir. I understand. But what does this have to do with Landry?" He knew damn well what it had to do with his friend, but he wanted to hear Edwards say it out loud. The general wouldn't get off that easy.

"The folks in the White House want us to make an example out of someone, to show we're serious about not letting any soldier shirk his – or her – responsibility. They want action – now. And Landry is their poster boy."

Josh lost it. "Landry is nobody's *poster boy*," he said with more vehemence than he should have. "He's just a sick soldier who needs medical treatment – not a court-martial."

A flicker of anger swept across the General's face, a reaction that disappeared as quickly as it materialized. "This isn't going to be a problem, is it Daniels?"

"No problem, sir. Unless someone intends to *make an example* out of Landry. In that case, yeh, there may be a problem."

Edwards stared at Josh long and hard. "You're a good officer, Daniels. I wouldn't want to see your career in the Army *impacted* by a personal situation."

Impacted. Situation. Josh didn't like the way the general expressed himself. But he knew better than to let his anger get him any deeper in trouble than it already had. He choked down his initial response and instead merely nodded. "I appreciate that, sir."

Edwards stared as if deciding whether to continue his harangue. He apparently decided against it. "Good. Then we're both on the same wavelength." He paused. "I'll ask around, see if I can find out who'll be sitting on the court-martial. Might be a help to the lieutenant."

Josh was taken aback. "Thanks, General. That would be... appreciated."

"Not a problem. And Captain?"

"Yes sir?"

"Just because the politicians want a poster boy, doesn't mean I want a kangaroo court. If this friend of yours is not a deserter, then he'll walk free. Understood?"

Josh managed a shaken nod. "Yes, sir. Thank you, sir."

"The Army needs men willing to stand up for their buddies, Captain. Now get out of here and go finish organizing his defense."

Edwards didn't even wait for Josh to leave, but turned back to the pile of papers on his desk and set to work plowing through them. As Josh left the office he couldn't help but wonder whether the officers on Landry's court-martial would have any of the common sense and integrity of the officer he'd just addressed. He could only hope so.

*****

"Are you getting enough sleep?" Kim-Ly asked as she worked to loosen the knots in Josh's shoulders. "You will not be able to help Landry if you become sick."

"I sleep," he said. "Maybe not as much as I'd like, but that's nothing new."

"Have they scheduled the court-martial?"

"Not yet. Could be any time, though."

When he'd first met Kim-Ly, her apartment had become something of a refuge, the one place he could go to get away from the War, if only for a short while. But as the date for Landry's trial came closer, not even that refuge could block the constant stream of questions, and strategies, and doubts that plagued him from morning 'til night, even in his sleep. Kim-Ly wouldn't give up, however, trying to distract, or dissuade him from worrying so much.

"You are as tight as a drum," she said, trying out one of her new-found English expressions. "Would you like a drink?"

He would've accepted gladly, but he'd been reaching for that crutch a little too frequently lately. "No, thanks."

"Something to eat?"

Josh grabbed her hand and gently pulled her around to sit on his lap. "Have I told you lately what an amazing woman you are?" He wrapped his arms around her and held her tight.

She smiled. "Not lately."

"Well, you are. And if I forget to tell you as often as I should, don't you think for one minute that I've forgotten."

"They say it is better to show than tell," she said, her smile widening.

"Oh?"

She disengaged herself from his embrace, stood, and took his hand to pull him up out of the chair. "Show me," she said, and she led him back to her bedroom.

CHAPTER 21

When Josh came into the strategy planning meeting at MACV, he thought at first he'd wandered into the wrong room. There were bottles of champagne and whisky scattered from one end of the long wooden table to the other, and the room buzzed with electricity. He'd just gotten back from Kim-Ly's and come straight to the MACV headquarters; a party was the last thing he expected.

Colonel Henry saw him standing slack-jawed at the doorway to the meeting room and called over to him.

"Hey Daniels, come join us for a drink! Did you hear – Uncle Ho is dead! The old bastard finally kicked the bucket!" A small cheer went up from the assembled officers.

"Ho is dead?" Josh asked, the import of the fact slowly making its way into his consciousness.

"As a doornail. It's been confirmed."

Henry handed him a paper cup of champagne. "To Old Man Ho – may he rot in hell!"

Josh took a sip of the lukewarm sparkly. "So, what does this mean as far as the War?" he asked the colonel as soon as the cheering died down. "Does it make any difference?"

"Exactly what I want to discuss this morning," General Edwards bellowed as he strolled into the room.

"Atten-shun!" Josh called out, and the officers jumped to attention.

"At ease, at ease," Edwards ordered as he eased into his chair. For the next four hours the group discussed the implications of the death of the enemy leader, everything from the effect on morale to whether a major offensive would be warranted because of the possible impact of Ho's death on North Vietnamese strategy. Debate was spirited, but Josh said little. His thoughts were focused on whether the bigger changes would somehow trickle down to Landry. Perhaps the bigshots in DC wouldn't be so adamant about prosecuting him if they thought the War was winding down. Maybe they'd let Landry go with a medical discharge. Maybe…

"You weren't very talkative today, Daniels," Colonel Henry interrupted his reverie as the meeting was breaking up. "That's not like you. What's going on?"

Josh shrugged. "Got a lot on my mind."

"How's it going with your buddy's defense?"

Josh rarely discussed Landry's legal problems with his fellow MACV staffers, but he understood that everyone at the table knew full well what was happening.

"Okay. I mean, I think we've got a pretty good chance of showing the court-martial that his problems are medical, and he had no plan to desert. I'm not even sure if he realized he was walking off his post."

"Poor bastard. I've seen a few dozen just like him during the two years I've been over here. Something just pushes the wrong button."

Josh understood the colonel was trying to be a good guy, but he didn't want to talk about it anymore. He *really* didn't.

"I'm sure it'll work out ok, Colonel," he interrupted. "He's a good man."

Henry stopped and exhaled deeply. "Yeh. Most of 'em are. Well, good luck, Daniels. We're all pulling for you."

'Most of you, anyway,' Josh thought. "Thank you, sir," he said.

By the time Josh left MACV headquarters and made his way back to his quarters, he was feeling the letdown that inevitably follows early morning champagne. He had a short while before he was scheduled for other duties and considered taking a quick nap. But when he got to his room he found a note pinned to his door.

'Landry's coming out of it,' the note read. 'Get over here as soon as you can.' It was signed by Colonel Lesser.

A bolt of adrenaline shot through Josh; he jogged over to the hospital complex despite the steaming hot temperature. Apparently Lesser had notified his people that Josh was expected, since he wasn't put through the usual processing but was shown straight through to the colonel's office.

"Daniels! You got my message?" the colonel asked as soon as Josh stepped through his door.

"I did. Thank you, sir. So Landry's conscious?"

"Off and on," the colonel explained. "But when he's with us he's responding to directions, and he asked for you."

Josh almost screamed for joy. "He *asked* for me?"

"I know, I know. It's a minor miracle. But now that we've eased him off the drugs, he seems to be bouncing back."

"Can I see him?"

"Actually, that's the subject of a very lively debate among our staff members. Some think it would do him good to see a familiar face; others think it might set him back."

"What do you think?"

The colonel hesitated. "I think I'd want to see a friend if I were in his place."

"So I can see him?"

"Yes, yes you can. Just for a few minutes, nothing about the court-martial or anything else that might get him agitated. Agreed?"

"Agreed."

"All right. Let's go take a look."

"You're coming?"

"I'm a doctor, Captain. My interest in our patients is more than just bureaucratic."

"I didn't mean to suggest…" Josh began, his face reddening.

"Don't worry about it," Lesser waved him off. "I realize full-well how we Army doctors are seen by many of the men. But I can tell you for a fact that there are a lot of good docs in the military, Daniels. Not all, but a lot."

Josh felt embarrassed. "I'm sure there are," was all he managed to reply.

As he followed the colonel through the dimly lit corridors of the hospital, Josh's heart began to beat faster. Would Landry recognize him? Did he understand his situation? What did he remember about leaving his post?

By the time they stopped at his friend's door, his stomach was tied up in knots.

"Remember, nothing to get him agitated," the colonel reminded.

"I remember."

When he stepped into the hospital room it took a second for his eyes to adjust to the even dimmer light in the tiny 12 x 12 foot box. As soon as he could see, Josh moved to the side of the bed where Landry lay unmoving, still strapped down, his eyes closed.

"Lieutenant Landry," Colonel Lesser said softly, "you have a visitor."

Landry's eyes fluttered open, blinking as if awakening from a deep sleep. At first he stared straight ahead, and Josh had the sinking sensation that the reports of his improvement might be exaggerated. But after less than ten seconds he turned his head slowly toward Josh and Lesser. His eyes opened a bit further.

"Josh?" he whispered through badly chapped lips.

"It's me, bro," Josh whispered back, his throat so tight he could barely speak. "How you doin'?"

A tiny smile appeared. "I've been better," Landry said.

"As your doctors have explained, Landry, you've been through a tough time," the colonel interrupted. "But you're on your way back. You're getting a little better every day."

"How long?" Landry asked.

"How long what? How long have you been here?"

The young lieutenant shook his head stiffly. "How long 'til I can get back to my platoon?"

Josh exchanged a questioning glance with Lesser. "We don't really know the answer to that one just yet," the colonel said. "We'll have to see how quickly you recuperate."

Landry nodded slowly as if digesting the information. "How 'bout the restraints?" he mouthed, each word a struggle. "When can I get my arms free?"

Lesser opened his hands to suggest his uncertainty. "I wouldn't think it'd be too long. I'll ask your doctors – how's that?"

"Appreciate it."

For several long seconds none of the men said a word. Then the colonel stepped back toward the door. "I'll leave you two to catch up. Just remember what I said, Captain."

"I will, sir. And thank you."

Lesser nodded. "You take care, Lieutenant. I expect to see you up and around before much longer."

Landry smiled wanly. "Hope so," he said.

As soon as the door closed, Josh turned back to his friend.

"How ya' feeling? You had us worried there."

Landry tried out a smile, but the lopsided smirk barely qualified. "Can't get rid of me that easy." He swallowed. "Josh, what the hell happened?" The pained look said it all.

"You don't remember?"

Landry shook his head. "It's kind'of fuzzy goin' back a ways."

"You were in some pretty heavy action," Josh ad-libbed. "Came out a little worse for wear. But the colonel says you're on the way back."

"Good, good," the lieutenant said, his eyes closing of their own accord.

"Is there anything you need? Anything I can get you?"

"Nice steak, medium raw?" He peeked out of the side of his eyes, his smile a bit broader.

"That may have to wait awhile. But anything else – candy, soda, any junk like that?"

Josh saw his friend's head jerk back as he fought sleep. "No, thanks," he managed.

"Well look, I can see you're tired. Let me get out of here just now, and I'll come back again later today or tomorrow. How'd that be?"

"That'd be fine, just fine," Landry drawled, on the verge of drifting off.

Josh didn't linger, but patted his friend on the shoulder and eased out of the room. He swung by Colonel Lesser's office, but the colonel wasn't in. He had some questions to ask, but they could wait. The main thing was that Landry was talking again, and making sense.

As soon as he could find a phone, Josh called Kim-Ly. She was on her way out to an interpreting job but immediately picked up on his improved mood.

"You have news?"

"Landry's awake and talking!" he explained.

"That is wonderful, Josh! We should go out tonight to celebrate."

He knew she was just trying to get him away from all the preparations for the court-martial, but he didn't care. For the first time in a long while, he felt like partying.

"Pick you up at 7:30?"

"Don't be late."

There was a little more bounce in his step as Josh left the hospital and headed off to take care of his daily activities. *'Maybe this whole mess will work out okay after all.'*

*****

A slight breeze cut through the steamy heat of the city as Josh made his way to Kim-Ly's apartment. He was in the best mood he'd been in since he'd heard of Landry's disappearance – perhaps longer. When Kim-Ly buzzed him in the front door to her building, he ran up the steps to her father's apartment.

"Someone is feeling better," she said as he emerged from the stairwell.

"My best friend is coming around, we've got his defense team pretty much all lined up, and I'm going out on the town with the most beautiful woman in all of Saigon. How bad can it be?"

"Just Saigon?" Kim-Ly asked with a seductive smile.

"Saigon, Vietnam, the whole darn universe!" he half-shouted.

He grabbed her tight and they kissed.

"You must not yell; Father is resting," she objected when they pulled apart, but only half-heartedly.

"Should we ask him to come celebrate with us?"

Kim-Ly looked at him as if he'd lost his mind. "I should get you out of here before you wake the entire building."

She had chosen a small, intimate restaurant just a few blocks from the apartment. With only nine or ten tables, it seemed an ideal spot to spend a quiet evening together, as far from the chaos and insanity of the War as possible. It was not.

They had been seated for just under an hour and were sipping after-dinner tea, when three American soldiers sauntered into the eatery. Josh looked up briefly; GIs were a staple at just about any decent eating or drinking establishment within several miles of the base. He had returned to his conversation, explaining to Kim-Ly some of the intricacies of the defense Landry's legal team was planning, when one of the soldiers called over to him.

"Hey, Captain, what 'ya up to to? Fraternizing with the enemy?" Drunken guffaws from his two companions.

Josh eyed the three closer. He didn't recognize them, but from their age and rank – all second lieutenants – he was pretty sure they were new arrivals. Probably from the Academy. Kim-Ly placed her hand on his forearm.

"Not worth the effort," she said softly.

"Maybe not," Josh answered, "but that never stopped me." He smiled at the three young lieutenants. "What brought you three downtown – you get lost trying to find your babysitter?"

Their sloppy, off-kilter smiles faded. "Actually, it was your Mama-san over there," one of the others called back. "She has three-for-one nights and we all chipped in to come up with a dollar for an hour with her." More laughs. This time the laughter was hard-edged.

"Josh, please," Kim-Ly plead quietly. "Let's go back to the apartment."

"Yeh, *Josh*," the first lieutenant sneered, "Mama-san's got some of that nice tight Vietnamese poontang she wants to share with you."

"Listen, *Lieutenant*," Josh said, standing to his full height and facing the three head-on, pronouncing the rank as if it were a swear word, "I think it's past your bedtime. You should be getting back to your quarters."

One of the officers spotted the name tag above Josh's right shirt pocket. "Daniels? You aren't that MACV guy who's been standing up for the deserter in the First, are you?"

"Yeh, that's who he is," the third officer chimed in. "A gook-lover and defender of traitors. Jesus, no wonder we're not winning this goddamn war."

Kim-Ly reached up to grab Josh's arm, but she was a second too slow. Before she could restrain him, Josh threw himself at the closest of the three with a furious roar. The two men crashed into the table and sent it tumbling onto its side, plates, glasses and silverware smashing loudly on the floor. The lieutenant's two buddies recovered quickly, grabbing Josh by his shoulders and pulling him off the screaming loudmouth. Kim-Ly yelled for help, and two young Vietnamese men came running out from the kitchen to enter the fray. In seconds nearly everyone in the restaurant had joined-in the massive brawl, with chairs and tables crashing, glass breaking, and bodies flying every which way.

It was only a few minutes before whistles shrieked and four MPs, their batons drawn and ready, came running into the restaurant. It took a short while and more than one barked order before all the parties could be separated. The MPs pulled Josh from the scrum with a bright red scrape just below his left eye and a bruise at his temple. And he was in better shape than most. One of the lieutenants had a bloody nose – probably broken – and another held his ribs as if they were badly bruised, or worse.

"What the hell is going on here?!" the senior MP demanded, his angry gaze directed at Josh.

"A misunderstanding, Sergeant," he answered straight-faced.

The MP turned to the three lieutenants. "Is that right – was it a 'misunderstanding?'"

"Yes, Sergeant," the three answered in near-unison.

"Who's the owner of this place?" the MP called out to the dozen or so Vietnamese who stood by watching the proceedings, chattering nervously.

Kim-Ly translated the request and then added more in the local language. An elderly man stepped forward.

"This man is the owner," Kim-Ly explained.

The MP eyed her suspiciously. "Tell him the U.S. Army apologizes for the inexcusable behavior of these four officers. And ask him if he wants to press charges."

Kim-Ly said something to the old man, who looked around his restaurant calmly surveying the damage. In fact, except for a handful of glasses and plates, the damage was minimal. He said something to Kim-Ly. She replied, receiving a curt bob of the head in return.

"He does not want to press charges," she said to the MPs. "Provided the soldiers pay for the broken dishes."

"Oh, here we go," one of the lieutenants, the one with the broken nose, whispered to his two buddies. "Here comes the shakedown."

"You should count your lucky stars this guy isn't pressing charges," the MP snapped at him. "You'd be facing a few months in the brig, and probably a dishonorable discharge on top of that."

The lieutenant shut up.

"How much?" the MP asked Kim-Ly.

She talked to the owner, and came back with a figure in local dong that equaled less than $20 U.S. When she told the assembled Americans, the MP laughed out loud.

"You think you four big spenders can handle that?"

"We can handle it," Josh said, and the lieutenants nodded.

"Okay, let's see the cash."

Josh pulled out his share from his wallet, and after brief negotiations the lieutenants came up with theirs. The MP grabbed the money and handed it to the owner.

"Please tell him once again how sorry we are that this happened in his establishment. He can be assured that these men will be punished for their actions."

Kim-Ly translated. The old man answered. "He says the three younger men should learn better manners."

"We'll see to it," the MP said, fixing the three junior officers with a stare that broached no contradiction.

With that the MPs stood guard as Josh and the three lieutenants straightened up the tables and chairs and apologized personally to the owner. Then the entire group moved outside.

"Where are you taking them?" Kim-Ly asked plaintively when it became obvious that Josh would not be returning home with her.

"We need to process some paperwork so their CO's know what they've been up to," the senior MP explained. "After that, it's up to the CO's."

"But…" she began, but was cut-off by Josh.

"Sorry, Kim-Ly. I'll call you as soon as I can."

She nodded her sullen understanding and watched as the big, burly MPs hustled all four officers into two Jeeps. The Jeeps drove off, leaving her standing alone amidst a knot of curious Vietnamese in front of the restaurant.

*****

General Edwards looked up from the paperwork on his desk and shook his head slowly.

"What in God's name were you thinking?" he said. "This doesn't seem like you at all."

Josh stood at attention. "I apologize, General. I have no good excuse."

"Was it those three yahoo junior officers? Did they say something?"

"I blame no one but myself, sir."

Edwards exhaled in exasperation. "The MPs' report suggests that the three lieutenants were the instigators, but you were the senior. You should know better."

"I agree, General."

Edwards shook his head again. "You're not making this any easier, Captain." He flipped through the report half-heartedly. "I'm afraid I'll have to discipline you. No real alternative."

"I understand, sir."

"All right then. You're confined to quarters for the next two weeks except for the daily planning session. No passes. No travel. Nothing. Understood?"

Josh blinked. "But, Lieutenant Landry is still in the hospital. I've been visiting him..."

"You should've thought of that before you decided to tear up that restaurant," Edwards answered. "One of those snot-nosed lieutenants is going to be out of action for at least ten days."

"Landry is just starting to come around."

"Which he'll have to do without your help. Is that clear?"

Josh hesitated, debating whether to pursue the subject. A glance at the general's expression dissuaded him. He threw back his shoulders and pulled himself up even straighter. "Yes sir!"

"Good. Now get out of here, and I don't want to hear anything more about this – got it?"

Josh saluted and pivoted sharply. Although his face showed nothing, his mind whirled.

*****

On his way back to his quarters, Josh stopped by a payphone and called Kim-Ly. The phone rang once before she answered.

"How are you?" she asked anxiously.

"I'm okay, but the general just confined me to quarters for the next two weeks."

"What? It wasn't your fault! Those three lieutenants…"

"I got off easy," he interrupted her. "He could've been a lot tougher on me. I screwed up."

"But they started it!"

"I was the senior officer. It was my responsibility to maintain military decorum."

She was quiet for a moment. "So what does this mean? Will it hurt your chances for promotion?"

Josh smiled wanly. He was constantly surprised by how much Kim-Ly knew about the American military system. "Don't know. If it does, it does."

"It's not fair," she muttered.

"It is what it is."

Another pause. "So, when will I see you again?"

"Two weeks and one minute from now." He tried to sound upbeat.

"That is so long!" she wailed.

"Nothing to be done about it." They both fell silent as they considered the two-week separation. Then, a thought struck him. "Could I ask you a favor?"

"Of course! What can I do?"

He told her about his concern for Landry, left all alone in the 'nuthouse'. "If I can get you access, would you mind stopping by every other day or so, just to remind him that someone out here gives a damn?"

"I would be pleased to visit him. But will they grant me permission?"

"We'll see," Josh said. "All we can do is ask."

He had his doubts, but he kept them to himself.

*****

The request for Kim-Ly to be allowed visitation privileges lumbered through the base bureaucracy. Josh tried to control his growing impatience but didn't quite succeed. He contacted both Max and Major Eastly a number of times to try to push the request forward, until finally taking their advice to let the process run its course. It was five days later when he received notification that Kim-Ly had been approved for on-base visits to the mental facility, though with both the frequency and duration of the visits tightly constrained.

Josh was eager to hear from her about Landry's state of mind, and so had arranged a phone call timed to his return from the morning meeting the day after her first visit. He could barely keep his focus on the planning meeting long enough to get through it, so when he was given a message to report to General Edward's office directly after the meeting broke up, his frustration boiled over.

"Damn it!" he snarled at the startled courier. "Why does it have to be now?"

"Because he's the CO?"

Josh took a deep breath. "Yeh, of course he is. Sorry – I've got a few things on my mind."

"No problem. Good luck with… whatever." The young NCO took off with a shake of his head. "Officers…" he mumbled.

When Josh knocked on the general's door, he had no idea what to expect. A discussion of his girl-friend's nationality and family ties was definitely not even in the mix.

"Sit down, Captain," Edwards directed as soon as he'd reported. Something was up; the general rarely called him by his rank unless official business was in play. "I understand a friend of yours, a Miss…" he glanced at a file open on his desk, "… Kim-Ly Tran has been granted visiting privileges over at the hospital," he began, his voice calm yet intimidating.

"That's right, sir. She's keeping an eye on Lieutenant Landry while I'm confined to quarters." He said it without emotion. He didn't want to rile the CO.

"Yes, well I'm sure the lieutenant appreciates that. But, were you aware that her family has very strong political ties in this country? Her uncle was Phan Khắc Sửu, the top dog a few governments ago." He stared at Josh with narrowed eyes. "Were you aware?"

"I was," Josh answered without even a moment's hesitation. "She told me all about it."

"And did you know her father is still politically involved and has been known to express some... opinions about the U.S. involvement here that might be considered... unfriendly?"

Josh fidgeted in his seat. "I, I didn't know about the anti-American sentiments, but I can assure you that Kim-Ly does not share his thinking."

Edward's stare intensified. "Can you? Did you know that one of her first cousins is under surveillance for possible links to the VC?"

Josh felt color rising to his cheeks. "Kim-Ly is not her father, or her cousin!" he said angrily. "She supports the American involvement and hates the Communists!"

The general leaned back in his chair. "And you know this how? Because she told you so?"

For the first time a hint of doubt crept into Josh's mind. He immediately felt ashamed.

"Yes, because she told me, and because I've spent considerable time with her over the past few months and I think I've gotten to know her pretty darn well." His words sounded weak even to himself. But he was not about to back down. Neither was Edwards.

"Look, Daniels, you're a good officer – this recent dust-up in the restaurant notwithstanding. But this is the kind of thing –

security questions – that can cause problems for even good officers. You understand?"

Josh nodded, trying to keep his face blank.

Edwards' voice grew softer. "Look, I'm not telling you to dump the woman. I can see you think highly of her. But perhaps you can keep her visits to the base to a minimum, and make sure she doesn't get 'lost' and wander around too much."

"Did she – get lost?" Josh suddenly pictured Kim-Ly wandering through the maze-like grounds of the huge base.

"No, not that I've been told," Edwards admitted. "But I can see where this all would be headed if she did. Do you catch my drift?"

Josh realized the general was looking out for him, trying to avoid any additional embarrassment, or worse. Still, it rankled. "I do, sir, and I appreciate your concern. I'll talk to Kim-Ly."

The general's eyes opened slightly. It was clear he'd picked up on Josh's irritation but had let it go. This time.

"Okay. Then enough said. How's your buddy, what was it – Landry? How's he doing?"

"I don't really know, sir. I was going to speak with Kim-Ly about it on my way back to quarters." He saw Edward's questioning look. "By phone," he quickly added. The general relaxed noticeably.

"Good. I hope he's coming along. For everyone's sake."

"Thank you, sir."

The general dismissed him and Josh made a beeline out of the office toward the nearest payphone. He was already late calling Kim-Ly. The phone rang several times and he thought he might have missed her, but on the seventh ring she picked up.

"How did it go?" he asked as soon as she'd told him she'd seen Landry.

"After some initial misunderstanding I did not have any problems getting into the base," she explained, "if that is what you mean."

It was clear to Josh that she was leaving something unsaid. "But…?"

"But your friend does not seem to be in a good place in his head. He is confused."

Josh winced. "How do you mean?"

"Well, he does not seem to remember the battle that left him 'injured', although he pretends that he does if you ask him about it."

"Then how do you know he doesn't?" Irritation crept into his voice.

"I asked him some questions based on what you told me. He did not know the answers."

"What's his mood? Did he seem fairly okay?"

"I do not know what 'fairly okay' means. He seemed…" She stopped as if to weigh her words. "… confused. And perhaps sad. Yes, he seemed sad."

"Damn," Josh muttered. He felt an overwhelming urge to sneak out of his quarters and hightail it over to the hospital, but he knew the consequences if they caught him. He decided to call Colonel Lesser and get a professional update as soon as he'd finished talking to Kim-Ly.

"It is a pity," she said, interrupting his reverie. "He seems like a good man."

"He is, he really is. Thanks for going over there. It must not have been the most pleasant thing to do." He'd heard her 'misunderstanding' comment and had a good idea what kind of 'misunderstanding' an attractive young South Vietnamese woman might have entering a highly secure American military base.

"It was not so bad. I am happy I could help."

Josh wanted to feel good about her visit, but he couldn't help hearing Edwards' questions echo in his head: *how do you know?* He tried to push those thoughts from his mind, to go back to the way he'd felt before the general's briefing. It wasn't so easy. "Did you have any trouble finding your way around?" he asked, ashamed at the subtext of his question.

"No. A soldier showed me the way."

Of course. There was no way they would allow a visitor to roam the base, credentials or no credentials. And a local would be scrutinized even more than an American. So why had Edwards brought it up?

"Look, there's something I need to tell you," he said. "My Commanding Officer called me in for a little talk this morning."

"General Edwards?"

"Yeh. He knows about your uncle's political career."

"Everyone knows about my uncle. He was the Chief of State."

"Yeh, but he also asked me about the rest of your family. Do you have a cousin?"

"I have many cousins."

He felt like a fool. Of course she did. Seemed like every Vietnamese had a dozen cousins, and nearly as many aunts and uncles. "This one would be a young man, who might have some friends who fight with the North." He could barely speak the last.

There was a long silence. "I do not know the political thoughts of all my cousins," she said without obvious rancor. "But I cannot say it is impossible. There are many young people in this country who admire the effort to free Vietnam from foreign influence. They cannot see what a future under the Communists might bring. I see."

His cheeks burned. He wished he could take her in his arms right then and there.

"I'm sorry, Kim-Ly. I had to ask."

Another long pause. "I understand. I should have told you more about my family."

"It's not your fault, it's the War. Everyone is nervous." He listened to his heart beat as he waited for her answer.

"Should I not visit Lieutenant Landry anymore?" Her voice was strained.

"No, no! I mean, yes, you should still visit Landry! But maybe we should keep it down to a couple of times a week. Just to be safe."

"I understand. I will visit your friend twice a week until either he is released or you are." She chuckled, and I realized she had made a joke. Sort of. "Will you be able to attend his court-martial?"

"I don't know. Why?"

"It is just that I am worried about Lieutenant Landry," she continued.

"So am I. We'll just have to wait and see how it plays out. At this point, it's up to the Judge Advocate. I would think he'd let Landry stay in the hospital until Colonel Lesser and his people declare him fit for trial, but who knows? This is the Army, after all."

"Yes, it is." Something in the way she said it made him nervous. *From the mouths of innocents...*

*****

Time dragged on all too slowly for Josh. Except for the morning planning meeting, his life was a tedious repetition of eating, showering, and exercise, with occasional breaks for reading or the radio. He had no visitors, no TV, he didn't feel like calling anyone except Kim-Ly, and she was busy with her interpreting work and her visits to Landry.

On the bright side, her second visit resulted in a telephone report that was at least a little more optimistic than the first. She thought Landry seemed more 'with it', a little less depressed.

"That's good news," Josh said.

"Perhaps," she answered.

"How do you mean?"

"I heard Colonel Lesser discussing Lieutenant Landry with one of his assistants in the hospital. He said that the 'powers that be' were pressing him to declare the Lieutenant fit for duty."

"By which they mean fit for his court-martial."

"That is what I assumed."

"Did he give any timeframe?"

"Not that I heard. But I was only waiting in the reception area, not eavesdropping." She sounded defensive.

"Of course not!" Josh reassured her. "Lesser speaks very loudly. I noticed that when I first met him." He hadn't noticed anything of the kind, but he didn't want to deter her from 'overhearing' anything else. "Does Landry know?"

"I am not sure. I did not tell him, and he did not mention it."

"Probably not, then. Let's just keep it to ourselves until we know more – okay?"

"Of course."

When he hung up, his mind was whirling. If the court-martial was imminent, he would not be able to attend without special dispensation from his confinement. He was pretty certain his absence would hurt Landry's chances. So if the Judge Advocate tried to speed the process up, he'd ask Landry's lawyer to stall, drag his feet until Josh was available once again. It was a good plan, but he had no idea what the likelihood of success was.

After all, it *was* the Army.

CHAPTER 22

Kim-Ly scheduled her next visit to Landry for the following Wednesday. Four days after that, Josh would be released from his punishment – IF nothing else came up. There had been no further word about discharging Landry from the hospital, and everything seemed to be going according to schedule. Until the night of October 18th.

Josh had gone to bed early, as had become his custom since he'd been restricted to quarters. He'd slept for just a couple of hours when a loud blast shook him awake. Moments later, another loud explosion. He leapt up from his bed and pulled on civvies. As he yanked open the door to his room, a fully-armed Ranger came running past.

"What's going on?!" he yelled after the soldier.

"Rocket attack!" the man yelled over his shoulder.

Josh ran back inside and pulled on his army greens. He was half-way out the door again when a familiar voice called out to him: "Where do you think you're going, Daniels?"

Josh turned to see the MP sergeant who had taken him into custody in the restaurant the week before. "Rocket attack, Sergeant! I'm reporting to my duty post."

"You are confined to your quarters, Captain," the MP said. "There has not been a general call to duty."

"But, the base is under attack!"

"And those of us who are *not* confined to quarters will take care of it. Is that understood?"

Josh felt like screaming. It wasn't bad enough the situation called for immediate action. It wasn't just that he was a Ranger and could definitely be of help. No, if he was honest about it, hearing an NCO order him to remain in his quarters stuck in his craw. *'I suppose that's why he's only a damn sergeant,'* he fumed even as he eased back into his room.

"Understood, Sergeant. I only hope the VC are as understanding."

The MP ignored his muttered reproach and ran off in the same direction as the Ranger. Josh was momentarily tempted to ignore the sergeant and follow, but when he heard no further explosions of any kind he did as he'd been told. It wasn't until an hour later that he learned the full extent of the attack: two rockets, fired from outside the base perimeter, landed in open areas inside the base. No one hurt, no real damage – other than to the pride of the joint U.S. – Vietnamese force. Josh could just imagine what the media – and yes, the politicians, would be saying come morning time: *'They can't even keep the enemy from shelling their principal base in Saigon!'* The realization brought a smile to his face.

He wasn't smiling the next morning, however, when General Edwards read his latest draft directive to the planning meeting staff. Among the many proposed security changes was one that hit Josh hard: "All base passes issued to non- MACV combatants, other than daily base workers properly identified and credentialed, are hereby withdrawn until further notice." Damn! Just like that, because of two stinking rockets lobbed over the perimeter to no effect other than perhaps embarrassment, Kim-Ly was going to lose her chance to visit Landry.

Right after the strategy session Josh requested a brief meeting with General Edwards, but the CO was unmoved.

"No exceptions, Captain," the general had explained. "If I let your girl come in, every other person with a pass – and there are quite a few – would come after me using her as a precedent. I'd never hear the end of it. Sorry."

Josh wanted to argue the point, to explain how Kim-Ly's visits were literally a matter of life and death. But he knew his CO well enough to know that he would've been wasting his time. If there was anything Edwards hated it was petty administrative hassles, and granting Kim-Ly an exception – for whatever reason – would open the door for a tidal wave of such hassles. Just plain bad luck, that's what it was.

Kim-Ly was not so sanguine. "We must do something!" she responded when Josh told her about the new regs. "He is all alone! Can you not call your father?"

Josh suppressed a grimace. He *could* call his father, but the results would almost certainly not sit well with Edwards and the other senior officers on-base. And that's if his father would even try to help. No, he had another idea.

As soon as he hung up with Kim-Ly, Josh called Colonel Lesser at the mental facility.

"Colonel, it's Captain Daniels," he introduced when the hospital Director finally came to the phone.

"I was kind of expecting your call," Lesser said. "You've heard about the new base pass regs?"

Josh was impressed. He didn't know that anyone beyond the planning group had been briefed on the changes. Apparently General Edwards thought enough of the colonel to share his thinking with him. "I have," he answered. "And as you've probably guessed, I'm not happy."

"It *is* unfortunate that Landry won't get regular visits. But I'm afraid the decision has been made."

"And I wouldn't think of arguing the point. But, perhaps we can make a small accommodation, at least until I get out of my quarters."

"I'm listening…"

"I still attend a strategy session over at MACV every morning, and on my way back to my quarters I pass this payphone that I'm speaking to you on right now."

"Uh huh. Okay, I get the gist. But how do you think General Edwards would react to your little plan? I mean, it seems to contradict the spirit of your punishment."

Josh shrugged. "I think the general is an officer who cares for his men, including Lieutenant Landry. A five minute phone call to a sick soldier will not undermine the military justice system."

"When is your confinement scheduled to end?"

"This Saturday. At noon. It'd only be a few days." He tried to keep the pleading from his voice.

The colonel was quiet for a while. "Okay, I think I can go along with you on this one," he finally replied. "But Captain, you'd better call me directly so I can put you through to Landry myself. The less people who know about our 'accommodation' the better. Agreed?"

"Agreed. And thank you, sir."

"Don't mention it. Literally." At that the colonel chuckled.

*****

The following day, after the morning meeting, Josh called the hospital. Colonel Lesser connected him to Landry's room.

"How's it going?!" Josh asked his friend, with perhaps a bit too much enthusiasm.

"O… kay," Landry said softly, the word coming out slurred. He didn't sound 'okay.'

"They got you on some kind of meds?"

"May… be."

Josh searched for something else to talk about. "Kim-Ly sends her regards. Did Colonel Lesser tell you about the new regs? She won't be able to visit you for a while."

"Oh." He sounded stoned to the gills. Whatever medicine he was taking, it was powerful stuff.

"Yeh. So, have you heard anything more from the Judge Advocate's office, or your lawyer?"

"Who?"

"Tim Jacobs – your civvy lawyer?"

"Oh. No."

"Well, no news is good news, right?" He tried to sound upbeat.

"I guess."

"So, Mason, I'm still cooped up here in my quarters until the weekend, so I'll only be able to call you – no visits until then. But if there's anything you need, you just get ahold of Colonel Lesser, and he'll contact me. Okay?"

"Okay." There was a short pause. "Josh – when can I get out of here?" For the first time he sounded halfway normal, albeit terribly sad.

"I don't know," Josh answered honestly. "I'm going to call your lawyer to see if he's learned anything more about the Army's plans. If I find out anything, I'll let you know."

""'Cause this place is like a prison," Landry continued as if he hadn't heard Josh.

"Yeh, I know bro. But hang in there. We'll get you out as soon as we can. You can count on that."

"Soon?"

"I hope so, Mason. I really hope so."

There was a long silence. "Me too," he finally said.

When Josh hung up he was not in the best of moods. He spoke to the lawyer Jacobs, but learned nothing new. As far as Jacobs knew, the Advocate was still putting his case together. He promised to give Josh a call if anything new came up.

*****

It was a few hours later, mid-afternoon, when Josh got a message that Colonel Lesser had called asking to speak to him urgently. Josh faced a dilemma: sneak out to return the call, or wait until the next day? Given Landry's state of mind, he decided to chance it. Trying his best to look both casual and inconspicuous, Josh made his way to the nearest payphone. He saw a few GIs along the way, but no one who knew him or his situation.

It took awhile to track the colonel down, and when he finally took the phone it was clear he was upset.

"The bastards!" he began with no introduction. "The goddamn bastards!"

Josh had never heard Lesser so angry. "What? What's going on, Colonel?"

"Four MPs showed up at lunchtime and took Landry into custody!"

"What?! I thought he was to be confined until you decided he was fit for service."

"They brought in their own guy — a Major Witherspoon, who interviewed your friend for all of five minutes before declaring him fit."

"He wasn't from your staff?"

"I've never seen the SOB before. From what I caught, they must've brought him in from the States."

From the States? That sounded bad. Really bad. If they brought in a ringer, they must be getting ready to make a move.

"Do you know where they took him?"

"No idea. But I'd imagine they took him to the base stockade."

Josh thanked him and hung up, his mind a blur. He debated with himself before calling General Edwards. He didn't want to get the CO involved but couldn't think of a better way to find out the truth about Landry. When the general's assistant put him on hold 'to see if the general is available' and then came back on to tell him that Edwards wasn't, he realized something was up. Josh was nearly certain Edwards told his assistant everything; the scuttlebutt was that the NCO even knew when the general was taking a crap. If Edwards wasn't available, the corporal would've known without asking. That meant he was ducking Josh.

Just for the heck of it he called Major Winshotz.

"Major, this is Josh Daniels," he began, hoping that Max might at least give him the lay of the land.

"You heard about Landry?"

Bad news traveled fast. "Yeh, I heard. I was wondering…"

"Sorry, Daniels, I can't help you."

"But you haven't even heard what I was going to ask you!"

"Doesn't matter. Word's out that Washington wants a court-martial, and so they're going to get one. Nothing I can do about it."

"But he's not guilty, Max! He was completely off his rocker!"

"I hear you, Josh, but they must think they have something on him 'cause they're gung-ho to wrap this up ASAP."

"Meaning what?" Josh was feeling sick to his stomach.

"Meaning you'd better tell his civilian lawyer to get his case together pretty damn fast. I don't think he has much time left."

Josh didn't know whether he meant the lawyer, or Landry.

*****

When Josh called Jacobs, the lawyer informed him that a courier had just delivered notification that the court-martial would begin the day after next.

"Seems like they're in a mighty big rush," Jacobs said.

"They're getting big pressure from Washington. They need a conviction."

"Unless they've got something new that we don't know about, they may be disappointed."

"What if they do – have new information?"

"Like what?"

"I don't know. Something. Do they have to tell you about it?"

"They do. But if they only just found out themselves, then they can probably get away with stalling until tomorrow, at least. Not leave us any time to dig up information to counter their new discovery."

"So what do we do?"

"I'm going to try to find out where they moved Landry and go see him – if they'll let me."

"He won't know what they've come up with. He'll be lucky if he knows where he is."

"I'm not going to talk with him to find out what the Judge Advocate knows – that's your job. I want to start getting him up to speed for the court-martial. I was hoping to have a week or more to prepare him, but it looks like it may be a good deal less than that."

Josh was confined to quarters and not even his friends were willing to buck Edwards and the political bosses in Washington on this one. How the hell was he supposed to find out what they had on Landry?

*****

He'd called everyone he knew, risking considerably more severe punishment than just confinement to quarters if anyone saw him stationed at the payphone for the hour or more he'd been calling around. When there simply wasn't anyone else to call, he made the call he'd been hoping to avoid: he called his father.

"Dad, it's Josh," he began.

"Josh? What's wrong?"

The Colonel knew him too well.

"I need some help."

"Are you in trouble?" He had to hand it to his father, he didn't shirk or dance around.

"It's not me – it's Landry." He explained the whole situation. "His lawyer thinks they might have come up with new evidence and are keeping it from him until the absolute last moment."

"And you want me to see if I can find out what they have?"

"You know Mason – he's a good guy. If he walked away from his post, he must've been really screwed up. Hell, he still is."

"No need to swear," his father said.

"So, will you?"

"You know the administration has its knickers all in a knot about GIs deserting. They won't be volunteering that information."

"So I found out when I called around out here. Nobody knows anything – or at least that's what they're telling me. I thought maybe a congressman might have more luck."

Josh had no idea what to expect. He never did with the Colonel. He held his breath.

"I've known Mason for what, five years now?" his father said after just a second. "I don't believe for a second he walked away on purpose. I'll do what I can."

Josh breathed a sigh of relief. "Thanks."

"You're welcome. So, how are *you* doing?"

"All right." Josh had no intention of telling the Colonel about his punishment.

"Don't sound so enthusiastic."

"It's… complicated."

"Want to talk about it?"

Josh was stunned. His father had never been the touchy-feely sort. But Josh could feel the clock running in the back of his mind. He needed to get back to his quarters. He couldn't help Landry much if he was confined to a cell as well. "I can't right now. I've got something I need to take care of."

A pause. "Okay. Call me when you've got the time."

"I'll do that."

They made a little more small talk, but both knew the conversation was over. When Josh finally hung up he shook his head in disbelief.

*****

He got a message from his father less than four hours later: "They've got a new witness. Corporal Alexander White." That's all it said. He debated sneaking out to make another phone call, but decided to wait until mess and make the call then.

Before he even sat down to eat, Josh headed straight to the pay phone in the officers' mess and called Jacobs' direct number. He hoped the lawyer was still in his office; he'd said he usually worked late, particularly when he had a court-martial coming up in just a couple of days.

"Tim Jacobs," the lawyer answered after just two rings.

"Tim, this is Josh Daniels. I think I know what the Advocate General has in store for us."

He explained that he'd contacted 'someone who has access to Defense Department sources' and found out about the new witness, Corporal White.

"What do you know about this soldier, White?" Jacobs asked.

"Nothing. I'm still confined to quarters and…" Just then Josh looked up to see a big, wide, mean-looking MP headed straight his way. The man did not look happy. "I may have to get off the phone directly, so try to find out about White," he told the lawyer. "I don't know that he's their secret weapon, but he might be."

"I'll see what I can dig up."

At that moment the MP's shadow blotted out the light behind him as he towered over Daniels.

"Captain Daniels, please come with me," he ordered in a flat, disinterested tone.

"Gotta go," Josh muttered into the phone as he hung up. "Where are we going?" he asked the MP.

"General Edwards wants to see you. Now."

It wouldn't do any good to argue, so he went along quietly. He knew the way. When he got to MACV headquarters the MP told him they'd have to wait in the outer reception room. After nearly a half-hour, he was called into the general's office.

As soon as he stepped through the door, he could tell he was in trouble. Max Winshotz stood off to one side of Edward's desk, another major Josh didn't recognize was on the right side, and Edwards sat between them. All three looked up from some papers on the desk to fix Josh with a look that was less than welcoming.

"Captain Daniels, come in, come in," the general said, motioning to him. Josh came to attention directly in front of the desk and saluted. He waited for Edwards to put him at ease. The order did not come.

"Captain, some disquieting information has recently come to our attention, and we wanted your input." Edwards fished around on his desk for a sheet of paper. He finally pulled it out and held it up to read. "Our people in the Pentagon are telling us there's been a 'high level' inquiry into the Landry court-martial. Would you know anything about that?" All three men stared at Josh, waiting for an answer.

Josh tried not to show the anxiety that surged through his body. "What kind of inquiry?" he asked, hoping to stall long enough for his brain to kick into gear.

"Don't play games with us!" the unknown major roared, his face plum-red with apoplexy. "You know damn well it was Congressman Daniels who initiated the inquiry. Do you think that interfering in a military investigation while you're confined to quarters is some kind of amusement?!"

Josh felt the breath in his lungs leak out in a sudden stream. "I... don't, sir. I don't think that at all."

"And yet you contacted your father and asked him to interfere in the investigation."

"No sir, I did not."

"You didn't ask you father to press the Pentagon for information concerning the Advocate General's case against Lieutenant Landry?" the major continued.

"I did contact him," Josh admitted, his voice now calmer, coming under control, "but I did not ask him to interfere in an investigation. Knowing my father, there's no way he would interfere even if I asked him."

"But you contacted him while you were confined to quarters," Max said with only slightly more empathy.

"I called him from a payphone, yes. But I didn't think I was disobeying any order..."

"You didn't think!?" the other major interrupted. "I would say that's an understatement."

General Edwards put up a hand to calm the officer. "Josh, I told you that this was an important case for the people in Washington – didn't that make any impression on you?"

"It did, sir. I understand why the politicians want to stop desertions and why they want to win this case. But I just don't think that Lieutenant Landry is the right soldier in the right circumstances to be the poster boy for deserting."

"Isn't it possible your friendship with the lieutenant might be clouding your judgment on this?" Edwards asked.

Josh hesitated. "He's my friend, General. One of my best friends. Because of that, I know – not think…" (he directed this at the unidentified officer) … "that Lieutenant Landry is *incapable* of deserting his post – IF he were in his right mind."

"Do you have any idea how many men would use the 'not in his right mind' defense if Landry wins this court-martial?" the major sneered. "We couldn't ever prosecute *anyone* for deserting!"

"I don't know about that, sir. I only know that Landry wouldn't desert. Period."

General Edwards let out a long sigh. "At ease, Captain." He looked Josh in the eyes. "Captain, I understand this isn't easy. I do. You think you know your friend, and you think he'd never do what he's been charged with. But you also must know the impact that war, this war, has on people. Maybe it changed your friend."

"It didn't." Josh didn't hesitate, but even as he mouthed the words a tiny inking of doubt swept through him. Could he be wrong? Could Landry have been aware of what he was doing? *'No, it isn't true,'* he decided just as quickly. *'He was screwed up.'*

"Yes, well the court-martial will ultimately decide whether it did or didn't, I suppose. For now, we've also received a request from Lieutenant Landry's civilian lawyer to allow you to appear at the court-martial as a witness for the defense. We've talked it over," he glanced at both Max and the other major, "and have decided that you can serve the last three days of your punishment after you testify. So, beginning today, and until you are called to testify, you are free to leave your quarters."

Josh blinked. Free? "Thank you, sir," he said.

"But no more inference in the court-martial," the stony-faced major said.

"I never had and have no intention of interfering in a court - martial," Josh answered.

"All right, that's good enough for me," Edwards spoke up. "Anything else?" He looked not only to Josh but to the two majors.

"No sir," the three answered in virtual unison.

"Good. Then you're dismissed, Captain."

Josh jumped to attention and saluted. "Thank you, sir!"

As he marched from the office Josh didn't know whether to feel relieved or even more anxious than when he'd entered. But he knew where he was headed next.

*****

He had no idea if she were home, but he wanted to see her so badly it was worth the effort to hike the half-hour or so to Kim-Ly's apartment on the off-chance she'd be there. All the boisterous sounds and myriad sights barely registered in his mind as he double-timed it through the crowded Saigon streets. Motorbikes wove in and out between old French automobiles and unmarked delivery trucks, horns blaring, with a constant stream of bicycles, pedestrians and animal-pulled carts just to add color to the chaos. Josh didn't see any of it. Or just enough to pass through the maelstrom without getting killed. When he arrived at the apartment he couldn't have said whether it had taken him ten minutes or an hour. It didn't matter, as long as she was home.

He pushed the buzzer and waited anxiously.

"Đó là ai?" a gruff male voice answered. Her father.

"It's me, Mr. Tran, Josh Daniels." He felt like a teenager calling on a date.

"Đợi!" came the reply after several painful seconds.

'Wait.' For what? Was she home, or…?

"Josh! Josh, is that you?" Kim-Ly called out over the intercom.

"Can I come up?"

"Of course! Come!" The door buzzed open and Josh ran up the stairs taking two at a time. At the top Kim-Ly stood waiting, a stunned smile on her face.

"How? I thought you were confined…" she began as soon as she saw him appear from the darkness of the stairwell.

Before she could finish her sentence Josh swept her up in his arms and kissed her as if he'd never kiss her again. By the time they came up for air, Kim-Ly's father stood in the doorway, a stern look on his face.

"Không trong hành lang!" he shouted.

"What's he saying?" Josh asked, his mind only half engaged.

"He says 'Not in the hallway!' she said with a grin. "Come!"

Kim-Ly took his hand and dragged him into the apartment, past her angry father, and straight to her bedroom. She slammed the door behind them and pushed him forcefully onto her bed. Before he could say a word, she began to madly unbutton the long black silken blouse she wore over black slacks. Josh responded without a second thought, tossing his clothes into a pile by the side of the bed. Kim-Ly had just pushed him back down onto the bed and climbed on top of him, her small pointed breasts bobbing wildly, when a loud knock sounded at her door.

"Nó là gì?" she yelled shrilly. Her father shouted something back to her.

"What?" Josh asked, unable to keep a smile from his face.

"He says he is going out to play cards," she said.

"Good luck!" Josh yelled out.

"No more words!" she ordered, and for once he obeyed without question.

*****

When they were finished, lying tired and satisfied in each other's arms, Kim-Ly traced the scar from the bullet wound on Josh's side.

"This was a wonderful surprise," she said dreamily. "How did you get off the base?"

Josh almost begged-off explaining what had happened, not wanting to spoil the moment with too much reality. But Kim-Ly was persistent, and so he explained. She lay silent, listening intently.

"They will bring Landry to trial tomorrow?" she asked, concern coloring her words.

"That's what we understand. They seem determined to get a conviction to slow the numbers of desertions they're seeing."

"But you told me that Landry did not desert." Her eyes shone with anger.

"I don't believe he did," Josh said. "But I wasn't there, and his lawyer thinks the Advocate General has a new witness that will give some damning testimony."

"Do you know what he will say?"

"I don't. The Army is supposed to inform his lawyer ahead of time, but as of this morning they hadn't told him anything. It could be they're keeping him in the dark as long as possible to make it harder to organize a solid defense."

"But that is not fair!"

Josh smiled a sad, worried smile. "No, it's not fair. But no one said the Army was supposed to be fair. They do what they think they have to do to win the War."

"And convicting Landry will help them win?"

He shrugged. "That's what they think, or at least what some politicians in Washington think. I really don't know about the Top Brass here in-country. It's not like they've discussed it with me."

"What can we do?" she asked, sitting up in bed, her jaw set with determination. "We cannot let them do this to your friend!"

He brushed a strand of hair from across her eyes. "You're something else, you know that?"

Her anger softened. "Am I?"

He kissed her gently. "You are."

They made desperate, passionate love twice more, and then sat up half the night talking about Landry and his upcoming court-martial. It was after three when they finally fell off to sleep.

CHAPTER 23

Josh slipped out of Kim-Ly's bed just as the sun was rising and made his way downstairs without waking either her or her father, whose loud snoring filled the apartment with rasping gasps. He tiptoed down the stairs and out into the early morning cityscape. As opposed to the night before few people occupied the streets and walks, with just a couple of ox carts lumbering along noisily on the main boulevard. A few drunks and even fewer merchants made their way through the relative quiet of the still-sleeping city, though more and more bikes and motorbikes appeared with each block he traveled.

As soon as he got back to his quarters he showered and pulled out clean dress greens. Dressing quickly, he sat at his desk and jotted a few notes about what he hoped to cover when Jacobs called him to testify. He'd been over and over it in his mind, but was worried that in the pressure-cooker of the court-martial he might forget key points. It was still too early to call the lawyer by the time he finished, so he went off to breakfast. He caught some ribbing from his fellow officers for wearing his Class A's and fruit salad, but did his best to ignore them. Truth was, his mind was a million miles away – or more accurately, the two or three miles between the Mess and the site of the court-martial.

At 0900 he called Jacobs and was put straight through. He explained what had transpired at the CO's office the day before, and the lawyer confirmed that Josh was still on the witness list. The court-martial was scheduled for 1100, and Jacobs was about to head over to the stockade to make sure Landry was ready for the ordeal. They arranged to meet at 1030.

The next hour and a half passed much too slowly for Josh. He tried to review his notes, but found his mind wandering. After repeated failed attempts to focus on the details of the charges, he abandoned the effort and headed for the Administrative building of the MACV complex. He would've walked, but he didn't want to arrive drenched in sweat and so took one of the old Peugeot taxis that filled the streets. The taxi dropped him off a little before 1000, and so he entered the air conditioned building and waited nervously for Jacobs to arrive.

At 1033 the lawyer stepped out of a taxi and hurried into the two-story stucco Admin building, an assistant – her arms full of black binders – hurrying to keep up.

"So, how's he doing?" Josh asked as soon as Jacobs came through the security check.

"Not so well. Not one of his good days."

"He understands what's happening?"

"I think so, but it's hard to tell for sure. One minute he seems pretty with it, the next…" He shook his head.

Josh felt his stomach sink. "Could that help him?" he asked, reaching for straws. "If they see how bad he is?"

"Who knows?" the lawyer said, but his tone suggested he wasn't optimistic. "I'm more worried about that Corporal White. Turns out he was a friend of a soldier in Landry's platoon who the VC captured and killed – nasty business. Come on – let's get inside so we're there when they bring Landry over."

The courtroom was small, with perhaps thirty folding chairs facing a table wide enough to sit six set on a raised wooden dais. An American flag and the Army banner sat on either side of the dais.

Two folding tables, one on either side of the narrow aisle in the center of the chairs, were topped with name cards – one for the defense, one for the prosecution. Jacobs excused himself and went with his assistant to the furthermost table and unpacked. Josh paced nervously.

It was nearly twenty minutes later, just ten minutes before the court-martial was scheduled to begin, when two MPs guided a chained and groggy Lieutenant Mason Landry into the room. Josh motioned to his friend, but he didn't seem to notice. They settled him into a chair next to Jacobs, and the two began to talk. Moments after, a team of three officers from the Advocate General's office took their place at the table to the left of the aisle, the lead officer stopping briefly to shake Jacob's hand and nod to Landry.

Just before 1100 a door opened at the back of the room, behind the dais; Josh prepared to stand while the military judges entered. But instead a solitary figure emerged, a figure that was all too familiar to Josh from their meeting the day before with General Edwards: the unnamed major who had been so intent on convicting Landry without the formality of a court-martial. The officer scanned the room, his eyes settling for just a second on Josh. He couldn't be sure from that distance, but Josh thought the man scowled. The major quickly made his way to a seat just behind the prosecution's table, where he exchanged a few words with the lead prosecutor before sitting heavily. A few other people came into the room, including two civilians, one of whom carried a thin notebook. They sat a few rows behind the prosecution and defense tables, a position from which they could take-in the entire courtroom. Josh didn't know what made him so sure, but he was confident that at least one of the two was a reporter.

An NCO came out from the rear door and loudly announced: "All rise!" Five senior officers came out, led by a military judge, and settled behind their table.

The judge motioned for everyone to sit. "We're here today to try docket number 322-A – the United States Army vs Lieutenant Mason Landry," the judge began. "Lieutenant Landry has been charged with a violation of Article 85 of the USCMA – desertion, which is defined as 'going or remaining absent from an armed forces unit, organization, or place of duty without authority and with intent to remain away therefrom permanently; or quitting a unit, organization, or place of duty with intent to avoid hazardous duty or to shirk important service.' Any person found guilty of desertion or attempt to desert in time of war 'shall be punished by death or such other punishment as a court-martial may direct.'" He turned directly to Landry. "Does the accused understand the charges made against him and the punishment should he be convicted?"

Jacobs took Landry by his arm and helped him to his feet.

"Do you understand?" he asked the blank-faced lieutenant.

Landry blinked repeatedly. "They say I deserted," he said in a flat, lifeless voice.

Jacobs looked to the judge. "Your honor, Lieutenant Landry has been hospitalized for over a week with battle fatigue…"

"Objection!" the lead Prosecutor roared, jumping to his feet. "The defense attorney is not a medical expert."

"I can read a doctor's reports," Jacobs answered coolly.

"Not in a court-martial."

"Okay, all right, that'll be quite enough," the judge intervened. He turned back to Landry. "Lieutenant Landry: do you understand that you face the possibility of execution if you are convicted of this charge?"

"I've already died many times," Landry mumbled.

"Counselor, direct your client to answer my question, please," the judge ordered Jacobs.

"Do you understand they can execute you?" he asked Landry softly.

"I know," he answered. Josh flinched.

"All right then," the judge went on. "Do either the defense or prosecution have any preliminary motions?"

Before he could finish his sentence, the prosecutor jumped to his feet. "The prosecution asks that the proceedings be closed to the public in accordance with USCMA regulations regarding the protection of national security."

"Your honor, this is outrageous!" Jacobs screamed, glancing back at Josh with a panicky look that matched what Josh was feeling.

"Enough!" the judge ordered. "The two of you – in back with me," he directed Jacobs and the Prosecuting Officer. "We'll take a ten minute recess," he explained to the five officers at the table and the handful of spectators. He didn't wait for responses, but rose and stamped off through the rear door. "All rise," the bailiff shouted, but by then the door was already closing behind the judge. Jacobs said something to Landry and followed the judge, the prosecutor close behind.

Landry was left sitting with Jacobs' assistant, two MPs standing just a few steps away. Josh didn't know the protocol for such a situation, but decided to push the envelope. He walked toward the defense table, his eyes focused on his friend. The MPs weren't fooled.

"Sorry sir, no contact with the accused," the larger of the two very large MPs said, stepping into his path.

"Can I at least speak with him?" Josh asked.

The two MPs looked to each other in confusion. Josh pressed his point. "No contact, just a few words from an old friend." He smiled innocently.

"Well, all right, but from right there – no closer."

"Thanks." Josh turned to Landry. "Hey, Landry, it's me, Daniels."

Landry didn't react. Josh caught the assistant's eye and nodded toward his friend. She tapped him on the shoulder and pointed back toward Josh. Landry turned painfully slowly.

"It's me, Daniels!" Josh said with as much enthusiasm as he could muster.

Landry's eyes flickered. "Daniels. They want to execute me." His voice was flat, as if he was discussing the menu for breakfast.

"Don't worry about that," Josh answered dismissively. "They don't have a case. You'll be back out in the field in no time." He didn't actually believe that, but thought it might give Landry a needed shot of optimism.

"You think so?"

"Yeh! These bozos are just going through the motions. They don't want to get embarrassed."

Landry started to say something in return when Josh saw his friend's eyes suddenly sweep to his left. Josh turned just in time to see the unnamed major arrive in full rush right at his side.

"Who authorized communication with the accused?!" he shouted, staring at the MPs. His voice and expression carried the full weight of his rank; maybe a bit more.

"I, ah… we…"

"There should be NO contact between the accused and *anyone* except his defense team," the major continued as if they hadn't answered.

Josh saw the impact his words were having on the MPs. He felt no such intimidation.

"Says who?" he asked, staring the major flush in the eyes.

"Says me!" the officer growled back.

"And who, exactly, are you – sir?"

The major's face turned from red to purple.

"Major Anthony P. Wilcox," he said. "Pentagon Office of the General Counsel."

"You're a little out of your sandbox, Major."

"My *sandbox* is the entire U.S. Army, *Captain*." He turned back to the MPs. "NO access to the prisoner," he repeated, and without waiting for any further conversation, glared at Josh before returning to the prosecution table.

"Seems the major doesn't want us talking to each other," Josh said to Landry.

The senior MP took a step in his direction. "Captain…"

"He's an asshole," Landry said softly.

Josh smiled. "Call's 'em like he sees 'em," he said to the two MPs, who shooed him away with their M-16s. "I'll be back here in the peanut gallery!" he added aloud in Landry's general direction. As he picked his way back among the folding chairs he felt a little better about Landry. At least he still knew an asshole when he saw one.

Ten minutes later the judge, Jacobs and the prosecutor all came back out from wherever they'd been huddled behind the scenes. Josh saw at once that Jacobs wasn't happy.

"Both the defense and prosecution have made their cases," the judge announced as soon as he'd sat down, "and I've weighed both arguments carefully."

'It's only been ten minutes!' Josh thought. *'How careful could he be?'*

"Although this *is* a capital case, the need to protect national security must take priority over competing interests. I do not see how allowing spectators in the courtroom will add to the defendant's protections under the law, while it is clear that an open court might jeopardize security concerns. Consequently, I have decided to close these proceedings to the public. Bailiff!" he continued, turning to the startled NCO, "clear the courtroom."

The soldier lurched into action, even as Jacobs stood and turned to the few spectators who even then were rising to leave the room: "I want it publicly noted that I protest this infringement of my client's Constitutional rights!" he shouted. "This smacks of backroom politics!"

"That's enough, Counselor!" the judge exploded, jumping to his feet. "I warned you in chambers…"

"Justice cannot be gagged!" the lawyer shouted back.

The judge stared for just an instant and then turned back to the Bailiff. "Get them out of here!" he ordered.

Josh gave Landry a thumbs-up as the NCO came to his seat to shoo him from the courtroom, although his friend gave no outward sign he'd seen or understood. As he walked from the chamber he glanced over at the prosecution desk. The major from the General Counsel's Office was smiling broadly, chatting with the prosecution team.

'Somehow I doubt Jacobs won Landry any new friends with that speech,' he thought cheerlessly as he was ushered out of the room. *'But I'm still glad he did it.'*

As soon as he stepped into the daylight outside the Admin building, Josh headed straight for the nearest payphone. But he'd gone less than a city block when he heard footsteps coming up quickly behind him. He stopped to look back. Captain Harris from the MACV planning group came to a huffing, puffing stop right next to him.

"Daniels, General Rattling requires your presence in his office – ASAP!"

Rattling? Josh hadn't said two words to the man since Day One at MACV. "Since when are you Rattling's errand boy?" he asked the red-faced officer.

"Just get your ass over to MACV – now!" Harris spit venomously. Not waiting for a reply, he pivoted and left Josh standing dumbfounded.

'What the hell does that old fart want?' he wondered. He'd always dealt directly with General Edwards. Whatever it was, it would have to wait. He had a call to make.

As usual, his father was not available, so he left a detailed message with the congressman's secretary. He couched his words carefully, telling just enough so that his father would understand the circumstances, but not so much that his secretary would grasp the importance and possibly blab to one of her office-mates. It wouldn't do to have the General Counsel's office tipped off before his father could ask around about the closing of the court-martial.

As soon as he hung up the phone, he walked across the large open plaza between MACV buildings and into the Headquarters low-rise. He went directly to General Rattling's office, where he was told to 'have a seat' by Corporal Wilding. A half-hour later he was still seated, still waiting.

"The general will see you now," Wilding announced after nearly 50 minutes. She didn't flirt with him like the first time he'd been there.

Josh half-expected to see Wilcox, or at least Winshotz in the Deputy Commander's office, but the general sat all by himself behind a big oak desk.

"Captain Daniels – thank you for coming over here so quickly," Rattling said with a smile, putting Josh on the defensive at once.

'What the hell is this?' he asked himself. *'First I'm ordered to report, now I'm thanked for doing what I'd been ordered to do. Something's not right.'*

Josh snapped to attention and saluted. "Sir."

"At ease, at ease," Rattling said, waving away the formalities. "Have a seat."

Now Josh knew he was in trouble, but he did as he was told.

"Captain, I'm well aware of the troubles your friend Lieutenant Landry is experiencing," Rattling went on, "and I just want you to know that all of us here at MACV Command are rooting for him."

Josh tried not to show any reaction, though he was tempted to yell 'Liar!' to the man's face. He knew damn well that the entire Command Staff was hoping the whole court-martial and especially 'the Landry problem' would just go away.

"Thank you sir," he said, keeping his voice as emotionless as possible.

"But the work of the U.S. military here in Vietnam must go on. You understand that, don't you?"

"Yes sir." He felt rather than heard the doubt creep into his voice.

"Good, good, I told them as much. Now what I'm about to tell you is classified, Captain. For the time being, it's not to be shared with anyone outside this room."

Josh tensed. *'What was going on?'*

The general leaned forward as if drawing Josh into his confidence. "Washington has just released a most disturbing report about a village up-country, a place call My-Lai."

Josh had never heard of it, though that didn't surprise him that much since there were thousands of small villages scattered all over the country.

"There was an... *incident.*"

Something about the way he pronounced the word made Josh's skin crawl. "What kind of... incident?" he asked.

"Well, reports are conflicting at this point, but whatever the details it seems clear that an American unit was involved in an unfortunate attack on a civilian population about a year ago, including a number of women and children." The general stared at Josh as if daring him to react. He held his poker face.

'A year ago?'

"Were there many casualties?"

"Quite a few. And there have already been press inquiries."

Ah. Now Josh was getting an inkling of why the Big Brass might be upset. Bad soldiering was one thing; bad press quite another.

He had a million questions, but held his tongue. This was the general's meeting; he'd get around to sharing when he was damn well ready.

"Now, you must be wondering why I'm telling you all this," Rattling continued as if he'd heard Josh's thoughts.

"It had crossed my mind, sir."

"Yes, well, it looks like this attack may stir up a real big shitstorm, another black eye for the U.S. military. We're looking for people who might be able to help us… handle the media inquiries."

'And a decorated congressman's son might be just the person,' Josh thought. He wasn't going to make it that easy on them. "I'm not very well-versed in PR," he said.

"I understand, but your name has come up in our discussions of soldiers who could be brought up-to-speed quickly. We've got some contractors from the States on their way out here to work with us here on the ground. We were hoping you might be willing to be a liaison between them and MACV."

Hoping? Since when did a general 'hope' that a soldier would do as ordered? "So it would be more of an administrative position, then?" he asked. "No direct contact with the press?"

"Well, let's just say it would *primarily* involve admin duties. However, I can't say that there wouldn't be opportunities to interact with certain media elements on occasion."

'Opportunities? 'On occasion?' Josh felt as though he was being sold a used car. His BS antennas were fully extended.

"I don't know sir. My duties with the Planning Group already take up most of my time."

"Those duties would be suspended," the general came back much too quickly. "Temporarily, of course."

Josh was still confused. "General, is this a request, or an order?"

The general's eyebrows arched appraisingly. "We'd prefer it to be voluntary," he said, the alternative clearly indicated.

Josh nodded. "May I take a while to think about it?"

"Of course, of course!" Rattling said, "But not too long. Let's say... tomorrow morning, 0800? We need to move on this before we get behind the curve with the press."

Josh realized full-well they wanted to use him, but wasn't that what the Army did – use people? No, it was more the timing, during Landry's trial, that made him have second thoughts.

"I'll need to testify at Landry's court-martial," he spoke his doubts aloud.

"Understood!" the general said with the salivating energy of a shark circling its prey. "I wouldn't think that would take more than an hour or two, would you?"

Josh wasn't sure how long it would take. Jacobs had said it would largely depend on the prosecution. If they wanted to hammer him with questions, it might be a drawn-out affair.

"I'm not sure. I don't think so."

"Good! Then are we agreed, or do you still need more time?"

Josh could almost see the sharp jagged teeth of a shark in his expectant smile. "I guess we are sir. When do I start?"

"Good man!" the general said, jumping to his feet and extending his hand. "I knew you'd see the light. The plane from the States arrives at 1330 hours. Can you be there to meet them and give a basic orientation?"

"If I'm not needed at the court-martial," he insisted.

"Of course, of course! I'll send word to the prosecutor's office to keep you apprised of the scheduling."

"All right, then I'll be there." From the little he'd heard it would be a nasty job, but *someone* had to do it. Rattling gave him the name of a colonel in Public Affairs who was coordinating the media control campaign, and told Josh to report to an office at MACV headquarters ASAP. He saluted and left the office, intending to contact Jacobs, General Edwards, and his father as soon as he could get to a phone. He'd get to the PA people in a short while.

As soon as Josh left his office, however, the general placed his own phone call. "Major Wilcox? General Rattling here. He's taken it on. Uh huh. No, no real trouble. Your strategy worked perfectly. Okay, I'll see what I can do." As he hung up, the general fell back into his chair, a worried expression reflecting the conflict he felt in his gut.

*****

As usual, Josh wasn't able to reach his father so he left another message. More surprisingly, he got a recording machine at Jacobs' office. At first he worried, since someone had always answered the phone after just one or two rings, but after a moment's reflection decided that the lawyer was probably still at the court-martial – with his assistant. He decided to call back later in the afternoon and headed back to MACV Headquarters to see if Col. Henry was anywhere to be found. Henry was probably his closest friend in the planning meeting. Well, perhaps *friend* was overstating it – *friendly acquaintance* was closer to the truth.

As luck would have it, the colonel was in his office when Josh arrived.

"Josh, what brings you down here to the worker bees' ghetto? Slumming?" Henry's brilliant white teeth contrasted vividly with a dark tan.

"Colonel, do you have a couple of minutes?"

The colonel told him to take a seat, and Josh quickly ran through the scenario of Rattling asking him to front the My-Lai situation, without revealing any of the particulars. Thankfully, the colonel knew what he was talking about.

"Ol' Ratbag asked you to work with the media?" the puzzled colonel asked. Josh got the sense Henry wasn't a big fan of the general.

"Strange, huh? I mean, I understand that I'm a congressman's son and all, but this sounds like it might make a real stink. You'd think they'd go with pros."

"You would, wouldn't you?" It was a statement, not a question. "So what are they up to?"

Josh told him about Landry and the court-martial. "And you think the media job might be somehow connected with Landry?"

"I don't know. Maybe not. I was hoping you might've heard something."

Henry shook his head. "Sorry. No clue. But I'm not in on a lot of the decision-making. Can't you wangle something out of Edwards?"

"Can't even reach him."

"Another coincidence?"

"Could be, I suppose. But I don't believe in coincidences."

"Yeh, neither do I actually. Look, let me make a few calls, and I'll see what I can find out."

"Don't tell them I told you – it's supposed to be hush-hush."

"Hush-hush?" Henry asked. "Everyone in this place has known about it for months, and I'm guessing even the media finally has the bone between their teeth. But I'll keep your name out of it. Call me around 1600."

Josh agreed and shook the colonel's hand before leaving for the Public Affairs office upstairs.

*****

Colonel Bradley Winston was a tall, heavyset man with thinning black hair and the kind of beard that made him look like he always needed a shave.

"Captain Daniels!" he greeted Josh with much too much enthusiasm. "Welcome to MACV Public Affairs!"

Josh's first instinct was to cringe, but he restrained himself. "Colonel. Captain Joshua Daniels, reporting for duty" He came to attention and saluted.

Winston looked at him as if he'd lost his mind. "Enough of that!" he said, waving off the salute. "This is PA, not the front lines. We take things a little more… relaxed down here."

"Except, of course, when all hell is breaking loose, the media are breathing down our necks, and the big shots in Washington are baying for our blood," an attractive young woman added as she strolled into the office unannounced. Josh glanced over to see the thin, strawberry blonde officer stride confidently in his direction with her hand held out. He strained to see the insignia on her shoulder to determine her rank.

"Hey, my eyes are up here," she said with a smile, "though I appreciate the vote of confidence."

Josh blushed in spite of himself and glanced up into her pale blue eyes.

"Give the captain a break, Gordon. He's not used to PA humor," the colonel chided.

"Lieutenant Linda Gordon," the woman continued, "who'd you piss off to get sent down here?"

"Josh Daniels," Josh replied numbly.

"I know *that*," she said. "We all know the courageous Captain Daniels. Hell, I wrote the release when you got your medals."

"Gordon – enough!" Colonel Winston barked, and this time the lieutenant paid attention.

"Just trying to make the newbie feel at home," she said, slightly abashed.

"Well try a little less," Winston grumbled. "Both of you, take a seat."

Josh waited for Gordon to sit and then joined her in front of the colonel's desk.

"Daniels, I take it you know why you're down here?" he asked.

"I, ah, I know about the… incident up north."

"Incident? It was a goddamn massacre!" Gordon chimed-in.

"Keep your opinions to yourself," Winston ordered without a smile. "It was a tragic incident that occurred over a year ago."

"That was a long time ago," Josh said. "It's just coming to light now?"

Gordon shrugged with an 'I told you so' look of exasperation.

"It has been under investigation by both the US and Vietnamese authorities," Winston said, as if that would explain the long delay.

"Smells of a cover-up," Gordon said. When she saw the colonel's reaction she threw up her hands as if to protect herself. "Not that it is!" she corrected. "But there will be those who see it that way."

"There are always people who want to think the worst, especially about this conflict," Winston grumbled, half to himself. "The point is, there were a number of casualties and we need to implement the public affairs strategy that's been developed over the last year plus."

"How many – casualties?" Josh asked.

"The exact number is in some dispute…" the colonel began.

"Somewhere between 350 and 500, including a large number of women and children," the lieutenant said, this time with cool professionalism. "And there are photos."

"My God," Josh said softly. His thoughts flashed back to the small village nearly a year earlier. He found it difficult to exhale.

Winston nodded with a pained grimace. "It's bad, there's no denying that. But we need to get our side out there before the rabid 4ᵗʰ estate runs off half-cocked. This isn't a case of the U.S. Army doing something terrible, it's just one unit that ran amok."

"Just?" Gordon said.

"Okay, bad choice of words. But you get the idea."

"*That's* our PA strategy?"

"Do you have a better idea?" the colonel challenged.

"I…" Josh could barely get his brain around the whole affair. "I'll have to think about it."

"Good luck," Gordon said. "They've had every beltway bandit in DC working on coming up with a palatable way to spin this for over a year, and calling it an 'unfortunate aberration' is the best they've come up with. Of course, calling it a *great victory* right after the incident didn't help much."

"What?!"

"Now Lieutenant, that's not quite true," Colonel Winston corrected.

"No? They put out information saying the majority of deaths were Viet Cong, and admitted to only a couple dozen civilian casualties. What would you call that?"

Only a couple of dozen? Josh felt like hitting something, or someone. What the hell had the War come to when killing dozens of civilians was considered collateral damage?

Winston passed a thick envelope across the desk. "Here – it's all in here. Read it through, and let's get together this afternoon to talk about it. How about 1600 hours?"

Josh was almost speechless. "Yeh, okay. I'll be back at 1600."

"Me too?" Gordon asked.

"Are you still part of this team?"

"As far as I know."

"Then be here."

"Okay… sir," she spit.

"You're both dismissed," Winston said wearily, turning to some paperwork without even looking up at the two officers. "Oh, and Daniels," the colonel said as an afterthought, "that material is highly classified – it needs to stay in this building."

Josh hauled himself up out of the chair and saluted from habit. Gordon sneered in his general direction.

As soon as they were out the door, the lieutenant grabbed Josh by the sleeve and pulled him to a stop.

"Look, Captain, I don't know what you did to get yourself assigned to this screwed-up duty, but I've got to warn you: it's gonna be messy. Real messy."

"I'm getting that feeling. How long have you been working on it?"

"I found out about the *incident* two days ago. Seems a writer for the New York Times has gotten ahold of the story and is about to go public. That's when the crap will really hit the fan."

"Any idea when he plans to publish?"

"He's been bugging the Pentagon for a comment, so they think the story will come out any day now."

"I guess I'd better read this stuff then, huh?" he said, patting the thick envelope.

"Do it on an empty stomach," she warned. "Those bastards went absolutely batshit."

Josh nodded. "I guess I'll see you at 1600."

"I'll be there," she said.

Josh managed to access an outside line in a nearby office and called Jacobs once again. He got the same answering machine. Anxious to learn what'd been going on, he debated running over to the Admin building to try to get a note to the lawyer, but one look at the amount of material in the envelope he carried made him decide to postpone any side trips until he'd plowed through it all. He hunkered down in the small office, locking the door behind him.

Gordon had been right: the pictures and descriptions of the attack portrayed an entire unit completely out of control. According to the Army investigation, the officer in charge lost it and the men followed his lead. It looked like charges would be brought, but the investigation was having problems getting the men in the unit to talk. Great.

By the time Josh read the detailed report and took several pages of notes, it was nearly time to head over to the Air Base and meet the incoming flight with the Washington contractors. A couple of Jeeps had already been put at his disposal by Rattling's office, so as soon as he locked the investigation material in a secure file cabinet he hurried over to the Base. Turned out the flight was just a few minutes late – a rare occurrence – and so Josh was barely in place when the jet rolled to a stop. He watched the passengers stream down the stairway, trying to pick out the contractors by sight. Since virtually every person on the plane wore the omnipresent drab green Army uniform, it wasn't all that difficult to pick out the PR professionals: four men, spanning the spectrum from 20-something to middle-aged, tie-and-jacket to flowery Hawaiian shirt and casual slacks, and two women – both in their late 20's or early 30's, both wearing tailored slacks and white blouses.

Josh had been given the passenger list by Rattling, so he knew the makeup of the team and headed in their direction as soon as they reached the tarmac.

"Welcome to Vietnam," he said with all the false enthusiasm he could muster. "I'm Captain Josh Daniels, and I'll be working with you on this assignment."

The senior member of the group, both in terms of age as well as authority, shook Josh's hand with more gusto than his exhausted appearance would've suggested. "Jack Denton," he introduced himself, "pleased to meet you." He went on to introduce the other five. As soon as the niceties were over, Josh ushered the entire group into the waiting Jeeps and then to their temporary quarters. Josh was eager to drop them off and be on his way, but Denton was just as eager to discuss the *situation*. So they discussed it. And discussed it. Until Josh didn't think there could possibly be another perspective or approach to consider. Denton seemed prepared to go on indefinitely, however when Josh glanced at his watch he was surprised to see it was quarter to four – barely enough time to get back to MACV Headquarters for the meeting with Winston.

"I'm sorry, sir," Josh announced as he pulled together all his notes, interrupting the talkative PR man in mid-sentence, "but I've got a meeting at 1600 hours with Colonel Winston and other members of his team. I've got to get going."

Denton glanced at his own watch – a Rolex, Josh noted – and his eyes opened wide. "My God, I'm supposed to be at the same meeting. May I come with you?"

What could Josh say, other than "Sure thing." Luckily he'd kept one of the Jeeps on standby for himself, so they made it to MACV on time. Josh desperately wanted to call Col. Henry to find out the real scoop about his assignment to the PA team, but with the civilian PR man in tow and both of them running late, there was no way to make it happen. They barely had time to stop at a bathroom. By the time they got upstairs, Lieutenant Gordon was already deep in conversation with several other officers, including Winston.

"Jack, you made it!" the colonel greeted Denton. They shook hands warmly.

"Looks like they're bosom buddies," Gordon whispered to Josh. He hadn't seen her sidle up to him and felt ill-at-ease chatting with the diminutive blond – at least until he knew better where she was coming from and who she reported to.

"Definitely not their first rodeo."

"Not likely. I wonder who's in charge."

"Probably neither of them."

"I think we'll find out soon enough."

Rather than stay put and continue the back and forth with Gordon, Josh moved to where Denton and Winston were chatting. The civilian put his arm around the captain's shoulder and pulled him into the discussion.

"Had a good session with your Captain Daniels, here," he told Winston. "He's got a good head for this sort of thing."

Winston smiled at Josh. "Had a feeling he might. He's been around the media most of his life."

To Denton's questioning look, Winston added, "He's Mark Daniels' kid."

The light went on in Denton's eyes. "Ah, so you're no stranger to press scrutiny then," he said to Josh.

"Not like *this*," Josh answered. "But I've been around the media some, yes."

"Good. It'll help to have an actual combat officer who knows his way around journalists. They lay a tougher minefield than the enemy in the field sometimes." He smiled at his witticism.

Josh didn't smile. "Are journalists the enemy?"

Denton looked to Winston, who quickly took the lead. "Just a figure of speech, Daniels. All Jack means is that they have their job, and we have ours – right Jack?"

"Couldn't have said it better myself," the PR man said, as he and the colonel exchanged a smug self-satisfied look. Josh suddenly wondered what the hell he was doing there. But before he could give it a second thought, the colonel called the meeting to order.

After introducing all the members present, and the four new arrivals in absentia, Winston turned the meeting over to Denton, who rehashed every detail of the incident just as he'd done with

Josh. After an hour listening to the PR man drone on, and suffering through too many impossibly naïve and just plain dumb questions from his fellow attendees, Josh thought he might vomit if he heard the word *incident* one more time. Finally, he couldn't take it anymore.

"Don't you think that people will see through an attempt to downplay this as an *incident*?" he asked in the middle of a strategy session. Ten eyes looked at him askance.

"What would *you* call it?" Denton asked him.

"A terrible mistake. A mistaken attack. Something that tells people we realize the unit screwed up and we're sorry about it."

The two officers Josh had just met both looked to the colonel for his reaction.

Winston hesitated, seemingly thinking it over.

"Makes sense to me," Lt. Gordon volunteered when the silence became oppressive. "Last thing we need now is for people to think there's a cover-up."

"There is no cover-up!" Winston bellowed with such vehemence that the other members flinched. "We will make all the facts known in good time."

"It's been over a year," Gordon whispered.

"It takes time to investigate this sort of thing," Winston went on, and Josh didn't know who he was trying to convince – them or himself.

An awkward pause ended when Denton suggested they "move on to the next order of business." Gordon shrugged at Josh, sharing his frustration.

By the time the group finally called it a day, it was clear that Josh and Gordon were a minority of two when it came to championing a more truthful approach to reporting the *incident* to the public. Everyone else seated at the table – which really amounted to just Denton and Winston since the two junior officers went along with everything the two more senior members said – agreed to couch descriptions of the attack in language that obscured more than it revealed.

"That was a very satisfying first get-together," Gordon said sarcastically as she shadowed Josh from the Headquarters building. "Why did they even bother to invite us if they had no intention of listening to our input?"

"I was wondering the same thing," Josh answered. "Seems they've already decided on their strategy."

"They're asking for trouble when the media finds out they've been dancing all around the truth. And the media always finds out, sooner or later."

"Doesn't make sense," Josh answered, his thoughts straying to Landry. "Hey, sorry to chat and run, but I've got a few calls to make."

"The New York Times?" she asked with a grin.

"Something like that. I guess I'll see you tomorrow." Winston had called another meeting for 0800.

"Yeh, see you then."

Josh headed straight for a payphone. First he called Jacobs' office, but got a busy signal. *'At least he's there,'* Josh thought, hanging up and immediately dialing Col. Henry's number. He was over an hour late getting back to the colonel, but he knew Henry often worked right up until dinner time.

Luck was with him; Henry answered on the first ring.

"Henry."

"Colonel, it's Josh Daniels. I'm sorry I'm so late…"

"Don't worry about it; I don't have all that much to tell you anyway. I checked with a few of my buddies, both at Headquarters and in the field, but none of them knew anything of interest about Landry. Most of them didn't even know he was being court-martialled."

"So what's the deal with adding me to the PA team for the My-Lai attack?" he asked. "Am I just being paranoid?"

"Don't know. Might be just coincidence, I suppose. It does happen, occasionally."

"Yeh, maybe. Well, thanks for checking. I'm going to run over to Landry's lawyer's office and see how that went this afternoon."

"They've really got you jumping, don't they?"

"Big time. I guess I'll see you when I see you."

"You're not coming to the morning meeting tomorrow?"

"I've got a PA meeting at 0800 that'll probably run all morning, if not longer. Those PA guys can really BS."

"That's why they're in PA, I suppose."

"So why am I?" He didn't expect an answer, and he didn't get one.

*****

By the time Josh arrived at Jacobs' office, the sun was disappearing behind the smoky, jagged skyline of Saigon. Late afternoon traffic had slowed his travel, and as his mini-cab pulled up in front of the lawyer's building he was beginning to wonder if he'd wasted a trip. But the handle to the office door turned easily in his hand and he found the lawyer bent over his desk, hard at work.

"Jesus Christ, Daniels, where have you been?!" Jacobs called out as soon as Josh stepped into the outer office. "I've been trying to get ahold of you for hours!"

The way Jacobs looked and sounded told Josh something bad had happened.

"I was called away to an important meeting," he explained. "Why? What's going on?"

The lawyer took off his glasses and dropped them wearily to his desk. He motioned to the lone chair in front of his paper-strewn desk. "Have a seat."

"What?" Josh asked again.

Jacobs took a big breath. "The prosecuting officer only presented three witnesses: that guy from his unit – Corporal White, a DC-based shrink, and one of the MPs who took him into custody. They all claimed that Landry was with-it enough to understand what he was doing when he walked away from his post, and still knew what he'd done when he was hospitalized and jailed. They basically made him out to be a malcontent who knowingly deserted."

"That's bullshit!" Josh exploded. "I've known that guy for years, and I'd bet everything I own that he was off his rocker when he walked away."

"I know, I know," Jacobs said, his face showing the pain of the afternoon encounter. "But without your testimony, and with no medical evidence of a pre-existing condition or even a visit to a medical unit, it came down to our Sgt. Makris versus Corporal White. Makris got shredded by the Prosecution, while I couldn't budge White from his testimony that Landry had been giving rational orders right up until the hour he walked."

"You know White is out to get back at Landry for not making more of an effort to rescue his buddy."

"I know."

"Did you make that point to the Judge?"

"I tried. White said it had nothing to do with his friend, and the Prosecutor kept objecting when I tried to make him change his tune."

"What about Colonel Lesser? Didn't he speak-up for Landry?"

Jacobs held his palms open in frustration. "He tried too. But he wasn't there when the alleged desertion took place. He never examined Landry before he was admitted to his hospital. And the

Prosecution's hired gun from DC contradicted everything he said. At best, it was a draw."

"Goddamn it, they're trying to nail Landry to the cross just to make a point!"

"I wish I could tell you something different, but it looks that way."

"Okay, okay," Josh said, trying to calm down, "so what's the plan? Will you call me to testify tomorrow? Maybe I can sway the Judge…"

"There is no tomorrow, Captain," Jacobs said softly. "They closed testimony and adjourned to reach a verdict. When you came in I thought you might be my assistant bringing word already."

"But I haven't had a chance to testify!"

Jacobs stared at the young captain with a look of undisguised sympathy. "I'm not sure if it would've made a difference. You weren't in the field with him, Captain, and as a friend of his everything you said would've been viewed as biased."

Josh stood and began to pace. "This is insane!"

Jacobs watched him trudge back and forth in front of his desk.

"What did Landry say? Did he testify in his own defense?"

The lawyer shook his head. "He refused. Once he heard White's testimony he shut down and kept mumbling he 'had it coming.' With him in that condition I couldn't risk forcing him to testify."

"Did you ask for a postponement?"

"Denied."

"How can this happen?" Josh asked. "How can they railroad a good officer just to make a point?"

"From their perspective they're helping the cause, reducing the number of soldiers willing to chance a court-martial to get away from this terrible War."

"'*Every* soldier is sacred,' that's what they told us at the Academy," Josh said, more to himself than to the lawyer. "I guess they meant every soldier except Landry."

"Look, Josh, there's still a chance they won't convict."

Josh glared at Jacobs with open incredulity.

"Okay, so not much of a chance," the lawyer admitted. "But we can still appeal. All the way up to the Commander in Chief, if necessary. Make a big stink in the media."

"After what the public is about to find out, I'm not sure they'll give a damn about one soldier more or less."

"How's that?"

Josh caught himself. "Nothing, just muttering out loud. So, can I see Landry? How'd he take all this?"

"Like I said, he sort of shut down. Didn't show much emotion one way or another."

"Are they letting him have visitors?"

"I don't know. I came straight back here to start drafting the appeal once I saw how things were headed. You'll have to ask the prosecution, I imagine."

"I may have a better idea."

Jacobs wanted to probe further, but Josh was in a hurry.

CHAPTER 24

By the time Josh got to the hospital, darkness had fallen and the buzz of the city had settled into its usual lower-pitched nightly hum. Josh hoped against hope that Colonel Lesser was still on the premises. But even if he'd gone home, Josh *would* see his friend.

He asked the guard at the entrance to call Lesser, and to his surprise the colonel answered on the first ring.

"It's that Captain Daniels here again," the guard said into the telephone mouthpiece, making no effort to disguise his irritation. "Yeh, okay."

The guard hung up the phone. "The colonel's in his office," he snapped. "Wait here for an escort." Josh didn't need any more information, and the guard didn't offer any.

It took several minutes for an MP to come out to the entrance and accompany him into the dimly-lit building. Moans and gut-wrenching cries greeted him as soon as he passed through the heavy security door. He led rather than followed the MP, making his way to Lesser's office as quickly as he could without running. The MP waited without saying a word as he knocked on the door with mounting impatience.

"Come in!" the colonel's familiar voice directed.

Lesser stood from behind his desk and stepped forward to greet Josh.

"I take it you've heard?"

"Jacobs told me. How's Landry taking it?"

Lesser pointed him to a chair. "Not so good. That corporal's testimony really hit him hard. I could see it from the gallery."

"They let you watch the proceedings?!"

"Medical exception. I told them I wouldn't be responsible for his competence unless I was present."

"You think he's competent?" There was no doubting Josh's opinion.

The colonel tilted his head from side to side. "Sometimes, yes. Sometimes, no. My main reason for being there was to pull him out if he lost it."

"But you didn't – pull him out. Yet the way Jacobs described it, he basically shut down when White told his story. You didn't consider that 'losing it'?" The edge to his voice was deathly sharp.

"No, I didn't. I spoke with him during a short recess immediately after the corporal's testimony, and it seemed clear to me he knew exactly what was happening in that courtroom. Or, if not exactly, pretty darnn close."

Josh stared at him with narrowed eyes. *Was Lesser in on it too? If so, they were lost.*

"Did the Judge know you were there to evaluate Landry?"

"Of course not! Like I said, I made it seem like I was there just in case the lieutenant fell into the deep end. If anything, I made him sound worse than he was. Oh - don't tell the Judge that."

Josh breathed a sigh of relief. At least Lesser was still on their side. He let the colonel's words bounce around his brain until he came to a decision. He had other questions, but one request outweighed them all: "Can I see him?" he asked, trying not to sound too desperate.

"Landry? I don't see why not. Although he may have gone to sleep already." Lesser picked up a large set of keys and stood. "Come on – let's take a look."

Josh waited for the colonel to lock his door and then the two of them walked through the long, eerie corridors to Landry's wing. Josh fought the urge to rush on ahead, instead keeping pace with the slow-moving doctor. At last they came to room D-417. Lesser pulled out his keys and flipped though several until he found the one he was looking for.

"Let me go in first," he said. "If he's sleeping, I don't want to startle him."

The colonel cracked opened the door, took one step, then stopped. Josh saw a look come over his face that nearly stopped his heart.

"What? What's the matter?" he asked. When the colonel didn't answer, he pushed past him and threw open the door. The bed was empty, disheveled. It took just a moment before he saw the silent shadow turning slowly on the wall; he looked up and saw the knotted bed sheet, the purple, bloated face.

Someone yelled out, a scream of pure, uncontrolled terror that echoed through the hallways like the cry of a wounded animal. At first, Josh didn't realize the voice had been his.

*****

It had been a nightmare, a real, living nightmare. Just minutes after they'd discovered Landry, MPs poured into the hospital, their eyes gleaming with purpose. They interviewed Josh three times. With each telling the facts became more unreal, more unbelievable. By the end of the third telling, the words held no meaning for him. They were just sounds, disassociated from events, necessary only to fulfill his duty.

His duty. The thought of it made him sick to his stomach. Landry had always wanted to do his duty, and now Landry was dead. Killed by the very people he'd fought for, killed for. Josh tried to make sense of it, tried to convince himself that it was because of the War — after all, bad stuff happened in wars. But the more he repeated the mantra, the less he believed it. *Wars don't kill, soldiers kill.* And in this instance, his friend's own people had done the job.

It was nearly two hours later when the investigating officers finally cut him and Lesser loose. The colonel tried to talk to him, tried to explain why *'things like this'* happened, but it seemed to Josh as if his voice were coming from a long ways away, from a different place than the place they both inhabited. He nodded, made believe he was listening, but the words never got past his ears.

The heavy night air shrouded him in blackness as he walked from the hospital building, an enveloping blanket that weighed him down, made breathing difficult. He made no conscious choice where to go, he could not, but his feet took him toward a familiar address in the city.

He pounded on the door to the apartment building for several long moments, until his eyes focused on the button for the buzzer; he stabbed at it like a rattler striking prey. The door buzzed open without any questions from the intercom speaker, not that Josh noticed. He trudged up the staircase, his feet increasingly unwilling to move. He felt tired, so tired…

When her hand came to rest on his arm, he looked up for the first time and saw her worried face. She said nothing, just grabbed him under the shoulder and struggled to guide him up the stairs and into the apartment. Josh barely saw her father standing silently in the middle of a large open space as she ushered him directly to a bedroom. The last thing he remembered, her arms held his head tight to her breasts as warm tears poured down his cheeks.

*****

When he awoke, Josh felt as though he were encased in a velvet cocoon. For just an instant, one short, fleeting instant, he lay there staring at the ceiling, unaware of where he was and why he was there. But then it all came crashing back down on him: the court-martial, the treachery, the shadow spinning ever so slowly on the hospital wall. He pinched his eyes shut, but when he opened them nothing had changed. It was not a nightmare he'd be awakening from.

"How do you feel?" Kim-Ly asked, and for the first time he realized she was sitting on the edge of the bed, looking down at him with sad, worried eyes.

"Landry's dead," he croaked, his voice raw and sore.

She closed her eyes as if in prayer, then opened them slowly. Tears hung in her lashes.

"How?"

"Killed himself. But they drove him to it."

She didn't have to ask who 'they' were. She put her hand on his cheek and held it there, tenderly.

"I'm so sorry."

He nodded, a lump forming in his throat. But he didn't feel like crying. He wasn't sure he'd ever cry again.

He looked past her, out a window at the gray morning light beyond.

"It's bullshit," he whispered. "It's all bullshit."

CHAPTER 25

He didn't report for the morning PA meeting. Instead, he went back to his quarters, alone. Kim-Ly had tried to convince him to stay, or to let her come with him, but he needed to be alone.

Landry was dead.

As hard as he tried, he couldn't get his head around that simple fact. He was dead.

Whenever he thought of the court-martial and his dubious assignment to the My-Lai task force – and he could think of little else – his pulse began to race and the blood pounded in his temples.

"Goddamn 'em! Goddamn 'em all!" he shouted. His words echoed in the concrete block room as he slammed his fist into the top of his desk, again, and again. The sweet pain brought him focus, and that's what he wanted more than anything right then – focus. He would make them pay, the whole damn bunch of them. He wasn't sure how yet, but he'd find a way. He owed Landry that much.

Josh had left his quarters just once since he'd awakened from a brief restless sleep – to call Landry's parents. His mother's stifled cry when he'd told her that their oldest son was dead still reverberated in his head. It was like no sound he'd ever heard before; it was a sound he hoped never to hear again.

Josh sat and stared at the wall in front of him, seeing nothing. He wasn't hungry. There was no one he wanted to talk to. There was nothing to do. Landry was dead.

A loud pounding on his door barely penetrated his grief and anger.

"Daniels, I know you're in there!" the voice of Colonel Henry called out. "Open the damn door!"

Josh considered ignoring the voice, but Henry was a friend. He pushed himself to an upright position and struggled to make his feet move toward the renewed pounding.

When he finally got to the door he stood there for several long seconds, debating whether to open it, until he turned the throw bolt and stepped back. The door swung inwards almost immediately.

"Jesus Christ!" Henry said as soon as he saw Josh's face. "Are you sick?!"

Josh turned away from him and shuffled back toward his desk. He dropped into the chair and stared at his feet. He was surprised to find he wasn't wearing any boots.

"Landry's dead," he said softly.

"Yeh. Real sorry to hear it. Seemed like a good guy."

"He was a good soldier!" Josh said with more vehemence than Henry would've thought he could muster. "They killed him. Those bastards back in Washington."

The colonel turned quickly and peeked both ways out the open doorway before shutting and locking the door. He crouched down so that his face was even with Josh's.

"Daniels... Josh – you gotta keep it down," he whispered. "They already have their doubts about you."

"Fuck those sons-of-bitches! They're not going to get away with this!" he screamed louder than ever.

Henry grabbed him by the forearm, tightly. "Okay, alright. But you're not going to be able to do much about it if you're locked up in a loony bin somewhere. Are you?"

Josh stared at the colonel. Suddenly a wave of cold fear swept through him. *Had they sent him? Was Henry one of* **them**?

As if he could read his thoughts, the colonel grabbed Josh's arm with both hands. "We can do it, Josh. We can make sure they don't get away with this. But we have to be smart. We have to be careful. Do you understand?"

The way he pronounced the last made Josh realize that Henry thought he might have lost it. A gray haze partially lifted from his brain.

"I'm not crazy, Colonel. Not by a long shot," he said, looking straight into Henry's eyes. "As a matter of fact, I may be more sane than I've been for a long time. Since I got to this stinking country."

A small smile crept over Henry's lips. "Good. Good! Now, let's talk."

*****

By the time Henry left his quarters, Josh had a plan. He hadn't told the colonel everything. Not yet. He trusted him, but only so far. Until he was ready to move, no one would know. Oh, he'd told Henry that he'd be contacting his congressman father back in Washington, and made it seem like they'd be using his clout to get at the people responsible for prosecuting Landry. And he would. At least try. But that was just a part of his plan. The rest he'd do himself.

The colonel had persuaded him to get back into his routine, to make it seem like he'd gotten over Landry's death. Josh had seen the logic in that and promised to do his best.

"Don't ever let them see your true feelings," Henry had said. "You're a Ranger – act like one."

And he would.

*****

The sun seemed to shine too brightly, the noise of the base seemed a cacophonous roar in his ears. But he forced himself to leave his room and make his way over to the hospital. He needed to speak to Lesser. Get his advice, *and* his consent.

"You sure you want to go this route?" the colonel asked when he'd sketched out the basic outline of his plan. No details, but enough so the hospital Director could understand what he was consenting to.

"They *killed* him, Colonel. They need to pay for that."

"You understand what they'll do when they find out it was you, don't you? Your career will be over."

"I'll face that problem if and when it comes to that. At this point, I don't know if I even want to be part of this Army."

"Josh, as your friend, I'm worried that Landry's death has made you lose perspective…"

"Perspective?!" Josh spit the word as if it were poison. "You and I both know they dragged Landry in front of that court-martial just to make a point. Well they made one, with me at least."

Lesser sighed deeply. "Okay. I'll give you what you need. But I still wish you'd talk to someone – the Chaplain, or Dr. Ellinsten." At the naming of the Base shrink, Josh laughed, a cold, bitter gasp of a sound.

"So they can lock me up too? No thanks. Call me paranoid, but I've seen what those people can do when they want to."

"The Chaplain then?" Lesser was almost pleading.

Josh began to answer, then hesitated. "I'll think about it," he finally agreed. "When can you get me the info?"

"Tomorrow?"

"Good. Thank you. I'll keep your name out of this – I promise."

"I know you will. But Josh, be careful. These people don't play games."

"Neither do I," Josh said as he stood to leave. "Neither do I."

*****

Josh spent a half-hour tracking down several other sources for the information he needed, before he called his father's office in Washington once again from an isolated payphone. This time the Old Man was in.

"Josh! To what do I owe this unexpected call?" the Colonel asked lightly. Josh knew at once the news hadn't reached him.

"Landry's dead," he said. There was no other way to say it. "Hung himself."

"My God." Josh heard the hurt in his father's voice, and it reassured him. He went on to explain the circumstances.

"This isn't right," the Colonel said. "Not right at all."

There was something in his father's voice that made him want to believe he could trust him. He explained what he intended to do.

For several long moments after he finished his explanation there was no response from the other end of the line. Disappointment began to well up inside him.

Then, his father answered. "They're going to come after you, you know."

"I know. But I've got to do it."

"Yeh, I suppose you do." Another long pause. "Look, I'll see what I can do on this end to provide some cover for you. But keep your head down and watch who you share this with. They'll look for any excuse to crucify you if they get word before you make your move."

"They won't know what hit 'em. And thanks, Dad."

Dad. The word had seemed foreign to him for so very long, but after so many years it finally seemed right. When he hung up the phone he felt as if he could take a deep breath for the first time since he'd seen that shadow on the wall.

Landry was dead, but the people responsible would pay.

*****

Josh found an urgent note from Colonel Winston tacked to his quarters' door ordering him to report for a meeting at 1300 hours. He nearly crumbled it up and tossed it in the trash. But instead, he folded it calmly and stuffed it in his pocket. *They'll never know what hit them.*

He forced himself to stop by the officers' mess and eat some lunch, knowing that word of his presence there would soon make its way through the Base grapevine to the people who had engineered Landry's trial. They'd be getting nervous. Just the way he wanted them.

At 1300 he made his way over to Winston's office, arriving just a minute or two late. *Make them sweat.*

"Captain Daniels, we missed you this morning!" Winston said with enough good cheer to elicit raised eyebrows from the other seven people at the table. "Feeling better?"

The implication that Josh had been sick was not lost on anyone in the room. Josh wondered if the colonel was just a good actor, or if he hadn't been told the truth.

"A little," he answered lamely. "Hope I didn't miss anything."

"Oh, I think we made some headway. Didn't we?" he asked the group. There were a few nods and mumbles of agreement. Josh got the opinion that several members weren't especially happy with the way things were going.

"I'm sure you'll get caught up quickly. In fact, let's run through everyone's assigned roles just to reiterate and give Josh a sense of where we're headed. Marsha?"

One of the two civvy women flipped open a notepad and read from the morning's notes with the bored professionalism of a full-time secretary. Apparently she'd been brought along just to keep track of the team's ramblings. It sounded like she was good at it.

It didn't take long for Josh to see that the Beltway Bandits had staked out the behind-the-scenes managerial roles, leaving Gordon and Josh to face the media, Lieutenants Alvarez and Holstace to serve as glorified go-betweens, and Winston as the titular CEO. From the dynamics of the meeting it was obvious to Josh that Denton was running the show, but deferred to Winston in public to make the PA officer feel like he wielded real influence. Josh didn't really care. Let them play their games.

He tried his best to look and sound involved, though it was difficult to listen to their smug platitudes without showing his true feelings. In a nutshell their plan was simple: leak just enough contradictory information to make it seem that there might be a disagreement as to what actually happened at My-Lai, stonewall any questions that might lead to the real truth, and throw the platoon commander, Lt. Calley, under the bus at the first sign that the charade was crumbling. The last wouldn't be too hard, since the lieutenant *had* apparently given the order to shoot the civilians. His own company commander called him 'Lieutenant Shithead'- in public.

"SOP," one of the Bandits said with a self-satisfied grin. *Standard Operating Procedure*. Lie, obfuscate and shift the blame. Nice. Of course the one thing they didn't want to see in the media was an examination of how the entire War had led to this *incident*. That would "embarrass" the Big Brass in Washington. Couldn't have that.

By the time the meeting adjourned about two hours later, Josh felt as if he'd been dipped in pigshit. The whole thing stank to high heavens. But he wouldn't be playing their little game for long. Not long at all.

When Winston finally dismissed the group, Josh was eager to get out of the building and get on with his plan. But the colonel had other ideas. He came straight for Josh, ignoring the entreaties of Gonzalez and even 'Jack', to intercept him before he could slip away.

"Heard about your friend – Landry, was it? Terrible thing. How ya' doing?" He sounded concerned, but Josh didn't buy it for a second. He barely kept his temper in check.

"As well as can be expected, I suppose, sir. It was quite a shock."

"I imagine, I imagine. And if it was anything other than this My-Lai thing, I wouldn't have called you in. But this is going to be big," he whispered, raising his eyebrows for emphasis. "REAL big."

"I understand, sir. I'll do the best I can."

"I'm sure you will, son. Now go get some rest," he said, laying his hand on Josh's shoulder. Josh fought the urge to throw it off. "We're going to need you at full speed, and soon. Maybe as early as tomorrow."

"Thank you, sir. I'll do that."

Perfect. If the assholes thought he was busy pulling himself together, they wouldn't be keeping a close watch on him. He only needed a few hours…

"Daniels!" Gordon called to him just before he could slip out the door. He tried to hide his impatience.

"Lieutenant. I was on my way out."

"I won't keep you long. I just wanted to tell you how sorry I was to hear about Landry." He could sense the pain she felt.

"Thanks," he said softly, his voice catching ever so slightly. "He was a good man."

"Those SOBs!" she whispered. "Should've been one of them."

"They'll get theirs. Maybe not today or tomorrow, but what goes around comes around."

She nodded, and then – to his surprise, she hugged him.

"Hang in there, Captain. Don't let 'em break you."

His eyes narrowed. "Ain't gonna happen," he said. "No way."

*****

As Josh left the headquarters building, he was so absorbed thinking about avenging Landry he didn't notice a senior officer coming up the outer steps to the building until he pushed open the door and nearly knocked him over. It was Major Wilcox, the bastard who'd been sent out from the Pentagon to railroad his friend.

"Daniels!" the major said, his surprise poorly hidden. "I was hoping I'd run into you before I went back to Washington."

Josh fought the urge to smash the guy's face, forcing himself to unball fists which had curled tight of their own volition. "Oh, how is that?" he said in a calm, even voice. He did not want to say or do anything that might make the major suspicious of where his true loyalties lay until he'd dropped his 500 pounder on him and the rest of the bastards in DC.

"I heard about Lieutenant Landry. A tragedy. No matter the outcome of his court-martial, you sure hate to see anyone end up like that." He sounded so convincing, Josh almost believed him.

"Yes, sir. The Army lost a good man."

"Yes, well, I'm headed back to the Pentagon on the flight at 1400 hours this afternoon. Leave the fighting to you experts." His smile never reached his eyes.

Josh couldn't think of anything to say that wouldn't alert the major to the depths of his anger. So he said nothing, or the next best thing.

"We'll do our best, sir."

"I'm sure you will!" Wilcox answered, seemingly relieved. "Your country should be proud of men like you."

"Thank you, sir."

At that, neither man had anything else to say. Wilcox saluted, forcing Josh to salute him back, and the awkward encounter ended with Wilcox hurrying inside and up the stairway that led to the senior officers' offices. Josh watched him go, grinding his teeth. *Not much longer…*

*****

Josh double-timed it directly back to his quarters, where he pulled out his old Smith Corona portable typewriter and finished the letter that had been running through his brain for hours. It was after one when he finished, folded the four sheets of white paper neatly and placed them in an envelope which he addressed by hand before affixing two first class stamps. He then put that envelope into a second one, which he addressed to his father and marked "PERSONAL" in big black letters. Two more stamps, and it was done. Josh admired his work: a very innocuous looking device to cause so much damage – or so he hoped.

He hurried over to the air base, where he made his way to the waiting lounge for the U.S.-bound aircraft scheduled to depart at 1400. Just as he hoped, he found Major Wilcox holding court with three other members of the Prosecution team, including the lead prosecutor himself. Josh caught his breath and walked straight to where the four of them were engaged in a lively, laugh-filled discussion. A First Lieutenant saw Josh first and elbowed the prosecutor who nodded in Josh's direction. Major Wilcox stopped in mid-sentence and wiped the self-satisfied grin from his face.

"Captain Daniels! I didn't expect to see you again so soon!" the major said without missing a beat.

"Major. Gentlemen," Josh said, recognizing the others with a nod. "I wanted to ask you a favor, sir," he said directly to Wilcox.

"Oh? What kind of favor?" Wilcox sounded relaxed, but his eyes darted back and forth anxiously.

Josh pulled out the envelope addressed to his father. "Since you're headed back to DC, would you please drop this is the mail when you get there? I owe my folks a letter or two." He thought he'd used just enough 'aw shucks' attitude to sell the request whole-hog.

Wilcox glanced at the address, saw the 'Congressman' title, and smiled. "Of course, Captain. I'd be happy to do it. Guys, I think you all know Captain Daniels?"

The prosecution team mumbled awkward hellos, which Josh accepted with utter neutrality. They made small talk for a few seconds, but neither Josh nor the four officers had any interest in continuing the discussion past polite chit-chat, and as soon as Josh could make his escape, he did. As he walked from the air base waiting room, he smiled. There was something utterly satisfying about using Wilcox to avenge Landry. *Utterly* satisfying.

*****

Josh spent that night with Kim-Ly. Of course he told her about his plans and tried to console her when she begged him to be careful. But after that, they didn't talk about the War at all – not his plans, not the PA assignment, not even about Landry. For just that evening, just the precious few hours they were together, he wanted to really *be* with her. To leave all the madness and depravity of the War behind. To talk about the future, *their* future. And above all, to celebrate life, the simple, ethereal pleasure of living.

For although he had long ago accepted his own mortality, and come to grips with the fact that he might not leave Vietnam alive, he hadn't fully realized how painful the death of someone close to him would be. Landry's suicide had shaken him to his core. It was the first time someone he cared about, someone he expected to spend many more happy days with, had suddenly, unexpectedly passed away. It wasn't just losing his closest friend that stung, but the realization that it was a harbinger of all the other friends and family who would die before him, if he were so *lucky*.

He looked down at Kim-Ly, at the curve of her jaw, the subtle pout of her lips, the way her eyes drew him in, and his breath caught in his chest – what would he do, what would he be, if she were to disappear from his life? As if she somehow understood what he was thinking, she slipped her hand behind his neck and slowly drew him down to her. Her lips were warm, soft, and her racing heart reassured him and calmed him.

He touched her cheek with the back of his hand. They would go on. They had to.

CHAPTER 26

The next morning Josh reported to the small TV studio the Army had built in the basement of MACV headquarters. It was a tiny room, not much more than an oversized closet, really, with a few massive spotlights hanging from pipes in the ceiling. Winston was already there, as were Lieutenant Gordon, Jack Denton and three other members of the Washington information control team. One member of the studio team, a young lieutenant not much older than Josh, gave them a quick tour of the studio, explaining to Josh and Gordon what each piece of equipment did and reassuring them they would have no problems adjusting to the glare of the overpowering lights needed for recording. Josh wasn't so sure. When they flipped the lights on to give the two of them a sense of what they'd be facing, he could barely keep his eyes open. He began sweating almost as soon as they flared.

"Don't worry – Greta's a whiz with makeup," Denton reassured.

"Can we wear dark glasses?" he asked, only half-joking.

"Oh sure, that would project the honest, open approach we're trying to create," Denton answered with the same half-serious tone.

"At least we'll get a good tan," Gordon chimed in.

After the studio tour, the group adjourned to an adjacent office where they ran through the kinds of questions to expect from journalists who would be invited to a press conference in the next day or two, and were given a rough draft of an announcement of charges being brought against Lt. Calley and others involved in the 'incident.' Josh felt queasy reading the half-truths and evasions of the release. It was as if they had an innate aversion to telling the truth.

"So, what do you think?" Denton asked when they'd completed the run-through. "No big deal, right?"

Josh knew he meant standing up in front of the media and their cameras, but he couldn't help but think he was also referring to the entire spin-control operation.

"It's do-able," he said, "but there's no way we're going to come across like polished professionals by tomorrow or the next day."

"We don't expect you to," Col. Winston replied. "In fact, the more you come across as plain old combat soldiers trying their best to explain a terrible mistake, the better it'll be. Right, Jack?"

"That's the plan: nothing too slick, nothing too polished. You two are the faces of John and Jane Q. Soldier."

Josh saw Gordon flash him a worried look.

"You know I've never done anything like this before, right?" he asked.

"Neither have I," Gordon added.

"We know. But we also know you're both trained infantry officers, used to standing up in front of people and telling them things with great authority. That's all we want here," Denton responded. Winston nodded his approval like one of those bobble-head hounds you see on the dashboard in redneck pickup trucks.

"And you *will* get some practice in front of the cameras," another of the DC team offered. When Denton shot him a withering look, he added, "Won't they?"

"Of course they will. In fact, this is as good a time as any," Denton assured. Turning to the studio manger he went on, "Let's get them set-up on the riser next door and get them used to reading off the prompter."

As Josh followed the others back into the tiny video studio, he felt the skin tingle and energy rush he'd always associated with impending combat.

'Not such a big surprise,' he thought. *'In a way, this will probably be my last battle here in Vietnam.'*

*****

That night, Josh went once again to Kim-Ly's apartment. Lt. Gordon had wanted to get together and practice their *delivery* one more time as if they were salesmen – or politicians – but he had demurred. He didn't care how he came across to the press. Just that they were there and recording.

Kim-Ly's was the only place he still felt comfortable in Vietnam, or at least Saigon. For a short time right after Landry died he'd considered going back out into the field, to lose himself in the minute-to-minute insanity of the War. But he knew how distracted he was, how lost in his plans. By leading his men into combat without 100 per cent focus, he'd be putting every one of them into unnecessary danger. He couldn't do that. He wouldn't.

When the door to the apartment opened, he was more than a little surprised to come face-to-face with Kim-Ly's father. He wore the light black jacket and inverted woven bowl hat that he always wore when he went out at night, and looked as if he'd been waiting for Josh to arrive.

"Mr. Tran," Josh acknowledged with a polite bow of his head. "Goin' out to play some cards?"

To his surprise, Tran spoke in English. "Play cards. Yes," he said, his face revealing nothing.

Josh was at a loss for words. He'd never exchanged more than two words with the old man. Looking past him, Josh scanned the room for any sign of Kim-Ly.

"She come," Tran said, following his glance. "But now we talk."

"We talk?"

"You do not hurt my daughter," he said, and in the set of his jaw and the glare of his eyes, Josh knew the man was deadly serious.

"I would never..!" he began, but the old man put up one hand to stop him.

"You hurt her, I kill you," he whispered, and drew his finger slowly across his neck to be sure Josh got the message.

"I... I..." Josh stammered, but before he could recover, Tran pushed past him as though he were a bag of yesterday's trash. The door slammed shut behind him. Josh was left stunned.

"Did you and my father have a good talk?" Kim-Ly asked, appearing from her bedroom while adjusting the comb in her hair.

"It was... interesting. He really loves you, you know."

She looked at him with a quizzical glance. "I know. What brought that up?"

"Oh, just something I picked up from our little talk. Wow, you look great!" he added to change the subject.

She smiled, a knowing 'don't think you're fooling me by changing the subject' smile that made him feel foolish, and then kissed him. "You are sweet. How did everything go today?"

Part of him wanted to withhold details of the plan. He didn't want her to worry. But she was the only person he felt comfortable discussing it with, and so he told her as much as he thought she could handle without freaking. They shared a cup of tea, and then a sip of the local snake wine. They were still sitting in the living room, talking quietly, when her father came back from his night on the town.

"Father! How did you do tonight?" Kim-Ly greeted him, jumping up from the loveseat to take his hat and jacket. She kissed him on the cheek.

The old man smiled, if the crooked grimace could be called a smile. "Not too bad. I win more than I lose."

"You always win. You would think they would stop playing with you."

He shrugged, a quick jerk of his shoulders. "They win sometime."

She invited him to join them for a sip of wine. He shook his head. "Too tired. I go to bed now. Leave you young people."

"Come join us!" Josh insisted, more to assuage the sting of their earlier exchange than because he wanted company.

The old man looked at him as if considering the offer, but then decided against it. "Thank you, but I must sleep – đêm tốt."

They said their goodnights, and Kim-Ly went with him into his bedroom to help him get ready for bed.

"He has trouble unbuttoning his shirt," she explained when she returned to the loveseat a few minutes later. "His arthritis is becoming very bad."

Josh stroked her long black hair. "He's lucky to have a daughter like you."

She looked honestly shocked. "I am lucky to have *him*. He is such a good man. I feel so sorry for him, now that my mother is no longer living."

Josh recognized the special bond between father and daughter, and for just a second felt a stab of regret as he thought back to his own family, so very far away. He had never had that kind of relationship with his father – he doubted anyone, even his mother, ever had – but he had always been his mother's Golden Boy, and she'd always been his fiercest protector and greatest cheerleader.

"What? What are you thinking?" Kim-Ly asked, looking intently into his vacant eyes.

Josh realized he'd been drifting. "Oh, just thinking about my parents. My Mom, really."

"Tell me about her."

It was difficult at first, explaining the family dynamics. But he knew instinctively that Tran shared a number of qualities with the Colonel and so he did his best to describe a childhood that was both trying and yet... happy. For the most part. Kim-Ly nodded with understanding, listening attentively until he drifted to a halt. Then it was her turn, sharing more about her youth than ever before. They talked for hours, until his eyes began to blink shut.

"You must sleep," she said, taking his hand and pulling him toward her bedroom. "You are a television personality now." She covered her mouth with her hand and giggled.

He tried to smile, but found it impossible. His thoughts kept turning to the upcoming press conference, and the endgame of his personal battle.

Sleep would not come easy that night.

*****

The next day was a whirlwind of meetings, rehearsals, and evasion. Josh and Gordon practiced with the teleprompters until both could read with something approaching fluidity; still, no one would mistake them for Walter Cronkite. Of course, they weren't supposed to.

None of them were sure when Washington would give the order for the press conference, so they were all on edge the entire day. Denton paced; Winston fiddled with a gold Cross pen; Gordon kept messing with her hair. Why was it, Josh wondered, that women always seem to play with their hair when they're anxious? He'd noticed Kim-Ly doing the same thing: pulling on it, running fingers through it, twisting it. *'Must be some kind of security blanket,'* he thought. He rarely saw men doing the same thing, even the longhairs back in the States. It was as if the need were a genetic predisposition. Or something.

For Josh the day crawled interminably. Once he'd made up his mind to do something, he couldn't feel comfortable until it was done. Probably got that from the old Davy Crockett show: 'make up your mind and then full speed ahead.' More likely from the Colonel. The Old Man never liked to see a project unfinished. Most of those projects, it had seemed to Josh as a kid, had been his.

Because of the time difference between Vietnam and the States, Denton figured that the Pentagon would probably ask them to convene the press conference around midnight local time to slot into the American evening news cycle live from coast to coast without requiring any overtime. Seems the networks hated overtime unless it couldn't be avoided. The Army, on the other hand, didn't give a damn. No overtime there.

At 1700 hours Winston told them all to go to dinner, but "Stay on call – this could be the night." No one knew for sure what would be the trigger to prompt Pentagon officials to call the conference, but rumor had it that the N.Y. Times would soon publish a second installment of their exposé of the incident. That would probably be it. The Army had used their usual 'lay low and wait it out' strategy for the first revelation, but a second one would mean that the story had 'legs' as Denton described it – wasn't going to die down quickly. That's when they'd call on Josh and Gordon to do their thing. If they only knew...

Lt. Gordon seemed particularly nervous that evening, as if she sensed that their time had come. When she asked if she could go to mess with Josh he wanted to say no – wanted to be by himself, getting his thoughts straight – but thought better of it. "What the hell – come on, let's see if we can choke anything down," he'd finally agreed.

Gordon couldn't stop talking; just burning off nervous energy, Josh decided. Most of it was about the answers they'd prepared for the questions they expected to be asked by the journalists. She tinkered relentlessly with the wording, challenging everything from punctuation to the guts of the strategy. In a way, Josh was happy she'd joined him. The constant chatter diverted him from fixating on his own strategy, getting so wound up in his reiterations he tied his tongue in knots. The one thing he wanted was to be clear, to be understood. He knew full well he wouldn't get a second chance.

At 1830 he excused himself, ignoring Gordon's pleading eyes and returning to his quarters to rest up. He hadn't been able to eat much, forcing down a few forkfuls to settle his stomach. It wasn't so much that he was nervous. Excited, yes. Ready, definitely. But nervous? Not really. He had made his peace with his decision and that was that. He knew full-well that his actions would cause a worldwide uproar. He didn't care. One way or the other, he was finished. By his calculations the Times might have received the letter he'd sent. By the next day at the latest. And then… then his career in the Army would be over.

He closed his eyes and tried to slow his breathing. He put Sergeant Pepper's on the stereo and stretched out on his bunk – the sitar music on *Within You and Without You* taking him to another place. For all their strangeness, there was something about that group…

A loud knock on his door startled Josh back to full awareness.

'*Showtime!*' he thought.

When he opened the door he wasn't the least surprised to see one of the lieutenants from the PA group with a message: "The order came from Washington!" he said, excitement visible in his eyes. "Report to the studio – ASAP!" Without waiting for a reply, he turned and hurried off into the warm, humid night. *'Probably has to notify some of the others,'* Josh thought languidly, his nerves suddenly placated. No more waiting. It was time.

He changed into a clean uniform, washed his face and combed his hair. Staring into the bathroom mirror, he gave himself one last motivational speech, one last moment before he changed his life forever. Then he took a deep breath, smiled, and walked out into that good night.

The video studio was alive with activity and jammed with bodies. Cameramen from all three networks and both news services had staked out their spots and were busy finalizing their set-ups. Off to one side, Denton held court with a small group of reporters, chatting informally, smiling, even laughing from time to time. Winston grabbed Josh as soon as he stepped through the door.

"This is it!" he said, his voice too loud, too eager. "The second article is coming out tomorrow in the Times. They want us to get ahead of the curve."

"Then let's get to it," Josh said calmly.

They took him to the small green-room behind the stage where Gordon was already seated getting light makeup.

"Ready for your close-up?" she asked him with a smile.

"As ready as I'll ever be."

"Remember," Winston interrupted, still over-amped, "there are only four or five journalists out there. No big deal."

"And only about a billion people who will watch their reports. No big deal," Gordon said without a smile.

Despite his protests, the makeup person dabbed a little powder on Josh's face as well ("keeps the shine down") and sprayed some hair spray "just because."

"You look like you're ready for the prom," Gordon teased.

"I feel like I should be wearing a gown."

"Okay, okay, enough with the wisecracks, let's concentrate on our mission," Winston said, beads of sweat appearing on his forehead. "You both ready?"

"Yes, sir!" Gordon answered.

Winston looked at his watch. Seven minutes left. "Good. I'll be back to give you the signal to move out."

Gordon began to chuckle as soon as the colonel left the room. "He thinks we're heading out on patrol. You okay? You're kind of quiet today."

"A lot on my mind."

"Yeh, well what's that Hollywood saying? 'Break a leg?'"

"I think it's Broadway, but yeh, you too." He forced a smile.

Josh felt utterly calm now that he was in place and ready to go. Just like in the field. He'd get a little wired in the lead-up, but once it started he was good. It was like everything slowwwed down.

"One minute!" Winston called out, sticking his head into the room.

"Sua Sponte," Gordon said softly. "Let's go get 'em."

Despite their rehearsals, Josh wasn't prepared for the glare of all the studio lights focused on their little riser. He squinted in spite of himself, trying to adjust to the white hot glow of the massive overhead lamps.

"Just like home," Gordon whispered as they made their way to the dual podiums.

"Yeh," Josh answered blankly, his thoughts elsewhere.

Through the electric white gauze of the lighting, Josh could barely make out the cameras in the back and the five journalists seated right in front of them. On the backdrop behind the riser someone had hung a banner with the Army insignia and 'Military Assistance Command Vietnam' artfully displayed in bold lettering. Somewhere in one corner of his mind Josh was impressed: *Looks halfway professional.*

Off to the side of the riser he saw Denton signal them to begin. Gordon spoke first.

"Welcome to the headquarters of the Military Assistance Command, Vietnam," she said in a strong, clear voice. "This press conference has been called to address your questions concerning the unfortunate incident at My-Lai in March of last year. We will NOT be addressing other issues today. If you have questions about other issues, please address them to the Public Affairs Office here at the Base or at the Pentagon. I am Lieutenant Patricia Gordon, and this is Captain Josh Daniels. Captain Daniels will begin with a prepared statement, after which we will accept your questions. Captain Daniels?" She turned to him as she had in the rehearsals.

Josh saw the reporters scribbling on yellow notepads. Heat from the lights warmed his face. He heard his heart beating, slowly, under control.

"Good evening. Twenty-one months ago Charlie Company of the America Division's 11th Infantry Brigade received word that VC guerrillas had taken control of the village of Son My in Quang Ngai province. Led by Lieutenant William L. Calley, the unit was sent to the village on a search-and-destroy mission on March 16, 1968. Those are the facts. But they do not tell the entire story."

Out of the corner of his eye, Josh saw a look of puzzlement come over Colonel Winston's face. Lt. Gordon, just a few feet away from him, looked as if she were frozen in time, afraid to draw a breath. He went on.

"You are here to try to find out the truth of what happened at Son My, and specifically at the My-Lai hamlet. But that's not why Lieutenant Gordon and I are here. We're here to feed you a bullshit story how Calley's unit thought there were VC in the village, and the women and children were just 'collateral damage'. But that's not exactly true."

Josh heard Denton mumble "Goddamn!" loudly and saw a bustle of activity off to his right.

"What's true is that this War, this pathetic excuse for a war, is turning soldiers, even good soldiers, into the kinds of head-cases who can shoot women and children in cold blood and not think a thing about it. Not all of us, but enough so this kind of thing will happen again, and again, and again."

Now the activity off to his right was heading his way. He knew he only had seconds more before they would reach the podium.

"They're going to tell you that a friend of mine died recently and I'm 'disturbed' – don't believe it!" he said loudly enough to be heard over the jumble of voices now erupting from all sides. "He died alright – Lieutenant Mason Landry – a good soldier, but I'm telling you this because I've had enough of all the lies and the half-truths and…"

A strong pair of hands grabbed him by the arm and pushed him away from the podium. Josh started to resist, but then decided it would be better – look better on film – if he went quietly. By now the buzz of voices had swelled to a torrent. Josh glanced back at the podium, where Lieutenant Gordon stood watching him with a small mischievous smile. Their eyes met for just an instant, and he could've sworn she winked.

Led by a red-faced Colonel Winston, two big MPs stepped onto the riser and ushered Josh none-too-gently behind the backdrop, into the green-room. In seconds the room filled with officers, Denton's people, MPs – so many that they could scarcely move.

"Get these people out of here!" Denton screamed.

"Clear the room!" Winston ordered the MPs, and in a minute or two only Josh, Denton and the colonel were left to confront the 'incident'. After all the sound and fury of the previous few minutes, the sudden quiet seemed eerie, almost funereal.

"What in God's name did you think you were doing out there?!" Denton exploded as soon as the door to the room closed.

Josh looked from Denton to Winston and then back again. Both of them wore expressions of shock, dismay, and above all anger. He didn't blame them.

"I was telling the truth," he said. "You do remember the truth, don't you?"

*****

For the first few hours Josh was confined to quarters with two MPs standing guard outside his door. They would've thrown him in a cell, but no one could figure out what to charge him with. At a few minutes after 1300 hours the MPs entered his room and directed him to accompany them outside.

"Where to?" he asked.

"You'll find out, soon enough."

It didn't take long to figure out where they were headed. Even before the large two–story hospital building appeared through the inky blackness, Josh knew what their next move would be. Just as he'd told the newsmen – make it appear as though he'd had a breakdown. Colonel Lesser met him at the front doors.

"Didn't think we'd see you back here again so soon," he said matter-of-factly.

"Didn't expect it myself," Josh answered. "Sorry to drag you out of bed so late. Seems the powers-that-be aren't too happy with having the truth about this War splashed all over the evening news."

"Ah, so that's it. I didn't get the whole story. I guess you'll be staying with us for a while then. Let's see if we can make you as comfortable as possible." He turned to the MPs. "Thank you, boys. We'll take it from here." Lesser didn't wait for an answer, but instead motioned for one of his orderlies to shut and lock the doors – with the MPs outside – while he led Josh to his room.

"You want something to help you sleep?" he asked Josh once they'd arrived at the room.

"I don't think I'll need it," Josh said as he began to unbutton his shirt. "For the first time in days, I think I'll sleep just fine."

The colonel nodded with a smile. "See you in the morning then."

He closed the door as he left, but Josh heard no sign of a lock being thrown. His curiosity getting the better of him, he tried the doorknob just for the heck of it. It turned easily and the door swung open. Josh stuck his head out into the dimly-lit hall and looked in both directions. When he saw no one – no guards, no orderlies, not a living soul – he closed the door quietly and climbed into bed. In moments, he was asleep.

CHAPTER 27

The next few days flashed by. Day One consisted of nothing but appointments with doctors: a shrink ("how do you feel about what happened to your friend, Lieutenant Landry?"), a general practitioner ("could some illness have caused you to go off like that?"), and even Dr. Lesser ("I'm supposed to be grilling you for answers, but we both know what's happening here, so let's just chat for a while so they think I'm doing my duty.")

The orderlies brought him his meals, escorted him to the shower and the bathroom, and repeatedly made it very clear that he was in custody – hospital or not. In between doctors' appointments he read a little (Lesser smuggled him a new book about WWII that had just come out by a guy named Vonnegut), looked out the window every now and then to remind himself that there *was* a world going about its everyday business out there, and spent a goodly amount of time stretched out on his cot, staring at the ceiling thinking about Landry, and Kim-Ly, and his family, among many other things. He tried to picture where his letter to his father sat right about then, and if his family back home had learned of his *performance* at the press conference.

Day Two was pretty much like Day One, except as soon as it got dark a couple of MPs showed up and escorted him to a small, nondescript building located somewhere between MACV headquarters and the air base. He didn't think he'd ever seen the building before, or at least never noticed it. He wondered if it were something like Brigadoon, the imaginary village that only appeared once in a blue moon.

Inside the building, two civilian interrogators (probably CIA, he decided) questioned him intensely for over two hours under the watchful gaze of a major he didn't recognize. The officer didn't say a word. The spooks obviously wanted to know if he was working for the VC, or the Chinese, or the Russians, or anyone else for that matter, but they didn't ask him anything about that for quite a while. At first they tried to be subtle and winning, offering him a smoke, joking about the food at the officers' club, trying to be his buddy. But as soon as it became clear that Josh either couldn't or wouldn't give them the information they wanted, they did everything but beat him with rubber hoses. They shined bright lights in his eyes, shouted at him, refused to let him go to the bathroom, even blared deafening music for a half hour (after they left the room.) Unfortunately for them, they chose *Green River* by Creedence Clearwater – it was one of the rock bands he actually liked. Even if he didn't, there wasn't much he could tell them that he hadn't already said. The Army lied. The Army killed its own. He'd merely told the truth.

*****

It was on Day Three that the shit really hit the fan. He'd been awakened at 0630 by his two new best friends – the MPs who accompanied him everywhere outside the hospital – and hustled into a waiting Jeep. At first he thought they were taking him back to the interrogation room for another friendly chat, but instead they sped through the dim morning light to MACV headquarters. There they ushered him upstairs to General Edwards' office. Edwards was alone in his big office, seated behind his desk, a bottle of Jack Daniels and two glasses placed off to one side but within easy reach.

Edwards looked like he hadn't slept. Drooping dark circles of flesh framed his red-rimmed eyes. His uniform was wrinkled, stained. Josh had never seen the general wear a wrinkled uniform, and it shocked him.

"Daniels, come in, come in," Edwards greeted him, waving off the MPs. "Shut the door – please," he ordered.

Josh stood at attention in front of the desk. "Captain Joshua Daniels, reporting as ordered," he said, saluting.

"Sit, sit," the general said wearily, pointing to the two chairs that flanked Josh. "Want a drink?" He motioned toward the Jack Daniels.

"A little early for me, sir."

"Yes, of course, early for you, but late for me. Mind if I take a sip?" Edwards didn't wait for an answer. He poured three fingers and took a long gulp. "Been a tough day. Tough couple of days."

Josh wasn't sure if Edwards was marshaling his thoughts or waiting for him to say something, but whatever the case, he stayed silent.

"I don't know if you've heard about your letter to the New York Times," he began, and Josh struggled to hide his reaction. "Ah, I see you haven't," the general continued. "Well, I just got word it'll be on the stands this morning, New York time – front page, with an accompanying editorial from the Times editorial board. Pentagon's in an uproar. They want to court-martial you."

"They may have to get in line," Josh said without a hint of a smile.

"Yes, I heard about your news conference rant. I told them it was a bad idea, using you as their My-Lai front-man. But you can't tell them anything…" The last was mumbled, the drink and lack of sleep catching up to him. "I suppose you know we'll have to send you back to the States." He seemed genuinely apologetic.

"I figured."

"Top Brass want their pound of flesh. Some are calling you a traitor."

"To what?!" Josh asked before he could censor himself. "Not to my country. Not to my men. And definitely not to Landry." He stared at the general as if daring him to disagree.

Instead, the commander shrugged. "Maybe you're right. I really don't know anymore. Probably doesn't matter. Your father's been making inquiries…" He looked away. "You know, this fucked-up war is like pissing down a mineshaft. No matter what we do, it's not going to make any difference."

Josh sat quietly, his eyes riveted on Edwards. He'd never heard a senior officer talk about the War like that, and certainly not the CO. It was as if he'd stepped into the Twilight Zone; nothing was what it appeared and everything was changing all the time.

"You know, I fought in Korea," Edwards continued, his eyes staring off into space. "Two tours. Just a kid. But there, everything was cleaner. Clearer. More like World War II. We were fighting the Chinks and their North Korean buddies, and the South Koreans were fighting right alongside us. Us versus Them. Democracy versus Communism. Easy. Here…" he waved his hands lazily in the air, "here it's everybody against everybody. I mean, who are our friends?" By now he was slurring some of his words, his eyes beginning to lose focus. "One day they smile at you and bring you fresh eggs, and the next they drop a grenade into the middle of your squad.

"What the hell are we doing here?" he asked Josh directly, his voice a plaintive cry. "How can we defend people who won't defend themselves? Sometimes I think… Sometimes…" his voice drifted.

"But who gives a shit what I think? I'm just another gear in their war machine. They say kill, and we say 'how many?'"

Josh took a deep breath. Despite his best efforts, despite every instinct in his body, he found himself feeling sympathy for the old S.O.B. He'd never even considered the possibility that the general might not fully support the orders he'd been given by Washington. Never thought about it much. He just assumed that Edwards moved in lockstep with the Brass at the Pentagon.

He'd been wrong.

"Anyhow," the general went on after a long lapse, "I jus' wanted you to know that I understan' what you were tryin' to do." His eyes fluttered from exhaustion. "I may not agree with how you wen' about it, but I understand. I do. So, if I don' see you again before they send you back, you take care. You're a good man, Daniels. A damn good soldier. Too bad it was here. Too bad it was Vietnam." His head drifted forward and then snapped back as he forced himself awake.

"Now get out of here! Go back to your quarters and pack your bags. You're goin' home." He snickered to himself. "So now who's the lucky one?"

Josh didn't move. He wanted to say something, do something, but he didn't know what. Before he could decide, Edwards waved him off.

"Go! Get the hell out of here, and don' look back," he said wearily. At that, Josh stood, came to attention and saluted.

The general pulled himself upright for just a moment and returned the salute with all the concentration he could muster.

Josh pivoted without a word. As he opened the door to the outer office he heard the loud ticking of a wall clock.

He didn't look back.

*****

Despite Edwards' words, Josh was still surprised when the MPs took him back to his quarters instead of the hospital ward. The entire time they'd been escorting him they hadn't said a word more than was necessary to carry out their duty. But now Josh needed a favor.

"Hey, sorry you guys have to drag me all over like this. But I'll be out of your hair soon," he said, hoping to spark some conversation. One of the two ignored him completely, but the other one, a big strapping kid who looked like he might've played football back in high school, turned to him with an inquiring look.

"How's that?"

"They'll probably be sending me back to the States. I don't think they want me here anymore."

"Not a big surprise," the other MP, a rope-thin black guy, mumbled.

"No, I suppose not," Josh said, smiling. "The thing is," he began, looking to the one who'd shown some interest, "I haven't had a chance to tell my girl that I'll be leaving."

"A local?" the big guy asked.

"Yeh. Translator for the Embassy. Beautiful girl."

"You can get yourself another when you get back to the States," the black guy said.

"Could, I suppose. But this one's special. Might be a keeper."

"So, what, you want to call her?"

The skinny guy looked to his partner in horror. "What you doin'?! They didn' tell us nuthin' about lettin' him make no phone calls!"

"Didn't say he couldn't, either," the big guy argued.

"Uh uh. This one's on you, bro. I don' wan' nuthin' to do with it."

"All right, you just close your eyes for a few minutes. You won't see nothing."

"Hey, thanks a million," Josh said before the kid could change his mind. "I'll be fast. Just have to say goodbye."

"Oh right, like that'll be fast," the skeptical one challenged.

"Come on, let's go if we're going," the big guy said, but before he could even open the door, a loud knock sounded that made all three jump.

Josh motioned for them to stay quiet and went to the door. He didn't know what to expect, but it wasn't Colonel Henry.

"Colonel! This is a surprise," Josh said, shaking his friend's hand. "What brings you out so early in the morning?"

Henry looked like he was about to speak, when he caught sight of the two MPs.

"I see you've got company."

"They were just leaving – right guys?" Josh said.

"Yeh, sure. We'll be outside," his big new friend said. Both MPs snapped lazy salutes as they went past the colonel, who all but ignored them.

"I guess you know what brings me here," Henry said as soon as the door closed behind them.

"I don't expect you just wanted to have breakfast with me."

"Could. But no, that's not it. Saw your orders come through – they're shipping you back to the States – today."

"Didn't waste any time."

"They're running scared. You're a big story now – on the nightly news, in all the papers…"

"And Landry? Did they mention Landry?"

"Oh yeh," Henry said nodding emphatically. "Of course, part of that's due to your old man."

"My father? What about him?"

Henry smiled. "You haven't heard? He's called for a congressional investigation. Not only about Landry, but the whole damn War! Those guys in the Pentagon must be shittin' bricks." Henry seemed almost as happy as he was.

"Wow." That was all Josh could say as he sat heavily on his bunk. The Colonel had come through.

"Yeh, wow. Edwards sent me over to make sure you get packed-up in time. You're on the 1400 milk-run out of here."

The news snapped Josh out of his reverie. "Colonel, I need to ask you a favor."

*****

It was after 1100 hours when a Jeep showed up at Josh's quarters. Josh had finished packing – there wasn't that much to pack – and had been waiting impatiently for word from the colonel. The corporal driving the Jeep told him to jump in, Col. Henry had sent him.

"Where to?" Josh asked.

"Not at liberty to say, sir," the corporal replied. He didn't look at Josh when he answered.

What the hell is this?' Josh thought as he climbed into the vintage four-wheeler.

The ride was brief, to a location he wasn't anticipating: the same nondescript building where he'd been interrogated after the press conference.

'Uh oh. Don't like the looks of this,' he worried as he climbed out and made his way to the guarded front door.

"Captain Joshua Daniels," he told the MP in the guard shack. "I think you're expecting me. Or someone here is, anyway." The sergeant looked at a long printed list of names and nodded.

"Captain. Just hold on one second, sir." He slid the glass window closed and Josh could see him dial a phone. A few seconds later he was back. "Someone will be here to get you in just a minute."

In less time than that a man dressed in preppy civvies opened the heavy steel door. He was young, probably younger than Josh, with close-cropped black hair and the kind of observant non-committal look that screamed *spook!*

"Captain Daniels? Follow me please." Without waiting for a reply the man turned and left Josh to catch the rapidly closing door; it was even heavier than it looked. The man led Josh down a familiar corridor, the worn carpet and cloying smell of cleaning products giving him an intense feeling of déjà vu. They proceeded directly to the same room he'd visited previously.

'Here we go again,' he thought as the young man stopped and opened the door for him, stepping aside to allow him to enter first.

"Josh!" a voice called out loudly. For an instant he was completely disoriented, his expectations shattered. Then Kim-Ly was in his arms, kissing him, and he felt as if he'd fallen down a rabbit hole. For the first time since the night of Landry's death tears came to his eyes; he struggled to keep them under control.

Kim-Ly reached up and tenderly wiped them away. "Your Colonel Henry told me. Oh Josh…" Now she was crying; she squeezed her eyes shut so tightly that just a single tear streamed down her cheek.

"It'll be okay," he heard himself saying. He didn't know if he believed his own words, but he knew he had to say them.

From behind them the civilian in the preppy slacks and button-down shirt cleared his throat. "She isn't supposed to be here, on-base," he announced with what the kid probably thought was authority. "She can only stay a few minutes."

Josh turned his head back and nodded. "Thanks."

As soon as the door closed, he took Kim-Ly's face in his hands. "I'm so sorry. I didn't want this…"

She put a finger to his lips. "You had to do what you did. You would not be you if you did not." She smiled wistfully. "So now you are being sent home? That is what Colonel Henry said."

"No choice. They think I'm a bad guy, I guess. But as soon as I get there I'll start the process for getting you into the country." Her smile faded to a pained grimace. "What?" he asked, his eyes scanning hers for some clue.

"I cannot leave," she whispered. "My father – he is getting old."

The words cut deeply. "But… I thought…"

She touched his lips once more. "I know, and if I could you know I would come. You know that. I love you with all my heart. But, I cannot leave."

The finality with which she spoke touched-off a shockwave that surged through his body. He struggled to find the right words, to convince her. But even as he did, he knew full well he would not succeed. Perhaps should not.

"Then I'll come back," he said, catching his breath. "As soon as all this blows over."

She nodded, tears coming again to the corners of her eyes. "Yes. That would be… wonderful."

He kissed her again and held her tight to his chest. He could feel her heart beat, smell the sweet scent of her hair.

He didn't know how long they stood like that, frozen as if two statues, afraid to move, unable to speak. But much too soon a pounding sounded on the door just an instant before it swung open.

"Sorry, but she's gotta go," his spook escort announced with perhaps the slightest hint of empathy.

"And we've got to get you over to the terminal for your out-processing," Colonel Henry said, stepping past the young man.

"Colonel!" both Josh and Kim-Ly cried out happily.

"Sorry to break up this little love fest, but we've got to get *you* off the base before they realize you're here," he said to Kim-Ly, "and *you* we've got to get moving toward your 1400 flight," he added to Josh. "Hope this little visit wasn't too short."

"It was, but I would not have traded it for anything," Kim-Ly said, looking up at Josh.

"Thanks, Colonel. We really appreciate it."

"Thank General Edwards. He's the one who pulled the strings to get her onto the base."

"I'll do that – although it'll probably have to be by phone."

Henry tilted his head in a half-shrug. "Life isn't always fair, Captain. Just know that there are people here who think what you did needed doing." He turned to the CIA operative. "And you can tell that to your bosses."

"I'm just doing my job, Colonel," the young civvie said defensively.

"Aren't we all. Okay, enough chit-chat, give the girl a kiss and let's get this wagon train moving." He turned away and ushered the young guy out in front of him.

Josh turned to Kim-Ly. Her eyes were red but she wore a brave smile. "I'll be back," he whispered. "I can't say when, but one day you'll answer your door and I'll be standing there."

"I will be waiting," she said.

They kissed then, with a passion that spoke of both pain and hope.

"Say goodbye to your father," Josh said when they parted.

"And you say hello to your parents. Tell them I hope one day to meet them."

"That day will come soon, very soon."

He smiled and led her outside by the hand. One last brief kiss, and Colonel Henry hustled Josh into a waiting Jeep.

"I'll call!" he yelled as the vehicle pulled off. The last thing he saw was Kim-Ly standing in the midday sun, waving goodbye.

*****

The processing at the air base took almost no time at all. His thoughts were elsewhere, though, and several times the clerks had to repeat themselves to get him to follow even the simplest of orders. Colonel Henry stayed with him the entire time, until finally they moved into the departure lounge where several dozen other soldiers – most of them waiting for the Freedom Bird to take them home at the end of their tour – sat talking or deep in reverie.

Josh and Henry were equally absorbed in their own conversation, when suddenly a strange sound rippled through the terminal. First it was just a single pair of hands, but within seconds the entire lounge broke into applause. And then they stood.

"What the hell...?" Josh said, but as Colonel Henry stepped away and joined the applause, he realized that the ovation was for him. Or not really him, but for Landry, and all those women and kids at My-Lai, and all the young men and women who'd been put through the meat-grinder that was the War.

He bowed his head slightly to all the men around him and tried to look each and every one of them in the eye. They deserved that, deserved to know that he appreciated all they'd done, all they'd suffered, for their country, for their fellow citizens, and above all for each other.

An announcement came over the loudspeaker: his flight was boarding. He shook Colonel Henry's hand, and surrounded by soldiers patting him on the shoulder and calling out their thanks, he took the short walk to the runway.

The heat and humidity of the Vietnamese afternoon fell upon him like a dripping blanket, but he barely noticed. He was going home, to remind people the War still raged, to find a way to share the truths he'd discovered in that strange little country on the far edge of the huge Asian continent. All those men and women needed someone to fight for them back there, to have their backs when the politicians and the Big Brass forgot what it was all about.

And when he was through, when he'd done all he could do to awaken America to the reality of the War, he'd be coming back to get Kim-Ly. Whether they stayed in Vietnam until her father passed, or moved somewhere else, it didn't matter. As long as they were together. For the one thing he'd learned during his time in-country was that one person can be your world, and without that person, your world was empty.

His world was full.